TEXAS
Orchids

samantha christy

Athena Books Publishing Group

Saint Johns, FL 32259

Copyright © 2021 by Samantha Christy

All rights reserved, including the rights to reproduce this book or any portions thereof in any form whatsoever.

This is a work of fiction. Names, characters, places and incidents are either the product of the author's imagination or are used fictitiously, and any resemblance to actual persons, living or dead, business establishments, events or locales is entirely coincidental.

Cover designed by Letitia Hasser | RBA Designs

Cover model photo by WANDER AGUIAR

Cover model – Kerry Smart

ISBN: 9798515746537

TEXAS
Orchids

Samantha Christy

PROLOGUE

Ten years ago

"Maddox," Dad says behind me for the tenth time.

I ignore him, mesmerized by the girl riding the horse around the barrels. How does she make it seem so effortless?

I'm not a complete stranger to horses. Dad brings us to Nana's ranch every few years when he can manage to get away from his booming production company. But how is it I still haven't figured out how to saddle a horse, yet this girl, who can't weigh more than a hundred pounds, is taking charge of a mare ten times her weight?

"Leave him alone," Mom says. "Can't you see he's busy?"

I climb onto the bottom fence rail. She flies by me so fast, she loses her hat.

"Busy doing nothin'," Dad says.

Mom chuckles. "Oh, I wouldn't say he's doing nothing."

I roll my eyes and hop the fence to retrieve the pink cowboy hat that landed in the dirt. I shake it off and walk over to the girl, who is still sitting on her horse, her back to me. I clear my throat.

She turns and the horse turns with her, as if they're one. Her eyebrows shoot up. "Didn't anyone ever tell you not to stand behind a horse?"

I back up and circle, giving a wide berth to the horse, eyeing it to make sure it won't kick me.

The girl laughs. "You're not much into them, are you?"

Her words are laced with a light southern drawl that sends tingles to parts of my anatomy I don't want to have to deal with, considering my parents are thirty feet away. I concentrate on the pile of horse shit to my left, hoping to stop my rising problem.

She leans over and holds out her hand.

I reach out to shake and then stupidly realize she wants her hat. I hand it to her and stuff my hands in my pockets. "Well, I'm from Connecticut, so no. But my grandma owns this ranch."

"You're Vivian's grandson?"

"The one and only."

Her horse neighs, and she leans down to stroke the side of her head. "It's okay, Baby Blue, he's friendly." She looks at me. "Aren't you, Connecticut?"

"Yeah, sure."

She takes her hat off and waves it. "Thanks." Then she plops it on her head and knees her horse.

"My name's Maddox!" I yell.

She looks back and smiles. "Your hat's crooked."

I fix it, feeling awkward. I'm used to baseball caps, not cowboy hats, but Nana insists we wear one whenever we're outside on the ranch. Even my two younger sisters wear them. I run back to the fence and climb over. Five pairs of eyes watch me. My sister, Jordan, breaks away from the pack. "Do you love that cowgirl?"

I choke. "I don't even know her, squirt."

"That's Andie Shaw," Nana announces. "One of the best barrel racers around these parts. Been doing rodeo for quite a few years now. Won her first buckle for roping calves at age ten."

Jordan cracks a smile. "Was she doing it at *my* age, Nana?"

"You're seven. She was a might older when she started." Nana gives me a look. "Now she's the same age as Maddox. Fifteen."

Jordan elbows me. "Are you going to kiss her?"

"Shut up."

"Maddox," Mom says. "Don't tell your sister to shut up."

"Sorry. Are we going to ride or what?"

Caitlyn tugs on Mom's coat. "Mommy, I'm sleepy."

Nana scoops her up and takes Jordan's hand. "You three go ahead. Dave will ride with you. I've got these two. I promised Jordan we'd make my famous chocolate cake during Caitlyn's nap."

"Better save me some, squirt."

"I promise," she says as Nana leads them away.

A ranch hand—Dave, I presume—comes out of the stable riding a horse. Another horse is trailing him. Two others are already saddled, ready to go, and tied to the fence. "Need help mounting?" he asks Mom.

"I've got it," Dad says. He pulls over a stool and helps her onto it, giving her instructions on how to swing her leg up and over.

Like me, she's ridden before, but we're far from experts. Truth be told, we're barely even novices. Dad grew up around here, back when it was a small ranch with only a dozen horses. Now they must have a hundred.

Mom slips and falls back into Dad's arms. They laugh and then kiss.

"Gross," I say.

Mom turns. "You're lucky to have parents who are madly in love." She kisses him again.

"Jeez, get a room."

"Not a bad idea," Dad says. "Maybe we will later."

I try not to gag. "Did anyone ever tell you there's such a thing as too much information?"

He chuckles and sets Mom down. "Okay, let's try again, darlin'."

Once we're ready to go, Dave leads the way. We go past the arena where Andie is still running her horse around the barrels. She stops, glances over as we pass, and does something with her hat.

Dave falls back even with me. "A lady like that tips her hat to you, you tip back."

"What?"

"She tipped her hat to you. That's a compliment. Some might even say an invitation into her—"

"Whoa there, Dave," Mom says. "He's only fifteen."

Dad and Dave share a laugh, then Dave shows me how to properly tip my hat.

Thirty minutes later we're on the top of a ridge. Dave points west. "That's the new land Vivian bought last year."

"How many acres?" Dad asks.

" 'bout three thousand."

"Three thousand *acres*?" I'm stunned.

"Your grandma has big dreams."

"You think she'll try and flatten the ridge?" Mom asks. "Make it more accessible from down there?"

Dave shakes his head. "Never. These two ridges are what gave the ranch its name. If you haven't seen it from the air, you should. My buddy over in Ft. Worth owns a helicopter. Maybe I can get him to take you up."

Mom stares out in awe. "These ridges are the Devil's Horns?"

"Yes, ma'am."

"Can we go up and see, Dad? That'd be so cool."

He cocks his head. "You just want to ride in a helicopter, don't you?"

"It would still be cool. You know, to see how the ranch got its name and all."

"We're leaving tonight," Dad says. "It'll have to wait until our next visit."

Mom says, "We'd better head back. I want to spend some time with Vivian before we leave."

The whole way, I wonder if Andie will still be there. She called her horse Baby Blue, but she's the one with the incredible blue eyes. Is that why she gave her horse that name? If my balls weren't killing me from the ride, I'd be hard just thinking about her.

When we get back, I don't see her anywhere, but when we approach the stables, I see the familiar pink cowboy hat. She's brushing her horse. She looks over, and I tip my hat the way Dave showed me. She smiles and looks away.

My horse unexpectedly makes an awful noise and rears up on his hind legs. I struggle to stay on but lose my grip and fall backward. Mom screams as I fall to the ground, pain slicing through my head as things go black.

"Maddox! Maddox, wake up!"

Everyone is staring at me. I reach up and touch my head, then I look at my blood-covered fingers. Dad takes off his jacket and holds it to my head. Andie is standing by the fence, crying. I try to sit up. She doesn't even know me. Why is she sad that I fell?

"Don't sit up. You could have a head injury."

"I'm fine."

"You blacked out for a minute. The paramedics are coming to check you out."

I look at Andie, feeling like a wimp. "I'm not getting in an ambulance. Take me to the hospital if you want, but I don't need to be put on a gurney. Please, Dad."

He helps me sit. "Fine, but I'm taking you right now."

Several ranch workers run over, but it's not me they're looking at. The horse I was riding lies on the ground, his rear leg a mangled mess. "Holy crap, what happened?"

Dad points to a dead snake a few feet away. "Your horse got spooked by a rattlesnake. He bucked you off and snapped his leg pretty badly."

One of the ranch hands gives Dave a large gun. He points it at the horse.

"He's not going to kill him, is he?"

"This isn't the type of injury horses recover from, son."

I glance at Andie. She's not crying because of *me*, it's the horse. Right before Dave pulls the trigger, she screams.

The ambulance shows up. They check me out and recommend I go to the ER for observation since I lost consciousness, not to mention I need stitches. Dad thanks them and pulls Nana's truck around to take me himself, like he promised.

I want to comfort Andie, but she doesn't know me from Adam. Nana has her wrapped in her arms as she sobs. As we drive away, I know I'll never forget the girl with the blue eyes and her devastating scream.

We leave the property, driving under the massive wrought iron archway that reads **Devil's Horn Ranch**. When we stop and wait for a car to pass, I keep the sign in focus, trying to ignore the ache in my head and the one in my heart. I wonder if coming here will ever be the same.

CHAPTER ONE

Maddox

Present day

I give the bar top one last wipe with my rag and flip off the lights. Kevin sticks his head in the doorway between the restaurant and the bar. "Some of us are going across the street for drinks. Want to come?"

"Nah. Long shift. I want to go home and watch the rest of the game. It's gone into extra innings."

"The Nighthawks?"

"You know it."

"One of these days you'll quit being a stick-in-the-mud and tag along, right?" Some of the waiters join him.

I laugh. "One of these days."

After they leave, I lock up and look at the marquee that reads **Mitchell's NYC**. This place is one of three started by Mom's parents and is run by Aunt Skylar. I've worked here for almost three years as Bar Manager. That is my official title. Sometimes I wonder if it's all I'll ever amount to.

During the walk home on the busy streets of New York City, I people watch, wondering how so many others seem to have found their path in life, their calling, their chosen careers so much sooner than I have. At twenty-five, I'm not getting any younger, and I'm pretty sure I don't want to be a fifty-year-old barback.

Reece, my best friend and former roommate, thinks I only feel this way because she got her big break and is following her dream. Dream may be an understatement. In the past year, she has gone on two tours, won a Grammy, and married her long-lost love. She went from an unknown to Reece Mancini, the famous up-and-coming artist who gets recognized wherever she goes. And to think only eleven months ago, she was waiting tables in the room next to the bar.

Maybe she's right. I feel like there's so much more for me out there. I just need to find it.

At home, I get a beer from the fridge and turn on the game in time to see Brady Taylor strike out three guys in a row, delivering another win to the Nighthawks. Maybe I should have played more baseball.

Dad pushed me to play soccer, and I did. Even played in college for a few years while I majored in business entertainment to placate my father, who owns two movie production studios. After working a few positions in his company, I knew it wasn't for me. Neither was working for Uncle Griffin's photography studio or the gym Dad owns with his two brothers-in-law.

My phone rings, and Reece's face pops up on the screen. I answer. "Hey."

"Did you see the end of the game?"

"Aren't you in L.A. shooting a music video or something?"

"It's a commercial. The Diet Pepsi one, remember?"

I sink back into the couch, amazed at how in-demand she has become in the past few months. "How'd you know I'd be home?"

"You're always home, Mad. Or at the restaurant. I wish you'd expand your horizons."

"You mean date."

"Or something."

"What's *or something?*"

"I don't know, try something new. Anything. You seem sad."

"I'm not sad. Bored maybe, but not sad."

"Maybe Garrett can get you a job at Indica Records."

"I don't know shit about music, Reece. I'm not going to empty trashcans, which is about all I'd be good for."

She sighs. "You're good for a lot more than that, Maddox McBride. You just haven't had the chance to find out what yet."

"When are you getting back to New York?"

"End of the week. How about we go on a road trip this weekend up to Vermont, like before? Just you and me."

"You don't think your husband would mind?"

"Garrett? No. He trusts me." She laughs. "It seems silly to say and believe it after everything we went through, but it's true. Say the word, and I'll have someone set it up."

"God, Reece, listen to you. You'll have someone set it up? You've come so damn far. Do you know how proud I am of you?"

My phone alerts me to an incoming call. It's Dad. Why is he calling after midnight? "Reece, my Dad's calling. I'll talk to you tomorrow, okay?"

"Night, Mad."

I switch over. "Dad, what's up?"

He sighs, so I know it isn't good.

"It's Nana." I can hear the thickness in his throat, and my spine stiffens against hearing what comes next. "She's... she's gone, partner."

Partner. He hasn't called me that since I was twelve, but I get why he does. Nana and I were close, especially when I was younger. I didn't meet her until I was seven, but she made up for lost time by becoming not only Nana but a friend. Early on I spent weeks at her house, which was a small horse ranch back then. My gut twists, thinking how I haven't been down to Texas since I was fifteen.

I trace the scar on my temple that goes back into the hairline—a nasty souvenir of the last day I was on Devil's Horn Ranch. The images of the horse's mangled leg, of him getting shot in the head, and the bloodcurdling screams from the girl—

After that, Nana always came here to visit. Suddenly I'm mourning the years of vacations we didn't have down in Texas.

"She's dead?" I say with a lump in my throat. "How?"

"She fell." There's a long silence as he gathers himself. "I was always telling her she should take the bedroom downstairs. At seventy-five she was getting too old to go up and down so many times each day. But you know Nana."

"Yeah. She's stubborn. Uh... was." I wipe a tear before it drips off my chin.

"I'd like the five of us to fly down tomorrow to plan her funeral. You'll come, won't you?"

"Sure. Whatever you need. I'm so sorry."

"I'm sorry too, son. We'll fly out at three. Can you meet us at the airstrip?"

"Of course. How are Jordan and Caitlyn taking it?"

"They're sad, but they weren't as close to her as you and I were."

"Right."

He sniffs. "See you at three?"

"Yes."

The line goes dead. I throw my phone on the couch and lie back. "Shit!" I scream at the ceiling.

I can't believe she's gone. It's bad enough we lost Grandpa twelve years ago. Technically he wasn't my grandpa. Tanner was Nana's second husband. I never met Dad's real father; he died when I was four, so it was only natural I called Tanner that. She's been running the ranch alone ever since. Well, she and her staff. What will happen to it now?

I go into my bedroom and riffle through the closet until I find what I'm looking for. Then I fall asleep, staring at the picture of me when I was seven, sitting on a horse for the first time, with Nana looking up at me proudly.

We have tiptoed around each other for days, not knowing what to say. Dad tries to be strong for us, but I know it's hard for him being back on the ranch. Pictures of Nana and Grandpa line the walls of the house. Her coffee cup is still on the counter, untouched. Nobody wants to be the one to put it away. Her favorite tattered cowboy hat hangs on a peg by the back door. She's gone, but she's still very much here.

A Border Collie named Beau, one of the farm dogs that I'm told took a liking to Nana, hasn't left the back porch much. We put out food and water for him, but it's clear he's missing her along with the rest of us.

Mom and Dad have spent the past two days at the funeral home, preparing for the service. I've been holed up with my sisters in the main house, unable to go outside because of the storms that never seem to end. I guess it's fitting—someone has died; there shouldn't be sunshine.

The doorbell rings, which I find funny. Nobody rings doorbells around here. They just walk in.

With no one else around, I hop off the couch. I'm surprised when I see Reece standing on the porch. She tears open the screen door and pulls me into her arms. I cry. I haven't let any tears fall since the night Dad called, but seeing my best friend opens the floodgates. I let it all go.

"I'm so sorry, Mad," she says, running her hands down my back in a soothing way. "I know how much you loved her."

"I was a bad grandson. I should have visited more."

"There's nothing you could have done to prevent this. There's nothing anyone could have done. I met her once, remember? She was definitely a force to be reckoned with. A strong, independent woman, for sure. I mean, look what she did with the ranch. God, Maddox, I had no idea. You've told me about it, but this place is like something out of a TV show."

"I barely recognize it myself." I pull away and lead her into the house. "It's twice as big as it was the last time I was here."

"Maybe you could show me around."

"If it ever stops raining, I'd like to see it myself. It's been a long time." I hug her again. "Hey, thanks for coming. It really means a lot."

"I was on my way back from L.A., so it was an easy ticket change. I'll stay as long as you need me."

"The funeral is tomorrow."

"What happens after that?"

I look at the couch where Nana read me books about horses. The old farm table in the kitchen Grandpa built from trees on the property. The pictures of her grandchildren on the bookshelves next to ribbons and trophies won by her horses. I sit heavily on a chair, wondering what will become of all of it. "Honestly, I have no idea."

Jordan appears in the doorway. Her eyes light up when she sees Reece. They have spent time together over the past three years. My sister is a celebrity at high school for knowing *the* Reece Mancini.

Reece fishes around in her bag and pulls out a CD. "Hi, Jordan. I brought you something."

She's excited. "Is that what I think it is?" She beelines across the room.

"An advanced copy of my soon-to-be-released album."

Jordan takes it from her and squeals. "Oh my god! Juliette will die when I tell her I have this. Wait, am I allowed to let anyone listen?"

Reece laughs. "Sure, but don't let my bosses at IRL know."

"Isn't your husband your boss?" Jordan asks.

"Yeah, so mum's the word."

Jordan crosses her heart. "I swear." She races through the house to find Nana's CD player.

Reece glances after her. "She doesn't seem too worse for the wear."

"She and Caitlyn weren't as close to Nana as I was."

Reece looks around. "I can't imagine growing up in a place like this."

I point to the doorway leading to the living room. "This is where the original house ended. When Dad grew up here, it was half the size it is now."

"At half the size, it would still be huge. Has she lived here alone since your grandpa died? What did she do with all this space?"

I shrug, guilty I don't know the answer to her question since I haven't been here in so long.

"Where are your folks?"

"Meeting with lawyers and stuff. They said not to wait up." Reece yawns. "You must be tired after the week you had. I'll show you to the guest bedroom, but tomorrow I want to hear all about the commercial."

"Tomorrow is all about Vivian. The rest can wait." She stops in front of a picture of Nana and me in the hallway. "She really loved you, Mad."

"I know. I wish I could have done more. Come on, the guest room is back here."

There's not a dry eye at the cemetery. Everyone loved Vivian McBride. Well, there are a *few* dry eyes. I keep looking at the old man standing behind everyone else as they lower Nana into the ground. He and the younger man he's with are wearing cowboy hats—disrespectful if you ask me. Everyone else has removed their hat. At least the woman with him isn't wearing one, but she's not wearing black. A springtime dress is more like it. None of the three were at the service, and they're hanging back, well away from everyone else. They don't even look sad. Just impatient.

"What's *she* doing here?" Mom whispers to Dad as the pastor says his final words.

He looks over and his whole demeanor changes. His hands ball into fists. His face goes red. He's downright pissed. He starts to stand, but Mom coaxes him down.

"Don't," she says. "Let's pay our last respects. Don't let her ruin that."

"What's going on?" Reece whispers to me.

I shrug, focused on the trio who look like they belong anywhere but here.

When it's all over, I ask Dad, "Who are they?"

"Karen Thompson, her brother Jon, and their father, Joel."

My eyes widen. "Karen Thompson, your ex-wife?"

"That's the one," Mom says, kicking the dirt. "Of all the places I thought I'd see her again."

The three of them approach. Dad turns to Mom. "Darlin', can you take Jordan and Caitlyn to the car please?"

"Gladly."

Mom eyes Karen with daggers as she guides my sisters away. Karen doesn't seem to mind. She has a smug smile on her face. "Gavin," she says as if greeting Dad at a nightclub and not a burial. "As I live and breathe. I wondered if we'd ever cross paths again."

"What do you want, Karen?"

"Why, to pay my respects, of course. Vivian was a great woman."

"She was, and you've paid them, so feel free to leave now. Jon. Joel." He walks away.

Before we take five steps, the old man says, "Gavin, I'd like to set up a meeting."

Dad looks at my grandmother's grave. "My mother's casket isn't even covered yet, Joel. Can't this wait?"

"I'll reach out to you in a day or two then," Joel says.

"We'll be gone in a day or two."

Joel takes a business card out of his back pocket. "Call me before you leave."

"Bye, Gavin," Karen says flirtatiously before the three of them turn and walk away.

The third one, Jon, never said a word. He watched, as if his job was not to speak but to learn. He shoots a look over his shoulder at Dad like he wants to kill him.

"Jeez," Reece says. "They look like trouble."

"What do they want, Dad?"

"Same thing everyone wants around here. Grandma's land."

My jaw drops. "And they thought coming to her gravesite was the way to get it?"

"The Thompsons have never gone about things the conventional way."

"So what's going to happen to it? Her land?"

"That's what your mom and I have been discussing the past few days. It's not like selling a house. It's a business. Lots of moving parts. It could take a while to figure out the best way to go."

We all look up as a pickup barrels through the cemetery, almost hitting the limousine we came in before stopping. It makes an awful noise shutting off—like a sick cow. Not that I've ever heard what a sick cow sounds like. The woman inside takes off her cowboy hat and rips off her shirt, putting on something in its place. Then it looks like she's trying to shimmy out of her pants. On this somber day it's kind of comical to watch. She puts her hat back on and opens the door. She runs a few steps in a black dress and cowboy boots, then stops, takes off her hat, and tosses it in the bed of the truck. She runs again, stops, and returns to the truck to retrieve a bouquet of flowers. Finally, she trots over to Nana's grave, shaking with sobs.

"I'm so sorry I missed it, Viv," she says, and it's barely audible.

"Who's that?" I ask Dad.

"Beats me."

The only other person near the grave is an old man. Mom said his name is Gerald. Word has it he was there when she died, though none of us know him. He envelops the woman in his arms, and they sob together.

One of the guys I recognize from the ranch walks over and comforts them. She turns and cries into his shirt.

"Should we go back over?" I ask.

Dad shakes his head. "Matteo has it under control."

"Matteo? You know the names of her employees?"

"I learned them all, Maddox. I'm responsible for what happens to them. I don't take that job lightly. If I'm going to put anyone out of work, I damn well want to know who they are."

We stroll to the limo, sidestepping puddles that have accumulated over the past few days. At least there was a break in the rain for her burial.

Mom and Dad seem to be having a conversation about Karen.

"I take it there's a story there," Reece says.

"There is, and you can read all about it if you want. Mom wrote a book about their lives together. That Karen bitch played a big part."

"I'm intrigued. And I've been wanting to read some of your mom's books. I'll be sure to get it for my flight home."

I continue to watch the woman at the grave. She takes flowers out of the bouquet and throws them on the casket. The older man kisses her on the temple like a father would, then the three of them go to her truck. She sees us and smiles sadly. Then she stops and stares at *me*. "Connecticut?"

I study her red, puffy face, but there is no mistaking those blue eyes. "Andie?"

CHAPTER TWO

Andie

"Wow. I haven't seen you in about—"

"Ten years," he says.

"I'm real sorry about Viv, uh, your grandma. She was a very special lady."

"Thanks. And my name is Maddox."

"I know, but I've always thought of you as Connecticut." The woman beside him raises her brows. Oh, gosh, that was a stupid thing to say. Now they think I think about him, which I have—or I used to anyway. But the way I said it. I look at the woman's hand. Wedding ring. Great, now she probably thinks I have a thing for him. "Sorry, this is all so much." I hold out my hand to the woman. "Andie Shaw. You must be Maddox's wife."

She chuckles. "You wouldn't be the first person to think that. No, we're best friends. Reece Mancini. Nice to meet you."

Feeling stupid all over again, I shake her hand. Of course he's not married. Viv would have told me if he was. She tells me everything about her family. Sadness washes over me. *Told* me everything. I still can't believe she's gone.

"I apologize for missing the service. There was an emergency over at Diamond Duce Ranch."

"Is everyone okay?" Maddox asks.

"Everyone except Diamond Duke. Jumped the fence again and got his leg stuck in a game trap. He's in the sling now. Still might lose him. Time will tell."

Maddox looks at me in confusion. "A guy steps in a trap, and you put him in a sling? What are you, some kind of hillbilly medic?"

Matteo steps forward. "Andie is a doctor, a vet. She works for half a dozen ranches. Diamond Duke is a horse."

Maddox turns red. "Oh, right."

Reece snickers.

"Andie?" a man by the limo says. "Are you the Andie who tried to revive her? I'm Vivian's son, Gavin McBride."

"Nice to meet you, Mr. McBride."

"It's Gavin. Are you the one?"

I nod, trying not to remember that horrible night. Tears escape my eyes. "I'm so sorry I couldn't save her. I tried everything I could think of."

"There wasn't anything anyone could have done. Her neck was broken. She died instantly."

"I know, but I hoped—"

Matteo says, "Andie did CPR on her for thirty minutes. She wouldn't give up even when she knew it was hopeless."

"You were there too?" Gavin asks.

"One of our boarder horses was showing signs of colic. I was with Andie in one of the stables when we heard Gerald scream from the main house."

My throat is thick with tears. I can't speak.

"Come now," Matteo says. "You're in no shape to drive. I'll take you home."

I nod to Maddox and his family. I know they are even more devastated than I am.

"Bye, Andie!" Reece calls after me jubilantly. "Hope to see you around."

I look back to see Maddox scolding her.

I drive onto Devil's Horn Ranch for my weekly rounds, knowing nothing here will ever be the same. My eyes become misty when I pass Viv's house on the way to the stables. I park my pickup in the usual spot and grab a few things from the back, wondering where everyone is. Usually on a Monday morning, the ranch is bustling with activity.

A semi pulls away from the barn. Some of the ranch hands are dealing with the hay delivery, but other than them and a few random horse owners milling about, it's a ghost town.

I enter the south stable and check on four pregnant broodmares. Daisy Mae is due any day, and the others should drop within the month. I peek at Henny, who foaled two weeks ago, and her baby, Lips. Lips dances around the pen, weaving between her mother's legs.

"Oh, my gosh, he's so cute," someone says behind me.

Reece and Maddox are walking past. "*She*, actually. This little one is Lips. She's a ball of energy."

"Lips?" Reece asks. "Kind of a funny name for a horse."

"It's her barn name. Her papered name is Lipstick Lollipop."

"What does that mean, papered name?" Reece asks.

She obviously doesn't know anything about horses. "You know how purebred dogs come with official papers? That's kind of like horses. The breeder picks their papered name and that is their unique official name which can never be changed. Most horses also have a barn name, like a nickname."

"Oh, neat." She walks to the stall across from this one. "What's *her* papered name? Are they all that funny?"

"That's Ingrid. She's a grade horse. She doesn't have a papered name."

"Why not?"

"Think of her as a mutt. No one is sure of her lineage." I cross the aisle and give Ingrid a pat. "But that doesn't mean she's any less special, does it, sweetie?"

"I never knew any of that about papers and grades," Maddox says.

I give him a sideways look. "But your grandma owned this place."

He shrugs. "She used to read me books about horses when I was little, and I suppose she tried to teach me things, but we weren't here much."

"I was surprised I never saw you come back after that time."

He runs a finger across his temple. "Yeah, well, I guess we all got busy."

"I'm sure someone could show you around; give you a tour of the place." I look around. "Normally there would be. I'm not sure where everyone is."

"My dad said there was a big meeting this morning in the barn office."

I nod. "Makes sense. There's a lot to discuss, I'm sure."

"Darn," Reece says. "It would have been fun to have a tour before I fly out tomorrow."

"I could do it."

"You?" Maddox says. "Do you work here?"

"I'm not an employee of DHR, but they contract with me for my veterinary services. I know the place like the back of my hand. I've been riding here for fifteen years."

"We don't want to impose," Maddox says, earning him a kick in the shin from Reece.

I laugh. "It's fine. I'd love to show you around." I look them over. "Come with me." I lead them to the tack room at the front of the stable. Along with all of the gear for riding horses, the room is lined with extra muck boots, gloves, hats, and basically anything a visitor to the ranch could need. I point to the boots. "Find a pair that fits. You do not want to walk around here in ballet flats or Nikes."

Reece explores the room. The DHR brand on the wall catches her eye. "I saw this on Vivian's front door."

"You'll see it all over, on every saddle, barn door, and fence post. It's the brand for Devil's Horn Ranch."

She traces the "horns" above the lettering. "I like it." She turns to Maddox. "Maybe I should come up with a Reece Mancini brand."

"Maybe you should," he says. "You could start a trend."

I wonder what she does that would have her needing a brand. Before I can ask, she pulls on boots and stands. "Ready," she says, smiling.

"Not quite." I reach for a hat and offer it to her. "Vivian had a strict rule. Anyone on the ranch has to wear one."

Reece takes it and puts it on backward. "How do I look?"

Maddox takes it off, turns it around, and plops it back down. "Your fans would love to see you like this."

She picks up a stray piece of hay, puts it in her mouth, and poses with one leg on a bench. I suppose she's trying to look like Annie Oakley or something. "Fans?"

Maddox laughs. "Reece is kind of a big deal."

"Shut up," she says. "Take the picture, but nobody sees it but Garrett."

While Maddox snaps a few shots, I google Reece Mancini. I'm floored to find out she's a Grammy-winning singer, and she's married to a guy who plays drums for one of the hottest rock bands in the country. I'm embarrassed that I didn't have any idea. "Oh, gosh, you're famous. I mean you know that. I've never met anyone famous before, and here I am, making you put on boots in case you step in horseshit." Oh my god, I said horseshit in front of a celebrity. "I'll shut up now."

They laugh. Reece says, "It's refreshing to run into someone who doesn't recognize me. Makes me feel like a regular person, which I am. Now how about that tour?"

I walk them out front so we have a good view of most of the buildings. "You're familiar with the main house." I point east. "There's also a guesthouse. It's currently vacant. There are two smaller houses over there, where Matteo and Miguel live."

"Miguel?" Maddox says.

"He's the barn manager."

"I thought Matteo was the barn manager."

"Matteo is the *ranch* manager. He pays the bills, orders supplies, and makes sure the buildings and equipment are maintained. He's basically the boss of everyone. Although there's a lot of administration, he does get his hands dirty. He even assists with minor vet duties. Miguel, on the other hand, oversees the hay and grain deliveries and supervises the workers who clean the stalls, turn out the horses, and mend the fences."

Maddox shakes his head. "There is so much I don't know."

"It's not your job to know things, Connecticut." I scrunch my brow. "What *is* your job, if you don't mind my asking."

"Bartender."

"He means bar manager," Reece says proudly.

"For my aunt's restaurant," he explains, as if he's *not* proud.

"She must really trust you if she made you manager," I say.

"It's not something I plan to do forever."

"What do you plan on doing?"

"I have absolutely no idea, but I know it's not working at a gym, a production company, a photography studio, or a restaurant."

"Miguel is looking for another barn worker. You ever mucked out a horse stall?"

"I'd probably get kicked in the head."

"Nah. You just need to understand how to act around horses. If they think you're afraid of them, they'll get scared. If you are comfortable around them, they sense it."

"I *am* afraid of them," he says, rubbing his temple again.

"We'll have to see what we can do about that." I'm smiling like a smitten schoolgirl. Victor, the man I'm seeing, would not be amused. I think the reason I'm drawn to Maddox is because of his connection with Viv. Oh, how I miss her. "To finish out the accommodations, there's a log cabin a ways in that direction. Owen, the assistant ranch manager, lives there. There's another small cabin near the cattle pens."

"Nana has cows?"

"About two hundred head. They are mostly used to train the horses." I point back at the main stable. "There are a few apartments behind the arena and a bunkhouse where some of the ranch hands and barn workers stay."

"Wow," Reece says. "Just how many employees work here?"

"Let me see." I do the calculation in my head. "Twenty or twenty-one, not counting me."

Maddox's jaw drops. "This place makes enough money to pay twenty-one people?"

"It does, and then some. Vivian wasn't only a great rancher, she was an incredible businesswoman." I see what's about to happen and pull Maddox aside. "Watch your step, cowboy."

He glances at the pile of manure he almost squished, then looks at my hand still on him. I quickly pull away, not knowing what has come over me.

"First rule of ranch life—walk looking down."

I don't miss how Reece's eyes dart back and forth between us. She thinks I'm flirting, but I'm not. At least I don't think I am, and I shouldn't be. Because of Victor and all.

Reece pulls out her phone. "Garrett's calling. Sorry, but husband trumps tour. See ya." She hurries away.

Maddox looks embarrassed. She didn't really get a call. "Sorry," he says. "She can be… she's always trying to… never mind. You were saying?"

Merle, one of the assistant horse trainers, appears from the stable. "Dr. Shaw, can you please take a look at June Bug's eye? I'm not sure the infection has cleared."

"Be right there."

Maddox has a strange look on his face. "You're a doctor." He chuckles. "I have a hard time picturing you as anyone other than the girl in the pink cowboy hat, riding a horse."

My insides tingle. He pictures me?

"I suppose I should call you Dr. Shaw."

"Don't you dare. I ask them to call me Andie, but some of them are set in their ways. At least Dr. Shaw is better than ma'am. I mean, I'm only twenty-five." I gesture to the stable. "I'd better go. Duty calls."

"Maybe we can pick it up later?"

I shrug like it doesn't matter to me. "If we're both still here, sure."

"I'd like that."

I trot to the stable and turn before entering. He's watching me. He tips his hat, and my insides melt. I turn and bump right into Victor. "Hey, uh, what are you doing here?"

"Most yards are still too wet to mow because of all the rain. Figured I'd take advantage and come take my girl to lunch." He eyes Maddox. "Who's he?"

"Viv's grandson. The family came for the funeral."

"They staying on?"

"I don't think so."

"Want to go to lunch?"

"I have to check on a horse first. Can you wait a few minutes?"

"I'll wait in the truck."

As I work on June Bug, it dawns on me that Victor called me his *girl*. He's never said anything like that before. We've only been dating a month. He's my best friend's landscaper. Christina told me he saw a picture of me and insisted she introduce us. It's still new. He's nice. Not from the south but a true gentleman.

After I join Victor in his truck, I see Maddox sitting on the front porch with Reece and his sisters. When they wave, I wave back. Victor leans over to kiss my cheek, something else he has never done before. I smile at him as we drive away.

CHAPTER THREE

Maddox

"That was a short tour," Reece says, looking disappointed.

"She had to check on a horse. It looks like she had other plans anyway. Suave exit, by the way."

She sighs. "Looks like my matchmaking attempt was all for naught."

I watch the dust being kicked up from the guy's truck as they pull away.

"Who's she?" Jordan asks. "She was at the funeral, right?"

"Andie Shaw. She's the horse vet."

"Cool job."

"I suppose."

Mom pops her head out the screen door. "Lunch." Her eyes linger on me. "Who was the attractive woman out front?"

"Horse vet."

"Oh, that sounds like a fun job."

Reece and Jordan snicker.

"What am I missing?" Mom asks.

"You're missing nothing. Let's eat."

After lunch, Mom contemplatively washes a plate. "I'm going to miss this place."

"We haven't been here in forever," I say.

"I know, and I regret it now." She addresses all of us. "Never take anything in life for granted. Your father and I spoke of the ranch on many occasions, and we intended to visit more often, but life always seemed to get in the way." She sits at the table, slumping in her chair. "You can never get back time with people you love once they're gone. I hope you all learn how to seize the day and do what you desire, despite life telling you otherwise. Okay? Promise me."

"We promise, Mom," Jordan says.

She gives us quick hugs before leaving the room.

Caitlyn retrieves Nana's old cowboy hat, hanging by the back door, and runs a finger along the rim. "I miss her."

"Cool hat," Reece says, taking it from Caitlyn and putting it on.

I quickly take it off. "Not this one." I put it back on the peg. "This one stays right here. It was her favorite."

Reece frowns, looking guilty. "Oh, gosh. I didn't know."

"It's fine. She wore the old thing everywhere. The only pictures we have of her without it are from when she came to Connecticut to visit, and only after we asked her to remove it. She'd come at least once a year, sometimes twice. She always showed up wearing it. I can't remember her any other way."

"You can take the girl out of the country…" Reece says.

I chortle. "Yeah."

We sit on the front porch, watching a horse trainer in action. He stands in the center of a circular pen with a horse on a long line, snapping his rope on the ground as it gallops around him.

"Do you think it's easy to train a horse?" Reece asks. "It's obviously not like training a dog. No 'sit' and 'stay'."

"Dunno."

"You really don't know anything about horses, do you?"

I shake my head. "Now I wish I had learned more."

"There's always time."

"We leave tomorrow."

She puts a hand on mine. "I'm sorry."

A truck pulls up. It's the one Andie left in before. It stops next to the house instead of the stables. The man leans over and kisses her. She looks embarrassed when she sees us watching.

"Later, babe," he shouts as she walks away. He turns the truck around and barrels out of the driveway like a bat out of hell.

"Boyfriend?" Reece asks.

"Not really."

Reece's eyebrows shoot up. "But he called you babe."

Andie scrunches her brows. "That's a new development. I guess we're dating. Uh, we've gone on a few dates. I only met Victor a month ago."

Victor. Why do I suddenly hate that name?

"Do you have more horses to tend to?" I ask.

"No, but my truck is here, and I wondered if you wanted the rest of the tour."

I stand. "Sounds good." I can see Reece smiling out of the corner of my eye. "You coming?"

"No. I have to pack."

"But you're not leaving until tomorrow."

"I have a lot of shit, Maddox. Now go ahead, and don't take anything for granted."

I shoot her a look. She smiles big, spins on her heels, and goes into the house.

"She's nice," Andie says.

"She is. She's not some rock star diva, like a lot of musicians."

"I'm still embarrassed I didn't recognize her. We don't listen to a lot of pop or rock down here."

"Where did we leave off?"

"Go get on your boots and hat, and I'll show you."

I go to the tack room and do what she says. When I look back at her, she's looking up, warming her face in the sun. I haven't seen a lot of women in cowboy hats, so I don't know what they normally look like. I wonder if they all look this good. She catches me staring, and I can't look away. Her blue eyes are stunning. They remind me of something. "Do you still have that horse… what did you call her? Baby Blue?"

"I do. Want to meet her?"

"She's here?"

"These are the best stables around. I've always boarded her here."

"The best ones, huh?"

She nods. "It will be a shame if the new owners aren't like Viv."

"Do you have any idea who they'll be?"

"No, but there's been talk. Hugh Jenkins owns a ranch nearby. He'd probably be the best. I know he's interested. I doubt he can afford it though. Then there's Dillon Patlinger. He's an old rodeo star, but he has no idea how to run a good horse ranch. I'm not sure I would keep Baby Blue here if he bought it. But it's the Thompsons who scare me the most."

"My dad used to be married to Karen Thompson."

"So I've heard. They have the money and the means, but they'd most likely mow it down and use the land for oil, if it's rich enough, or break it up and sell it off in bits and pieces. Maybe even put condos on it. Who knows? They do what makes them the most money regardless of whether or not it's best for the community."

We pass several people in the stable. Andie greets all of them by name and tells me which horses they board here.

She stops in front of a stall. "Here she is, my pride and joy." She opens the gate and we walk in. "Go ahead, you can touch her. Do it with confidence. Run your hand down her like this."

I do it exactly the way she did. The horse paws the ground. "Oh, man, she's not going to kick me, is she?"

Andie laughs. "Quite the opposite. That means she's happy."

"Good. So did you name her after yourself, because your eyes are so blue?"

She turns pink. "Her papered name is Caribbean Blue. It's too formal, so I gave her a barn name when I got her."

"How long have you had her?"

"Fifteen years. My granddad bought her for me for my tenth birthday. She always loved Viv. All the horses loved Viv. Sometimes I wonder if they know she's gone."

"You call her Viv. Nobody else did. Why?"

"Your grandmother was like a mother to me. My mom was a single parent. She died when I was eight. Cancer. Granddad raised me after that. He called her Viv, so I did, too. She took a special interest in me when I started coming around. At first I think she felt sorry for me, but then we became friends. Family. She even paid my way through vet school. I owe her everything."

"I'm sorry about your mom."

"Thanks. Hey, do you want to go riding? It'll make the tour easier. There's a lot of ground to cover."

"You should know I suck at it."

"Duly noted, but if this is the last day you'll ever be on a horse ranch, you should spend it on a horse, don't you think?"

"Which one?"

She steps back and looks around, appraising the dozens of horses in the stalls. "Tadpole," she says, approaching a brownish horse.

"Why him?"

"He's a gelding, which means he's gentler than a stallion, but he's big, like you. He's also good with beginners."

"I wouldn't say I'm a beginner."

"When's the last time you were on a horse?"

I touch my scar. "Ten years ago?"

She looks shocked. "Ten years ago when I saw you? You were hurt. Is that why you haven't been back? It wasn't the horse's fault, you know. Horses are gentle animals. They're flight animals, which means they won't fight, they flee. He was afraid of the snake and took a bad step."

"You remember an awful lot about that day."

"It was the day that shaped my entire future."

I narrow my eyes in curiosity.

"I felt helpless when they shot the horse. I wanted to do everything in my power to make sure it wouldn't happen again. That was the day I knew I wanted to become an equine vet."

I laugh incredulously.

"What's so funny?"

"You knew at age fifteen what you wanted to do with your life, and here I am still trying to figure it out."

"Maybe it'll come to you when you least expect it."

She calls to a barn worker to saddle up Tadpole, then she guides Baby Blue to the tack room and saddles her up so quickly, my eyes can't keep up.

Tadpole is led over to me. My heart pounds. What if I screw up trying to mount and fall on my face? It's been a while.

Andie takes the reins. "You remember how to do this?"

"Will you hold it against me if I fall off and cry like a baby?"

She laughs. "You won't fall. Throw your weight up and over as you swing your leg across."

"Like riding a bike, huh?" I joke.

"Well, no, but…"

Thank God I'm successful on my first attempt.

"Remember, horses respond to pressure. If you squeeze your legs too tightly, he'll go. Release and he'll slow down. Say the word if you need help. We'll take it slow."

We exit the stable. I don't do much to guide Tadpole; he's good following Baby Blue. I can hardly blame him.

"What do you want to know about the ranch?" she asks.

"Tell me everything you know."

"Okay, but I know a lot. Stop me if you get bored. Devil's Horn Ranch is about ten thousand acres, which is fifteen square miles."

"Jesus, that's big, isn't it?"

"To give you some perspective, a football field, minus the end zones, is about an acre."

"Holy shit."

"This is nothing compared to some ranches in Texas. DHR is barely considered a mid-sized ranch. The largest one I know of is over eight hundred thousand acres."

"Wow."

"There are almost two hundred horses here. Fifty of them are owned by your grandma's estate, some of which are elite broodmares and valuable Quarter Horse stallions. All the others are boarders, like Baby Blue. Three thousand acres of land are dedicated to the horses. That includes three stables, the hay barn, a large and small pavilion, indoor and outdoor riding arenas, four round training pens, thirty paddocks, six pastures, outbuildings for tractors, four-wheelers, and other large equipment, a hot walker and, let's see, what am I forgetting?"

I chuckle. "I'm going to pretend I understood half of what you said. What's the rest of the land used for?"

"There's about two thousand acres of hunting ground, rich in deer, quail, elk, turkey, and antelope. It gets rented out to hunting clubs and for private parties. Another two thousand acres are leased to a local windmill contractor. Five hundred acres are dedicated to the cattle. The rest is undeveloped land used for riding trails. It's beautiful and pristine, with rolling grassy hills. Oh, and there's an airstrip by the far west fence, but it hasn't been maintained, so I wouldn't go landing a plane there. Rumor is teenagers sometimes break in and have motorcycle races there—but you never heard that from me."

"Is that so?" I shake my head in awe. "My grandmother did all this?"

"I told you, Viv was an amazing businesswoman."

"When I was a kid, the ranch was maybe a tenth the size it is today."

We're approached by a man on a horse. He slows. "Hey, Doc."

"Owen, this is Maddox, Vivian's grandson."

"Damn glad to meet you, Maddox."

"You too."

"Owen is the assistant ranch manager. Youngest one ever, right, Owen? What are you, twenty-one?"

"Recently turned twenty-two, ma'am." Andie gives him a hard stare. "Sorry, Doc."

"I was giving Maddox the grand tour."

"You thinkin' of hanging around?" he asks.

"No, just wanted to see everything before, well, whatever happens."

"Your daddy owns all this now?"

"I guess he does."

"Well then maybe it's your responsibility to make sure you help him keep it from fallin' into the wrong hands."

"I think you're confusing me with someone who has power, Owen."

"Maybe so." He makes a clicking sound, and his horse walks away. "Nice meeting ya. Hope to see you around."

"You, too."

Sprinkles of rain fall. "Damn," Andie says. "And here I was hoping we'd get an entire day without precipitation. We'd better head back."

We turn the horses in the direction of the stables, going slower than the other riders making their way back from the trails. As they pass us, Andie has short conversations with each of them.

"Do you know *everyone* who boards horses here?"

"Pretty much. Devil's Horn Ranch is like a community, everyone knows everyone and they're always helping each other out."

The last of the horses trot ahead of us. "Have you saved many animals?" I ask.

"Sure. I save them all the time. It's my job."

"I mean like the horse I fell off ten years ago."

She shakes her head. "Sadly, horses that get injuries like that one can't be saved. Their legs are fragile. They have to carry a lot of weight. Certain injuries they just can't recover from."

"That sucks."

"It does, but I still love my job. I can't imagine doing anything else."

We make small talk on the short ride back. As we reach the stable, three sleek black pickup trucks pull up, looking like a presidential motorcade.

"Oh, boy," Andie says.

"What?"

"It's the Thompsons."

Andie calls someone over to help with the horses. Then a dozen people come out of the building next to the stable, the one with the offices. Dad is among them. I pull Andie aside. "Who are all these people?"

"You met Matteo already. The one in the red shirt is Miguel Avila, the barn manager. The guy with the scar on his face is Mickey Underwood, the head trainer. Hugh Jenkins, the ranch owner I mentioned this morning is in the gray shirt. Oh, wow—that's the mayor in the blue suit. The other men I don't recognize."

Joel Thompson gets out of a truck. He walks up to the mayor. "I wasn't aware there was a community meeting, Patrick."

"There isn't."

"Then what's Jenkins doing here?"

"He was passing by when he saw my car and popped in to sit in on our conversation."

"Conversation. Right." Joel looks mad.

The men in the other black trucks get out and stand behind him, arms crossed. I lean over to Andie and whisper, "What is this, a rumble?"

"The funny thing is, you probably aren't wrong."

Joel goes over to my dad. "Why didn't you call?"

"Hadn't gotten around to it yet."

"My offer will beat Jenkins', I guarantee it."

"I haven't accepted any offers yet. Truth be known, he hasn't made one."

"Good." Joel motions to someone, who brings him a file folder. He takes it and hands it to Dad. "Here's mine. Look it over. You'll find it's more than generous. Enough so your kids won't have to work a day in their lives."

"That's hardly the point. I want my kids to work."

Joel laughs like Dad is crazy. "You get any other offers, let me know." He hands Dad a business card. "In case you lost the other one."

"I didn't."

"Well, then, I'll be off."

The six men get into three trucks and drive off, leaving dust in their wake. I turn to Andie. "Does he always ride with an entourage?"

"That's what mobsters usually do, don't they?"

My eyes widen. "Seriously?"

"No, not seriously." She cocks her head. "Well, maybe."

Dad shakes hands with the remaining men and then joins us.

"Big day?" I ask.

He blows out a big breath. "You could say that. If I was staying here a while, it would be ideal, but I can't. I'll have to do this from back home."

"Do what, sell the ranch?"

He puts a hand on my shoulder. "What choice do we have? But I can't sell it until it's officially in my name. Your grandmother was in the process of putting it in a trust, but it hadn't happened yet, so now it goes through probate. I'm named as her sole heir, so there won't be an issue, but it could take anywhere from six months to a year before we'll be able to sell."

"Then why are all these people here?"

"This is a big deal, Maddox. We're standing on a lot of prime land. People will fight over it, and it's up to me to decide what will happen."

Andie clears her throat. "Sorry," I say. "Dad, you remember Andie Shaw from yesterday. She's the veterinarian here and was a good friend of Nana's."

They shake. "Any friend of Mom's is a friend of mine," Dad says.

"She was a fine woman."

"Thank you."

"I'd better go," Andie says. "Looks like your family has a lot to discuss."

Dad gives me a look and inclines his head to her truck.

I say, "I'll walk you."

"I hope everything works out for you."

"And for you and Baby Blue."

"Thanks." She stands by the truck door.

There's an awkward silence. "Thank you for the tour."

"Sorry you couldn't see the whole thing."

"Maybe it's for the best."

"I suppose." She gets in and turns over the engine. "See you around, Connecticut."

"See ya, Doc."

She smiles, backs up, and drives away. Damn. Another place, another time maybe.

I look around, almost sad we're leaving tomorrow, which is funny, because I am so out of my element here. Maybe that's what makes it so interesting. I go over to the house.

Reece says, "You got her number, didn't you? Please tell me you got her number."

"I'm leaving tomorrow. I live in New York. We're selling this place, and I'll never have a reason to come back."

She shakes her head over and over. "There is a land called Missed Opportunity, and you, Maddox, are its king."

"Dinner's ready!" Mom shouts from inside.

We pile into the kitchen and sit around Nana's table, knowing it's probably the last time we'll do it. The air is thick with emotion.

"Matteo said he might know someone I can hire to watch over things and report back to me," Dad says. "Said he'd do it himself if running the ranch wasn't such a big job."

"It has to be someone you trust," Mom says.

"Why do you need someone here?" Jordan asks. "The employees take care of everything."

"Let's see," Dad says. "I'll need a caretaker for the house, not to mention the guesthouse. The mayor wants someone local to sit in on council meetings regarding the ranch. And the list goes on."

"What are the qualifications you're looking for?" Reece asks.

Dad laughs, "Are you applying for the job?"

"No, but I think Maddox should."

"Me?"

"Why not? It's not like you have some burgeoning career to go home to. Or a girlfriend. Or even a pet, for that matter. Your mom said they need someone they can trust. Who more than their own son?"

"But I don't know anything about running a ranch."

"Matteo runs the ranch, right, Mr. McBride? Maddox would just be here as your proxy, so to speak."

Dad's face lights up. "It's not the worst idea."

I shake my head. "It's ridiculous. I can't do it."

"Why?" Reece asks. "Name one reason you can't do this."

"I…, uh…, I guess I can't."

Reece is about ready to jump out of her skin. "Good, then it's settled?"

I turn to Dad. "Do you really think it's a good idea?"

"It's a great idea, sweetie," Mom says. "Right, Gavin?"

He laughs. "It's not one I'd have considered, but it kind of makes sense. So, yes, I guess it's settled."

CHAPTER FOUR

Andie

"Just keep an eye on her, Mr. Hendrix. She should be as good as new in a few days, but we want to keep her up and moving as much as possible."

"What would we do without you, Andie?"

"I'm happy to be of service. See you next time."

He nods to my truck. "Looks like someone's waitin' on you."

I try not to roll my eyes when I see Jon Thompson, the thirty-two-year-old illegitimate child of Joel and his Mexican housekeeper. While Jon looks ethnic, and nothing like his father, he sure did inherit his dad's unpleasant demeanor. Actually, I think Jon is in many ways worse than his father, because he thinks he has something to prove.

"Jon," I say politely and put my things in the truck bed. "What brings you here?"

"Saw your truck when I was passing by. Thought maybe you were hungry. It's almost lunchtime."

"I am hungry, and thanks for the offer, but I'm meeting someone for lunch—your wife."

"At least it's not that Victor guy. He's a real ass."

"Vivian always said it takes one to know one."

He laughs. "Old bat was as stupid as a rock. No wonder she fell down the stairs."

I push him. "Don't you ever talk about her that way."

He grabs my hand and holds it to him. "I'll talk about anybody any way I want to. You know why? 'Cause I'm a real fuckin' cowboy. Not some transplant like Victor what's-his-name. A girl like you needs a real cowboy." He pins me to the car with his body.

"Everything okay over here?" Mr. Hendrix asks.

Jon turns. "Buzz off, Henry."

I take the opportunity to squeeze my way out and get in the truck.

Jon calls after me, "Until next time!"

"Saw your husband today," I tell Christina.

She takes a sip of her mimosa. "That makes one of us."

"He was in rare form."

"Tell me again why you're still married to that asshole?" Tara asks.

"Because that asshole comes from a family that has more money than half of Texas."

"You'd get some of it if you divorced him," I say.

"Nope. Joel made me sign a prenup."

My jaw drops. "You never told us that."

She shrugs. "I was young and stupid. Now I'm stuck. But we have an understanding."

I cringe in disgust. "I've seen your understanding. He hits you, and you get a new bracelet."

She fingers the diamonds around her wrist. "It wasn't a hit as much as a push. You're making way too much out of it."

"You're better than that," I say.

"I have a housekeeper, three cars, a wardrobe most celebrities would die for, and a five-figure monthly allowance. I can put up with a little shove once in a while."

Tara scoffs. "I have a three-year-old, a dead-beat ex, a dead-end job, and I'm thousands of dollars in debt. I still win because I don't have to put up with your douchey husband."

"Touché," Christina says, raising her glass. "You're in debt? Why didn't you say something?" She pulls out her checkbook.

Tara shoves it away. "I don't want your money. I want you to see that living without it isn't as bad as you seem to think it is."

"I didn't go to college, like you guys did. I'm not good for anything other than planning dinner parties and sitting on social committees." She laughs. "How did the three of us turn out to be so different?"

"As if my psychology degree did me a bit of good," Tara says. "I'm waiting tables, in case you forgot."

"Are you guys happy?" Christina asks. "Like, are you where you thought you'd be in life?"

Tara looks at her son as he shoves a French fry in his mouth. "I may not be where I thought I'd be at twenty-five, but I'll take it."

They look at me.

"I have my dream job. Losing Viv was a blow, but yes, I'm happy."

"Let's not forget the hot new guy," Christina says. "How's that going?"

"Okay, I guess. He was acting strange the other day. Called me babe. We're definitely not to the babe stage yet. We haven't even had sex."

Christina chokes on her drink. "You haven't done the deed with the hot landscaper? Have you not seen his body?"

"No."

She fans herself. "Girl, you need to come by Thursday at three. He usually takes off his shirt by three-thirty. Believe me, you'll want to sleep with him after that."

Tara laughs. "Oh, my god, you and Jon *do* belong together."

"Hey, I'm married, not dead. Plus, like I said, we have an understanding."

"Meaning you can both have affairs or just *him?*"

She shrugs. "I haven't tested the theory yet."

"Watch yourself. In my experience, the apple never falls far from the tree. We've all heard stories about how Joel treated his ex-wife."

"What about Quinn?" Tara says. "He seems nice."

"Karen's kid?" I ask.

"Helped me change a flat last week. I hope he goes off to college and gets far away from his toxic family."

"Not likely," Christina says. "They keep close tabs on family. I have it on good authority that he smokes pot, and he's the gigolo of his high school. I get it though; he's gorgeous."

I elbow her. "He's seventeen and your nephew."

"I'm not saying I'd do him or anything. I'm just saying he's cute."

"Mama!" Trey screams, trying to get Tara's attention for the tenth time.

She pulls out crayons and a coloring book. "I'm sorry I couldn't get a sitter."

"Are you kidding?" I ruffle the hair of her adorable son. "I love this kid."

"What's on your agendas for the rest of the day?" Christina asks.

"I work second shift," Tara says. "What's new?"

"I have a date with Victor."

"How many will that be?" Tara asks.

"Five, I think."

"You definitely need to have sex," Christina says. "I can't believe you made it past three or four. His balls must be three shades of blue."

"He is pretty hot," Tara says. "In a mysterious sort of way."

"I guess he's attractive, and he can be funny. I don't know. Maybe we don't have much in common or something."

"Because you haven't slept together," Christina says. "You'll have lots in common after you've seen each other naked."

"You think?"

"How long has it been?" Tara asks. "Tony Ramsey was the last one, right? And that was what, six months ago?"

"Seven."

Christina laughs. "If you're counting how long it's been, you're ready. Just do it."

"Maybe I will."

They squeal. "We're going to need details," Tara says. "Lots and lots of details. I'm living vicariously, you know. There are cobwebs growing between these legs."

I check the time. "I have to get out to Thousand Acre Ranch." I leave a twenty on the table and kiss Trey's head. "See you guys later."

"Details!" Christina yells after me.

I'm so busy, the rest of my afternoon flies by, and before I know it, Victor is picking me up. "You look amazing," he says and peeks past me into my apartment. "Are you ever going to invite me in?"

"Play your cards right, and we'll see."

He straightens. "All right then. I promise to be on my best behavior."

I shut and lock the door. "Where are we off to?"

"I thought barbeque and then mini-golf."

"Sounds good."

All through supper, I try to picture Victor without his clothes on. Why am I not getting hot and bothered? I order another glass of wine. Maybe I'm nervous and need to drink more. After a while, though, I come to the conclusion I'm not nervous. I'm bored.

"Shall we?" he says after paying.

We make small talk in the car. Again I ask about his family, and again he's hesitant to offer information. For someone who seems so interested in a relationship, he sure is tight-lipped.

"There's not much to tell," he says.

"But what do they do? Is your dad in the landscaping business? Is that how you learned?"

"Why is my family so important to you?"

"I don't know. I guess because mine was. Mom and I were close. I miss that. It's why I was so drawn to Vivian. With my granddad in the retirement home now, I think family is important."

"Okay, fine. If it means that much to you, my dad was a construction worker, and my mom was an accountant."

"Was? You mean they aren't anymore?"

"No. They still are." He grabs my hand. "I'm kind of distracted by the possibility of seeing your apartment later."

Suddenly I'm regretting what I said. "We're here." I glance around the packed parking lot the mini-golf place shares with Target. "It looks busy."

He drives down the rows looking for a spot. We end up parking quite a distance from the entrance and closer to Target. On foot, we weave through the cars to get where we're going. I see a familiar face and stop.

"What is it?" Victor asks.

I can't answer because I've locked eyes with Maddox McBride. And suddenly, this date just got a lot more interesting. He rolls his packed shopping cart over. "Hey, Doc."

"Hey yourself, Connecticut. I thought you went back home days ago."

"Change of plans."

"Your name is Connecticut?" Victor asks.

"Victor James, meet Maddox McBride, Vivian's grandson. He's from Connecticut."

Victor's eyes dart between Maddox and me as they shake hands.

"My dad wanted someone to stay at the ranch, be a proxy for him since he couldn't stay any longer."

I'm aware of my heartbeat for the first time all night. "How long will you be here?" I glance at his cart. "Based on the amount of toilet paper, a while."

He laughs. I really like his laugh. "I'm not sure."

"Andie, the line isn't getting any shorter," Victor says.

"Right. Well, nice to run into you. I'll see you around the ranch."

"Yup."

"Bye."

Victor leads me away. I look back over my shoulder to see Maddox watching. He lifts his chin.

"What's up with that guy?" Victor asks.

"What do you mean?"

"He has no business being on a ranch if he's from Connecticut. What could he possibly know about it?"

I chuckle. "He knows absolutely nothing about it."

"You seem to think that's funny."

"I'm surprised is all."

"Surprised good or surprised bad?"

"Neither. Just surprised."

He looks at the line, then he puts a seductive hand on the back of my neck. "Maybe we should skip it and go back to your place."

"What? No. You promised mini-golf. I was looking forward to it. I haven't played since I was a kid."

"Whatever my lady wants. My dad used to say that to my mom when she asked him to rub her feet after she'd had a tough night shift."

"Night shift? Your mom worked nights as an accountant? And why would her feet hurt?"

"Uh, well, you know, during tax season and all, she'd have to work late. I don't know why her feet hurt. Maybe she wore high heels." He takes my elbow as the line moves forward. "Are we going to play or not?"

I breathe a sigh of relief. Despite what I told my friends earlier, regardless of what I said to Victor when he picked me up, I know *he's* not the guy I want coming to my apartment. I look back at the parking lot, but Maddox is long gone.

CHAPTER FIVE

Maddox

The FedEx truck pulls away after leaving four large boxes on the front porch.

Owen runs over. "Let me give you a hand with those."

I awkwardly pick one up. "Thanks. I think my parents must have sent every single piece of clothing I own."

He holds the door open for me and I go inside and turn toward the back bedroom. Owen says, "You don't want to take the master?"

"It was my grandmother's."

He follows me with one of the boxes. "There are a lot of memories in this house, huh?"

"My parents told me I should pack up her stuff. They thought we should donate her clothes."

"Good idea. Vivian would have wanted that."

"I'm not sure I can do it. It makes everything seem so final."

"It's not final if you still have these."

I glance back; he's looking at the pictures lining both sides of the hallway.

We drop the loads in the second largest bedroom in the house. I don't feel guilty staying in this one. We retrieve the remaining boxes.

"Can you tell me how things run around here? Like, how often do we get deliveries of hay? Is there a list of chores or whatever I should be tending to? And personnel—how often does the vet come around?"

A smile cracks his face. "I'll start by telling you what you're really after. Andie comes around a lot. At least a few times a week—more when it's foaling season, which is now. Do you really want to know about the hay?"

I laugh. "I guess not. I mean, yes, I'm interested in how things work around here, but I'm not sure how much I really need to know since my dad is selling and all."

"Word is that won't happen for months. That's enough time for you to learn everything there is to know about Devil's Horn Ranch. Hell, you might even end up stayin'."

"In Texas? I doubt it."

"Never say never. That's my motto. If you need anyone to show you the ropes, I'm your guy. Matteo is usually busy with paperwork and other business stuff. My time is more flexible."

"Thanks. I appreciate it. I don't want to seem like dead weight, so if you can think of anything for me to do, I'll do it."

"You might regret sayin' that, but if you're serious, you should start from the bottom up—it's how all ranchers learn."

"What's the bottom?"

"Mucking out stalls, mending fences, and hauling hay."

"I may have to buy some more appropriate clothes first."

"Jeans and T-shirts, man. That's all you need on a ranch." He glances at Nana's hat on the peg as he opens the back door. "And one of those. And some proper boots. Those Nikes won't last long around here."

"Sure thing. Thanks."

"Looky there," he says in the doorway. "Speak of the devil." I follow his gaze and see Andie entering one of the stables. "She's good people, and she deserves to be treated right."

I snicker. "Aren't you twenty-two or something? You talk like you're her father."

"You'll find everyone around here is protective of her. Vivian made sure of it. She's somethin' special. Don't know what she sees in that Victor guy she's taken up with."

"You think it's serious?"

"Nah, but maybe someone should make sure it don't get that way." He trots down the back steps then turns and raises his brows at me.

I grab a Coke and sit on the steps, waiting for her to come out. I don't want to seem desperate, because I'm not. I'm not even sure why I'm drawn to her. Could be she made an impression on me ten years ago. Could be I've gone so long without a date, it's starting to wear on me. Could be those incredible blue eyes.

Beau trots over and lies at my feet. He's black with a single white stripe running from the top of his head down between his eyes and around his nose. A large white patch of fur spans his chest. Three of his paws are black, the lone white one gray with dirt. I rub his ears. "I miss her too, buddy."

After my second Coke, I wonder if she's ever going to emerge. Owen crosses from the stable to the barn, smirking at me.

"Fine," I say to no one as I hop off the steps and stride to the stables. I look inside one, but she's not there. I go to the next stable. I hear voices and follow them until I see her. She and Matteo and someone I don't know are standing outside a large stall.

She sees me. "Come here. Look."

I go to the stall door and lean over. A horse is busy licking a newborn foal. "Did she just give birth?"

"About thirty minutes ago," she says.

"He's trying to stand already?"

Andie nods. "Healthy foals stand and start walking within an hour."

"That's incredible."

She smiles. "It is."

"Can I touch the foal, or will the mom get mad, like a mama bear?"

"You can touch them, but we like to give them time to bond. I'll hang around to make sure Kenzie expels the placenta and then I'll examine them, but they look good." She turns. "Have you met Romeo Sanchez? He's our farrier. Romeo, this is Vivian's grandson, Maddox."

"Pleasure to meet you," Romeo says with a heavy Spanish accent.

"And you. A farrier shoes horses, right?"

"That's my specialty."

"Don't let him fool you," Andie says. "He could definitely take care of a lot more than hooves if he needed to."

"The torturer," I say. They look at me sideways. "I used to think horses were being tortured when shoes were put on them. I must have been thirteen when Nana told me they aren't actually nailed into their feet."

"They still don't like it much," Romeo says. "I've got a few scars to prove it."

I reach up and touch mine. "I've got one of my own."

Andie looks at me sympathetically.

"I'll let you get back to work." I take no more than half a dozen steps when my Nike squishes into a pile of horse shit. "Aw, damn it."

Andie tries not to laugh and fails. "I did warn you."

I sit on a nearby bench and take the shoe off. Matteo nods down the way. "You can hose it off in the wash room."

"I might just throw it away."

"Get used to it, *hermano*," Romeo says. "You live on a horse ranch now. You're going to smell like shit whether you step in it or not."

I look at Andie. "*You* don't smell like horse shit."

Romeo snickers.

"I mean, you smell nice."

"Thanks," she says turning as red as I feel. "I usually change my clothes and boots at least once a day."

"I'll have to remember to do that."

"What size are you?" Romeo asks. "I'll go grab you one of our extra pairs of muck boots."

"Eleven. Thanks."

"I'm off to pick up a few supplies," Matteo says. "You need anything?"

I laugh. "A hat. Jeans. T-shirts. Boots. At least that's what Owen said."

"One man cannot buy boots and a hat for another," he says stoically.

"I was kidding. Not about needing them, but about you getting them. Except I have no idea where to get them. I found my way to Target, but that's as far as I've gotten."

"I can show you," Andie says. "You'll want to go into Ft. Worth to do the bulk of your shopping. I'm free on Sunday."

"That would be great. I'd really appreciate it."

Romeo drops the boots at my side and he and Matteo leave. I put on the boots and pick up my shit-covered shoe. "I better wash this off."

"I'll show you how the hose works. It can stick sometimes."

"Don't you have to stay here with the horses?"

"They'll be fine for a while. They don't need me staring at them while they bond."

She takes me to the wash room and shows me how things work. I hang my wet shoe out to dry. "I guess I should get used to this," I say. "Owen said he'd show me the ropes. Said I should muck out stalls to get a feel for things."

Her jaw goes slack. "He wants you to clean stalls? There are barn hands for that."

"I know, but I'm here. I'm not going to sit on the porch sipping whiskey and watch others do it. Might as well earn my keep."

"You're one of the owners, Connecticut. You don't have to earn anything."

"That's not what my grandmother would say."

She looks at me thoughtfully. "You're right. Viv would want you to clean stalls. Come on, I'll show you how."

"You muck out stalls? But you're a vet."

"Everyone had to start somewhere. I spent weekends and summers shoveling horse manure. It's the deal I made with my granddad in order to get Baby Blue."

I laugh. "I can't believe I'm going to say this, but let's shovel some shit."

She takes me to a nearby stall. "First put on some work gloves. You'll probably get blisters anyway, but they'll help. Grab that wheelbarrow there, and the shovel and shaving fork—that thing that looks kind of like a rake." She opens the stall door. "This one's not so bad. Looks like it was cleaned recently. Use the shovel for the manure and the fork to clean up the wet pine shavings. Put it in the wheelbarrow. There's a place out back to dump it. Then put fresh pine shavings on the floor and spread it evenly. Pile hay in the corner until it's about knee high. Finally, check the water trough. They use automatic waterers, but they get gummed up sometimes. I also habitually check the latches on the stalls. More than a few horses have escaped and wandered off over the years."

She stands aside and watches me follow her instructions precisely.

"You'd make a great ranch hand. I'd say you passed your first class with flying colors."

"Ranch Hand 101," I say. "My first *A*."

"First of many, if you have your grandmother's work ethic. What's next on your agenda?"

"Mending a fence?"

"That I can't help you with. But Owen, Miguel, or any of the ranch hands can. With a property this size, there's always a fence to mend."

"Guess I'm off to find a broken fence then," I say, taking a step back.

"Maddox, watch—"

I stop and turn, barely missing the same pile of shit I stepped in earlier. "Right, eyes down." I shovel it up and toss it in the wheelbarrow.

"And next time—wear a hat. You're breaking Vivian's cardinal rule. Besides, you're a real cowboy now."

"I doubt I'll ever be one of those. I'm from Connecticut, remember?"

"You think there aren't cowboys in Connecticut? You'd be hard pressed to find a state without them. Besides, you've mucked out a stall, and you've ridden horses. Maybe you should look up the definition."

I laugh. "Maybe I will. Good luck with the foal, Doc. I'll see you Sunday."

"Noonish?"

"Come hungry. We'll stop for lunch. It'll be my treat as a thank you."

"See you then, cowboy."

My pants get a little tighter, hearing her call me that. I wish I had on a hat. I'd tip it to her. After dumping the wheelbarrow out back, I go in search of someone who can help me be the man she thinks I can be.

CHAPTER SIX

Andie

Loaded up with everything Maddox needs, we return to the ranch. He eyes all the bags in the backseat of the pickup. "I can't thank you enough for this. Looks like I'm ready for anything."

"You'll want to go easy with the boots," I say. "It takes a while to break in a good pair." I put a foot up on the dash. "I've had these since I was nineteen."

I feel the heat of his eyes as he looks at my boot and then farther up my leg. When he realizes what he's doing, he quickly turns away. "Seems like a long time to have a pair, especially with what you do."

"I've only been a vet for a year, and not a lot of people wear cowboy boots in Ithaca, New York."

"You were in Ithaca?"

"I went to vet school at Cornell."

"Damn, really? Good school."

"Number two in the nation for veterinary medicine."

His eyebrows shoot up. "You must be pretty smart. Well, of course you're smart; you're a doctor. I meant you must be smarter than the average vet."

"Thanks. I like to think I am."

"Ithaca is only a few hours from New York City."

"We used to take the train there for long weekends."

"I live there, you know."

"I thought you lived in Connecticut."

"Grew up in Connecticut. My parents still live there. I moved to the city a while ago."

"Well, that stinks. Calling you 'New York' just doesn't have the same ring to it."

He laughs. "I wonder if we were ever at the same place at the same time."

"It's a big place."

"It is. Still…"

I wonder the same thing. Were we ever at the same restaurant? Did we pass each other on the sidewalk? He has no idea how much I've thought about him over the years. How I hoped one day I might run into the boy who fell off the horse. I thought he would show up at the ranch someday, but I never said anything. Not even to Viv.

"I've been meaning to ask you how you became a doctor so fast. I mean, you're my age. Isn't vet school like medical school? Don't you have to go for four years?"

"You do. But when I graduated high school, I had so many credits from my AP classes, that it only took two years to get through college. After four years at Cornell, I graduated at twenty-four. And here I am a year later."

"I still think it's great you know exactly what you want to do with your life."

"I know I'm the exception to the rule. Most people have no idea what they want to do. Take my friends, Christina and Tara. Tara went to Baylor with me for undergrad. She studied psychology. Now she's waiting tables at La Cocina. And Christina… now that I think about it, she's doing exactly what she set out to do. She's a rich Texas housewife."

"Women aspire to be housewives?"

I elbow him. "Hey now, it's the twenty-first century. Didn't you get the memo saying we can be whatever we want to be?"

"So one of your friends is a socialite, the other is a waitress, and you're a veterinarian. The three of you make quite the trio."

"We do, and we all hate Christina's husband. Even Christina."

"Then why is she with him?"

"Did you not hear the part about her wanting to be a rich Texas housewife?"

"So she's in it for the money."

I sigh. "She claims she is, but I think there's more to it. He's a Thompson. Thompsons don't give up easily. Her divorcing him would make him seem like a loser. His family would never stand for it."

"Your best friend is a Thompson?"

"By marriage, yes."

"Oh my god, is she married to the old man?"

"Joel? No. His son, Jon."

"The way you say his name… you really do despise him, don't you?"

"He hits on me."

He glances at me. "He hits on you? But he's married to your best friend."

"He's a Thompson. You'll learn soon enough that family doesn't care about rules. They take what they want."

He grips the steering wheel so hard his knuckles turn white. "Has he—"

"Whoa, cowboy. He hasn't crossed that line, but he sure does like to stand smack dab on top of it sometimes."

"You tell me if he bothers you. I'll handle it."

"Oh, you'll handle it. Maddox, I'm not sure you understand the Thompsons. They aren't a family you 'handle.'"

"If he touches you—"

"He hasn't. He won't. I'm sorry I said anything. Can we talk about something else please?"

"What does your boyfriend think of Jon hitting on you?"

"You really don't get the point of talking about something else, do you?" He stares me down with his side-eye. "And Victor is not my boyfriend."

"Does *he* know that?"

"He's nice. I don't want to hurt his feelings."

"So Christina is with Jon because she's afraid of them hurting her, and you're staying with Victor because you're afraid of hurting him."

"Relationships can be complicated. What about you? Did you leave anyone behind in New York?"

"No one is crying in their wine over me. I haven't had a serious relationship in a long time."

We pull into Devil's Horn Ranch, where I left my truck. A car is parked behind it that looks conspicuously out of place on a horse ranch. "You expecting someone?"

"Considering I don't know anyone here, no."

He parks around back. By the time we get out, a man and woman wearing black suits are walking over.

"Looks official," I say. "You haven't killed anyone, have you?"

"Not yet. But if Jon hits on you again…"

I roll my eyes.

"Andie Shaw?" the woman behind the reflective sunglasses asks.

"Did *you* kill anyone?" he whispers, then steps forward. "Who's asking?"

The woman flashes an FBI badge. "Special Agent Katherine York. This is Special Agent Michael Watkins. Is there someplace private we can talk?"

"I'm confused," I say. "Am I in trouble? How did you find me? I don't live here."

"They're the FBI, Andie."

The woman motions to the house. "So, inside?"

I glance at Maddox, unsure what to say. What does the FBI want with me? I realize my hands are shaking.

"Yeah. Yes. Of course," he says. "Right this way." He ascends the porch steps and opens the door.

The man doesn't walk in but stands at attention outside. Agent York says to Maddox, "Mind waiting out here with Special Agent Watkins?"

"It's my house. I'd rather not. Look at her," he says, touching my shoulder. "You've got her scared out of her mind."

"And you are?" she asks.

"Shouldn't you already know that?" Maddox says. York isn't amused. "A friend. Maddox McBride. My family owns this ranch."

I say, "I'd like him to stay, if it's okay."

She thinks about it. "This conversation is confidential, understood?"

He nods. We go inside and sit around the kitchen table. Maddox says, "Can I offer you anything? Water?"

"No thank you." She pulls a photo out of her inside jacket pocket and slides it across the table. "Do you recognize this man?"

Maddox and I share a look. "It's Victor James." I laugh nervously. "Did *he* kill someone?"

"That's what we're trying to figure out, ma'am. He's a person of interest in a missing person's case."

I cover my mouth with my hand. "I was joking. I mean, really? Victor?"

She retrieves a piece of paper from the same pocket and shows it to me. "His name isn't Victor."

Maddox leans over my shoulder, and we stare at a photocopy of a Missouri driver's license that belongs to Tim Dorsey. On it is a picture of Victor, with longer hair and no facial scruff. She shows us another driver's license belonging to Neil Richmond. This one is from Vermont. He's a redhead, not a dirty-blond, like he is now.

I'm stunned. "Who is he?"

She points to the Missouri license. "Tim Dorsey."

I study the license and look up, surprised. "He's twenty-three? He told me he's twenty-seven."

"He also told you his name is Victor," Maddox says. "Just who is this guy, and who do you think he killed?" He gets up and paces. "Holy shit, Andie, you're dating a goddamn murderer. You guys are going to arrest him, right? Andie can tell you where he lives. In fact, why aren't you out arresting him now? You obviously know he's in the area." He runs a frustrated hand through his hair. "Why are you wasting your time here?"

"Do I need to ask you to step outside?" York says. "Or can you calm down so we can finish?"

He sits, clearly brooding. I can hardly blame him. I'm more than a little freaked out myself. I have never been more glad that I didn't invite him back to my apartment the other night.

"Eleven months ago, while living under the name Neil Richmond, a woman went missing. Someone he worked with at a landscaping business. As of now, he's a person of interest in a missing person's case, not a murder."

Maddox snorts. "At least he didn't lie about his profession."

"It may have been the only job he could get that allowed him to get paid under the table," York says. "We got a tip last week that he might be in the Ft. Worth area. We've been following him around for a few days and that's how we found you, Ms. Shaw."

Maddox smacks the table. He's pissed. "You've been following him around? Are you shitting me? While Andie's life could be in danger? Who the hell do you think you are? What if something had happened to her?"

"Like I said, we've been following him. We would have stepped in if he'd tried anything the other night."

My heart races. "What if I'd asked him to my apartment?"

"We had it covered. My partner was ready to pose as building maintenance, checking a gas leak."

"I'm confused. Why not just arrest him?"

She hesitates. Maddox scoffs in disgust. "Because they can't prove it, and now they're here talking to you." He gets up again, this time so fast his chair falls backward. "Oh, hell no," he says to her. "You want to use her to get to him, don't you?" He points to the door. "I think you should leave."

York pushes another photo at me. "This is Jennifer Grossman, single mom. Left behind a six-year-old girl who's being raised by her grandparents. Don't you think this little girl deserves some closure?"

Maddox picks up the picture and then looks at me. "This could be you, Andie. Blue eyes. Dark hair. Around your age." He turns to York. "You think this guy has a thing for women who look like this?"

"It wouldn't be the craziest thing I've ever come across."

"What is it you want from me?" I ask. "I don't know much about him. I'm not sure how I can help. In fact I was thinking of calling it off." I laugh. "What am I saying? I'm *definitely* calling it off. I never want to see him again." I study the woman in the photo. "This is all so creepy."

"We'd rather you didn't call it off," she says.

"Why would I—"

"No fucking way," Maddox says. "These special agents want you to keep seeing him so you can feed them information. Maybe do a little digging."

I laugh. "I think you watch too much television."

"Actually…" York says.

"You're kidding. No. No way."

York nods. "You'll be safe. We'll have eyes or ears on you at all times."

"You want me to pretend I like him? After seeing all this? I don't want to do that. I don't think I *could* do that."

"How well do you know Tim, er, Victor, Mr. McBride?"

"I don't know him at all."

"What if Maddox goes with you on your next date?"

"Oh, that wouldn't be obvious at all," he says.

"I'll be there, too," she says. "I'll pose as your girlfriend. It will be a double date. We'll have fun, have a few drinks, get him to trust us. Eventually we might end up at his place. You'll distract him, and I'll do some digging."

"Eventually?" I say, terrified. "Exactly how long do you expect me to do this?"

She produces a picture of a six-year-old girl. "As long as it takes to find out what happened to her mother."

"It's too dangerous," Maddox says. "Find someone else. Andie can break up with him and then *you* can swoop in and be his girlfriend."

"He trusts her already."

"What if he shows up at her apartment unannounced?"

"She can call us. We'll have agents standing by."

"Way too risky. You'd have to protect her at all times."

"We don't have the resources for that."

"Find them or no deal."

"Excuse me," I say. "I'm sitting right here. I do have a say in this."

"You're going to agree to see that slime bag?"

I pick up the picture of the little girl. "I'm not wild about it, but if I'm their only hope."

Maddox blows out a long breath. "I can't believe you're considering this. You're vulnerable. Does your apartment have security?"

"No."

He crosses to the window and looks out. "Move here. There are a dozen guys around who can help keep an eye on you."

"Like moving into your house won't raise any red flags for Victor. Are you crazy?"

"Not here with me." He points out the window. "There. In the guesthouse."

"How could I justify it?"

"Student loans," York says. "You're a vet recently out of school. You must have a lot of debt."

Maddox laughs disingenuously. "If you're so good at your job, you'd know she didn't have any student loans. My grandmother paid for her schooling."

"Does Victor know that?" she asks.

I shake my head.

"Good. Then that will be your reason. Say they're raising your rent and you can't afford the increase. You were close to the woman who owned this property?"

I nod.

"Tell him she was always nagging you to move to the property since you're here a lot anyway. Tell him when we all go out together. With me there, he'll have no reason to be jealous of Maddox. He'll see we're a couple, and Maddox isn't competition. Maddox can become his friend. You can help him find common ground, something Victor brought up he could use as an in."

"Why do you keep calling him Victor?"

"Because *you* need to keep thinking of him as Victor. We all do."

This all feels like a dream, and I keep waiting to wake up. "This is a lot to take in."

"I know, and I'm sorry to put you in this position."

Maddox sees my shaking hands, pulls a bottle of wine from the rack, and pours me a glass.

York watches him pour. "Learn how to water down drinks. It'll help when we're out together. You'll need clear heads."

I raise the glass. "Well, I don't need a clear head now." I gulp it down.

York stands. "I'll be in touch. We'll want to do this soon, in a day or two. Set something up the next time he calls, then let us know."

"Aren't you tapping his phone or something?"

"It's not that easy." She pulls out her card and hands it to Maddox. "Don't let him find this. Add me to your contacts as Melina Scott."

"If his real name is Tim, and whatever he did to that woman he did as Neil, why was he posing as Neil?"

"We don't know the answer to that yet."

"As in he could be a serial killer?"

"Let's not get ahead of ourselves. It could turn out to be a dead end. Using other identities doesn't necessarily mean he's a murderer. It's only one of a few avenues we're exploring."

"So he's not the only person of interest?"

"We're looking at her ex-husband as well."

I exhale a relieved breath. "You know, you could have led with that. Maybe Victor isn't to blame at all."

"I didn't tell you because I don't want you to let your guard down."

Maddox rests his hands on the back of his righted chair. "She won't. I won't let her."

The agent smiles for the first time since we met, and I realize she's actually very pretty. "Looks like you're a good man to have around. I'll be in touch."

"Bye, Special Agent York," I say.

She turns. "Nuh-uh. Melina. Get used to it."

"Okay. Bye, Melina."

She leaves with the other agent. I close my eyes and try to take in what happened. Maddox taps me on the shoulder and hands me my glass of wine, then pours one for himself. We sit at the table, finishing the bottle, and wonder what the hell we just signed up for.

CHAPTER SEVEN

Maddox

"Does this stream provide water for the entire ranch?" I ask, looking at the flowing water below the ridge we're on.

"No," Owen says. "Not even close. We have two main electric water wells, four additional submersible water wells scattered across the property, and miles of water lines feeding into small ponds and water troughs."

I'm trying to listen to what he's saying, but all I can think about is Andie. It's impossible for me to be with her twenty-four seven, and although I'm a big guy, could I protect her from a criminal?

My horse starts to trot. Owen rides up beside me. "Ease up. You seem tense, and he can sense it. You're probably squeezin' him with your legs and sending mixed signals. Did you even hear a word I said? You seem distracted."

"I guess I am."

"You miss Vivian. I get it. I'm sure touring the ranch has you thinkin' of her."

"Can you teach me how to shoot?"

"Sure. You got a permit? Do you own any guns?"

I shake my head.

"Why does a city boy want to learn how to handle a gun?"

"I'm not a city boy when I'm on the ranch. I want to learn everything."

"Coulda fooled me with how your mind has been anywhere but here."

Someone on a horse approaches in the distance. I squint until I can make out who it is.

Owen laughs. "I get it now. It isn't Vivian's memory that's distracting you, it's the pretty veterinarian."

"What? No."

"I'm calling horseshit, friend. All morning you've been about as interested in what I'm saying as a box of rocks. Then Suzie Sunshine comes ridin' up, and all of a sudden you're sitting tall."

"Hey, guys," Andie says, bringing Baby Blue to a stop. "Owen, Matteo needs you. Something about a mix-up with the grain."

"He didn't call. My phone not gettin' a signal?" He pulls it out of his pocket. "Four bars."

"I told him I'd ride out. He said you were probably with Maddox on the ridge."

He's amused. "I see. Okay then, you two have fun." He glances at the hot sun, then takes off his shirt and wipes his brow. I'm shocked to see what's tattooed on his left shoulder blade.

"Did you see that?" I ask Andie after he rides away. "He's got the DHR brand tattooed on his back."

"Several of them do. It's their way of pledging themselves to the ranch."

"But what if they go work somewhere else?"

"You don't get it, do you? Ranchers are a family. When they find somewhere they fit in, most of them stay for life. Few will ever have enough money to buy their own spread. *This* is their ranch, and they treat it like their own."

"How come you came all the way out here?"

"I figured I'd pick up where Owen left off. We never did finish the tour."

"Don't you have better things to do than show me around?"

"I'm waiting on one of the mares to deliver. Could be a few hours. I don't have to be present for every delivery, but I like to be. It's one of my favorite parts of the job."

I motion. "Lead the way."

We ride past an empty pasture and then see several mares and foals in another.

"Why do they keep most of the horses in that pasture when there are so many others vacant?" I ask.

"Devil's Horn Ranch has six pastures on a rotational system. Each one needs to rest for at least six weeks, twice a year. You don't want the horses eating them down or you'll get weeds."

"And why is it only the moms and babies are out most of the time?"

"Ideally, horses should be kept outside all the time, because it's closest to their natural environment, but it's not practical on a ranch. Their coats get dull and thick. They get bitten by bugs. They just look rougher. But that doesn't matter with broodmares. They don't need to be as pretty as the other horses. People who board their horses like them to look well maintained."

"So they live out here?"

"For the most part, but don't worry. They are well taken care of. There are run-in sheds if they need to escape the weather, and most days they get brought in for a few hours to be groomed and handled." She stops her horse and turns her around. "Look. Isn't this amazing? Everything you can see in every direction is Devil's Horn Ranch. We're smack dab in the center."

I take it all in. "I can't believe she did this all by herself."

"She did, assisted by the twenty people she employed."

I frown. "What'll they all do when my dad sells? Do you think the new owners will keep everyone on?"

"Doubtful. Ranchers like to use their own people. They don't tend to trust outsiders. But who knows? It's a big place. Maybe some of them will get to stay on—unless the Thompsons or another developer get their hands on it."

I think of Owen's tattoo and wonder how painful it is to have a tattoo removed. "What about you? Will you lose the business?"

"Possibly. There are a few other vets around here with a lot more experience than I have. DHR is my largest ranch."

"That sucks."

"I'll be okay. I can always branch out into bovine medicine."

"As in cows?"

"I'm a large animal vet. I can work on most livestock—cattle, sheep, pigs, goats—but equine medicine is my specialty."

"And your passion."

She smiles and pats her horse. "Yeah."

"I'm glad to see you can still smile. How are you doing with everything?"

"You mean about the Victor situation? I'm still trying to wrap my head around it."

"Has he called?"

"He left me a message. I haven't gotten around to replying."

"This must be terrifying for you."

"I can't believe I was that close to ending it. If the FBI had only come one day later, I wouldn't be in this situation."

"Can I ask you a question?"

"Sure."

"Why were you going to end it?"

Her lower lip is drawn into her mouth as she shrugs one shoulder innocently. "I think it's because we didn't have much in common."

I snort. "I'll say. He's a killer, and you're—"

"I'm what?"

"I don't know. Sweet. Generous with your time. Empathetic."

Her lips turn up into a wide grin. "I could say the same thing about you, offering me your guesthouse and all."

"One could say *we* have something in common." Her face turns pink, and it's adorable. "My grandmother would have wanted you there."

"So this is all about Vivian?"

"Well no, not *all*."

"I'm only kidding, Connecticut. I appreciate your kindness, but I'm still not sure I'll be any good at this."

"Good at what?"

"Lying. Viv always joked that I should never play poker, because she could always tell when I was keeping something from her. What if Victor will be able to tell?" She rubs her temple. "Oh lord, I feel sick."

I lean over and touch her shoulder. "You're not in this alone. I won't let you be."

"Thanks, but you can't always be there. It would be weird."

"Remember what the agent said about me becoming friends with Victor? I'm thinking that's a good idea. What angle should I use?"

"Angle?"

"Something he likes. Hobbies, interests, something we can bond over."

"I don't know a whole lot about him. He's pretty tight-lipped." She laughs. "Now I know why. Oh, but he does like football."

"Does he have a favorite team?"

"The one in New England, I think."

"The Patriots?"

"That's the one."

"Sweet. I can talk football until I'm blue in the face. I'll order some Pats shirts online as soon as we get back."

"I don't know if he'll go for it. He doesn't have many friends. He drinks with the guys he works with, but I don't know of anyone else."

"You underestimate my charm."

She scrunches her brow. "You're going to *charm* him?"

"My charm works on both men *and* women."

She smiles. "Does it now?"

"How about you tell me?"

There's the blush again. "Let's finish the tour. We have a lot of ground to cover." She makes a clicking sound, and Baby Blue trots off.

CHAPTER EIGHT

Andie

"'Evenin', Ms. Andie," Kevin at the front desk says. "You here to eat supper with your granddad?"

I lift a bag of food. "You know it."

"I could tell you were coming by how he's acting. He sure does look forward to your meals together."

"How is he? Since Vivian McBride died, he's been depressed."

"That's true, but it's hard to find someone here who hasn't lost a loved one. They get each other through it. His pinochle buddies provide distraction."

"Good. Well, I'd better get this to him before it gets cold."

I walk down the hall past the elevators and social rooms, past the dining hall and offices. I turn right to apartment 118 and knock. It takes a minute for Granddad to answer the door. It's difficult for him to get out of a chair sometimes, and with his arthritis, he finds it hard to cook, which is why he moved here. But he's still sharp as a tack and one of the wisest men I've known.

He opens the door and pulls me in for a hug. "Andie, my girl. So nice to see you on this lovely day."

"You too, Granddad." I jiggle the bag. "I brought your favorite, barbeque from the place on Main Street."

"You're too good to me."

That's far from true. "If I was too good to you, I'd bring you dinner every night."

"Nonsense. You're young. You have a life and a busy career. I'm one of the fortunate ones. Most folks here are lucky to get a monthly or even yearly visit from their grandchildren."

"Those grandchildren should be ashamed of themselves." I pull containers out of the bag and place them on his small dining table. "I'll never be too busy for our suppers." I cut up his brisket; it's hard for him to do. He looks sad. "What is it?"

He swallows hard. "Last time I had brisket was at Vivian's. It's been a while, but it feels like yesterday."

I put a hand on top of his. "I miss her too."

"Tell me what's goin' on out at her ranch."

"The McBrides are going to sell it."

"Shame."

"Vivian's grandson is staying there to keep an eye on things until that happens. Funny thing, I met him on the ranch when we were fifteen, but he never came back until the funeral."

He puts down his fork and gives me a look.

"What?"

"Your eyes just lit up like fireworks on the fourth of July. Tell me about this grandson."

"He's my age. He doesn't know much about being a rancher, but I think he's having fun learning. I gave him a tour of Devil's Horn Ranch."

"Why you?"

"Because I was there."

He smiles, then his bushy white eyebrows draw down. "What about that other fella, Victor?"

For a moment I consider telling him everything, but he would be livid knowing I might be in danger, so I lie. "We're still dating. Sort of. We're going to the rodeo this weekend with Maddox and, uh, Melina."

He cocks his head. "Your eyes don't sparkle when you speak of Victor. Seems to me you should be with the other one. Or has Melina already got her hooks in him?"

"It's complicated."

He laughs. "All good relationships are."

I think of his relationship with Vivian. They'd been companions, maybe even lovers.

"Make sure whoever you end up with treats you like a lady and makes you happier than all git-out."

"I sure will."

"And he best know you'll take a backseat to no one."

"Yes, Granddad."

"And you'd better tell him your ol' granddad is expecting at least one ankle-biter before he buys the farm."

He always manages to work that in no matter what we're talking about.

"All y'all know I ain't gettin' any younger, but maybe not with that Victor fella and for sure not with anyone with the name Thompson."

"Both of those you can be sure of."

"Good girl. You need to stay as far away from those Thompson hoodlums as you can."

"My best friend is married to one," I remind him. "I do see them occasionally, but you can be sure I want nothing to do with them."

He looks a little pale.

"You feeling okay? Should I get someone?"

He takes my hand. "Promise me, pumpkin. They're dangerous, them Thompsons. Been a long time since I seen any family try and control a town like they do. They don't much care who gets in the way."

"What are you saying?"

He releases my hand and picks at his supper. "Don't mind me. I'm a crazy ol' coot."

"You're far from crazy, and you're no old coot. You have a lot of years left in you."

"You should bring him to see me sometime."

"Victor?"

"No, not him. The one who makes your face light up."

"Maddox? But we're only friends."

His attention travels to a framed picture of Vivian on his bedside table. "Like I was friends with Vivian. He's her grandson. I'd like to meet him. I'm old and dying, so you have to fulfill my dying wish."

"You are not dying, Granddad."

"I will be someday. Tell him that."

"Fine. I'll tell him, but no promises, okay?"

I clean up our trash, and he gets out the backgammon board. "You reckon you'll beat me today?"

"As always, I don't think I stand a chance."

He points to his temple. "Other parts of me may not work so well, but the noggin is fully intact."

"I'm glad to hear it."

"You're a good girl, Andie. Make sure he knows it."

"I'm quite sure you'll make sure of it for me."

"Damn straight I will. Now—your move."

CHAPTER NINE

Maddox

I watch in awe as a young girl runs the barrels, then I lean over Victor and shout, "Andie, I can't believe you used to do this."

"That's my girl," Victor says.

Hatred of him crawls up my spine.

"We don't have to stay and watch all of it," she says. "I only wanted to pop in for a few minutes. I'm sure you boys would much rather see the bronc riding. It's over in the other arena."

"Now that's what I'm talking about," Victor says and stands. "A real man's sport. Well, that and bull riding." He turns to me. "Think you'll ever try it?"

I fake laugh. "I'm still trying to figure out how to get a horse to turn around."

"At least you're honest about your shortcomings. I like that in a person. No bullshitters. You and I might get along yet." He nods at my Patriots shirt. "Not to mention you're a fellow fan."

I try not to sneer, remembering why we're here. *He* doesn't like bullshitters. *Him.*

"Easy, boy," Agent York whispers and takes my hand.

I don't miss how Victor seems to like it when "Melina" and I touch. She was right—he doesn't see me as his competition this way.

On our walk over, Victor asks her, "What do you do, Melina? I haven't seen you around before."

I stiffen. I'm sure Andie told Victor about her before the date. He'd naturally be curious about who they were going to hang out with. I pray Andie stuck to the script or this night will be over quickly.

"I'm a writer," Melina says. "I'm down here researching horse ranches for my next novel. I had only planned to stay a few weeks, but now"—she looks at me as if she's in love—"I might stay here for as long it takes to write the whole book."

"How long will that be?" he asks.

"Months. Maybe longer." She looks at me and giggles. "Perhaps I'll make it a trilogy."

I lean down and peck her on the lips.

"A noble profession," Victor says. "Who's your publisher?"

Andie and I share a quick look of panic before Melina rattles off a name. "I've only recently signed a contract. This will be my first book with them. Before now I self-published. You'd be amazed how easy it is to do it. But I wanted more exposure. I longed to see my books lining the shelves of bookstores."

"What's your last name again?" he asks, taking his phone out.

"Why do you need to know that?" Andie asks, looking scared.

"Scott," she says without hesitation.

Victor taps around on his phone and whistles. "Damn, you've written ten books? Your bio says you live in Spain. You're an awfully long way from home."

"I did live there. Now I'm in Tucson. Spain makes me sound more exotic."

"Here we are," Andie says in front of the bronc arena.

Victor thumbs to the bathroom near the entrance. "Beers are going through me. I'll only be a minute."

We are silent until he's out of earshot. "Holy shit," I say to the agent. "I about died when he started asking questions. How did you come up with the story so quickly?"

"Not to sound too cliché, but this isn't my first rodeo. My childhood best friend is Melina Scott. She's a bit of a recluse. Doesn't allow any photos of herself to be posted on the internet. Gives me credibility. And she lives in Spain, which keeps her far away from any danger I might put her in by using her name."

Andie blows out a relieved breath. "You're good at this, Agent York."

"You're both doing great. Keep it up. And please call me Katherine, but only when Victor isn't around." Her eyes twinkle. "We're going to be spending some time together, so we may as well drop the formality." Her eyes flit to the bathroom. "He's coming." She grabs my hand. "Kiss me."

I lean in and kiss her. More than a peck but less than would be publicly indecent. My back is to Victor, so I open my eyes. Andie is watching. Her eyes meet mine and then she looks away.

"Ready, babe?" Victor says.

Andie cringes. I pray Victor didn't see that.

As the three of us discussed before coming, I say, "Andie, your turn to make the beer run."

She puts on an award-winning guilty face. "I can't. I'm a little behind this month. My landlord decided to raise my rent. I have to save every penny."

"Want me to rough him up?" Victor jokes. "Maybe put a little poison on his bushes?"

We all laugh, but deep down I know we're all thinking he's capable.

"Don't you dare," she says. "He's a nice old man trying to make a living, like the rest of us. But with that and my student loans, I'm in way over my head."

"Do you have a lease?" I ask, as scripted.

"I'm month-to-month."

"Then I happen to know a place you can get for a lot less."

"Really?" she says, feigning excitement. "Where? And how much less?"

"How about utilities, and we'll call it even?"

"What are you saying?"

"The ranch has a guesthouse. It's just sitting there vacant. You'd be doing us a favor actually. Empty houses can develop issues."

Victor doesn't look happy. He puts his hand on hers. "I'm sure he could get a lot of money renting it out. Doesn't seem right to be taking handouts. I'll help you out if you get in a bind."

Oh, shit. He's not going for it.

"Are you crazy, Victor?" Melina says. "Your girlfriend was just given the golden ticket. Do you know how much debt she could pay off if she's living rent free? You wouldn't want to deprive her of that, would you?"

"My grandmother would have wanted me to offer," I add.

He still looks unconvinced, though he seems pleased that Melina called Andie his girlfriend.

"I'll be at the main house a lot," she says with a big smile as she elbows Andie. "Just be sure to keep your windows closed at night unless you want to hear me screaming this one's name."

Victor almost spurts beer through his nostrils. "Maybe you should do it. Tell me when, and I'll help move your stuff. Hell, it may be the only way you'll let me in your apartment." He leans toward me. "Looks like you're the only one getting lucky lately."

"Hey now," Melina says. "Cut her some slack. She went through a bad breakup. Those can take time to get over. Though we won't be convening at *her* place, that doesn't mean we can't go to *yours*. How about Maddox and I bring the booze. Next weekend maybe. We could have a game night."

"Yeah, sure." He eyes Andie. "I thought you said it had been a while since you'd dated."

It's almost imperceptible, but her hand trembles. Jesus, how I wish I could reach out to her.

"It had been," she says. "A few months is a while."

"And you told *Melina* about it? You barely know each other."

"Girls talk," Melina says. "I'm nosey, what can I say. While you were getting our tickets for the events earlier, I gave her the third degree. I mean, if we're going to be friends and go on lots of double dates, I need to know *everything*."

"Sounds like you need a real man to get you over the douchebag," he says to Andie.

"A real man wouldn't pressure her," Melina says, giving him a pointed look. "Would he?"

"No, of course not." He brings Andie's hand to his mouth and kisses it while she looks at me, terrified.

My gut twists into a knot.

"Now that that's all settled, let's go watch some bucking broncs," Melina says. "Maybe I can get some pointers for later." She winks at me, and Victor gives me a thumbs-up.

I wish we didn't have to do this. I can tell how nervous Andie is. My grandmother was right; she's got a terrible poker face. Good thing it's not usually her face he's looking at.

But somehow that does not make me feel any better.

Agent York and I circle around the building, park, and wait for Victor to leave her front stoop. It kills me to leave her alone with him for even two minutes, but some things are inevitable. When he goes in for a kiss, I want to puke.

"Let him do it," Katherine mumbles. "Good girl."

He walks down the steps, gets into his car, and drives off. I start to exit the truck, but Katherine holds me back. "Best to wait a few minutes. Make sure the coast is clear."

"I fucking hate this."

"She did great. You both did."

"You did all the work. I'm not sure how you got him to agree to the move and then drinks at his place. You're good."

"It's amazing what men will agree to when they're sure they aren't in competition with anyone."

"Quick thinking about the screaming and stuff."

"I thought it was a nice touch."

"Can we go in now? I need to make sure she's okay after that creep kissed her."

She takes one more look around. "I think we're good. You really care about her, don't you?"

"I haven't known her very long, but yes, I do."

"Good, because she may need a real man to help her get over the douchebag."

"Now where have I heard that before?"

I get out hastily and almost run to get to Andie.

CHAPTER TEN

Andie

Driving down the road, I think of how many excuses I've made not to see Victor this week. Animal emergencies, girlfriend problems, packing. Katherine made me agree to a game night at his place. I did so reluctantly. She keeps reminding me we have a job to do. I keep wanting to ask her when I can expect my paycheck. But every time I think of blowing the whistle, I recall the picture of the little girl she showed me. Her family deserves answers. If anything ever happened to me, I would want Granddad to have that closure.

I slow my truck when I see Maddox along the side of the road on the outskirts of Devil's Horn Ranch. Looks like he's doing fence work today, and he's shirtless. Oh my. My insides tingle.

I pull over so I don't drive into a ditch, gawking at him. I wave, and he smiles.

"Out here alone, eh?" I say from inside the truck. "You must be getting the hang of things."

"Miguel went back to get more supplies."

"You look very capable, if you ask me."

"Thanks," he says and kicks a broken post. "But this one is being stubborn."

"Need help?" I'm five-foot-five. He towers over me and is pure muscle. I can tell he's trying not to laugh. "What? I work out."

He puts a chain around the old fence post and anchors it to the back of his four-wheeler. He climbs on, starts it up, and tries to pull the post out of the ground. The front wheels come up, and I see a disaster waiting to happen.

"Maddox, you aren't heavy enough!" I yell.

"It's fine."

"It's going to—" I watch in horror as the ATV up-ends and falls back on Maddox after he's thrown to the ground. I jump out of the pickup and run over. "Are you okay?" When he laughs, I feel relief, then help him get out from under it.

"Not exactly the way to impress the ladies."

He's trying to impress me?

He stands and brushes himself off. His sweaty torso is covered with dirt. I resist the urge to help clean him off. He turns to try and right the four-wheeler, and blood trickles down his back. "Maddox, you're injured."

"Where?"

He reaches around to investigate, but I stop him. "Don't touch it. It's dirty enough already. Sit on that rock and wait here."

He continues to work on the ATV.

"Sit. Doctor's orders."

He looks up, amused. "Yes, ma'am."

"What have I told you about calling me ma'am?" I get my first-aid kit and a bottle of water from the pickup. I pour water on the wound. "Looks like you might need a few stitches."

"It barely even hurts." I dab it with gauze, and he flinches. "Okay, *that* hurts."

"I'm serious, Maddox. You should get this looked at."

"I'm a little busy."

"It'll get infected."

"You're a doctor. Can't you do something about it with all the vet things you carry?"

"I fix animals, not humans."

"Surely you can deal with a little cut." He looks at the first-aid kit. "This isn't for animals, is it? You must have something in here you can use."

I look through it. It's well stocked, though I've never had to use it. "I do have some skin glue." I go back to the truck for antiseptic and iodine. I hold them up. "This could hurt, but it might do the trick."

"Do it."

I pour more water on the wound, dab it dry, clean it with antiseptic, roll a swab of iodine on it, then apply the skin glue. After it dries, I bandage him up, impressed he didn't complain about any of it. Maybe he's still trying to impress me.

"It may rip open if you move the wrong way. You might want to tackle something easier than this fence today."

"Not a chance. I can't have Miguel and the guys thinking I'm a pus— uh, wimp. If I rip it open, I'll go into town later and get it stitched up."

I put my things back in the truck. I turn, and he's standing right behind me. I can't help but stare at his chest like a smitten schoolgirl. In my defense, it is a *very* nice chest.

"You okay?" he asks. "You were a little shaken up the other night."

"I'll be fine. Did Katherine tell you about game night? Friday. You, me, Melina and Victor. At his place."

He pulls his phone from his back pocket and waves it at me. "You do know how to use one of these, right? If I recall, I programmed in my contact information the day the FBI showed up."

"I didn't think you'd want to be bothered with the details. You have a lot on your plate, what with fence mending and all."

"Please, Andie, bother me with details. Day or night. I mean it. Plus, I get tired of talking to Owen, Miguel, and the guys all day. It'd be nice to have a friend who looks a lot better in a cowboy hat than that mangy lot."

I feel heat in my cheeks. "Fine. I'll call." I open the door to get in my truck. "Put your shirt back on. It'll help keep dirt off your bandage. Get it checked out if you see more blood."

"What if I don't see any? I still need to put on a fresh bandage after I shower, right? I can hardly change the bandage myself. Maybe you should come by tonight and do it."

"When will you be done?"

"By dinner. How about you come by after you've eaten? Heck, come for dinner. I'm not much of a cook, but I can boil pasta."

"Supper."

He cocks his head. "Huh?"

"We call it supper around here. Are you sure? I don't want to impose."

"You wouldn't be imposing. I'm tired of eating alone. We can go over the details of game night."

"Okay then. Seven o'clock?"

"Perfect."

I start the engine.

He runs up to the door before I take off. "Park inside the hay barn. We wouldn't want Victor nosing around and seeing your truck on the ranch before you move in. Even though you work here, it would be hard to explain why you're in the house and not the stables."

I raise a brow. "Already thinking like an FBI agent."

"I'm only thinking about your safety. Just be careful not to run over Patch's new litter of kittens in the barn."

"Patch?" I say, amused. "You're naming the barn cats?"

"Maybe you're not the only one with a soft spot for animals."

I eye him in the rearview mirror as he watches me pull away. A horn blasts, and I swerve back into my lane. My heart beats wildly, but is it because of the near miss or something else?

The big doors to the hay barn are open, and I drive in, get the bottle of wine off the passenger seat, and exit the truck. Matteo is walking from one stable to another and stops to help me close the doors. "It's about time you kids got together," he says, noticing the wine.

I flush. "It's not like that. I'm, um, with Victor. This is just a thank you for Maddox letting me crash in the guesthouse for a while."

The weathered lines around his eyes stand out prominently when he smiles. "Sure it is."

Does he know? Has Maddox told him about the FBI? Katherine warned us not to say anything, and I haven't told anyone. Not even Tara and Christina.

There's a jeep off to the side of the house. Did Maddox buy a car? I knock. Someone comes to the door but it's not Maddox. It's Katherine. I try not to show my disappointment; he did say we were going over the details of game night. I was obviously reading way too much into this.

She looks amused. "It's a good thing you were a better actress when we went out the other night."

"What do you mean?"

She gestures to my hands. "The wine. The look on your face." She steps closer. "Don't worry, I'll be out of here before dinner."

"You mean supper." Maddox appears around the corner, and I wonder how much he heard. "Hey, Doc. Come on in." He reaches around Katherine and opens the screen door for me.

I hand him the wine. "I hope red is okay."

"Red is great. Can I get you both a glass?"

"None for me," Katherine says. "I'm on the clock."

"But you drank the other night," I say.

"A few sips maybe. When nobody was looking, I poured it out to make it look like I was."

"Is there a handbook we can read?" Maddox says. "Covert Operations 101 or something?"

"This isn't funny, you know."

He huffs through his nose and then glances at me. "Oh, believe me, I know."

He pours himself and me a glass, then we sit and listen to Katherine tell us how Friday night is going to go. She has us repeat back the details before she leaves. I'm relieved she doesn't want me to do any of the snooping—just the distracting—but it's *how* she wants me to do the distracting that bothers me. Judging by the look on Maddox's face, it bothers him, too.

He walks her out and then joins me in the living room, where I'm holding a picture of Vivian on her favorite horse. He stands next to me. "I still can't believe she's gone."

"Her old cowboy hat is still on the peg by the back door. How long are you going to keep it there?"

"I'm not touching it. It's Nana's hat on Nana's peg in Nana's house. It would feel wrong to remove it."

"Any word from your folks about interested buyers?"

"There's a lot of interest, but we can't move on anything for a while. Probate."

"Karen Thompson came to see me at the Diamond Duce Ranch the other day. She asked about things."

"She broke up my parents back in college," he tells me. "I didn't meet my dad until I was seven because of her."

"Why does that not surprise me?"

"Did you know she tried to push off her illegitimate kid as my dad's?"

"Quinn? I feel sorry for him. He's just trying to find his own way. Must be more like his father, whoever that is. As far as I can tell, he's not happy being a Thompson."

"Then why not leave?"

"He's seventeen and still in high school. Besides, I'm not sure they would let him leave. They probably want him to go into the family business."

"You make them sound like the mafia."

"I told you before they might be."

He laughs. "The Cowboy Mafia. Kind of has a ring to it." A timer goes off in the kitchen. "Dinner's ready—I mean supper." He pulls a casserole out of the oven.

"I thought you said you could only boil pasta."

"I did. Look closely. It's a spaghetti bake. I may have overdone the cheese a bit."

I inhale. "It smells delicious, and crispy cheese is the best kind."

"It's better than sandwiches anyway."

"Is that what you've been eating? Sandwiches?"

"They're simple and quick." He scowls at the sauce-spattered counter. "And easy to clean up."

"I love to cook. When I move into the guesthouse, I'll be happy to cook for you. It's the least I can do."

He refills my glass. "I'll have to check the FBI handbook to see how you can covertly get it to me."

"We should install one of those things they have at bank drive-throughs. I can stick it in a tube and press a button, and it comes to your house."

We laugh through our meal, coming up with silly ways to share supper between the houses.

After we finish, he starts to clear the dishes, but I shove him out of the way. "Sit. You cooked. I'll clean." I don't miss how he watches as I wash the dishes. Suddenly I'm aware of my every move. Does the way I'm standing make my pants look baggy? Is the back of my hair matted from the hat I had on earlier?

"How do you know where everything goes?" he asks. "I live here, and it took me ten minutes to find a baking pan."

"Vivian had my granddad and me over for supper a lot, especially after he moved into the retirement home. I think she felt bad that he wasn't eating gourmet meals there. And wow, could she cook. Taught me everything I know."

"They were a thing, huh? It must have been awful for him to have been here when she fell."

"He still feels guilty about it. I think he might have loved her. They always insisted whatever they were doing was casual, but I'm not so sure. He hasn't been the same since she died." I put away the last dish. "Let's check out your injury. I forgot my first-aid kit in the truck, so I'll have to use yours."

"I have a first-aid kit?"

I open the cabinet under the sink and take it out. "I insisted Vivian have one. Even packed it myself. Now sit and take off your shirt."

His eyebrows shoot up. "Are you always this demanding?"

I'm sure I turn crimson. "Shut up and do it."

He laughs.

I lay out my supplies, pull up a chair behind him, and remove the old, soiled bandage that got wet when he showered. The adhesive must catch a few tiny hairs because he flinches. "Sorry." I'm close enough to smell his body wash. He smells like rain. I palpate the area around the wound. He turns his head and looks at me from the corner of his eye. "I'm checking for swelling. Looks good. I'll clean it and put on a dry bandage. I'm glad to see you didn't open it back up again."

I can't look away as he puts on his shirt. His back muscles bunch when he lifts his arms. He catches me staring and moves toward me. "Thank you," he says, so close he has to look down at me.

My breathing quickens. My heart races. He's going to lean in and kiss me, and I'm not sure I have ever wanted anything more.

Instead, he wipes my cheek. "You had a spec of red sauce there."

I put my hand on the spot and rub it. "Oh… thanks. I should… I should go. Thank you for supper."

"Anytime."

I walk through the door and down the porch stairs.

"Andie," he says behind me.

Is he coming after me? Does he regret not kissing me?

I turn and he hands me my purse. "You forgot this."

"Right. Thanks." I take it and head for the barn.

"See you Friday, Doc."

I wave, not looking back. I've had enough embarrassment for one night. I climb into my truck and bang my head on the steering wheel.

CHAPTER ELEVEN

Maddox

"Let her have a minute with him before we join them," Katherine says from my truck after we park in front of a house a few doors down. "It might seem suspicious to arrive at the same time."

"I don't want her alone with him."

"Nothing's going to happen, Maddox. We're right here. He knows we're coming."

"He killed someone. You can't tell me nothing's going to happen. Hell, Andie even looks like the missing woman. How long do you think it will be before he decides to do it again?"

"Hold on there. We're not even sure he did anything."

"The guy disappeared shortly after the woman went missing. Of course he killed her." I get out of the truck.

She hops out and blocks me. "One more minute. Trust me."

I fidget, pissed as hell we're allowing her to be in danger.

"Calm down," she says. "He'll pick up on your body language."

"I wish I knew what he was saying to her."

"Would it make you feel better if I outfitted her with a microphone next time?"

"It would make me feel better if there *wasn't* a next time. And, no, not if he can find it. I don't want to risk her safety any more than we already are."

"He won't find it. It's amazing how far technology has come."

"If you're sure, then yes. Do it."

"Take some deep breaths." I do as she asks. "Who am I?"

"Melina Scott."

"Let's go then." She gets a board game out of the backseat and hands me two bottles. One is wine, the other is whiskey.

Andie looks relieved when we come through the door. She shoots me a "where have you been" look, and I try to apologize with my eyes. Katherine squeezes my hand, reminding me I should be looking at her, not Andie.

Victor eyes one of the bottles. "Ah, you're a whiskey drinker, too. Nice. How do you like yours?"

I hold up a six-pack of Coke. "With this. You?"

He laughs. "I don't like to water mine down. Straight up for me."

"Point me to the glasses, and I'll pour us some."

He points to the kitchen counter. I'm glad he's letting me fix them. Mine will be a lot more Coke than whiskey, and I will give him a heavy pour. The drunker he gets, the better it is for us.

"You ladies want wine?" Victor asks. "Andie brought a bottle too."

"I wish I could afford better," she says.

"It's okay." He puts an arm around her. "All that is about to change. Do you have a move-in date yet?"

"Thursday."

His brow scrunches. "Babe, Thursday is my busiest day. Why would you do it then?"

"It's the only day this week I can manage it. I'm booked solid every other day, and I told my landlord I'd be out by the weekend."

She knows Thursdays are his busy days.

"But who's going to help you move?" His eyes momentarily flick my way, and I don't like what I see behind them.

"The guesthouse is furnished," she says. "All I'll really need are my clothes and personal items. I'll put my stuff in storage until I pay off my loans and can find a new place."

"But you still have to move it." He looks at me. "You planning on doing it all by yourself?"

Katherine smiles at me and runs a finger down my arm. "Maddox was nice enough to ask a few ranch hands to do it." She cups my chin and turns my face to hers. "You are the nicest cowboy I've ever met." She plants a kiss on me.

"I can't be there to help either," I say. "I've got meetings that day."

Victor shrugs. "I guess if the guys at the ranch don't mind." He taps his glass against mine. "Looks like we dodged moving duty." He kisses Andie's temple, and she looks at me in disgust. "Not that I didn't want to help, but if the grunts will do it, all the better."

What he doesn't know is Andie isn't moving out at all. She's keeping her apartment and her furniture. This could be over in a matter of days or weeks, but we were fully prepared to go along with moving her for real if he'd insisted on helping.

"Ready to play?" Katherine says, holding up the game.

Victor laughs. "I thought you were kidding about Trivial Pursuit. People still play this?"

"Unless you have something else in mind."

He looks at Andie. "Babe?"

"If y'all are okay with it, I'm good."

Katherine goes to the kitchen, which appears to be farthest from the living room and bedrooms. "This looks like a good place to set up."

Victor takes a seat on the couch. "Nah, let's play here. More comfortable than those hard chairs."

That's unfortunate. Katherine was hoping to rummage through some of his personal things while Andie and I distracted him in the kitchen.

"Whatever floats your boat," Katherine says, rolling with the punches. After a few minutes, she proclaims she has to use the bathroom.

Victor points to a door off the kitchen. "It's right there."

The three of us share a look. This isn't good. We all expected the bathroom to be back by the bedrooms.

"Thanks," Katherine says, popping off the couch. When she returns, she picks up her glass and mine. "Looks like we could all use a refill. Andie, want to bring in yours?"

Andie grabs her glass and Victor's, and they disappear into the kitchen. I wish I knew what they were saying. I know Katherine is plotting something. When they return with the drinks, I hope Victor doesn't notice the lighter color of their watered-down wine.

After an agonizing hour of watching Victor's hand on Andie's thigh, Katherine says she has to use the bathroom again.

"Oh, gosh," Andie says. "I really need to pee, too. Like badly. Victor, is there another bathroom I can use?"

He points. "Down the hall, second door on the left. Don't judge me if there's toothpaste in the sink. I wasn't expecting anyone to use it."

Andie flashes me a look before going down the hall. What is she doing?

My heart is pounding. Does Katherine want *her* to snoop? I'm both pissed and scared at the same time. I should do something to distract Victor so he isn't aware of how long she's taking. "How long have you been in the landscape business?"

"I've never done anything else."

"How many guys are on your crew?"

"Five."

"Do you enjoy it?"

"Not the maintenance so much. That gets old. I like the jobs where I'm hired to do a complete redo or plant a new house."

"Kind of like a blank canvas," I say.

"Exactly. You're from New York? What do you do there?"

"I was a bartender at my aunt's restaurant."

His eyebrows shoot up. "Bartender to rancher. Kind of a big change."

"You can say that again."

Katherine returns as if she hasn't a care in the world. "What are you two discussing?"

"Our occupations."

She takes her time coming back to the couch. She's looking at his bookshelves. I know what she's thinking. Where are the pictures? Everyone has family pictures somewhere. But his shelves are full of landscaping books and sports memorabilia. She turns. "You're the quintessential bachelor, aren't you? No photos. No mementos. I'm a writer. A researcher. I pick up on things others might not pick up on, but I'm not getting a vibe about you. Exactly who is Victor James?"

What the fuck is she doing? I'm about ready to stand up and fetch Andie. Take her through the bathroom window if I have to.

He eyes her suspiciously. Duh. I would too. Then he laughs. "What you see is what you get. Everything you need to know about me is right there. I'm a landscaper and a Pats fan. End of story. What's with the twenty questions anyway?"

I rise. "Yeah, Melina. You didn't know that much about me until our third date." I laugh awkwardly, then grab our drinks. "Come on, Victor, let's get a refill. You can show me your junk food. I'm starving."

As he gets out chips and salsa, I pour him another large drink and me one that's almost all Coke. I peek through the sliding glass doors. The sun is just setting. "Nice yard."

"You're full of shit, McBride," he says. "It's not nice at all, but you know what they say, you rarely take what you do for a living back home. I should spruce it up, but it's a rental. I don't need to sink my money into something that's not mine."

"How long have you lived here?" Katherine asks.

"Not long." He moves away. "I'd better go check on Andie."

"I'll do it," Katherine says. "You know how girls like to use the bathroom together." She giggles like she's had way too much to drink.

"Your girlfriend asks a lot of questions," he says. He gets out his wallet, extracts a ten-dollar bill, and tosses it on the counter. "I'll bet you she can't go twenty minutes without asking me another one."

I laugh even though I want to puke. I fish in my pocket and pull out a ten. "You're on."

He leaves his wallet on the counter and returns to the living room. The women appear.

"Everything okay?" Victor asks.

Andie nods. "A little too much wine, I think. I could probably use some fresh air. Can you take me outside, Victor?"

"Sure. Grab your drinks. We can all sit on the porch and enjoy the sunset."

It's not what Katherine was hoping for. She wanted time in the house without him.

Andie goes to the end of the raised porch and looks at the sky. Victor walks up behind her and traps her against the railing, encapsulating her in his arms. My nostrils flare. I want nothing more than to rip him away from her and throw him to the ground, and not just because of who he is or what he might be, but because *I* want to be the one whose arms are around her.

I've wanted it since the day I set eyes on her at the funeral. I wake in the night, wishing she was already living in the guesthouse. Not because she's getting away from a killer, but because she wants to be near me.

We had a moment the other day at the house. We've had several if I'm being honest. But maybe it's only me wanting to protect her. Maybe it's me remembering the fifteen-year-old girl screaming as the gun went off.

Then again, there's the way she looks at me and how she touched my back when she patched me up. She was going to break it off with Victor before she knew about any of this. That has to mean something.

She's watching me out of the corner of her eye. Does she wish it was me behind her? At this point, I'm not sure she would care who it was as long as it wasn't him.

I give her a nod of encouragement.

She smiles and turns away, looking at the yard. She flinches suddenly.

"What's wrong?" Victor asks.

"Nothing. Got a chill."

She turns around, and he hugs her. She looks at me over his shoulder, and there is terror in her eyes.

"This wine is going right through me," Katherine says. "I'll be back in a jiff."

This is her opportunity to find whatever she thinks she's going to find here. I only hope she has enough time. It takes, what, three minutes for a girl to pee?

"We should go back in," Victor says.

"No!" Andie says a bit too boisterously. "Can we wait until the sun is down? It's so pretty. Viv and I used to watch sunsets together out on the ridge."

He wipes a wisp of her hair off her face. "Sure."

She turns back around. I'm a few feet away. She is not looking at the sunset. She's trying to get my attention with her eyes, but I don't know what she's telling me. Victor still has his arms wrapped around her. She brings a hand to her chest, hiding it from him, and points down and to the side. I look where she wants me to, and my heart falls. Part of what looks like might be a grave is sticking out from under the decking. Weeds are sprouting on top of it, but it's clearly different from the grassy earth around it. It's old, but not that old.

Many things go through my head, the first of which is that I should grab Andie and run out the door with her. Part of me is scratching my head. He's a landscaper; surely there are better places and better ways he could have done it. Another part of me is oddly happy. As soon as we show Katherine, this will all be over. Yet another part is thinking that now Andie won't have to move into the guesthouse, and that makes me sad.

I go for the stairs, hoping to get a better look before it gets too dark. Victor stops me. "Best to stay up here. I have a massive fire ant problem. Been meaning to take care of it."

Sure he has.

Katherine appears in the doorway, but I can't get a read on her. Did she find what she was looking for? Before I can get her to come out to see the grave, Victor corrals us back inside. "Feeling better?" he asks Andie.

"A little, but no more wine for me. Why don't we finish the game and call it a night?"

"Lightweight, huh?" Katherine jokes. "We'll have to do it again soon. Next Saturday? We can go to Andie's new place for a housewarming party."

I cringe. I don't want Victor on the ranch, let alone in the house she'll be living in. Behind Victor's back, I make the cutthroat sign; Katherine doesn't know about the grave out back. But she ignores me.

We finish the game and get up to leave. Victor hands me my ten and his. "I don't want your money," I say too harshly.

"Take it. A bet is a bet."

Katherine raises a brow. "Something you want to share with us?"

"Just a friendly wager between men," Victor says.

I hesitate on the way out. I don't want to leave Andie with him for even a second. I don't care if we blow our cover.

"It's dark," I say. "Melina and I will walk you to your truck."

"I think I can walk my girl to her car," he says, following us out. "Catch you two later."

Katherine drags me along. "Come on," she whispers firmly.

"Stop," I say when we're out of earshot. "We have to go back. There's a fucking grave in his backyard."

She looks at me strangely. "You saw a grave right out in the middle of his yard?"

"No. It was mostly under the porch, but I know what I saw. Andie saw it too."

"I think you two might be paranoid. Despite what you've seen in the movies, people rarely bury their victims in a backyard, especially if it's a rental. It's probably a dog."

"Katherine, a woman is missing, and we saw a grave in the yard of a suspect. Are you fucking kidding? If you're not going to do anything, I'm going back—"

"Calm down. He'll hear you."

I glance back. He's kissing her, and I feel sick. I can't even begin to imagine what she must feel, having to kiss him.

He may be the murderer, but in all my life, I have never wanted to kill someone so badly.

CHAPTER TWELVE

Andie

I follow Maddox back to the ranch, barely able to keep my truck on the road because I'm shaking so hard. I hope Victor didn't notice.

Maddox parks and runs over to open the hay barn door for me.

I storm out of my truck and over to Katherine. "Why aren't you taking the cavalry over to his house to arrest him? Didn't Maddox tell you about the grave?"

"He did, and I'll tell you what I told him. It might not be her."

I huff in frustration. "What if it's someone else? What if he's a serial killer?"

"That's not what I meant. It could be an animal. If we rush over there and blow our cover, he could run, and who knows how long it will take us to find him again."

Maddox seems as upset as I am. "We have to keep up this charade?" I ask. "I have to pretend to like the guy with a grave in his backyard that may or may not contain the remains of a missing woman?"

"Yes."

"He kissed me," I say in disgust. "Do you even know what it feels like to have a person like that touch you?"

"I do."

Maddox steps forward. "But you're trained for this, Katherine. She's not." He turns to me. "You're not going back to your apartment. I don't care what story we have to come up with, you're staying at the ranch."

"Busted pipe," Katherine says. "You can tell Victor your upstairs neighbor had a busted pipe and your floors got wet so you decided to move out immediately. You came over with what you needed early in the morning and will send the ranch hands back on Thursday to move your furniture into storage."

"So we're really having him here next weekend?" I say.

"It's the best way for us to figure out what's in the grave," she says. "We've been watching him. His daily routine is erratic. He goes home for lunch almost every day, but at different times. We can't risk him finding anyone in his backyard with the grave half dug up. We need to get in and out without him knowing we've been there, and the best way to do that is to know he's going to be here for several hours."

Maddox says to me, "Did you find anything in Victor's room?" I shake my head. "What about you?" he asks Katherine.

"I found something in his wallet." She pulls up a picture on her phone of a photo. It's old and weathered and had been folded and unfolded so many times, it's starting to tear.

"Who do you think it is? A victim?"

"Perhaps, though she doesn't look like the missing woman or Andie, if that's his MO. She's young. Still in her teens by the looks of it. I can't be sure, because it's old, but see here? It might only be a shadow on her face, but it could also be a bruise. I'll send it to my people, see what they can come up with. Andie, are you going to be okay? Can I send Special Agent Watkins to your apartment to get any of your belongings?"

"I'd rather go myself."

"I'll take her," Maddox says.

Katherine nods. "I'll park outside Victor's house, so we'll know if he tries to leave. Call me when you're back."

We cross to Maddox's truck, and he opens the door for me. I slide in and slump, exhausted.

"You don't have to do this, you know," he says. "Say the word, and we'll call the whole thing off. They can get someone else to do the dirty work."

"I have to do it. Victor doesn't trust people easily."

"But he kissed you." He slams the door harder than he needs to, then runs around and gets in.

"As long as that's all he does, I can deal with it."

"He hasn't tried anything else?"

"No, which surprises me. He's actually quite, I don't know, gentlemanly. He hasn't ever pushed me to do more than I'm comfortable with. Doesn't that seem odd for a criminal?"

"Or he's waiting to get you right where he wants you. Or maybe it's not about sex for him. Could be he has some strange fetish about women who look like you and the missing woman. Maybe you look like his dead mother or something."

I gaze out the window as we leave the ranch. "I'm not sure you're helping."

"Sorry." He puts his hand on mine, and I feel something I haven't felt all day: safe.

He leaves his hand on me longer than a friendly pat. When he finally moves it, I realize how much I miss it. The warmth. The security. The feeling I had inside when he was touching me.

We are quiet most of the way. I wonder what he's thinking. Is he thinking about the touch? Or maybe he's still focused on the grave and what could be in it. I shudder to think that poor six-year-old's mother could have been discarded in such a way.

At my apartment, I pull out my suitcases and stuff them with as many clothes as will fit. I get my laptop and a few books and put them in a box. Maddox hands me pictures. One is of Vivian. Another is Granddad and me at Devil's Horn Ranch when I was younger. The last is of my mother.

"Is this your mom? Wow, you look a lot alike. She's beautiful." Though he's speaking about my mother, he's looking at me.

I feel warmth and avert my eyes. "Thanks." I touch the photo, missing her still, then I put the pictures down. "You forget I'm not really moving. These can stay."

"*You* forget Victor thinks you are, and he's coming to your new place next week. It has to look like you live there."

I sit heavily on the couch and look around my living room, wondering what else I should bring. "At least he's never been in my apartment. He has no idea what I have. I won't need much more than those photos." I get up and go to the kitchen, perusing my supply of pots and pans. "How's the guesthouse set up for cooking? I haven't been in it for years."

"Pretty sure you could cook a full gourmet meal with what's there." He laughs. "Don't think I've forgotten what you said last week about cooking for me."

"It would be my pleasure. It gets old cooking for one. Speaking of food, I should take over anything that's still good and throw out the rest."

We pack food into plastic bags and put them with my other things.

"Is this it?" he asks. "Are we ready?"

I wonder how long it will be before I come back. I pick up the box, add a few bags to my forearms and pull a suitcase behind me.

Maddox laughs. "You're unbelievably strong for your size."

"I do work with thousand-pound animals."

He picks up the rest, and we leave.

"You think he'll buy the story about the pipes?" he asks when we're back in the truck.

"I'm not planning on telling him unless he asks. We don't normally see each other much during the week."

"Kind of risky, don't you think?"

"We're not at the stage where we tell each other everything, so I don't think so."

"What stage are you at?"

"We're not at any stage. I'm pretending, Maddox."

"Right."

"I keep thinking about what would have happened if I'd been sleeping with him. Would Katherine have expected me to continue to do it?"

Maddox sneers. "No fucking way."

I try not to smile. I don't know him very well, but he's already protective of me. "Tell me about the guesthouse. Vivian gave me a tour a long time ago. I seem to remember brown walls."

"They're white now," he says. "Actually, they're 'summer linen' in an eggshell finish."

"How do you know that?"

"I painted them last week. The old color made it too dark inside. I didn't want you to feel closed in."

"It's a three-bedroom house. I hardly think it'll feel small." I stare at his profile. "You painted it for me?"

He shrugs. "Had some free time."

"You've had *no* free time. You spend your days mucking out stalls, mending fences, and learning all there is to know about ranch life."

"Okay, I've had some free nights."

We pull up to the ranch and park. He goes straight to the guesthouse, which shares a driveway with the main house. The back doors of each can't be much more than fifty feet apart. My skin prickles as I imagine sneaking over to the main house in the middle of the night.

He helps me bring my belongings inside. Everything I see reminds me of Vivian. She loved to find furnishings at antique stores. I run a finger along the edge of a breakfront bookcase and stop when I come to a picture of me sitting on Baby Blue.

"She obviously thought of you as family," Maddox says.

"And I her."

My stroll through the living room is like a walk down memory lane with all the pictures. Maddox picks up a photo of him. "You'll want to stash this for now, and any of the others we don't want Victor seeing."

"It feels wrong."

"It's just temporary, Andie. You won't have to keep up the act forever."

Temporary. Just like Maddox's presence here.

I inhale. "Still smells like paint."

"I can get you some air freshener if the smell bothers you."

"It doesn't. It reminds me of my granddad. When I was growing up, I was always changing my mind about what color I wanted my bedroom. One month he painted it twice. I thought I wanted black, but it creeped me out, so he painted it pink. If I recall correctly, he had to give it three coats to cover the black. He never complained. I think he felt bad about me losing my mom at such a young age. I suspect that's one of the reasons why I want to help Katherine. I got to say goodbye to my mom. That little girl didn't have the opportunity."

"Must have been hard for you." He takes the picture of her out of my box and puts it in a prominent spot on the bookshelf.

"I was young. Kids bounce back quicker. It would have been harder if I'd lost her during my teen years."

"I lost someone once," he says. "She was my nanny, and I was seven. I know it's not the same, but she lived with us for years. She was part of the family."

"What was her name?"

"Callie." He laughs. "She used to call me Mad Max. She used the nickname so often that Dad ended up naming his production company after it."

"Mad Max Productions?" I smile. "I like it. If you don't mind my asking, why are you a bartender if your father owns a business?"

"He owns a gym, too. He and my uncles. I tried working there. It seems like I've tried working everywhere." He walks to the window and looks out into the darkness toward the stables. "Nothing ever felt right until…" He checks the time. "It's not important. Listen, it's late, and I'm sure you want to hit the hay. Let me help you change the sheets. I wasn't expecting you until Thursday, so I hadn't gotten to that yet. Who knows how long it's been since they've been changed."

"I can do it, Maddox. You don't have to treat me like a guest. I'm grateful this place was available and you offered it to me. You need to let me pitch in where I can."

He ignores me and goes to the master, where he removes the decorative pillows and starts stripping the bed. "It's not a big deal."

"Where are the sheets?"

"Bathroom closet. Top shelf."

When I'm in the bathroom, I quickly check my appearance in the mirror. Then I roll my eyes at myself. I return to the bedroom with the sheets. It's so domestic, making the bed together, and oddly intimate. Our eyes lock momentarily and I wonder if he's thinking the same thing.

When we finish, he starts to pile the decorative pillows back on. I toss one at him. "I'm only going to take them off in about five minutes."

"Right." He throws a small one at me.

I catch it and throw it back. He dodges, grabs a larger one, and runs around the bed to hit me on the backside. I squeal and jump up on the bed to escape him, but my foot slips, and I fall back, right into his arms.

His face is inches from mine, and we're both laughing. My heart is beating wildly. We're silent as we stare at each other. Surely he can feel my chest thundering.

Kiss me! I'm screaming in my head.

And then he does.

The moment his lips touch mine, I melt. He lays me on the bed, climbing on top of me on all fours. Our lips are the only parts of us that are touching. He kisses my top lip, then my bottom one. Then my cheeks, my chin, my neck. Then he's back at my mouth, his tongue swiping my lips. I tilt my head, allowing him to deepen the kiss. Only one thing is going through my head right now: how have I never known kissing could be this good? He's way better at it than Victor.

Victor. I close my mouth and pull away.

Maddox hops off the bed, confused.

I sigh. "You're—"

He stuffs his hands in his pockets. "A jerk? An opportunist? A terrible host?"

"I was going to say a good kisser."

He smiles. "Thank God."

"But we shouldn't be doing this."

"Why not?"

"What if Victor saw us? You'd be in danger, not to mention I work for you."

"You don't work for me. You work for the ranch, and even so, you're not an employee, you're an independent contractor. Don't worry about Victor. I'll make sure he never sees us."

I sit up. "You're leaving soon. It's probably best that we don't."

Disappointment crosses his face. "Maybe you're right."

My head is screaming at me, telling me what an idiot I am.

"You'll let me know if you need anything?" he asks.

We go to the living room. "Of course. I can't tell you how much I appreciate this."

"It's no problem."

I call him back before he reaches the front door. "Connecticut? What's your favorite meal?"

"Lasagna. Why?"

"Because I'm going to cook it for you, that's why."

"But I thought we weren't doing this."

I nod to the bedroom. "Just because we're not doing *that* doesn't mean we can't be friends. Friends eat together, don't they?"

"Sure. Sounds great."

"Seven o'clock good for you?"

"Seven tomorrow?"

"Seven *every* night. I mean, unless you have other plans. I'm not about to cook only for myself when I know you're over there eating sandwiches. Plus, it's easier to cook for two."

"I'd better get to work building the bank teller drive-through sucker thingy." He winks at me and leaves.

I chastise myself. How is it possible that I made it twenty-five years without experiencing a kiss like that? I've made out with my share of guys. Dozens of them. I thought I knew everything there was to know about kissing.

I was wrong.

I might have to go my whole life settling for boring, mediocre kisses, because I kicked out the one guy who made me feel more with his lips than any other man has ever made me feel in his bed.

CHAPTER THIRTEEN

Maddox

I'm early. I lean against the truck and watch a few private planes land as I wait for Dad's. There's a big town meeting tomorrow. A lot of people will be talking about the future of the ranch. He wanted to be here.

A couple emerges from a small single-engine plane. He picks her up and swings her around, then they kiss. She can't stop looking at her left hand. Damn, what a way to get engaged. They seem to be about my age. I watch them almost skip with happiness to a waiting car and drive off.

Seeing them has me thinking of Andie and how happy I am when we're together, despite the whole thing of her pretending to date a murder suspect.

We've had dinner together the past three nights. We've been careful. Matteo and the guys know to alert us if Victor comes around, but we haven't told them why. They probably think Andie is stepping out on him with me. It upsets me to have them thinking she would treat someone in such a manner, but they'll know the truth soon enough. Either way, they treat her like a sister and, surprisingly, they have welcomed me as one of their own.

Andie is an amazing cook. We sit and talk until well after the sun goes down. She tells me stories of her granddad, Nana, and horses. I tell her about my family, my string of failed career attempts, and my famous best friend. I'm not sure I have ever learned so much about a person in such a short period of time. I can't seem to get enough of Andie. After every story she tells me, I want to know more. After every moment of silence, I come up with something else to ask so I don't have to leave.

Her blue eyes—I swear they put me in a trance. She's beautiful. Maybe the most beautiful woman I've ever seen. But she only wants to be friends. I can't blame her. Look at where her last relationship got her. She's right about one thing: I'm not going to be here forever.

I sigh and lean against the truck. I glance at the boots I've only recently broken in. I think about my hat and how it no longer feels awkward when I wear it. I feel like something is missing when I'm not. Leaving this place will result in an emptiness inside me. For once in my life, I feel like I belong. I snicker, because if someone had told me a month ago that I'd feel at home on a horse ranch in Texas, I'd have called them crazy.

"What's so funny?"

I was so preoccupied, I didn't even see his plane land. "Hi, Dad."

He comes in for a hug, then takes a step back to appraise me. "Well, look at you. Hat, boots, scruff, tanned skin. If I didn't know any better, I'd think I was looking at a genuine cowboy." He pats my mid-section. "They puttin' you to work, son? I've never seen you in such good shape."

"*They* aren't putting me to work. I asked for it. I had no idea how much was involved in running a ranch." We get into the truck, and I tell him all about it on the way home. "When I was a kid, I thought having horses meant you rode them, cleaned them, and fed them, but there's so much more to it. Rotational grazing systems, semi loads of hay, hundreds of pieces of equipment for training, boarding, and showing. Land contracts, leases, building maintenance. Did you know there's even an airstrip on the property?"

Dad's eyebrows shoot up. "An airstrip? Why did we just land forty miles away then?"

"It hasn't been maintained. I rode Tadpole out there the other day. Lots of cracks in the asphalt."

"Tadpole?"

"He's the gelding I ride. Seems to have taken a liking to me. We have an understanding."

"What's that?"

"He understands I'm not a very good rider, and I understand he knows it."

Dad laughs. "Seems you know an awful lot about Devil's Horn Ranch."

"That's why you wanted me here, isn't it? To help you with the sale. Well, what better way to help than to know everything there is to know about the property?"

He pats my shoulder. "Looks like I made the right choice, then."

Andie's truck is at the ranch when we pull in. She, Matteo, and Owen are standing around outside one of the stables, talking. Are they all here to greet Dad?

I park, and we get out. None of them look happy. "What's up?

"Another mare and foal are presenting with colic," Owen says. "They were fine yesterday when they were turned out, but this afternoon when Merle rode out, they were rolling. Add them to the mare with colic we found yesterday, and this is becomin' a problem."

"Is that bad?"

"It can be," Andie says. "When a horse has colic, which is mainly an upset in their digestive system, they tend to lie down and roll when they're in pain. But when they do this, their intestines can become twisted, which can cut off blood supply and make them necrotic. It's a real emergency and one of the most common reasons for equine mortality. We treat colic with pain medication, which should keep them on their feet, but it's important to keep them walking."

"Colic isn't that unusual, is it?" Dad asks.

"No, but to have three horses in the same pasture over a period of two days experience it, that could mean something."

"Like what?"

"We don't know," Matteo says. "Colic is caused by a lot of things. Changes in diet, adverse weather, inadequate water intake, ingestion of foreign material, even worms." He shakes his head. "We monitor them closely. I don't get it."

"We've moved the remaining horses in the pasture," Owen says. "We're checking it now for animal carcasses and other possible culprits. We'll keep the three sick ones inside until Andie gives them a clean bill of health."

"Good," Dad says. "Keep us posted." He turns to Andie. "Maddox tells me you're quite the veterinarian. I have complete confidence in you."

Her cheeks turn pink. "Thank you. I'll do my best to make sure they have a complete recovery." She pulls me aside. "Before

Owen called, I'd just put supper in the oven. Should be ready in about twenty minutes. Just take it out. There's plenty for you and your dad."

"You're not joining us?"

"I want to stay with the horses."

"You need to eat, Andie."

"I'll grab a protein bar later. Don't worry about me." She nods to the stable. "Worry about them."

Dad's having a conversation with Matteo, and after they finish, we go inside the main house. He takes his suitcase to the downstairs guestroom and immediately comes back out. "You're not staying in the master?"

"Doesn't seem right."

He looks at the family pictures lining the walls. "No, I suppose not. Guess I'll take my old bedroom upstairs."

"It's strange to think you grew up here."

"It was a lot different back then. We lived in a house with horses out back. We had a lot of property, but it was just that: property. It's amazing what your grandmother turned it into."

He climbs the stairs, and I look at the time. "I have to run next door for a second. Be right back."

When I return with a steaming casserole dish, he looks confused. "Your oven broken?"

"Andie made it. I invited her to live in the guesthouse."

His eyebrows shoot up.

"Before you go getting any ideas, it's what Nana would have wanted. She's drowning in student loans, and she's here a lot anyway since DHR is her biggest client. The house was just sitting empty."

"I wasn't going to argue with you. You're the one running things here, and you seem to know what you're doing."

"It would take years to know what I'm doing. I've barely scratched the surface. I really am in awe of Nana."

I put the casserole on the kitchen table. Dad gets three plates. I put one back. "We only need two. Andie will stay with the horses. She's really dedicated." I scoop us each some supper. "Did you know she went to Cornell? It's one of the top vet schools in the country."

He looks amused. "So you and the vet—"

"No. I mean, I would. I want to. But no."

"Why not?"

"It's complicated."

I tell him more about the ranch over our meal. Sometimes I amaze myself with all the knowledge I've acquired over the past month.

"You really like it here, don't you?"

I laugh. "I shovel horse manure, mend fences, groom horses, clean equipment, paint barns, and do a dozen other odd jobs I've forgotten, but yeah, I like it here. In some way, it's the most satisfying job I've ever had."

"I'm pleased to hear you say that, because there's another reason I wanted to come down here in person. I'm glad I did, because now I know Aaron will be in good hands."

"My *cousin*, Aaron?"

"Seems he's taken up with the wrong crowd in high school. Been suspended for fighting, and Griffin found drugs in his room." He makes a face. "His grades have taken a turn for the worse."

"What are you saying?"

"Your mom and I were talking to Skylar and Griffin about him last week. They're at their wits' end. Skylar had heard of places where you can send unruly children, where they work them hard and instill good values."

"Like boot camp or military school?"

"Yes, but then when they asked about you, the conversation took a turn. They were wondering if we'd be willing to have Aaron here for the summer."

"You think his living here will somehow turn him into a good kid?"

"It'll get him away from his delinquent friends. You'll put him to work. All those things you told me you do—he can help. No partying, no gaming with friends. Just good old-fashioned manual labor. Would you be willing to do it?"

"You want me to be his babysitter?"

"Yes and no. I'm going to talk to Matteo and the other guys, see if I can get them on board. But I suppose you'd be the one keeping tabs on him and reporting back to Skylar and Griffin."

"As in rat my cousin out if he doesn't toe the line?"

"It's what I would have wanted for you if we'd found ourselves in the same situation. It would be a huge favor to me. To all of us."

I push around what's left of my supper. "I can hardly say no to Aunt Skylar after all she's done for me at the restaurant."

He pats me on the back. "I'll make the arrangements." He takes his dish to the sink and then gets a plastic container out of a cabinet and hands it to me. "Put some of this delicious meal in here and take it out to the gracious woman who made it for you."

"She said she was going to eat a protein bar."

He stares me down. "You're really not gettin' how this works, are you, partner? You're in Texas now. Things are different here. Your grandmother had a saying: 'If you're gonna be from Texas, you might well know how to ride a horse, play poker, and treat a lady right'."

I laugh. "Some of the guys have been teaching me how to play poker."

"It looks like you've gotten two out of three then. Fill that container."

"Yes, sir."

I wrap a fork up inside a napkin, put a lid on the container, and take my hat from the peg above Nana's before going outside. Dad snickers behind me.

I stroll through the stables, but I don't see her anywhere.

Owen points. "She's out back."

She's past the arena, standing on the bottom rail of the fence surrounding the hot walker. Three horses—two mares and a foal—are slowly being walked in a circle by the large machine that is programmed to move them along at a certain speed. I've seen horses here before, but usually it's to exercise them six at a time without having to ride them, and it's usually going much faster.

"How's it going?" I ask, climbing up next to her.

"I gave them each a shot of Banamine, which is a pain reliever. I've got this set on the slowest speed. So far so good."

"How long do you have to watch them?"

"All night. Colic usually resolves itself in twelve to twenty-four hours. If it doesn't, I might have to use a nasogastric tube to relieve the pressure."

"Won't they just throw up if they aren't feeling well?"

"Horses don't throw up. It's why colic can be so dangerous."

"You're not really going to stay with them all night, are you?"

"Not all night. Only until ten. Miguel said he'd have the guys take shifts after that."

I hold out the food. "You should eat this."

She takes it and sits on a nearby bench. "Thanks. How's your dad settling in?"

"Fine. He told me my aunt and uncle are sending my cousin, Aaron, down here for the summer for boot camp or something."

She scrunches her brow. "Boot camp?"

"They want me to put him to work. They think it will make him a better kid. Guess he's gotten into trouble at school."

"How old is he?"

"Fifteen."

"The same age we were when we met." We lock eyes for a moment and I'm sure we're both thinking of that day. "They're sending him for the summer? It's only May. Does this mean you're staying longer?"

I shrug. "Guess so."

"Are you okay with that? You don't need to get back to your job?"

"My exciting bartender job, that can easily be done by about a thousand other people in the city, in a restaurant owned by the same people who want me to watch their kid? Believe me, there's no reason I need to hurry back. Besides, I kind of like it here."

"You do?"

"Yeah."

She picks at her food. "What do you like about it?"

"A lot of things. The ranch, the weather, the horses. I really like the horses."

"Oh."

I elbow her. "The people aren't bad either."

"Won't you miss being in the city? This is so completely opposite."

"That's why I like it. In New York City, it's almost expected that you be on the go twenty-four seven. Bars. Restaurants. Ball games. I like doing those things, but they get old after a while. Sometimes I just want to, I don't know, enjoy a good sunset."

"Unless there's a grave under you."

I give her a disgusted laugh. "Unless there's that."

"If you like sunsets, you should ride up to the ridge. It's the best place to watch one."

"Wouldn't it be dangerous to ride home in the dark?"

"Horses have great night vision, and if you pick a night with a full moon and clear skies, even better."

"Will you go with me? I wouldn't trust myself not to get lost."

She gets out her phone and taps around. "Tomorrow is supposed to be clear. Not a full moon but almost."

"Great. It's a date. I mean, it's not a date, it's, well, you know."

She blushes. "I'll pack some food."

One of the mares makes a noise. Andie lowers her fork and looks through the fence. "Yes! Ginger just pooped."

I laugh. "I've never met a person so excited to see shit before."

"Half my job is analyzing, monitoring, and sometimes even sifting through shit."

I turn up my nose. "Seriously?"

She giggles. "Bet you're re-thinking me packing food for the ridge, aren't you?"

"Not on your life."

She turns off the hot walker. "They've had enough for now. I'll move them back to the stable and monitor them there."

I put her empty food container on the bench. "I'll help. Then I'll go back to the house for supplies."

"Supplies?"

"You don't think I'm letting you stay out here alone after dark, do you?"

"It's my job, Maddox."

"Somehow I doubt your job is to sit here and watch other people's horses all night. The ranch hands can do it."

"I want to be here when the pain reliever wears off to make sure they don't try to roll again."

"I hope all your clients know how dedicated you are."

We move the horses, then I take off for the house. Ten minutes later, Beau is on my heels as I come back with two folding chairs, blankets, a thermos of coffee, and a game.

"Backgammon?"

"If you don't like it, I'll run back for another."

"I like it." She smiles and starts to set it up. "I like it a lot."

CHAPTER FOURTEEN

I lay out baguettes, deli meats, cheeses, fruit, and wine on the table. I find cheap plastic put-together wine glasses and tuck everything into a large satchel I can hook on my saddle.

Packing for our sunset ride feels an awful lot like preparing for a date. I'm not sure why I agreed to it. Could be I miss those sunsets with Vivian. Or maybe it's because he said he's going to be here all summer. In some ways that's even worse. I already feel things for Maddox. If he's here for three more months, and I get attached, it will be hard when he leaves. I don't trust myself around him. I'm afraid it will be like Bobby Monahan all over again.

There's a knock on my door. I grab my jacket and pick up the satchel. When I see Maddox holding a picnic basket, I laugh. "Where do you think you're going to put that thing? The trunk?"

"I thought I'd carry it."

"Connecticut, you can barely ride a horse, let alone balance a picnic basket." I hold out my hand. "What do you have in there, anyway?"

"Wine. Chocolate. A blanket."

I eye him suspiciously. "Not a date, huh?"

He nods to the satchel. "What's in yours?"

"Baguettes and stuff."

"No wine?"

I roll my eyes. "There may be a bottle."

"But this isn't a date."

"This is definitely not a date."

I open his basket, get everything out, and stuff it into my satchel.

We run into Miquel on the way to the stables. "Where are you kids off to?"

"Ridge," I say. "Maddox wanted to see the sunset."

"*Andie* wanted to see the sunset," Maddox says.

Miguel chuckles and wanders off.

I turn to Maddox. "Can we agree we both wanted to see the sunset and this is not a date?"

"Whatever you say, Dr. Shaw."

Tadpole and Baby Blue are saddled and tied to the hitching post. I turn to Maddox. "You did this?"

"I did. Go ahead and check it. I saddled her just the way you like it."

He chose my favorite saddle. I check the cinch to make sure it's not too loose or tight. I look at the headgear and the bridle. "You even used the double bridle. I'm impressed."

"Only for Baby Blue. Tadpole has the regular one. I'm not sure I'll ever be good enough to use the double."

"Most people don't like to. It's only for advanced riders and dressage competitions, but I like the precise control it gives me." I attach the satchel and mount Baby Blue, then we're on our way. "You're very observant, aren't you?"

"You prefer the horses you ride to wear a breastplate, you like to mount horses on the right side, even though most people do it on the left, and you think horses can understand you, even though it's not possible."

"They *do* understand me. Maybe not my exact words, but my tone and demeanor." I reach down and pat Baby Blue. "They're much smarter than you think. And out of curiosity, how does Owen prefer to tack his horses?"

"Hell if I know."

I can't help but smile.

We head for the mouth of the trail leading to the ridge. A bark sounds behind us and Beau runs up next to Tadpole. "He likes you," I say. "Must be a McBride thing."

"Beau, stay!" he shouts sternly.

The dog lowers his head and obediently turns back. I silently wonder if Maddox has found a friend.

"How are Ginger and the others today?" he asks.

"Much better. How was your day?"

"I sat in on a council meeting. There have already been several offers on the ranch. Joel Thompson's is by far the best. He even claims he won't sell it off in pieces."

"Do you believe him?"

"I don't know him well enough to answer that, but there were more than a few people there who didn't. Most people wanted Hugh Jenkins to buy it. Even the other guy, Dillon what's-his-name, but their offers aren't as strong. Someone even suggested the county subsidize their offers. Thompson about had a conniption.

There's been interest from commercial developers who just want it for the land."

"What do you think your dad will do?"

"I don't know. It's not about the money for him, but he's trying to do his due diligence."

"He seems like a nice man. Viv used to tell me stories of him growing up here. She said he and his father, the politician, didn't get along so well."

"I never met my real grandfather, but I know he wasn't happy about Dad going into the movie production business. He wanted him to follow in his footsteps. Do you know some people thought my grandfather might have gone on to be president one day?"

"Vivian mentioned it. Can you imagine what your dad's life would have been like? And yours?"

"I wouldn't be here, that's for sure."

"I'm glad it worked out the way it did." I stiffen when I realize what I'd said. "Not that I'm glad your real granddad died or anything."

"I know what you meant."

"I wonder why Vivian didn't push your father to become a rancher."

"Probably because she saw what happened when her husband tried to push him into politics."

"I can't imagine not living this life. If I ever have kids, I hope they want to grow up around horses."

"It does seem pretty awesome."

"It's a shame your dad didn't want to run the ranch."

"Not likely. He knows only slightly more than I do, which is this side of nothing."

"That's not true. Look at all you've learned the past month."

"I've learned how to be a barn worker."

"You have to start somewhere. Are you unhappy doing what you're doing?"

He cocks his head and studies me for a moment, then he looks out across one of the pastures. "It's quite the opposite. I love it." He chuckles. "Who knew I'd enjoy getting up at the crack of dawn and shoveling horse manure?"

"There are two kinds of people in this world. Those who are happy and those who want to be. In other words, those who love ranch life and those who don't. I'm convinced those who don't either haven't had a chance to try it or refuse to entertain the possibility that corporate life is a bunch of suits, running around trying to see who can make the best deal, build the tallest skyscraper, or buy the largest diamond for their pretentious wives. They think happiness is found in money, so that's what they covet."

"Are you saying everyone should work on a ranch? Kind of unrealistic and nineteenth century of you, don't you think?"

"Even in the eighteen hundreds, there was corporate wealth. Look at Vanderbilt, who made his fortune in shipping and railroads. Or Rockefeller, who at one point controlled ninety percent of the oil in the United States."

"You don't think they were happy?"

"Are your parents rich, Maddox?"

"By most people's standards, yes."

"Case in point. You grew up with rich parents, probably wanted for nothing, yet you worked in a dozen different jobs trying to find happiness. And here you are, shoveling horse manure and being happy."

"Dang."

"What?"

He stares at me. "Nothing, just… dang."

We stop in the east pasture and water the horses.

Maddox points to something by the large oak tree. "What's over there?"

"A graveyard."

"On the ranch?"

"I've told you, ranchers do this for life."

We tie the horses to a tree and go inside the small, fenced in, overgrown cemetery. Maddox walks around the dozen or so grave markers, brushing them off to make the names readable. "This one says Thompson. Is that why Joel wants the land?"

"Joel? He'd probably bulldoze these graves faster than you can say *high-rise condo*. He's not the sentimental type, if you know what I mean. This one was his great-granddad, Earl. Earl didn't own the land. It was his father-in-law's. That's his wife, Selma and two of their sons. Their third son, Joel's namesake and his granddad, moved away from the ranch and started an oil business. He had one oil well over fifty miles from here. *One*. Lived in a small house the size of Owen's cabin for sixty years. He had only one son, Jeb, who inherited the small plot of land and got a loan to add five more oil wells. His one and only son, Joel, inherited it when he passed. Joel was only eighteen at the time. How he managed to turn that into one of the largest oil fields in East Texas is beyond me, but rumor has it, he did anything. Beg, borrow, even steal."

"How do you know all this?"

"I spent a lot of time with Vivian. She bought this part of the property twenty-three years ago from Selma's great-granddaughter, Helen. Helen was one of those people whose happiness was tied to money. She took the proceeds and moved to Los Angeles to be an actress."

"Was she successful?"

"Drove her car off a cliff on the Pacific Coast Highway five years later, after she squandered the money on drugs."

"Okay, I get your point. Money can't buy happiness. But neither can a hard day's work and shit on the bottom of your boots. Not for everyone anyway."

"I suppose you're right. There are people who would rather do nothing than an honest day's work."

We leave the graveyard, and he latches the old, rusted gate. "I wonder why Nana didn't want to be buried on the ranch."

"I think she knew it wouldn't be in the family forever, and she didn't want to have her final resting place be on someone else's property."

"Do you think it made her sad, knowing my dad didn't want to run the place?"

"I don't think so. All she wanted was for him to be happy. She said your mom makes him very happy."

Maddox looks at the ground thoughtfully, then leans down to pick a few flowers. He bunches them together and hands them to me.

"I love these. They're my favorite. Thank you."

He looks shocked. "Orchids are your favorite flower?"

"Have been since I was a little girl. You seem surprised."

"They're my mom's favorite too."

I smile. "I know. I read it in her book."

"You read my mom's books?"

"I'm working my way through them. The first one I read was the one about her love story with your dad. It's incredible. She's a wonderful author. The way they met in college and then got torn apart by that horrible woman. And how your father saw you the first time. It was priceless."

"That's not embarrassing at all."

"You're embarrassed by her books?"

"She writes sex novels, Andie."

"That's not true. She writes love stories. It just so happens they have hot sex scenes in them."

"I'll take your word for it."

"You haven't read your own mother's books?"

"In case you haven't noticed, I'm a dude. I did see one of the movies once. Definite chick flick."

I laugh. "Read them, Connecticut. It's the least you can do out of respect for her."

"I'm not sure I could ever look at her the same way."

"It's just sex. Everyone does it."

He gives me a pointed look. "Not *everyone*."

Heat crosses my face and chest. Time to change the subject. "We're going to miss the sunset if we don't get up on the ridge." I look east. "I hope those clouds hold off for a while."

We make it up to the ridge, spread the blanket, have a snack, and pour the wine moments before the sky turns an incredible shade of orange.

"Wow," he says, mesmerized. "I'm not sure I've ever seen one quite like this."

"You wouldn't in the city. Out here, there are no lights and no pollution. Not even the sound of traffic. Call me crazy, but if you try hard enough, you can even *hear* the sunset from here."

"Says the woman who thinks horses understand her."

"So you *are* calling me crazy?"

"Will you shut up so I can listen?"

We sit in silence, sip wine, and watch the sky make its transformation. I can't think of a better fifteen minutes in my entire life.

When the sun has dropped below the hills, he removes his hat and lies back, fingers laced behind his head. "I think I could stay here all night. I'll bet when darkness sets in, you can see a lot of stars."

"Maybe not tonight. Clouds are rolling in. But on a clear night, you can see the Milky Way. Without all the light pollution, it's amazing."

He leans up on an elbow. "What's your curfew?"

"Gee, I don't know," I say sarcastically. "Dad usually wants me home by eleven."

"Tell me about your father."

"There's nothing to tell. I don't know him. I'm not even sure my mom knew him. She didn't have a picture. His name isn't on my birth certificate. It's listed as unknown."

"I'm sorry."

"Don't be. I had an amazing mother until I didn't. And then Granddad stepped in. If you never have something, you don't know what you're missing."

He leans over and runs a finger along the rim of my hat, then looks back at the sky. "I sure as hell know what I'll be missing when I go back to New York."

Holy hell. He might as well have been running his finger across my skin, because I swear I could feel it all the way to my toes.

"Did you hear it?" I ask, taking in the last moment of orange sky before it gives way to darkness. "The sunset?"

"I might have." He sits up. "Then again it could be my pounding heart."

I'm certain he's going to lean in for a kiss, but then a drop of rain hits my cheek. Then another. Before we have time to react, the skies open up, and it's pouring. Maddox scoops everything up in the blanket and shoves it in my satchel. We get on the horses.

"Follow me." I lead him across the nearest pasture and into a run-in shed. We dismount and tie the horses to a pole, then huddle in the center, dripping wet. I shiver. Maddox peels off my jacket and rubs his hands up and down my arms.

"What about you?" I ask.

He takes off his wet jacket and gets the blanket from my pack. "There's only one. We'll have to share." He wraps it around me and then steps close. I try to hold it around him, but Maddox is big, and the blanket is so small it barely covers him.

"Turn around," he says. "Try it this way." He pulls my back to his front and wraps us both in the blanket. I lean into him, and my hat collides with his shoulder, making it fall off.

"Leave it," I say when he starts to bend down. "Let's just warm up before we freeze to death."

"Who knew it could get so damn cold in Texas in May?"

We silently stand like this for minutes, watching the rain.

"I hope it lets up soon," he says. "You're really shivering."

I don't tell him I'm warming up. I don't say *he's* making me shiver, not the rain. The way it feels with his arms wrapped around me, I want to stay here forever.

His breathing quickens. I can feel his chest rise and fall, and his hot breath comes quicker on the back of my neck. I close my eyes and sink into him. Does he know what I'm feeling? What I'm thinking?

His hand grazes my breast when he adjusts the blanket. A noise bubbles up within me.

"Sorry," he says.

"It's okay."

He pulls me tightly against him. "Is it?"

I spin around, look up at him, and nod. The blanket falls to the ground as he cups my face and kisses me. Suddenly I don't care about the rain, the cold, or my wet clothes. All I care about is that his lips are on mine again. All I know is how much I want them there. His hands find a way under my top to caress my bare skin. I untuck his shirt and do the same. His skin is soft, with hard muscles underneath. I trace the small scar on his back that remains from his accident.

We kiss until Baby Blue shoves her face in my hair. We pull apart, and I run my hand along her mane. "Easy, girl." I turn to Maddox. "What does this mean?"

Maddox laughs. "I think it means she wants you all to herself."

"That's not what I meant, Maddox."

"I know what you meant." He wipes a wet piece of hair off my forehead. "And to be honest, I'm not sure. But what I *do* know is I'm going to want to do way more than stick my nose in your hair the next time you have to kiss Victor. More like stick my fist down his throat."

I giggle. "Way to ruin the moment."

"Look, it stopped raining. We should head back and get dry."

We mount our horses and leave the shed.

"Andie?" Maddox says. "I think it means something else, too."

"What?"

"That we should do that again. That we should *definitely* do that again."

I smile and trot away.

CHAPTER FIFTEEN

Maddox

She wanted to know what the kiss meant. The first time we kissed she said she just wanted to be friends. But last night, her lips were a hell of a lot more than friendly. I was honest when I told her I don't know what it means. I like her. And although I'm here for the summer, I'll leave sooner or later. I don't want to hurt her. With everything going on with Victor and her losing Nana, she has already been through a lot.

Through the kitchen window, I see Andie running across the yard to the stables. I go out on the back steps. "Where's the fire?"

"It's Baby Blue. Owen said she's sick."

I fetch my boots and hat and run after her, arriving at Baby Blue's stall just after she does. Owen, Matteo, and Merle are already there, urging the mare to stand up.

"Looks like colic," Owen says.

"Over here," Miguel calls. "There's one more." He's next to Tadpole's stall.

"Don't make no sense," Merle says. "Five of the turned-out horses got sick this week. But these two stay in the stable."

They get Baby Blue upright, and Andie examines her, then Tadpole. "Let's get them both out and walking around. I'll get the Banamine." She shakes her head. "I've never seen so many get sick in so short a period of time." On the way to get the medicine, she checks a few other horses in the vicinity. They all seem fine.

Outside, one of the ranch hands, looking upset, slowly walks a mare toward us. Andie is visibly worried. "Not another. What pasture was she in?"

"Number five."

"Not the same as the others." She turns to me. "We may have a real problem here. If whatever this is affects all the horses, odds are we're going to lose some and word will get out. People will move their horses. You'll lose a lot of business."

"Then let's figure out what's going on."

She gets her medical kit, and we return to Baby Blue and Tadpole. She rubs Baby Blue on the back like a mother might rub her child. It would kill Andie if anything happened to her. She whispers something to the horse, then turns her attention to Tadpole. I love the way she talks to them as if they are humans.

"What's going on with you two, huh? You were both fine last night on our ride." She turns abruptly. "Oh god, our ride. Maddox, we were out by the pastures, but they didn't eat. They only drank. It has to be the water supply." She yells for Matteo and Owen. "We have to test the water in the stream by the ridge. Get some of your men out there. Don't let any other horses drink from it until we have the results."

"We're on it," Matteo says and yells for half a dozen hands to hop in the truck with them.

"What do you think it is?" I say.

"Could be any number of things, from a diseased animal carcass upstream to a poison hemlock outbreak."

"Poison?"

"It's not poison per se. It's a plant that grows along streams. If enough of it got in the water, it could potentially make animals sick. Also humans, by the way, so stick to bottled water if you're out there. We normally don't see a lot of the plants, but it's been rainy this year, which can spur growth."

"Hopefully they can take care of either of those problems."

"They can, but we'll have to test the water daily for a while to make sure it's good." She glances at the barn. "Looks like Miguel is already getting water tanks and troughs ready to take out there to water the horses."

"We have water tanks?"

"You have *everything*."

We take the horses over to the hot walker. It's only now I realize Andie is wearing a Cornell sweatshirt and sleep pants. It looks like she just rolled out of bed and pulled on a pair of boots.

"I'll watch them," I say. "Get dressed and grab a bite to eat."

She shakes her head. "I want to stay with her."

"Okay, then. *I'll* get you something to eat."

"You don't have to."

"Andie, you might have just saved Devil's Horn Ranch. The least I can do is bring you coffee and eggs."

"You cook eggs? I thought all you make was pasta."

"I *scramble* eggs, and I make a mean piece of toast."

She laughs. "Sounds great. Thank you."

"They're going to be okay," I say, watching the horses being pushed along in the hot walker. I thumb toward the house. "I'll be back in a jiff. Then I'll sit with you."

"What about your dad? Don't you want to spend time with him? It could be hours before they're out of the woods."

"He flew out at the crack of dawn. Besides, I've become kind of attached."

She raises a brow.

"To Tadpole," I say, smiling as I walk away.

But as I make breakfast, I know the gelding is not the only one worming his way into my heart.

When the horses started to show improvement, I helped the barn workers unload the newly delivered hay. I'm leaving the barn when I see Andie heading to the guesthouse.

"How are they doing?" I ask.

"Much better."

"We don't have to do this thing with Victor and Katherine tonight. Everyone would understand if you cancel."

"The sooner they dig up the grave, the sooner we can be done with this. The horses will be fine. Let's just get this over with." She approaches and leans toward me.

My chest pounds as she gets closer. I've thought about her all day, about the walk and the kissing in the rain.

She brushes hay off my shoulder. "You might want to take a shower."

"I'll see you in about an hour?" As she heads toward the guesthouse, I think about tonight. Then I blurt, "I don't want him kissing you."

She turns. "Just the thought of his hands on me makes me sick to my stomach."

I take a step closer. "To be clear, that's not the only reason I don't want him kissing you."

I watch her chest rise and fall with a sigh before I walk away.

Forty-five minutes later, I emerge from my bedroom to find Katherine in the kitchen, looking out the window. "Well, come in," I say sarcastically.

"As I recall, most ranches have an open-door policy. Besides, Victor and I arrived at the same time. It would have looked weird if I'd knocked. Thank goodness your front door was unlocked."

I pick up a bottle of wine. "I thought you were going to outfit her with a microphone."

"I am. I have it with me for next time."

"Hopefully there won't be a next time." We cross the yard to the guesthouse.

"You mean if they find a body in his backyard? Maddox, don't pin all your hopes on that."

"Are agents at his place now?"

"Yes."

"Are they going to text you when they know anything?"

"They will."

"So we could be having dinner when you find out he's got a dead body in his backyard?"

"If that happens, backup will be here before she even knows about it."

"But you'll let *me* know? How about you give me a signal, like rub your nose if they find a body."

She rolls her eyes. "You watch way too much television."

I knock, and the front door opens.

Andie's there, looking relieved. "Oh, good. You're here."

Victor appears behind her, putting his hand on her lower back. I hand her the bottle.

"Thanks," she says. "I thought you were going to bring games."

"Damn, I forgot."

"That's okay," Katherine says. "Come on, Andie. Let's pick a few out. I know right where they are."

She doesn't, but Andie does. She knows the house like the back of her hand.

"We'll be right back," Andie says. "You boys open the wine."

They leave, and I'm left alone with the enemy. Victor steps back, inviting me in. We move to the living room.

"Andie said you've had some sick horses," he says. "I'm sorry to hear that."

I'll bet he's not sorry at all. A guy like this couldn't care less about human life, let alone animals. "They're much better now."

"When do you head back to New York? You're probably eager to get home."

"I'll be here for the summer at least."

"So you like it here?"

"I do. I'll miss it when I go back."

"Do you think Melina will go with you?"

"Who knows? We haven't talked about it. We're not to the moving in stage yet."

"She seems like one you wouldn't want to let get away. We're both lucky in that respect."

My stomach turns. I go to the bar. "Pour you a drink?"

"I should be pouring you one." He puts down the bottle of wine and picks up the whiskey. "I'm not sure if she has any Coke. You good with it straight up?"

"Sure," I lie.

He pours far too much into my glass.

"How long do you think *you'll* be staying around?" I ask.

He narrows his eyes. "What makes you think I won't be?"

I take a drink and try to come up with a reason. "I heard Andie telling Melina about how you like to move around the country and see different places."

He looks almost sad. "I've never stayed in one place long. Do you think Andie would ever want to leave?"

I go on high alert. "I don't think so. She loves it here. Her job, the ranches, her granddad—I can't imagine her wanting to leave."

The women return with armfuls of games. I start toward Andie to relieve her of a few, but Katherine clears her throat, reminding me who my date is. I change direction smoothly. "Let me help you, Melina."

Victor laughs, eyeing the stack of games. "How long do you plan on being here? I was sorta hoping I could have some alone time with my girl later."

Andie closes her eyes and swallows. I eye Victor's glass, debating if I should try to get him piss drunk so he'll pass out. It could backfire, though, and make him more aggressive. Maybe Andie should slip some horse tranquilizer in his drink or something.

All through dinner, I notice that Victor doesn't ask many personal questions. He doesn't ask about Andie's family, Vivian, or her past. I'll bet Katherine would say it's because criminals don't want similar questions to be asked of them.

I'm getting a little drunk, or maybe I'm just stupid, but I say, "Victor, you're what, twenty-eight?"

"Twenty-six… uh, seven."

I fake laugh and grab the whiskey bottle. "Sounds like you need another drink if you can't even remember your age."

He pushes the glass away. "Maybe that's why I *don't* need one."

"You ever come close to getting hitched?"

Katherine gives me a swift kick under the table. "Babe, that's not polite to ask with Andie sitting right here."

Victor takes Andie's hand. "There'd be nothing to get jealous about. I haven't had many long-term relationships. I'm kind of a loner."

Katherine puts an arm around me. "It's a good thing this one's not. Did you tell them I might be moving to New York with you?"

I about shit my pants. What is she doing?

Victor cocks his head. "Is that so?"

"I thought we were keeping that to ourselves, *babe*," I say to Katherine.

"Oops. Guess our secret is out." Katherine kisses my cheek. I don't miss the brief look of jealousy that crosses Andie's face. I try not to look happy about it.

Andie clears the table and brings a game over. Halfway through it, I can't stop looking at the clock on the wall. Surely there's been enough time to dig up the grave.

"Is there someplace you need to be, man?" Victor says. "You're staring at the clock like it's going to jump off the wall and bite you."

There's a knock on the door. I hope it's the FBI to arrest him. I'm so ready for this to be over.

"You expecting someone?" Victor asks Andie.

"No."

He goes to the front door as Katherine discreetly tells us she knows nothing.

"It's Matteo," Victor says.

Matteo storms past Victor on his way to Andie. "What's wrong?" she asks.

"Anticoagulant rodenticides," he says. "That's what's fucking wrong."

"What's that?" I ask.

"This." He throws something on the table.

I pick up the package. "Rat poison?"

"The stream is full of it. The water tested positive for it. One of my guys found this about fifty yards north of the property line near the mouth of the stream."

Andie shakes her head. "One bag wouldn't be enough to pollute the entire stream."

"I'd say about a hundred bags is more like it," Matteo says.

"Jesus," I say. "Who would poison the water?"

"Don't touch the bag," Katherine says. "There might be fingerprints." She uses a pencil to take it from me. "Andie, do you have a large Ziplock bag we could put this in?"

"Who are you, the FBI?" Victor jokes.

Andie looks like she's about to pass out.

"No," Katherine says. "They do this on TV."

"It could have been a lot worse," Matteo says. "If you and Maddox hadn't taken your horses to the ridge last night, we might never have tested the water."

Victor looks more than a little unhappy. "You and Maddox went riding last night?"

Andie goes completely ashen.

Katherine jumps in without missing a beat. "One of the mares was giving birth in the pasture. Maddox wouldn't let Andie ride out alone in the dark. Isn't that right, babe?" She leans in and kisses my cheek. "You're so chivalrous."

Matteo looks confused. Before he can say anything that might blow our cover, Andie urges him toward the door. "Thanks for getting to the bottom of it. You'll contact the authorities?"

"Already have."

She rejoins us. "I hate to cut the evening short, but I need to check on all the horses in the pasture." She turns to Katherine, looking nervous. "Is it okay if we continue this another day?"

"Of course. We'd be happy to."

"It's dark outside," Victor says to Andie. "I'll go with you."

"No. Go home. I'll probably be working all night. I won't ride, I'll drive my truck."

"I'll have a few of the ranch hands go with her," I say.

This seems to satisfy him. "Okay, but I want a rain check. Maybe next time we can fly solo."

"Yeah. Sorry, I really have to go. The horses might need me."

Victor leaves, and Katherine and I pretend to go back to my place. "You two almost blew it," she says. "You can't go galivanting around together after dark when *they're* supposed to be a couple. You're lucky I was there to diffuse the situation."

"Us? What about you? I told Victor we hadn't talked about my going back to New York yet and then you practically announce we're moving in together."

"You were getting too personal. Men don't ask other men about their relationships. Andie is the one who needs to do the asking, not you."

"Who cares about any of that? What did you find out? They're obviously done digging if you let us end the evening early."

"It was an empty grave."

I'm dumbfounded. "Maybe he saw us looking at it last week and dug it up."

"If anything was there, it was a dog. It looks like a canine tooth was found—they sent it off to be sure. Could be the previous tenants wanted to take their pet's remains with them."

My jaw drops. "Who would do that?"

"People get attached to their pets, Maddox."

"Still, digging them up. That's sick." I blow out a long breath in frustration. "So we're back to square one, and Andie needs to keep seeing that prick."

"I wish it didn't have to be that way."

"Then why don't you do your damn job and figure this out without her help?"

"We're trying. I promise you we are."

"I need to get to the stables. I have problems of my own."

"Let me know if I can help. I'd be happy to run the rat poison bag for prints if you don't get anywhere with the local police."

"Thanks. I'll keep it in mind."

Since Victor is long gone, we simply shake hands. "I'll call you soon with our next move."

"Andie is not doing anything else without a microphone. I won't allow it."

"She already has it. Gave it to her when we got the games."

"She was wearing it tonight?"

She nods. "I told you it wouldn't be obvious." She opens her car door. "Be careful. You don't want to put her in danger. Might want to cool it with the nighttime pony rides."

After she leaves, I join the others in the barn office. "Do you have any idea who would want to poison the stream?"

"Someone who has something to gain from it," Matteo says.

Repulsed, I ask, "Who could possibly gain something by killing horses?" Several pairs of eyes stare me down, like the answer should be obvious. "The Thompsons?"

"Who else?" Owen says. "They are the only ones who would benefit from DHR getting bad press. Hugh Jenkins sure as hell wouldn't want to buy a ranch that had lost a bunch of horses."

I sit down. "You think they'd kill horses to get what they want?"

"I think they'd do just about anything," Owen says.

I get out my phone and step into the hallway. Andie pops her head out. "The police are already on their way."

"I'm not calling them. I'm calling my father. No way in hell will I let him sell to those pricks."

CHAPTER SIXTEEN

Andie

In Matteo's office, I sink down on the couch in defeat. "How can they have come up with nothing?"

"The police questioned every retailer of that particular rat poison," he says. "Even went as far as Oklahoma."

"And there were no prints on the bag you found?"

He shakes his head.

Maddox is clearly as upset by this as I am. He's pacing. "So that's it?" he says. "Case closed and whoever did this gets away with it?"

"They haven't closed the case," Matteo says. "They're looking into online purchases, but the sheriff told me not to expect much."

"What about footprints?" I ask. "Or tire tracks. There must be *some* evidence they can find."

Matteo gazes out his window, brooding. "Apparently, a few sick horses don't get us to the top of the priority list at the sheriff's office."

"A few sick horses?" I say in revulsion.

"Andie, I know Baby Blue is more than just a horse to you. She's family. I'm willing to do what it takes to protect her and the rest of them. I sent some of my men upstream the past few nights. I thought maybe they'd see if anyone tried to do anything."

"They didn't or you'd have said something."

"It's a long stream, and the poison could have been dumped in anywhere."

Maddox sits on the arm of the couch. "But Thousand Acre Ranch hasn't had any problems, and they are directly north of us."

"We're doing everything we can," Owen says. "I've got someone testing the water twice a day. The horses are healthy."

"For now," I say. I get a text and stand. "It's Hugh Jenkins. I have to check on one of his pregnant mares."

Maddox walks me out. "See you for supper?"

I smile. Meals with Maddox have become the highlight of my day. "Absolutely."

"And *I'm* cooking."

"Spaghetti casserole?" I say, laughing.

"It's a surprise."

"I'll be over at seven."

"No. I'll bring it to you. Remember what Katherine said about you not being at the main house."

I kick dirt when we reach my truck, frustrated. "Someone's poisoning horses, and I could be dating a murderer. How did I end up here?"

He strokes my arm. "Everything will be okay. I'm going to make sure of it."

"How? You don't know the Thompsons. If they did this, who knows what they are capable of. And Victor—I don't even want to think about those possibilities."

"I don't know how, but I'm going to keep you safe, Andie." He glances at the stables. "And them."

He can't possibly mean it, but hearing him say it makes me feel better. When I was young, Granddad always looked out for me. Then it was Vivian. Now him. My whole life, even though I never had a father, and Mom died so young, someone has been there for me. Despite all the terrible things going on around me, I am a lucky girl.

"See you tonight," I say, then drive away.

On the way to Hugh Jenkins' place, I call Christina.

She gets right to the point. "You're not calling to cancel Thursday's lunch, are you?"

"No. I wanted to ask you something. Please don't get mad, but I don't know what else to do."

"You know you can ask me anything."

"Is Jon working?"

She snorts. "He's always working."

I tell her about the rat poison and the horses getting sick and the police having no evidence. "Christina, I know he's your husband and all, but—"

"You think my rat bastard husband and his family might have done it because they want the ranch. Say no more. Tell me what you need. But it's not like I can just ask him, you know. He doesn't tell me anything, least of all Thompson family business."

"It's a long shot, but y'all have the biggest shed I know. You've told me Jon sometimes hangs out there with his buddies. I was thinking maybe you could, I don't know, snoop around a little."

"Ooooo, a covert operation. This is something I can get onboard with."

Christina is a bored housewife. If she's so gung-ho on this, I bet she would have a field day if I told her about Victor.

"This is serious business, Christina. If he did this—"

"If he did this, he'll go to jail, and I could live off the conniving shithead's money, so hell yeah, I'll help you."

"I'm sure you won't find anything, but someone did drop a bag of rat poison. If we could find another like it, we might have something to go on. But Christina, if you find anything, do not confront him. Call me, and I'll have the guys at Devil's Horn Ranch deal with it."

"Fine. Now let me go, so I can find my black ski mask and gloves."

I laugh. "See you Thursday."

"You know it."

When I arrive at the Jenkins place, a caravan of trucks is pulling out, kicking up dust as they spin their tires. I'd recognize that motorcade anywhere. Joel Thompson was here.

I park and go to the stable. Mr. Jenkins is sitting on a bench in the tack room, eyeing a huge pile of tack on the floor. "You okay, Mr. Jenkins?"

He's startled when I speak, then quickly stands. "Andie. I am now. Thanks for coming so quickly. I'm worried about Henny. She seems agitated."

"What were the Thompsons doing all the way out here?"

"Oh, you know them. They were politely letting me know how much they'd like to be the ones to purchase Devil's Horn Ranch."

"Politely?"

He gestures to the tack, which I realize wasn't removed for cleaning but has been forcibly ripped off the walls—nails, pegs, and all.

"You should report this."

"Won't do no good. They got everyone in the sheriff's office in their pocket. Joel Thompson was the largest contributor to Sheriff Wheatly's re-election campaign."

I sit next to him and close my eyes. "Is that so?"

"The sheriff doesn't even like old Joel. I'd bet my bottom dollar he'd love to see him go down, but I can almost guarantee it won't be on *his* watch."

I help him clean up and then we check on his horse. All the while, I tell him in confidence about the stream and the poison.

"You know it's him, don't ya?" he says. "Or at least his henchmen."

"Matteo thinks he wants to run the ranch into the ground and make it so nobody else wants to buy it."

"It's what I'd do if I were him. Nobody in town wants DHR to fall into his hands."

"I don't think it will. I know the owner's son. He assures me they won't sell to him."

He shakes his head. "They might not have a choice if he's the only one left standing."

"It won't come to that."

"You don't know Joel very well. Let me tell you a story, Andie. He and I go way back. We were friends even, though that seems like a lifetime ago. He was tight with my brother, Roger. They were a few years older than me, and I looked up to them. They both did everything first: dated women, drove trucks, bought ranches. They were who I wanted to be. One day when I was twenty-five, after saving my whole life to buy a stallion, we went to a show. I did my biddin', won the auction, and trailered my new stud back home. I'd never been so happy, but don't tell Thelma I said that. The next day I was eager to get things started. I knew ranchers would have their broodmares lining up to breed with him. He was going to make me rich."

It must have happened almost fifty years ago, but I can see how fresh the memory still is for him. My heart races. "What happened?"

"Come mornin', damn horse was dead in his stall."

I gasp. "What? How?"

"Vet said his reins got tangled up in the stall door. Died of asphyxiation. Blamed me for leavin' tack on him. But the thing is, I didn't leave him tacked up. I knew better. I mean, yeah, sometimes we leave halters on them, but the rest? Never."

"You think Joel did it?"

"I know he did. He practically gloated the next time I saw him. Bragged about his oil business and how he was the richest man under thirty in the county."

"And the police never did anything?"

"How could I prove I didn't leave his bridle on? Everyone knew how excited I was. Roger and I had drinks that night to celebrate. The police said I probably had one too many. Besides, Joel didn't have a bad rep back then. Everything he did was under the radar. No one would have believed me. They'd have said I was jealous, that Joel was rich, and he had nothing to gain by killing my stallion. But they were wrong. He had everything to gain. A few months later, he bought two stallions. Had them shipped from Europe even. He became the go-to guy around these parts if you wanted the best Quarter Horse bloodlines, and he never let me forget it."

"Mr. Jenkins, that's terrible."

"Been here my whole life, Andie. I could tell you a dozen more stories about backhanded tactics, corrupt deals, and lowlife antics concerning that family. I suspect every town has a Joel

Thompson. It's something you learn to live with. I'm over seventy years old. I've had a good life, despite what he did to me. Got me a lovin' wife, a prosperous ranch, and God-fearin' children. What more could an old man want? I'd love to buy Devil's Horn Ranch, but I won't jeopardize what I have to take it from the Thompsons."

"Please fight for it, Mr. Jenkins. There's no one who could run Devil's Horn Ranch better than you."

"I appreciate the vote of confidence, Andie." His attention turns to his pregnant mare. "She gonna be okay?"

"Henny will be fine. She's overdue is all. Like any female, she's going to be uncomfortable and irritable at this stage of her pregnancy. Is there anything else while I'm here?"

"Not today."

"Then I'll see you Friday on my normal rounds."

"You're a good girl, Andie. You remind me a lot of Thelma when she was your age. But good girls don't need to go stirrin' up trouble, you hear me? Best to steer clear of the Thompsons. You let others deal with the issues out at Devil's Horn Ranch."

"Okay, Mr. Jenkins."

He walks me out. "Why do I feel like you just fed me a line of horse manure?"

There's a knock at six fifty-five. I check my appearance one last time before answering the door.

Maddox is engaged in a balancing act. He's got a picnic basket draped over one arm, a bottle of wine in one hand, and a bunch of wild orchids in another. I quickly glance around to make sure we're unobserved.

"Get in here," I say, taking the bottle of wine before he drops it.

"Stay, Beau," he says then walks in. "If I had a third hand, I'd have brought your mail. It's sitting in my kitchen. I'll run it over later."

"You shouldn't be seen with all this stuff. People will think we're on a date."

"Who cares what the guys think?"

"Me. I care. They know I'm seeing Victor, and they'd think I was cheating on him. They probably call me a slut behind my back."

"They don't."

"How would you know?"

"I'd know. I'm getting tight with some of them."

"Still, we shouldn't be giving people the wrong idea." I inhale. "Maddox, what is that incredible smell?"

He puts everything down, opens the picnic basket, and pulls out a dish full of short ribs. My eyes snap to his. "You made these? But you can't cook."

"I've been learning. Well, I've only learned how to make this one thing, but I heard you say it was your favorite."

"So you thought you'd start *there?* That's not ambitious at all. How did you make them?"

"Dutch oven."

"You make sandwiches and pasta. I'm surprised you even know what a Dutch oven is."

"Wait until you taste them. You'll want to marry me."

My cheeks heat.

He smiles. "I'm kind of the whole package. I can cook, play backgammon, and I look damn fine in a cowboy hat."

He's not wrong. He does look good in a cowboy hat. "Cocky much?"

"Where do you want the food?" I point to the dining table. He takes more dishes out of the picnic basket. "I hope you like mashed potatoes and cooked carrots. I googled what goes well with short ribs."

"It all sounds wonderful."

He takes the flowers to the kitchen and starts to throw them out. "Stop!"

"If this isn't a date, no flowers."

I grab his hand. "You can't throw them away. They're beautiful. Where did you find them?"

"By the ridge."

"You rode all the way out there to pick orchids?"

"Didn't have anything better to do just then."

I pull a vase from a cabinet and fill it with water. "Well, thank you. That was very sweet." I put the vase on the dining room table. "We should eat before it gets cold."

He opens the bottle of wine and pours us each a glass. "What should we toast to?"

"Not much to celebrate around here lately."

"To orchids," he says. "And sunsets." He starts to drink, then stops. "And to unexpected rain showers."

We eye each other over our glasses as we drink. Has he thought about that night as much as I have?

I take a bite of short ribs. They melt in my mouth. "Oh my god, Maddox, these are amazing."

He smiles. "I know."

"But you haven't tasted them."

"I already made them two times this week. Ate them for lunch."

"Seriously?"

"They're your favorite. I had to make sure I got it right."

I take another bite. "Mission accomplished. Mine aren't even this good. You'll have to share your recipe."

"Things always taste better when someone else cooks. I found the recipe in one of Nana's cookbooks."

"Whenever she'd have Granddad and me over, she'd cook like it was Thanksgiving."

He grins. "That's Nana."

"Every time I leave this house and look over at yours, I think she's going to come bouncing down the stairs with a smile on her face, like she always did."

"I know. It's still strange living in her house when she's not there."

We reminisce about Vivian through supper. When we're almost finished eating, there's a knock on the door.

"Andie?" someone calls.

My heart pounds. "It's Victor. He can't find you here."

"He won't." He speedily picks up his plate, napkin, utensils, placemat, and wine glass. "I'll go out the back."

I swallow. "You're leaving me?"

"I'll find an excuse to come over in a minute. Now go answer the door."

"Coming!" I yell as Maddox runs through the kitchen and out the back door. Taking a quick glance around to make sure he didn't leave anything incriminating, I throw a book on his side of the table, then open the door. "Hi, Victor. What brings you out here?"

"I had to pick up supplies in Ft. Worth. Thought I'd stop by on the way back. We haven't seen each other much lately."

"I know. There's been a lot going on with my job."

He sees Beau lounging on the porch. "What's up with the dog?"

"There are several of them living on the ranch." I reach down and fluff his ears. "This one is Beau."

"Can I come in?"

I try to think of an excuse why he can't. "I was just finishing supper."

"Smells good." He crosses the threshold. "Too bad I ate earlier."

We enter the dining room, and I glance out the window to see Maddox running back to his house, Beau trailing behind. Does Victor somehow know he was here?

"What took you so long to answer the door?"

"I was in the bathroom."

He eyes my almost empty bottle of wine. "Drinking alone?"

"Just having a glass with my meal. One bottle lasts me all week."

"Nice dinner. Do you always cook this much?"

My throat goes dry. Why is he asking so many questions? I'm sure he can see right through me. "These were leftovers. I cook enough to last a few meals."

"Good idea. Maybe one of these days you'll cook for the two of us." He picks up my plate and the dish of potatoes. "Let me help you with these."

"I can do it."

He heads for the kitchen. "So can I."

I panic, knowing what he'll find there, and try to block the way. "No, really."

"It's no big deal. I showed up unannounced, the least I can do is make myself useful."

I almost run for the door. He's going to see Maddox's dishes, then he'll know for sure. What will he do?

I tensely wait for him to say something, but he returns with a clean glass and pours himself a couple fingers of whiskey. "I hope you don't mind if I stay for a drink. I've missed you."

"Sure, but only one, okay? I've had a long day."

"One then, but only if you agree to go out with me this weekend. No Maddox and Melina."

"I, uh…" I pray for Maddox to show up with some horse emergency.

"You have to agree. I've been very patient, Andie."

"You have."

"Dinner then. My house on Friday. You don't even have to cook."

"Okay."

He fills my glass with the last of the wine. "Great."

There's a knock on the door. I've never been more relieved.

"Looks like you're a popular girl," he says, going to open it. "Maddox, what brings you all the way out here?" He laughs at his own joke.

Maddox holds out his hand. "Andie has mail."

"Thank you for bringing it over." Victor starts to shut the door.

"Melina wanted me to ask if she could get the recipe for Andie's famous apple pie."

"Now?" Victor is clearly not pleased Maddox is barging in on our alone time.

I hurry over and fully open the door. "It's in the kitchen. Victor, sit and have your drink. I'll be back in a second."

Maddox trails after me. "While you're at it, can I get the recipe for whatever you cooked tonight? It smells great."

I scan the kitchen and don't see Maddox's dishes. "What did you do with everything?" I whisper.

"Dishwasher. I threw them in." He looks guilty. "I might have broken the wine glass."

"They're *your* glasses."

"Andie, give me a recipe."

"Oh, right." I pull out the old recipe box Vivian gave me and take a few. "Don't leave."

He puts his hand on mine. "You're shaking."

"Shh, he might hear you. Of course I'm shaking. He's in my living room."

"I've got it handled."

"How?"

"Trust me."

"Everything okay in here?" Victor says, appearing in the doorway.

I hand Maddox the recipes. "Tell her not too much butter in the crust. It'll make it less crumbly."

"Sure thing. Thanks."

Victor hands me a letter. "You should open this one. It looks official."

"I'm sure it can wait."

"I'm serious. Open it."

I examine the letter. It's from an insurance company. I open it and almost faint. I sit on a chair, staring at the check made out to me.

Victor takes it from me. "Holy shit. Two hundred fifty grand?"

I read the enclosed letter. "It's from Vivian. She named me beneficiary of her life insurance policy." I look at Maddox. "I had no idea. I can't accept this. This should go to your family."

"Hell no. She wanted you to have it, Andie. She left my family enough, believe me."

"This is huge," Victor says. "Now you can pay off your loans and move back to your apartment."

I think about what this means. He's right. I have no excuse to stay in Maddox's guesthouse. Why did I have to open the envelope? "I can't believe she did this."

"She loved you, Andie," Maddox says.

Tears come to my eyes. "She's still taking care of me."

Maddox puts a hand on Victor's shoulder. "We should take off. Andie looks like she has a lot to deal with. How about you come over to my place for a beer? Or I could rustle up some of the guys for a game of poker."

"I think I should stay with her," Victor says.

I shake my head. "I'm no good to anyone right now. All I can think about is Vivian. Go have your drinks. I'll be okay."

Reluctantly, Victor moves to the door. Maddox glances back and smiles, and I mouth *Thank you*. He nods like he gets me. Like he knows me better than anyone ever has.

Except maybe Vivian.

CHAPTER SEVENTEEN

Maddox

"Thanks for doing this," I tell Owen. "I know you have better things to do."

"Are you kidding? Any excuse I can get to shoot a gun." We examine the target. "This right here? This was yours. You're getting better. Want to try the shotgun?"

"Hell yeah."

He gives me a demonstration and hands it to me. "Watch out, it's got quite a kick. Make sure your feet are planted."

I shoot, then rub my shoulder. "Why do I feel like this is going to hurt later?"

"You get used to it. Kind of like working out at the gym—you build up a tolerance."

I take the handgun, aim at another target, and sprinkle bullets on and around it.

He laughs. "Whose face are you picturing?"

"No one."

"Maybe that's the problem. In my experience it's easier to hit the bullseye if you're motivated."

"Who do you picture?"

"Elly Michaels."

I lift a questioning brow.

"Broke my heart when I was sixteen. Ran off with my best friend."

"Seems you ought to picture *his* face then."

"My best friend's name was Janice Kessleman."

I laugh. "Oh." I squint at the target, aim, and pull the trigger. I hit it slightly off-center.

"Damn," he says. "Now we're talking. Let me guess. It's Victor, isn't it?"

"Why would you say that?"

"Everyone with eyes would say that, partner."

"That's ridiculous."

He holds up his hands. "I'm not one to judge. The vet is hot and considering the way you look at her, I'd say you agree."

"We're friends."

"Friends who sneak around and eat supper together every night."

"She cooks for me in exchange for my letting her live in the guesthouse."

"I'm willing to bet her boyfriend doesn't know that."

I kick at a stump.

"Hey, it's okay. We're family around here. Doc is part of that, and now you are too. Family take care of their own. You got nothin' to worry about."

"It's not what you think. There are things you don't know."

"Like I said, you'll get no judgment from me. Just so you know, if you ever decide you want to be more than friends, everyone thinks you're a good fit."

"Everyone? You guys talk about us?"

He pats me on the back. "It's getting late. You wouldn't want to miss supper, would you?"

While riding back, we pass a building covered in vines. "What's that?"

"The old hunting lodge. Before Vivian bought this piece of land, it was rented out for parties. But that came with a lot of liability she didn't want to take on. Get a dozen drunk hunters together and you got yourself a recipe for disaster. We still rent out the land for hunting but not overnight."

"What's it like inside?"

"Empty. Vivian cleaned it out years ago and shut off the electricity. Matteo inspects the place from time to time. You know, runs the water, checks for squatters. I can't remember the last time I was inside. It's probably dusty as all get out."

"Looks like a great place. Seems like someone should live there. In fact, why don't *you* live there? Your cabin is a fraction of the size."

"Now what would someone like me do with all that space? I only need a place to sleep. I work a hundred hours a week."

"Why do you work so much?"

"We all do. It's all we know."

"Do you enjoy it?"

"Maddox, I see you. You're up at dawn and busy until you go over to the pretty vet's house for supper. You're one to talk." He shakes his head. "The thing is, you don't even have a horse in this race. You're here temporarily. Your daddy's gonna sell out, and you'll probably never set foot on a ranch again." He gives me a pointed stare. "Now lie to me and tell me you're not enjoying the hell out of it."

"You got me. I do love it."

"Maybe I'm wrong then. Maybe you'll hang around."

"For what? They'll be nothing here for me."

He peers in the direction of the houses. "Oh, there'll be *one* thing."

He rides off, leaving me with my thoughts. Thoughts of a future standing behind a bar, serving drinks to ungrateful socialites. When I pass the run-in shed Andie and I took shelter in last week, I stop Tadpole and gaze at it. Owen is right. I can't imagine going back to my old life.

A black truck is parked by the stables. Damn it, I recognize it. Andie and an older man come out of the guesthouse. I dismount. "Looks like we have company."

"I saw Jon earlier," Andie says. "I think he's talking with Matteo." She turns to the man. "Granddad, this is Maddox McBride, Vivian's grandson. Maddox, this is my granddad, Gerald Shaw."

"I saw you at my grandmother's funeral." I hold out my hand. "It's a pleasure to meet you, sir."

"The pleasure is all mine."

"Granddad is here for supper. You'll join us, won't you?"

"I don't want to impose. I can just make a—"

"Sandwich? No, you won't. I've got enough stew to feed an army."

"I insist," Gerald says.

"I can't argue with that. Let me brush down Tadpole and jump in the shower, and I'll be over."

Jon Thompson exits the stable, pissed as hell. He beelines over and gets in my face. "You got somethin' to say to me?"

"Man, I don't even know you. Why would I have anything to say to you?"

He glares at Gerald. "How 'bout you, old man? You got something to say?" Gerald looks positively terrified. "I didn't think so." He turns to me. "Cops been sniffin' around. Don't stand here and lie to my face like that spic, Matteo."

"Spic?" I laugh in disgust. "Aren't you half Latino?"

"Don't mean I'm a spic like those fuckers you got working for you."

"They don't work for me."

"Your daddy then. It's all the same."

"I'd appreciate if you'd take your truck and your racial slurs off this property."

"Why don't you call off the dogs?"

"Now why would the cops be interested in you?"

"Don't play fuckin' dumb."

Andie steps forward. "Jon, we all know who poisoned the stream."

Gerald tries to hold her back. "Andie, don't."

Beau trots over and leans against Andie's leg as if protecting her.

"Maybe you should listen to the old man and mind your own business, sweetheart." Jon inches closer and looks her over like she's a piece of prime meat. "Unless you want to get all up in mine."

I step between them. "I said get off my property."

"You just told me it ain't yours."

"Leave or I'll throw you off."

Beau growls.

Jon bends over laughing. "You and what army? Oh, right, the spics. I'm shakin' in my boots."

I grab his arm. He jerks lose and lifts the front of his shirt, revealing a gun. "Might want to think twice before layin' a hand on me a second time."

"And you might want to think twice about coming back here."

"You have no idea who you're dealin' with, do you, boy?"

"Looks like an asshole with limited education and vocabulary. A loser whose only claim to fame is his corrupt father, and whose only aspiration is to belittle those around him, because he knows he'll never really amount to anything."

He makes a *ts*king sound. "You done messed with the wrong cowboy, asshole."

"Get the fuck off my property."

He blows Andie a kiss. "See you around, sweetheart."

He drives away. Matteo, Owen, and some of the guys witness his departure. Owen gives me a low whistle. "Damn. Not many people will hand him his ass like you just did."

I blow out a deep breath. "I guess not many people are as stupid as I am then."

"Granddad, are you okay?" Andie asks.

Gerald is pale. I help him to a bench. "Someone get him a bottle of water."

He waves off my comment. "I'm fine."

"You're as white as a ghost," Andie says.

"Those Thompsons have a way of doin' that. You stay far away from the lot of them, Andie, you hear me?"

"I plan to."

"That's a good girl."

Merle tries to hand him water, but he bats it away.

"I'll be needin' something a bit stronger. Now help your ol' granddad up so I can get a whiskey."

I make sure he's steady on his feet. "You sure you're okay, Gerald?"

"You get to be my age, you're okay if you're still breathin'. Now git on with that shower. Andie's stew is a callin'."

"Yes, sir. I'll be over in ten minutes." I lean down and pat Beau's head. "Good boy."

Merle takes care of Tadpole as I race to the house, shower, and change. I'm knocking on Andie's door in record time.

Gerald answers. He takes my bottle of wine, shakes my hand again, and gestures to the couch. "Andie will be out soon. Why don't we sit? Can I get you a drink?"

"I'll wait for supper, but thank you."

"You're a bartender, eh?"

"I was. I'm not really sure what I am anymore, to tell you the truth."

"Livin' on a ranch can do that. Gives you perspective."

"I hear you and my grandmother were close."

He nods. "No disrespect to your granddad."

"Of course not. He died a long time ago. I'm glad she was happy."

"One of the happiest people I've ever come across. Boy did she love you and your sisters. Talked about you all the time. Counted down the days until she was going to fly up for a visit."

Guilt consumes me. "I feel bad we didn't come here much in the last ten years."

"Wasn't for you. There's no blame in that. Your pop had a lot goin' on up there, with his businesses and raisin' three kids. It was easier for Viv to travel to you. She didn't mind one bit, so put that guilt right out of your head."

Andie appears with a large bowl of stew. "Supper's ready."

"Sorry we got to eat so early," Gerald says. "The old folks' home feeds us at five o'clock on the dot, so these days if I don't fill my belly by six, you can call me grouchy."

"It's a retirement home, Granddad. I hate it when you call it an old folks' home."

"It's where old folks live, ain't it?"

Andie returns to the kitchen for biscuits. During dinner Gerald asks me about my childhood, my sisters, my jobs, and he tells us stories about my grandmother. Between his stories and Andie's, I feel like she's still with us somehow.

"What happened to that old hat?" he asks.

"Still where it always was," I say.

"The peg by the back door?"

I nod.

"As it should be."

I pick at a spot on the table. I don't mention that someday, probably soon, it'll have to be removed because the house will no longer belong to a McBride. I feel a sense of sorrow I haven't felt before.

"You chokin' on a bone, son?"

"No, sir. Just thinking."

"If thinkin' put that glum look on your face, you better darn well fix whatever it was you were thinkin' about."

"Some things can't be fixed."

"Nonsense." He stands and takes his plate to the kitchen. "I reckon you'd better get me back, pumpkin, before the old folks' police declare me a missin' person."

She says harshly, "Granddad."

"But first I want to go say hello to that mare of yours."

"I'll go with you," she says.

"Nope. Maddox will show me the way."

"You know the way," she says.

He taps his temple. "I'm old. I might get lost. Come on, Maddox. Help an old man out, will you?"

"I'd be happy to."

We go outside and cross the driveway to the stables. He knows right where to find Baby Blue.

"Andie says you bought this horse for her on her tenth birthday."

He gives the mare a pat on the side of the head. "Best thing I ever did."

"She adores you," I say. "Uh, Andie, not the horse."

"And I her. She's kept me goin'. I lost my wife before Andie was born. When her mother died, it was Andie and me for more than ten years. When she went away to college and then vet school, I started comin' around more to check on her mare. Never took up with another woman until Viv. She was something special, that one."

He starts back to the driveway. "What you did out there with the Thompson boy? Be careful. They can't be trusted. Not a one of 'em."

"So I've been told."

"I'd keep Andie as far away from them as I could."

"I'll watch out for her, sir."

He stops walking. "You're a good boy, aren't you, Maddox?"

"I like to think I am."

"You are. I can tell that about folks."

One of the ranch hands hurries by. Gerald shouts at him. "You there. You drive?"

"Yes, sir," Zac says.

"You can take me home then."

"Sir?"

"It ain't but ten miles. You can use Andie's truck."

"I don't mind driving you, Gerald," I say.

He nods to the guesthouse. "I reckon you got better things to do."

"If you mean help Andie with the dishes, I planned on it. I always do the dishes when she cooks."

He laughs heartily and pats me on the back. "Your grandmother and I used to 'do dishes.' We used to do *a lot* of dishes." He turns to Zac. "What you waitin' for? An invitation from the president?"

"Yes, sir." Zac runs over to Andie's truck. Everyone knows she leaves her keys in it.

I have a thought. "Can you wait one minute, Gerald? I'll be right back."

He glances at his watch. "Time's money."

I chuckle and run to the back door of the main house. I'm back in twenty seconds. I hand him Nana's hat. "She'd want you to have this."

He looks at it for a long moment before taking it and running a finger lovingly along the crease. "I don't need anything to remember her by. Havin' this around might not be good for my old ticker." He hands it back to me. "I appreciate the gesture, I surely do, but the hat is exactly where it belongs." He swallows hard, then turns to Zac. "You got ten minutes to get me home. If I'm late, I'll have Miguel put you on manure duty for a month."

Zac looks ill, but Gerald winks at me.

I chuckle as they drive away. I place Nana's hat back on the peg, wondering just how long it will stay there.

Andie appears when I step outside again. "Who's driving my truck?"

"Zac. Your granddad made him take him home."

"I was going to do it."

"I think Gerald was hoping you'd do something else instead."

"What?"

"Me."

She turns as pink as a sunset.

"I'll help you with the dishes."

"They're done."

"Then let me help you finish the bottle of wine."

"It's almost gone."

"Andie, do I have to hit you over the head with it? I'd like to come inside and kiss you, if that's okay with you."

"In that case…"

I pull her inside, shut the door, and cage her against it with my arms. "Do you know how long I've wanted to do this again?"

I kiss her. She tastes like beef and wine and strawberries—the lip balm I see her use so much. I explore her mouth, jawline, and neck with my tongue. She sighs when I hit a spot under her ear.

She throws my hat on the floor and runs her fingers though my hair. I press into her so she can feel what kissing her does to me.

"Maddox," she exhales breathily.

I untuck her shirt and shove my hand under it up to her bra. I cup her breast. She leans into me. I reach around and unclasp her bra, then push it up. I want to see her. Feel her under me. I want to be inside her like I've never wanted anything before.

I pull her shirt over her head, and she lets her bra fall to the floor. She's gorgeous. My lips travel down her neck to her collarbone and then lower. She moans when my tongue finds her nipple. She claws at my shirt until I take it off. Her hands explore my back and shoulders.

I toy with the button on her jeans. She grasps my ass. I swear we can't get enough of each other. I'm about to pick her up and take her to the bedroom when a knock on the door ruins the moment.

Andie stiffens, terrified. I peek out; it's Zac. I hadn't realized we'd been kissing for so long. She quickly picks up her shirt and puts it on, kicking her bra under the entry table. She pushes me behind the door and opens it.

"I wanted to let you know your granddad got back okay."

"Thanks, Zac. I appreciate it."

"Might want to fill up your tank. You're almost empty."

"Will do. Goodnight."

She closes the door and sinks to the floor. "What if that had been Victor?"

I put my shirt on. "You can always not answer the door, you know."

"But my truck is outside."

"You're in the stables or a pasture."

She stands and paces. "Katherine thinks we're being reckless."

"She said the same thing to me."

"I told her this is, you know… casual."

"Right. Because I'm leaving in a few months."

She eyes me skeptically. "This *is* casual, isn't it?"

"Isn't that what you want?"

"I can't do more than casual, Maddox. Not if you're leaving. I've been burned by that before."

"So it's settled. I should go."

"Okay."

"See you tomorrow?"

She nods.

I turn and give her a searching look. "What exactly does casual mean? I want to make sure we're on the same page."

"It means I'm not your girlfriend. We won't get attached."

"Oh, okay." I turn to leave but spin around. "One more thing. Does casual mean I can't take off your pants?"

She laughs and covers her mouth. "Well, I don't know. Can you take off my pants and still be casual?"

"I'm pretty sure I can do that. What about you? Do you think you could take off *my* pants and still be casual?"

Her eyes travel to my fly, and I'm instantly hard. "Yeah," she says as if saying duh.

"So if we can take each other's clothes off and be casual, that means we can still be casual, say, in your bed or on the couch."

She blushes. "Maybe we could even be casual on the kitchen table." She shoves me out the door. "Bye, Connecticut."

I took a shower not ninety minutes ago, but damn it if I don't need another.

CHAPTER EIGHTEEN

Tara comes in for a hug. "You look amazing. One might even say glowing."

"Oh my god, did you finally shag my landscaper?" Christina squeals.

"Stop it. Can we just find our table?"

We're seated. I'm on Christina's right. That's when I notice the bruise on her cheek. It's faint, mostly covered by makeup, but it's there. My heart lodges in my stomach. "Did I do this to you? Did he catch you snooping?"

She touches her cheek. "What? No. Don't be ridiculous. I ran into a door in the middle of the night. It was stupid really."

Tara and I stare her down.

"Okay, fine. He caught me on Facebook. He hates it when I go on social media. Thinks I'm going to reconnect with a high school boyfriend or something. Speaking of high school, have you guys seen Dan Hickman?" She fans herself. "He's some hotshot lawyer in Dallas, and his status says he's single."

Tara and I don't give a rat's ass about Dan Hickman. "He *hit* you?"

She waves off my comment. "No, nothing like that. He reached over my shoulder to get my laptop and accidentally pushed me off the chair. I hit the edge of the table on the way down."

"Christina, that's as bad as hitting you."

"Not hardly."

"Are you telling us the truth?" I turn to Tara. "I asked her to nose around Jon's shed. I shouldn't have. Be straight with me, Christina, did he find you there?"

She puts a hand on mine. "He didn't, I swear. I didn't find anything either. Well, I found plenty but not what you're looking for."

We fall silent as the waitress takes our order, then Tara asks, "What'd you find?"

"Guns. Booze. Porn. A weird collection of those Russian nesting dolls. File folders full of things I can't understand. I'm also pretty sure there was a brick of coke."

Tara goes ashen. "As in cocaine?"

I shake my head. "You have to get out of there."

"I'm telling you, it's not that bad. I've seen those movies on Lifetime. So many people have it worse than I do, and most of them don't have a personal chef, a hot gardener, and a closet the size of Rhode Island."

I've known Christina since we were kids, and I believe she values her lifestyle over what that bastard is doing to her. She even seems happy. I don't get it.

"Enough about my delinquent husband. I want to hear about the hottie who put that smile on your face when you walked in.

You've actually done the deed, huh? Is his bottom half as amazing as his top half? What am I saying. Of course it is. But is he, you know, hung like a cowboy?" She giggles.

"I'm not sleeping with Victor."

Christina narrows her eyes. "But you're still dating, right?"

"It's complicated."

Tara bounces in her seat. "It's the new guy, isn't it? Elsa from the diner told me she saw the two of you shopping in Ft. Worth last month. Is he the McBride people are talking about?"

My eyebrows shoot up. "People are talking about Maddox?"

Christina's lips curl into a wry grin. "Maddox? You're on a first-name basis with the hot transplant from Connecticut?"

"He's from New York, actually. His family lives in Connecticut."

She laughs. "Well, I stand corrected."

I figure now is as good a time as any to tell them I moved. "Just so you know, I'm temporarily living in the guesthouse at Devil's Horn Ranch."

They're practically drooling.

"Guesthouse, huh?" Tara says.

"It's not like that. DHR is my biggest client. I'm there at least two or three days a week. I'm using this as an opportunity to pay off my student loans."

"As in you're living there for free?" Christina says. "What gives?"

Our food arrives, but no one so much as picks up a fork.

"Wait a minute. You don't have student loans," Tara says. "Vivian paid your way."

"I've got bills." I reach for my burger.

"You're a terrible liar," Christina says. "Something's up."

"Like I said, it's complicated."

"Why can't you tell us?" Tara says, pouting.

"I promise I will when there's something to tell. But there's nothing, so let's eat."

Christina is busy on her phone. She shoves it in my face excitedly. "*This* guy is living fifty feet from you? Holy shit, Andie."

I take her phone and scroll through the Facebook pictures Maddox was tagged in. A lot of them have his friend, Reece, in them. Some are of him behind a bar, others in the wings at concerts. There's even a picture of him with the famous rock band, Reckless Alibi. I stop on a selfie some girl took with him. Looks like they could be on a date. My eye twitches. I tap on his name to go to his profile, but he doesn't post much. The last one was over a year ago. It's mostly people tagging him. He's got a great profile picture. I can't pull my eyes away.

"Girl, you are so smitten," Christina says, snatching her phone back.

"I am not." I pick up my burger and take a bite.

"If you're not a thing, you wouldn't mind introducing us," Tara says.

"Well... I... he's so busy with the ranch."

Tara laughs. "I'm only kidding, Andie. He's all yours."

"He is *not* mine. He's only here until his family sells the ranch."

Christine nods. "Oh, I get it now. You're stringing Victor along so he's still around when the hot one from New York goes back to New York and leaves you with needs you'll want fulfilled."

I rub my temples, wishing I could tell them everything. "I love you guys, but there are some things I can't talk about right now. I promise I will soon."

"We should do lunch at your place," Christina says. "I'll have it catered. You won't have to lift a finger."

"I'm not sure that's a good idea."

"Sunday?" she says, ignoring my objection.

"Sounds good to me," Tara says.

Christina claps gleefully. "I'll set it up."

I drop it. There's no arguing with these two when they set their minds to something.

Halfway through lunch, I get a text from Matteo. "Sorry, guys, I have to run. Emergency at Devil's Horn Ranch."

"Tell McHottie I said howdy," Tara says.

Christina laughs. "OMG, yes. McHottie. I love it."

I roll my eyes. "It's not even from him." I shove my phone in Christina's face. She reads it. "What's choke?"

"Tara will explain it to you." I leave money on the table. "I'll see you guys on Sunday."

"Three horses have choke?" I say after meeting Matteo at the stables. "Seriously?"

"Four!" Owen yells from inside.

Maddox runs over. "What's the problem?"

"Choke," I say.

"A horse is choking?" he says, distressed. "Which one?"

I put a hand on his arm. "It's okay. I mean, it's not okay, but it's not an emergency. When something gets lodged in a horse's throat, unlike humans, they can still breathe. But it does panic them."

Owen joins us. "What's concerning is that four of them have it. Choke is fairly uncommon, so to have four at once, something is going on."

I silently curse. "It's like the water all over again."

We quickly go back to where the horses are. It kills me to see them suffering.

"Two of them passed the obstruction," Merle says.

"What can I do for the others?" Maddox asks. "Do we give them water to wash it down?"

"No water." I go to drain the water bin, but it appears Owen or Matteo beat me to it. "And don't rub their necks. The best thing we can do is encourage them to keep their heads low and keep them calm. Also, wipe away any nasal discharge. As they produce more saliva, their esophageal muscles will relax, and the blockage will pass. After that, I'll be on the lookout for lingering coughs, fever, or runny noses, which could indicate aspiration pneumonia."

"So choke itself isn't life threatening, it's the potential pneumonia that could follow."

"Exactly. Some horses have a propensity for choke. We need to monitor those who do."

"Is it always like this on a ranch this size?" Maddox asks. "Going from one emergency to another?"

"No. You're just lucky enough to be here when it all happened. Or should I say unlucky?"

Minutes later, the last horse seems to pass his obstruction.

"What causes choke?" Maddox asks.

"Eating too quickly, dental problems, esophageal trauma," I say. "But no way did that happen to all four. My guess is bad hay."

"Jesus," Owen says. "We got a load last week, but now that I think about it, we were using the last shipment until this morning. Shit."

"Get your guys to remove all the hay from the stalls," I say. "Start with these four. Did you put any in the pastures?"

"Not yet."

Maddox appears concerned. "But what'll we do for hay in the meantime? It'll take time to get a new load."

I lean against the wall, knowing he's right. *That* could be our real emergency. "We're going to need a lot of it. Horses can eat twenty pounds a day. That's three flakes per feeding. What's our head count?"

"One hundred eighty-three," Owen says.

"I'd send everyone you can spare with a truck to local feed stores to buy up anything similar to what we normally get."

"Might be hard to find as much as we need," Matteo says.

"What's so special about the hay we get?" Maddox asks.

"We order a combination of alfalfa and orchard grass. We need to keep it close to twenty-percent alfalfa. Anything higher might cause colic, and we sure as hell don't need more of that going around."

"Let's turn out as many as we can," I say. "They can graze for a day or two until we get a good supply." I turn to Matteo. "Get on the phone with the hay supplier. Find out what happened. And have someone analyze the hay. Could be moldy."

"I'm on it."

"Owen, can you head over to the Jenkins' place, then to Thousand Acre Ranch and the Double Duce, see if they have any to spare? They all use good quality hay."

"You think they'll do it?" Maddox asks.

"Ranchers help each other out. Unless they're low, they won't have a problem with it."

Everyone leaves. Maddox and I sit on a bench, keeping an eye on the two who just recovered.

"I hate this part of the job," I say. "The wait and see part. It's more rewarding when I can simply give a shot, patch a wound, or birth a foal. At least then I know I'm *doing* something."

"You're invaluable around here, Andie. I'm really sorry you might end up losing business when we sell."

"It's okay."

He stands. "No it's not. I'll do everything I can to make sure my dad sells to someone who will keep you on."

"I'm more worried about everyone else, especially Matteo, Owen, and Miguel. Management positions are always harder to find. Ranchers have their own people. Even the ranch hands and barn workers might have a tough time. Vivian always paid better than most."

"I wonder if my dad can write it in the contract to whoever he sells to that everyone gets to stay on in some capacity, even if only for a year or so."

"That would be amazing. Someone like Hugh Jenkins might agree to that."

"I'll bring it up the next time we talk."

"You're a good man, Maddox."

He snorts.

"What?"

"Your granddad said something along those lines last night."

"He's always been a good judge of character."

He brushes a stray hair behind my ear and adjusts my hat. "He'd change his mind if he knew what I wanted to do to his granddaughter."

I catch my breath. "Is that so?"

"What are you doing later?"

"Well, that's subtle." I stand and pat one of the geldings.

"That's not what I meant. Yes, I'd love to, but… okay, let me start over. My cousin is coming next week, and I thought I'd free up some room for him at the house. I was wondering if you'd help me pack up Nana's things."

"I'd be honored, but what if Victor stops by?"

"We'll deal with it. He knows you were close to her. It makes sense you'd help me go through her stuff. Besides, I doubt he will. You have a date tomorrow."

"Ugh. Don't remind me."

"Are you scared?"

"Of course I'm scared. I'm going to be alone with him."

"Katherine, her partner, and I will be close by, and we'll hear everything. The more you can get him to talk, the quicker this will be over."

"She gave me a panic word. You know, something to say so you guys can bust in if I feel in danger."

"What is it?"

"Beer. She figured I wouldn't usually say it, because I drink wine, and Victor drinks whiskey."

Matteo appears, and he's not happy.

"What is it?" Maddox asks.

"Our supplier said someone called to change the order two weeks ago. They were told we had to cut costs and to send only the cheap stuff. He said they even warned the caller about the possibility of choke, but the caller said we were transitioning from horses to cattle."

"Who did they say called?"

He looks stressed. "Me."

"Shit." Maddox paces. "You know it was the Thompsons. Who else would do that?"

"What'll we do?" I ask.

"Get rid of the bad hay for starters," Matteo says. "We'll clean every inch of the barn."

"Good idea," Maddox says. "Just watch out for the cats."

Matteo's brow shoots up.

"I'm just saying there are a lot of them in there. Be careful."

Matteo paces. "Owen and I are going to call all our suppliers—grain, water, produce, even the gas deliveries for the machinery. We'll set it up so this can't happen again. I, or one of my guys, will call and verify our orders the day before delivery."

"You shouldn't have to go through all that trouble. There's got to be a way to stop them."

"Stop the Thompsons when they have their sights set on something?" Matteo asks. "We may have to fight fire with fire."

"You want to sabotage them?" Maddox says.

"They've got oil wells, ranches, restaurants, hotels. I'm sure we could come up with something."

Maddox shakes his head. "If we sink to their level, we'll be no better than they are."

"I'm with Maddox. We can't play their game."

Matteo leans against one of the stalls. "I'll keep on top of things, but everyone here needs to be on their toes. If anything looks or smells different, or somethin' just don't feel right, I want to know about it."

"Agreed." I nod to the horses. "They seem much better. I'll check on them tomorrow."

"We were lucky," Matteo says. "Caught this one quick. Might not happen like that next time."

He leaves, and I sit. "Maybe it's not worth it. We're putting the horses at risk. Maybe your dad should sell to Joel. At least then nothing else bad will happen."

"You mean nothing bad except twenty hard-working people losing their jobs, and Nana's land—her whole life—being mowed down and turned into condos or a shopping mall."

"You're right. It was a dumb idea."

Maddox heads to the house. "See you later then?"

"I'll bring supper."

"I was thinking we could just order pizza. I'll run into town and pick it up."

"Pizza was Vivian's favorite," I say.

"I know, that's why I think we should get it."

I feel a lump in my throat. "See you at seven."

He leaves, and I wonder how one man can be so caring, hardworking, and selfless. So… perfect. Except he's not perfect. If he were, he'd be staying in Texas, not going two thousand miles away.

CHAPTER NINETEEN

Maddox

Andie knocks on the back door at seven. What I see takes my breath away. She's wearing a sheer top that reveals the black tank underneath, jean shorts, and cowboy boots. Holy god. Cowboy boots have never looked so sexy.

"Cat got your tongue?"

I try to stop staring but can't. "I've never seen your legs before. You're always wearing jeans."

"Have to for work, but the nights are getting a lot warmer." She looks past me. "Can I come in?"

I chuckle. "Right." I open the screen and move out of the way, grabbing a treat and throwing it on the back steps for Beau.

She takes her hat off. I put it on an empty peg by the door.

"Granddad told me you tried to give him Vivian's hat. That was really nice of you."

"I don't understand why he didn't take it."

"Maybe he sensed it wasn't time for you to let it go."

I motion to the table. "Have a seat. We can eat before we tackle everything."

I get the pizza box warming in the oven. "I figured you for a pepperoni and veggie girl, but just in case, I ordered half with only cheese."

"I'll eat anything but anchovies and pineapple."

I make a face. "You and me both. Wine?"

"Sure. I have a feeling we might need a glass or two to get through tonight. Are you sure you're ready to do this?"

"It has to be done sooner or later, and with Aaron coming, I figured now was a good time."

"Your dad didn't want to be here for it?"

"He took some things with him the last time he was here. He asked me to box up most of the family photos and save any nice jewelry for my sisters. The rest, her clothes and stuff, can be donated."

"It's what she would have wanted."

I put plates on the table and fill up our glasses. "I really like your granddad."

"He likes you, too."

"What did he say about your inheritance?"

"I haven't told him yet."

I'm surprised. "Why not?"

"I want to do something nice for him. If he knew about the money, he'd insist I use it all for myself."

"What do you want to do?"

"I'm not sure yet. I'd love to get him out of the retirement home. I know it's a nice place, but he misses being around horses. I've been thinking about getting us a house with a stable where I can keep Baby Blue. I could have help come in a few hours a day to make sure his needs are met."

"There are three bedrooms in the guesthouse, you know. Why not have him come stay with you? If it's horses you want him around, there are a hundred and eighty of them just steps away, and there are plenty of people on the ranch who can pop in and make sure he has everything he needs."

"I don't want to move him twice. I'm only here until the Victor thing is over."

"You can stay as long as you like, Andie. I'm not going to kick you out when they haul that lowlife to jail."

"While I appreciate the invitation, we both know the guesthouse is getting sold with the ranch. It would be harder on him to be here with the horses and excitement and then have to move somewhere else. There are a few places I've been looking at online. Small houses on an acre or so of land, with a couple of stalls."

"I'd be happy to go with you to check them out."

"I'd like that very much."

"You're a good granddaughter. All grandparents should be so lucky."

"He raised me. The least I can do is make his last years happy ones." She puts down a piece of crust. "I'm stuffed."

I shove the rest of the pizza in the fridge and refill our wine glasses. "I guess we should get started then."

"What do you want to do first?"

I go in the living room and get the boxes and tape I bought earlier. "Let's clean out her bedroom."

She grabs the packing paper, and we head upstairs but stop in the doorway. I don't come in here much. The book she was reading is still on her nightstand, next to a half-full glass of water.

"What do you want me to do?" she asks.

"Can you pack up her jewelry? I think it's all there on top of her dresser." I hand her one of the small boxes. "Use this. I'll start emptying out the closet."

We work mostly in silence, I'm sure both of us thinking of Nana as we pack away her things. As I tape up a box of clothes, I notice Andie staring at a necklace. I remember Nana wearing it a lot. The charm on the end of the chain is an outline of Texas, and there's a small diamond seemingly floating right where DHR is located. She traces the outline of the charm and then wipes a tear before she wraps it in paper and puts it away.

I get to my feet. "I'm going to put this down with the others."

While I'm downstairs I make a quick call. Then I rejoin Andie and fish through the jewelry she wrapped up until I find what I'm searching for. I undo the clasp and place the necklace around her neck.

"What are you doing?"

"I'm giving it to you."

"This belongs to your family. Your father said to save her jewelry for your sisters."

I turn her around to face me. "Not this piece. This is yours. I cleared it with Dad just now after I saw you admiring it. We want you to have it."

Her eyes turn misty, and she fingers the charm. "I can't tell you what this means to me. Thank you."

We finish the bottle of wine as we tape up the last box in Nana's room. I sit on the bed, wondering if I can ever see myself sleeping here. Even without her things, it's still *her* room.

Andie sits next to me. "We'll donate the bedding, lamps, curtains, and area rug, then we'll go out and buy something that's more you."

"How did you know what I was thinking?"

"Everything in here has flowers on it, Maddox. It's hardly appealing to a twenty-five-year-old man. I'm thinking something more rustic. Blues and grays maybe. Once you redecorate, you'll feel more comfortable here."

"Will you help me? We could go into town on Saturday."

"Now *that's* something I can look forward to."

I run a hand through my hair. "I hate that you have to do this thing with Victor tomorrow. Here's the thing, though. You *don't* have to do it. Say no. Stop putting yourself in danger. Don't we have enough to deal with around here without throwing that asshole in the mix?"

Her gaze drops. "Don't you think I ask myself that every day? But if I don't do it, he might get away with it. If I don't do this, a little girl might never know what happened to her mom, and a mom and dad might never know what happened to their daughter."

I put my hand on top of hers. "I'm going to be right outside with them. If he tries anything—"

"I know. Beer." She pulls her hand away and stands. "Come on. Let's finish the job."

I lean over to pick up a box, and she gasps.

"Maddox, what are you doing with a gun?"

I straighten and pull the back of my shirt down. "I know how to use it. Owen has been giving me lessons, and I've been to the range."

"But why?"

I try not to laugh. *"Why?* Let's see, you might be dating a serial killer, and a family of nut jobs is trying to ruin Nana's ranch. Do I need more reasons?"

"Are you licensed?"

"Not yet. I've filled out all the paperwork, and I'm allowed to carry on the ranch. People have a right to protect their property."

She looks scared. "You won't have it with you tomorrow, will you?"

"No, but Katherine and her partner will be armed."

"Be careful, Maddox. I don't want you getting hurt. What if Jon comes back?"

"Jon is one of the reasons I'm carrying."

"And if you both draw your guns, what then?"

"It won't come to that."

"You don't know the Thompsons as well as I do. They have politicians eating out of their hands. Remember that before you do something stupid."

I smile. "Andie, are you *worried* about me? Isn't that crossing the line of casual?"

She moves to the door. "I'd worry about anyone who tries to mess with the Thompsons. Or Victor."

"So it's not just me. You'd have the same feelings if, say, Owen were having this conversation with you?"

"Owen can take care of himself."

"Are you saying I'm a wimp?"

"I'm saying you're a bartender from New York who has no idea what he's dealing with."

I pick up a box and follow her downstairs. "You'd be amazed what bartenders have to deal with."

"Drunken sorority girls and men cheating on their wives?"

"Okay, yeah. But things get out of hand sometimes. I've had to threaten people with the baseball bat we keep behind the bar."

She stops, and I run into her. "A baseball bat? That won't kill someone."

"It will if you hit them in the head."

"You know what I mean. Promise me you'll be careful with that thing."

I put the box with the others. "I promise. Speaking of weapons, there's something I want you to do when you're with Victor tomorrow. I hate to ask, but you should hug him when you arrive. Really pat him down before going inside. See if he's carrying a gun or knife."

"How on earth can I do that without him knowing what I'm doing?"

"Say you had a bad day. You lost a horse or something. He'll hug you to comfort you. Maybe even fake cry—guys eat that shit up. He'll be so happy you're in his arms, he won't care where your hands are."

"Unless he has a knife or a gun."

"If he does, we'll be out of the car in two seconds. Better to know on his front porch than after you're behind closed doors."

"Did Katherine say to do this?"

"No."

"So this is *you* being worried about *me?*" She grins. "Isn't *that* crossing the line of casual?"

"Shut up."

CHAPTER TWENTY

Andie

"Stop fiddling with the ring," Katherine says. "You don't want to draw attention to it."

"*That's* the microphone?" Maddox asks. He takes my right hand and examines it. "You tested it?"

"We tested it when I gave it to her," Katherine says.

"But you haven't tested it today?"

"No."

"Test it," he says.

"It's fine," Katherine's partner, Michael says. "These things have a high reliability rate."

Maddox stares him down. "Test it."

"Fine. Andie, go in the back room. Keep your hand by your side and speak in a normal tone."

I go into Maddox's bedroom. "Testing one, two, three. Can you hear me?"

"We're good!" Katherine shouts.

Maddox opens the door. "We heard you. We're good." He sits next to me on the bed. "You okay?"

I nod.

"Your voice came right through the speaker on Michael's phone. I'll be able to hear whatever you say."

I swallow. "I don't know if that makes me feel better or worse."

"Why would it make you feel worse?"

"It could be weird, considering… you know."

He laughs. "Considering the casualness of our state of affairs?"

"Something like that."

"You think I'll be jealous, you having to hug him and all?"

"I would be."

"You would?"

"Casual doesn't mean dead, Maddox. Of course I would."

"Are you saying you want us to be exclusively casual?"

I smile. "Is that even a thing?"

"It could be."

I sigh. "I told you, I don't want to get burned."

"So you're saying you want to be casual with other people?"

"Ha ha." I fight a laugh. "No. Do you?"

"No. Okay then. Nobody is going to burn anyone, Andie. We enjoy each other. There's nothing wrong with spending time together while I'm here." My phone pings with a text, and I scan it. "Good news. Matteo says our supplier is rush shipping a new order of hay. Should be here Sunday."

"That *is* good news. You should be fine until then with what the other ranches loaned you."

"We ordered extra so we can pay them back with more than what they gave us."

I smile. "I think you're getting the hang of things, Connecticut."

He smiles, too, but it's sad.

Katherine pops her head in. "We'd better get going."

They accompany me to my truck. Katherine hands me a bottle of wine.

I take it and apologize. "I should have thought to bring one. I guess I don't have my head on straight."

"This one's on us," she says and puts a hand on my shoulder. "I need you to be sharp. There's only so long you can string him along without him expecting"—she glances at Maddox—"more."

Maddox scowls.

"The more we can get out of him tonight, the better. Keep him talking. Even the smallest details could give us something to go on."

"I'll do my best."

"I know you will. Now go. We'll be right behind you. Don't look for us when you arrive at his house. We'll be close."

I get in my truck, wait for them to get in Michael's car, and then I drive. My head buzzes the entire way to Victor's. What if I can't get him to talk? What if I slip up, and he realizes what I'm doing and hurts me before they can get to me? What if he says scary stuff, and I have to sit there and pretend I'm not terrified?

I pull over a block from his house to calm my nerves but end up banging my forehead against the steering wheel. "How did this happen to me? I just want to be with Maddox." I inhale deeply, hold my breath to a count of ten, and blow it out. I catch sight of the ring, remember who's listening, and realize they probably heard everything I said. I pull the ring close to my mouth. "I, uh…" I try to think of something to say but can't. "Oh, forget it."

At least now, instead of being scared of Victor, I can be mortified that the three of them heard my inadvertent confession. I continue to Victor's and park in the driveway. My phone rings. It's 'Melina.' "Hello?"

"Don't talk into the ring, Andie."

"I know. Sorry."

"You've got this. We're right here."

I hang up, pull down the mirror in my visor, and practice my fake pouty face. Then I take the bottle of wine to the front door.

Victor appears. "What's wrong?"

I hand him the bottle. "I could really use a hug."

"Of course." He steps aside. "Come in."

I panic, step back, and lean against the porch railing.

He comes toward me with open arms. "Hey, it's okay. What's going on?"

I wrap my arms around him, making sure to graze his sides. "I lost a horse today."

He holds me tightly and runs a hand down my back, so I do the same to him. "I'm sorry. I know how much you care for them."

I run a hand along the back waistband of his pants and over his back pockets. "I've lost animals before, but it's hard every time."

He lets me go and turns. "Looks like you need a drink."

I put my hands around him and touch his front pockets, pulling him back. "Just one more hug." I feel something, but it could be a wallet or a pack of gum. What would a knife feel like in someone's pocket anyway? He pulls me into his arms again. I don't think he's got a weapon on him, so I move away. "Thanks. I guess I needed that after the day I had."

"I'm available anytime. Let's get you a glass of wine."

I have to remind myself not to scan the street before going inside. I know they are out there somewhere. I'd just feel better if I knew where.

He pours us each a glass. "Do you know how happy you just made me?"

"I did?"

"Lately I've felt like you're pulling away. It's nice to know I'm still needed."

"There's been a lot going on with my granddad and my job. I've been distracted."

He leads me to the couch, and we sit. "I'm glad to know that's all it is, because I really like you, Andie. I haven't felt like this in a long time, so when I feel you're holding back, it's upsetting."

I sip, wondering what Katherine would have me say. "I don't know much about you, Victor. It's always been hard for me to open up to someone I don't know."

"Maybe we've been spending too much time with Maddox and Melina."

A timer goes off in the kitchen, darn it. I had a good opening there.

"That's dinner," he says. "Made my famous chicken and rice recipe."

"Famous?"

"Handed down from generations of—" He stops talking.

"Generations of James'?" I ask, wondering if he almost said Dorsey.

"Yeah."

As we walk to the kitchen, I realize he's given me another opening. "Tell me about your family."

He gets the casserole out of the oven, places it on the table, and dishes it up. "Not much to tell."

We sit at the table, and I push my food around with a fork. "Then what about you? Tell me about you."

"You know everything worth knowing, Andie. I'm a landscaper. This is my house. I live a pretty simple life." He glances at my plate. "What do you think of it?"

I take a bite. "It's good. Thank you for cooking." I persist in asking questions. "How was your day? Anything exciting happen?"

"I almost ran over Mr. Kasim's cat with my mower. In fact, I think I may have clipped its tail a tiny bit."

"Oh gosh, I hope the poor thing is okay."

"It'll be fine. The damn thing has eight lives left."

"I wish *we* had nine lives. That way Vivian and my mom would still be here. Is there anyone you'd bring back if you could?"

I hear myself talking and know the three people in the car are calling me stupid. Nine lives? Bringing people back from the dead? I'm so bad at this.

His expression becomes wooden. I've never seen him tense up like this. I've obviously hit a nerve. He clears his throat. "That's morbid, Andie. Hey, have you made any decisions about your inheritance? How soon can we move you out of the ranch?"

I wish he'd quit changing the subject. "I'm thinking of buying a house, actually."

"I'll help you look."

I smile like that makes me happy. "Okay. Thanks."

After supper, I behave like a girlfriend and help him clean up. Then I excuse myself to the bathroom, where I turn on the water and whisper into the ring. "I'm trying, but he keeps shutting me down." The meal is over. What will he want from me now? The thought terrifies me.

He's taken our wine glasses into the living room and turned on music. He pats the space on the couch next to him. "Join me."

I swallow, smile, and sit, but not right next to him. He hands my wine to me and scoots considerably closer. Our legs are almost touching. "Do you like this song?"

"I'm more of a country music gal, but it's fine."

"I didn't grow up in the south. I'm a staunch fan of rock. I love the band Reckless Alibi."

I perk up. "This is a Reckless Alibi song?"

He nods. "I saw them in concert last year in Boston."

"I thought you said you moved here from New Orleans."

"I did. I was in Boston on business."

"Landscaping business?"

He drinks. "I won't bore you with it."

"Maddox knows this band."

"No shit?"

"His best friend, Reece Mancini, is married to their drummer."

"Maddox's best friend is Reece Mancini? The singer?"

"Yes."

"Well, damn."

Here we are making chit-chat, and Maddox, Katherine, and Michael are probably wondering when I'm going to dig in. I remember what they told me to say, but everything flies right out of my brain when he puts his arm around me.

"I'm glad you're here," he says.

"Me too." I try not to choke on the words.

His thumb is caressing my shoulder in slow circles. The feel of his hand on me makes me sick. I need to get this over with.

I notice his empty glass and hop off the couch. "You need a refill."

"Top off your own while you're at it."

I take our glasses into the kitchen. I pour my wine down the drain and refill my glass with more. It's silly, I know, but if he looks at what's left in the bottle, he needs to think I've been drinking it. When I return, I put the glasses on the coffee table but don't sit. I pretend to be interested in his bookshelves. "You have a lot of Patriots stuff. How come you don't have any family pictures?"

He comes up behind me and wraps me in his arms. "Not everyone likes to display things like that, you know."

"Everyone I know does. I'm not sure I can name one person who doesn't have at least one family picture in their house." His frustrated huff displaces the hair on the top of my head. I must be getting to him. "You're close to your parents, aren't you?"

His arms tense around me. "The fire destroyed everything."

"Fire?" I'm genuinely surprised.

"It was a long time ago."

"I hope nobody was hurt."

He takes my hand and pulls me along. If he takes me to the bedroom, I'm going to scream, but he takes me outside. "I know you love sunsets. I'm glad there's a good one tonight."

I sigh with relief even as he cages me to the railing with his body. I glance down at the empty grave, noticing they were careful to put it back precisely the way it was, weeds and all.

He pushes into me, and I can feel his erection. I swallow the bile rising in my throat. "I really want this to work, Andie. It's been a while since I've felt like this about anyone."

"How long?"

"To be honest, I don't usually get close to women. Haven't wanted to until now."

"You've never been close to someone?"

"I've never had a serious relationship, and the last person I was close to isn't around anymore. Maybe that's why I have a hard time letting anyone in."

I turn slightly. "What do you mean, she isn't around anymore?"

He's looking at the sunset. "She died."

I tense. Is that a confession? Are they going to storm through the door? I wait and listen but don't hear anything. They need more.

"How did she die? What was her name?"

"I can't talk about it." He turns me toward him and tilts my head back. "The way you look, with the sun setting behind you—I've never seen anyone more beautiful."

He leans down to kiss me, and I panic. "Beer."

He pulls away. "You want a beer?"

I don't want him to kiss me, but we're so close to getting what we need, I can't ruin it. "No," I say quickly. "I *do not* want a beer." I tuck my hair back with my right hand so the microphone is close. "I definitely don't want a beer. No beer for me. Got it?"

"Andie, you're acting kind of strange."

"Just nervous."

"Because I'm going to kiss you? It's not like we haven't kissed before."

"I know. I'm being silly. And I am thirsty. Could I get a drink of water?"

"Whatever you need."

Inside, he fills a glass at the sink, hands it to me, and I gulp the water. I don't know whether I'm relieved or disappointed they aren't barging in.

"Better?" he asks.

I nod.

He takes my glass and sets it down. "Good. Then where were we?" He cups my face and gives me an "eyes half-hooded" look that from Maddox would be sexy as hell, but all I feel is an intense desire to run away. "Oh, right. I was about to kiss these fantastic lips."

In some ways, Victor is the complete gentleman. He's been nice, courteous, complimentary, and most of all, patient. If he weren't a suspect, he'd actually be quite a catch.

I close my eyes and do something I never thought I would do again. I let Victor kiss me passionately.

It takes everything I have not to stiff-lip him. I try to pretend it's not him kissing me. I remind myself I'm an actress playing a part. This isn't real. But the voice in my head reminds me I may be acting, but *he's* not. What if he likes me too much? What if he's obsessed with me? Was he obsessed with Jennifer Grossman?

"You're shaking," he says.

I laugh shakily. "I don't do a lot of kissing."

"I'm hoping to change that… as long as *I'm* the only one kissing you."

I smile at him. He takes it as an invitation to kiss me again. I let him but only for a minute. When his hands travel to my breasts, I pull away. "Victor?"

"Yeah, babe?"

"Am I competing with a ghost?"

His brows draw down. "You're not competing with anyone, Andie."

"But the woman you lost."

He picks up his glass and takes a long drink of wine.

"I'm not sure you realize how the female brain works. I wonder how I can ever measure up. Have you placed her on a pedestal?"

"I haven't."

"Maybe if you told me about her."

"I can't."

"It might make me feel better about us. About how you feel about me."

"You want to know how I feel about you? I'll tell you. I think about you all the time. I worry about you. I fantasize about you. I ask myself how in the hell I can be falling in love with a woman I haven't even been on a dozen dates with."

"You're falling in love with me?"

He closes his eyes and his head falls back. "No matter how much I've tried to fight it, I am. I don't want to, but I'm not sure I can help it."

"Why don't you want to?"

He paces. "It's complicated."

"Victor, tell me. Why don't you want to fall in love with me?"

"Because then I'll want to stay in Ft. Worth forever, and that's just not possible."

"Why isn't it possible?"

He huffs. I can tell he's getting irritated. "I've told you, I move around. It's what I do."

"But that was before we met. You don't have to move around if you don't want to. You could stay."

"Not forever."

"I don't understand. If you're in love with me, you should want to stay here. Give me one good reason why you can't."

"Because I can't, okay?" He punches the wall—puts his fist through the drywall—then cradles his hand. "I wish I could, but I can't."

I jump back, terrified of what he might do next. He's agitated. *I* agitated him. My phone rings, and I immediately answer. It's Matteo. "Hi, Matteo. What's up?"

"We need you, Doc."

I suspect Maddox and Katherine put him up to this when they heard how upset Victor was getting. "Is it an emergency?"

"Yes."

"I'll be right there."

Victor stares at the hole in the wall, then at me. "You have to go, don't you?"

"Emergency at Devil's Horn Ranch."

"I'll drive you."

"Thanks, but I need my truck." I glance at his right hand. "Ice it to keep the swelling down."

He looks guilty. "I shouldn't have done that."

"I know. All of us can probably say that about something."

He walks me to the front door. "Can I get a do-over? You know, without all the drama?"

"Sure. Call me next week."

He runs a hand along my jaw, then leans down and pecks me on the cheek. "Until then."

I leave, grateful he punched the wall and not me. Happy I'm alive and in one piece. Terrified I will have to do this again.

CHAPTER TWENTY-ONE

"Oh my god, oh my god, oh my god," Andie says through the app on Michael's phone as she runs down the sidewalk to her car. She gets in, backs out of his driveway and takes off like a bat out of hell. "He did it, right? He said he was close to someone, but now she's dead. Why didn't you come inside?" She speeds off ahead of us.

I pick up my phone and call her. When she answers, I say, "Andie, slow down or you'll hit something."

"Why didn't they come inside?"

I put the phone on speaker. "It wasn't a confession," Katherine says. "Listen, Andie, you did a fantastic job tonight. Confessions are hard to get, and he's guarded, but he loves you. People say things to those they love. We could be close."

"I don't know if I can do it again."

I cringe at the terror in her voice.

"Did you hear what he did? He punched a hole in the wall. When I was pressing him, he punched the wall. It could have been me."

"Calm down, Andie," Katherine says. "Take a deep breath. Let's meet back at the ranch."

The phone goes dead.

"She's not doing it again," I say.

"That's up to her, isn't it?" Michael says.

"You two think this is a game, but she's not trained. She couldn't defend herself if he tried anything. I'm telling you, she's not going to be alone with him again. I'm ending this."

Katherine and Michael share a look.

"What?" I spit from the backseat.

"Looks like Victor isn't the only one declaring his love tonight."

I grimace and gaze out the window.

The moment the car is parked in the yard at home, I dart across the driveway to Andie's truck. She's getting out, and her hands are shaking. "I don't know what more they want," she says. "Do they think he's going to lead me to the body or something? The holes in his story are gaping. He's obviously covering something up, and he talked about a dead woman."

Beau runs up, licking Andie's hand as if he senses she's in distress.

"We can't arrest him without evidence," Katherine says, joining us.

"But he's guilty of something. He's been using fake names."

"If he killed that woman, we want to put him in prison for life," Michael says. "Not get him for stolen identity or tax evasion."

Katherine leans against Andie's truck. "I was telling Maddox how close we are. You made real progress tonight. We just need a little more."

Andie wipes her lips aggressively. "I had to stand there and let him kiss me. His tongue was in my mouth. Do you know how hard that was?"

"I know." Katherine looks over at the stables. "What if we could arrange a more controlled environment? One where it was impossible for him to kiss you?"

"How would you do that?"

"Take him riding. The microphone has a range of up to five miles. We'll stay out of sight but won't be too far away. It'll be romantic, but on a horse, he won't be able to touch you. Watch the sunset. Make excuses not to dismount. One more time is all I'm asking."

I want to protest and yell and put my foot down, but I've already made it clear how I feel about this, and they're not listening.

"The ranch hands," Katherine says. "Does Victor know them?"

Andie shakes her head.

"Good. Michael can pose as one. We'll station him wherever you're going to end up. Maddox and I will be on one of those four-wheeler things. If we get too close, no harm, no foul—this is Maddox's land, and I'm his girlfriend."

"That could work," Andie says. "One last time. Then you find someone else to be your pawn."

"Tell us when."

"As soon as possible. I'm ready to get this over with. Sunday? I'll have to ask him."

"Sunday sounds great."

Owen comes out of the stables. "Doc, glad you're here. Cupcake is getting ready to foal."

Andie asks me, "Is this the emergency Matteo called about?"

"This is a coincidence, and I've got some explaining to do to Matteo. I needed you out of there quickly, but these guys wouldn't let me blow your cover, so I had him call you."

"So he knows?"

"About Victor? No. He probably just thinks I'm some jealous stalker."

She smiles. "How are you going to explain that?"

"Honestly? I have no idea."

Katherine and Michael take off.

Andie gestures to the stable. "Want to watch?"

"Hell yeah, I do."

We run to our respective houses and get changed and emerge at the same time, both wearing boots, hats, jeans, and T-shirts. We look at each other and laugh.

"How close is she?" Andie asks Owen on our way to Cupcake.

"Close."

"Has her bag of waters ruptured?"

"Not yet."

When we reach the large foaling stall, Cupcake is lying on her side, clearly restless. She stands and circles the stall, repeatedly looking at her sides. She lies down and gets up several more times.

"Is she okay?" I ask.

"She's doing great. Her behavior is typical."

There is a gush of fluid and then Cupcake lies down.

"Her water broke," Andie says. "It won't be long now. Fifteen or twenty minutes."

"You don't want to go in there?"

"She can do this all on her own." But fifteen minutes later, Andie is the one who's restless.

"What is it?"

"She's in distress. And the foal's hooves should be visible by now." She goes to a glove dispenser attached to the side wall, puts on two plastic gloves that go up past her elbows, then enters the stall.

"Andie, what are you doing?"

"I'm going to help her deliver."

"Uh, you're going to stick your arm in *there?* Up to *here?*" I point to the top of my arm.

She laughs. "This is my job, Maddox."

Owen goes into the stall with her.

Someone walks up beside me. I'm surprised to see it's Victor.

Andie looks up. "What are you doing here?"

"I—"

"Tell me later," she says. "I have to help her."

Andie sticks one of her gloved arms into Cupcake. "Holy shit," Victor says.

I shake my head in amazement. "You can say that again."

"She's breech," Andie says. "I'm going to pull it out."

What I see next is truly remarkable. Andie's arm emerges with a leg. Then another leg appears. Then a few seconds later, the whole body slides right out.

Andie and Owen immediately get out of the way as Cupcake appraises her foal. She makes a few noises and then licks it. The foal immediately starts moving, and we all cheer.

Andie comes through the stall door, removes her gloves, and goes to the sink to wash up.

"That was incredible," Victor says, going over and kissing her hair.

"What are you doing here?"

"I felt bad with how we left things. I thought I'd scared you off, and you faked the phone call because you didn't want to stay. I came to apologize."

She laughs nervously. I can hardly blame her. What if he'd shown up and Andie was at home *not* dealing with an emergency? Or worse, if she was at my house with Katherine and Michael?

"I'm glad I did," he says. "Now I know you really were needed, and I can put my paranoia to rest."

"We're good."

"Are we really? I punched a wall and scared you." He spares a look for the horses. "Are you finished here? Can we go back to your place so I can apologize profusely?"

"I can't. I'm going to be here a while. I need to examine them both."

"The drive out here was still worth it. I'll leave you to it then." He kisses her cheek and walks away.

Andie flashes me an anxious glance and calls after him. "How about you come back Sunday? The weather is supposed to be good. We can ride up to the ridge and see the sunset."

He appears pleased. "Now *that* sounds like a date. See you at six for dinner?"

I clear my throat. "Andie, we have a meeting Sunday. We already ordered supper for everyone."

"Oh right," she says, turning back to him. "I forgot. I'm showing some of the ranch hands how to deal with minor injuries. Why don't you come right after supper, around seven-thirty, and we'll ride out then?"

"Sunset on Sunday. Raincheck on dinner. Got it."

After he leaves, Andie says, "Quick thinking. I did *not* want to have supper with that man again, let alone some romantic sunset picnic."

Our gazes lock, and I'm sure we're both thinking about *our* non-date but romantic picnic on the ridge.

Owen interrupts our moment. "If you're good, I'm callin' it a night."

"I'm good," Andie says. "I'll hang around for a while, make sure they both check out okay." She turns to me. "You don't have to stay either."

"I *want* to stay."

She sits on a bench and stretches out her legs. "I haven't had a chance to breathe."

"I can't imagine what it must have been like for you, being in his house, alone with him." The vein in my temple is throbbing. "He kissed you." I can't get the image out of my mind. All I can think about is her kissing him. The thought of her kissing *anyone* has me seeing red but especially him. "I felt like *I* wanted to punch a hole in a wall."

She elbows me playfully. "You're not jealous, are you?"

"Actually, yes."

Her smile fades. "Maddox."

"So sue me. I don't want you kissing anyone else."

She wipes her mouth. "I swear I can still taste him."

"Well, fuck that." I pull her into my arms and kiss her. Hell if I'm going to let the taste of him linger on her lips. If she's going to taste anyone there, it's sure as shit going to be me.

She pushes me away and glances around nervously. "Someone will see us."

I open the door of the empty foaling stall next to Cupcake's and pull her inside. I latch it and walk her to the back corner, where it's dark, and shove her against the wall. "Nobody will see us now."

I lean down and put my mouth on hers. Her arms go around me and pull me tightly against her. When we're breathless, her mouth moves down my neck. Her tongue flits out to taste me. She pulls the neck of my T-shirt down and kisses my upper chest. It's pure heaven.

My erection strains against my jeans. Every swipe of her tongue makes me harder. When I can't take another second of it, I lay her down on the fresh straw.

I lift her shirt and my lips blaze a trail between her breasts. I push one bra cup out of the way and take her nipple into my mouth. She arches against me. I toy with her, sucking, licking, blowing on it as she squirms under me. The mewling sounds coming from her throat are enough to bring any man to his knees.

When she says my name in that sexy, breathy voice of hers, I need more. I skim a finger under the waistband of her jeans. She doesn't object, so I go for the button. Then the zipper. Knowing I'm about to touch her makes me feel like the luckiest son of a bitch alive. I've dreamt of this moment. Fantasized about it night after night. I slip my hand under her panties and past her barely-there hair to find her totally slick. I can't help my moan.

She utters my name a second time when I insert a finger. She pushes her pants down to give me more room to work. I move her wetness up and around her clit, keeping one finger inside her as I work her with my thumb. Her eyes are closed and her head lies on the straw. Her tongue comes out to wet her lips, then she arches her back and bites her bottom lip. Hard. Jesus, I've never seen anything so sexy. She tenses, then shakes as shouts of pleasure echo off the walls of the stall.

Her eyes fly open, as if she suddenly remembers where we are, and she stiffens. She covers her mouth with both hands and mumbles, "Did I just—"

"Scream?" I remove her hands. "Yeah."

She scrambles to do up her pants. "What if someone heard?"

"I guarantee you the horses did."

She smacks me on the arm, then stands, peering down at me. "Get up. Someone might come to investigate."

I stand and brush off her backside, then turn her around. "That may have been the hottest thing I've ever done."

She blushes. "But you didn't even—"

"Doesn't matter."

"I owe you one."

I chuckle. "If you insist on keeping score, I'm not going to stop you."

Footsteps echo down the aisle. We quickly slip out of the stall and move in front of Cupcake's.

Merle appears. "Thought I heard somethin'."

"My fault," I say. "I crept up on Andie, and she screamed."

His eyes bounce between us, then he focuses on Andie's hair. A few pieces of straw are sticking out of it. Merle laughs and leaves.

"You don't think he suspects anything, do you?" she asks.

"Now why would he have reason to do that?" I pick the straw from her hair and toss it.

She covers her face. "I'm never going to be able to show my face around here again."

"I'm sure we're not the first people to fool around in a stable, Andie."

"*I* never have," she says. "I work here. It's unprofessional."

"It was *very* unprofessional. When can we be unprofessional again?"

She retrieves her vet things from a nearby bench. "I'm going to check them over now."

"I'll stand back here and watch."

She thinks I'm talking about watching the horses, but I'm watching *her*. The way she uses her delicate hands. How her mouth moves when she speaks. The position of her head when she looks at things. Everything about her is graceful, beautiful, and utterly amazing.

She may be worried about getting burned, but I'm the one who'll be left in ashes.

CHAPTER TWENTY-TWO

Andie

"You didn't have to do this." I help Christina unload several tins of food from her car.

She stops to look at the ranch hands by the stable.

Zac tips his hat to her. "Ma'am."

She grabs my hand. "How do you live around all this hotness twenty-four seven? The amount of testosterone in this place!"

"Who's *that?*" Tara asks, ogling Owen.

"The assistant ranch manager."

"Is he single?"

"Yes, and twenty-two."

"You have to set them up," Christina says. "I need to live vicariously."

I wave to Owen, and he runs over. "Owen, these are my friends, Tara and Christina."

"Pleasure, ladies." He shakes Tara's hand and then narrows his eyes at Christina. "Have we met?"

She snickers, gazing at him like he's a piece of decadent chocolate. "I'm quite sure I'd remember meeting you."

"Christina is married to Jon Thompson," I say.

"Now why'd you have to go and ruin it," she says. "He probably thinks I'm a pretentious bitch."

I raise a teasing brow. "You *can* be kind of pretentious."

She rolls her eyes.

Owen turns to Tara. "And what about you? Don't tell me you're secretly married to Joel."

"Tara's not married to *anyone*," Christina says. "She's completely single. Like you, right?"

He chuckles. "I suppose so, ma'am."

"You think she's pretty?"

"Christina!" Tara scolds, turning deep red.

"Lunch is getting cold," Christina says. "We have to move this along. She's pretty, wouldn't you say?"

"Yes," Owen agrees. Tara looks like she wishes the ground would swallow her.

Christina is not deterred. "Tara is an amazing catch. She can cook, ride a horse, dance like J-Lo, and she makes the best apple pie this side of the Mississippi. As a bonus, she comes with an adorable three-year-old son but no ex. You don't hate kids, do you?"

"No, ma'am."

"Good." She gets out a piece of paper and pen, and scribbles something, then shoves it at him. "Here's her number. She's free Tuesday and Saturday nights."

"Okay then." He tucks the paper in his pocket and looks at Tara. "I'll be calling you."

Tara smiles awkwardly as he strolls away. Then she hits Christina in the arm. "I'm going to kill you."

"She got you a date, didn't she?" I say, smiling.

"Someone needs to remove those cobwebs between your legs," Christina adds.

Tara pouts. "I didn't say one word to him. He probably thinks I'm stupid or something."

"You talked to him."

"I did not. I yelled at you, but I definitely did not speak to him."

"There will be time enough for that on your date." Christina picks up a bag and hands it to her. "Carry this in." She looks at the remaining food in the trunk. "We'll have to make another trip."

Maddox emerges from the stable, and it's almost comical how Christina watches him. For a married woman, she sure does like to objectify men.

She licks her lips overdramatically. "Who needs lunch when you've got McHottie living next door? Excuse me!" she yells. "We don't have enough hands. Can we borrow you for a sec?"

Maddox trots over. "How can I help you ladies?"

Christina empties her hands and pulls him in for a hug. I glare at her.

"Finally we meet McHottie," she says.

Maddox looks at me, confused.

"Don't mind Christina," I say. "She's a little over the top. And this is Tara."

"Nice to meet you." He reaches into the trunk. "Let me help you."

We go inside and spread the food on the table. I survey it. "Christina, you brought enough to feed an army."

She pats Maddox's abs. "You'll stay for lunch, soldier?"

He backs toward the door. "Another time?" He looks nervous, and I can't blame him. Christina is like a steamroller when she wants something, and she's got Maddox in her sights.

"Nonsense. You'll stay." She takes tin foil off the dishes. "There's sliced tenderloin, sweet potatoes, corn on the cob, pole beans, potato salad, and cornbread. Everything a cowboy needs."

Maddox grins. "Everything *twenty* cowboys need."

"We'll give the leftovers to the ranch workers."

"*I'm* a ranch worker," he says.

"You're the owner, as I hear it."

"My dad's the owner. I'm here to…" He glances at me. "I'm not sure what I'm here to do."

"Right now, you're here to eat," Christina says.

I laugh. "You'd better sit. Christina won't stop until you pull up a chair."

He holds up dirty hands. "Need to wash up first."

"You know where the bathroom is."

He leaves the room, and my friends are all over me. "Oh my god," Tara says. "He's even hotter in person."

"You're telling me you aren't all over that?" Christina says. "Victor is hot, but this guy." She fans herself. "And he's a cowboy."

"He's a bartender from New York. He's just playing cowboy until his daddy decides what to do with this place."

"Who cares if he's playing?" Christina says. "*I'd* play cowboy with that man any time, any place."

"I think I have to agree," Tara says.

Christina gives her a biting stare. "Already cheating on Owen, are we?"

"Shut up."

"Will you quit trying to set everyone up," I say. "He's leaving in a few months, and I'm—"

"You're what?" Maddox says from the doorway. "With Victor?"

I pick up a plate and pile food on it. "We have a date tonight, in fact."

"Is that so?" he says, like he has no idea. "Where's he taking you? Mini-golf? Laser tag?"

I shove the plate at him. "He's not taking me anywhere. I'm taking him on a sunset ride to the ridge."

"You don't say? Kind of a bold move, Andie."

"Well, I do live here, and you said I could have the run of the place." I give him a pointed look. "You did say that, didn't you?"

"I suppose I did. I hope the weather doesn't turn on you. I'd hate for it to rain and ruin your night." The right side of his face turns up in a half-grin. I can't help but smile back, thinking of our night in the shed.

Christina and Tara stand back and watch us continue to banter. I'm not sure why we put on a show for them. They wouldn't care if I was dating both Victor and Maddox. Judging by the way they are hanging on our every word, I think they'd prefer it.

"We could leave," Christina says. "Give you two a minute."

"Eat," I command.

They fill their plates and sit. I say, "I'll get some lemonade."

Maddox follows. "I'll help."

"What are you doing?" I whisper in the kitchen.

"Having a little fun."

"Well, don't. They would like nothing more than for me to be dating both of you. They have no clue about Victor. They think this is funny."

He leans against the counter. "It is kind of funny."

I cringe. "My dating Victor is funny?"

"I was talking about the way they think you're juggling two men. What did she call me outside?"

"Never mind."

"McHorny?"

I choke. "Kill me now. No, not McHorny. If you must know, it was McHottie."

He laughs quietly. "What do they call Victor?"

"They don't call him anything."

His smile is full of pride. I hand him two lemonades. "Don't get cocky, Connecticut." I walk away.

"Tell me why your family doesn't want the ranch," Christina asks.

"We're from New England," Maddox says. "My dad runs a production company there. He owns a gym, too, and my mom runs her author business from there."

Tara looks curious. "Your mom is an author?"

I fetch a book from the coffee table. "She writes bestselling romances."

Surprised, she gushes, "Oh, I saw this movie. Your mom wrote this?"

He nods.

She thumbs through the book. "Can I borrow this? Books are always better than movies."

"Sure. I've got more in the bedroom if you want them."

Maddox's eyebrows shoot up. "Just how many of my mother's books have you read?"

"All of them."

Tara holds the book open and points. "Your dad must be some guy if he inspires her to write *this*."

Maddox rarely gets embarrassed, so it's adorable to see him blush.

"Maddox doesn't read his mom's books," I say.

"Why not?" Christina asks.

He shovels sweet potato into his mouth, then speaks around it. "I prefer movies."

"The movie is pretty hot, too," Tara says.

"Don't remind me. Listen, this is my mother we're talking about. I'd prefer not to believe she thinks that way."

"She's a woman, Maddox," Christina says. "We all think that way. Men don't have a corner on the market."

He glances at me. "Is that a fact?"

I stand. "If we're finished, I'll wrap up the rest and take it to the bunkhouse kitchen. The guys will appreciate this amazing food."

Maddox gets out his wallet. "Since you're feeding them, I want to reimburse you."

Christina bats his hand away. "Totally my pleasure."

"No, really. Will a few hundred cover it?"

"She's a Thompson," Tara says. "She eats hundred-dollar bills for breakfast."

Maddox stiffens and gets a sour look on his face. "You're the friend who's married to Jon?"

"I take it you've met my infamous husband." Christina sighs. "Why do I feel like I should wear a sign saying I'm a Thompson in name only?"

"He threatened me the other day," Maddox says.

"I'd say it's more like the other way around," I tell her. "You should have seen the way he stood up to him."

Christina touches her cheek. "You might want to think twice about doing that. He doesn't take kindly to those who question him."

Maddox snorts. "I gathered, but he was on my land, and your husband or not, I won't put up with that shit."

"Wow." Christina looks impressed. "I didn't think I could like him any better."

"What am I missing?" Maddox says.

"Christina and Jon don't have a traditional marriage," Tara says.

"What kind of marriage do you have?"

"The kind where he can do anything and any*one* he wants, and I get to spend his money while he does it."

He glances at me, and I shrug.

I pack the food into bags. Maddox takes them. "You enjoy time with your friends. I'll take this to the guys. It was nice meeting you both."

"Don't be a stranger," Christina says. "Her door is always open."

"I live fifty feet south. Being a stranger isn't really an option."

He leaves, and I stare her down.

"What?" she says.

"Will you stop trying to fix everyone up? You and your questions and your pushing. You'll scare him away."

"You *do* want him," she squeals. "I knew it."

"Can we not do this again?" I wipe down the table.

Christina picks up a bottle of vodka and pours shots into our lemonade glasses. "Lunch with McHottie and a sunset ride with my gardener. You're the most eligible bachelorette in three counties, Andie. Now tell us everything about the guy next door, and I mean *everything*."

I take a drink and savor the burn. "There's not much to tell. Or not much I *can* tell. Not yet anyway."

They look at each other, confused. "Why are you being so secretive?" Tara asks.

"You guys are my best friends. When the time is right, I'll share."

"You're trying to decide which one you want," Tara says. "That's it, isn't it? Who better to help you than your best friends?"

"It's not that, I swear." I hit the table. "I hate this!"

"What do you hate?" Christina narrows her eyes. "Is one of them married? It's Maddox. I knew he was too perfect. He's running away from a bad marriage and hiding at his daddy's ranch. Damn, I really wanted to like him. You know what? I still like him. I'm the last person who should frown on someone staying in a bad marriage."

"I should probably go to work."

"It's Sunday, Andie."

"Horses don't only have issues Monday through Friday."

Christina stands to leave. "And *he's* out there."

I hug them and walk them out. "Thanks for doing this. See you guys for lunch on Thursday?"

"And you'll tell us what's going on then?" Tara asks.

"I think so. I hope so."

"Are you working for the FBI or something?" Christina jokes. "Andie Shaw, undercover vet."

I laugh awkwardly, then go inside to prepare for my undercover operation.

CHAPTER TWENTY-THREE

Maddox

Katherine and I observe from my kitchen. Victor approaches the guesthouse with a bottle of wine. Andie sees him coming and steps onto the front porch. I'm amused that her shirt is buttoned almost to the collar. Not exactly a recipe for a romantic sunset ride.

He holds out the wine. "I thought we could bring it and have a toast at sunset."

She puts the bottle inside the doorway. "Let's save it for when we get back."

He leans in and kisses her. "I like the sound of that."

Beau appears on her porch, barks once, and worms between them. I like that dog more and more every day.

I turn to Katherine. "They are *not* going into her house after."

"Agreed. We'll figure something out."

"If he reveals enough this evening, we may not have to. Are you ready to arrest him if he does?"

"We've been ready. Agent Watkins is already in position, armed and standing by."

I lift my shirt. "So am I."

"No. Take it off."

"It's my land."

"Take it off, Maddox. You're too close. This is personal for you. I'm not risking you hurting someone in the heat of the moment."

"The only person I'm going to hurt is him."

"We play this right, and nobody needs to get hurt."

I look out the window. "They're going. You ready to follow them?"

"Don't be so eager. He can't do anything while they're on horseback. We can stay a safe distance behind and still hear them."

"How was your meeting?" we hear Victor say. "Learn a lot?"

"Excuse me?" someone says.

"The meeting. Andie was teaching you basic first aid for horses."

I feel ice cold. "Shit."

"Zac wasn't at the meeting," Andie says.

"Who was it for then?"

"Some of the other guys. Zac has been here a long time. Here we are. They're ready to go. You'll be riding June Bug."

He snorts. "Sounds like a girl's name."

"It is, but don't let it fool you. She's more of a workhorse than half the geldings around here."

"It's been a while since I've ridden," Victor says. "Take it easy on me."

"We'd better get going. The sun is due to set in half an hour."

As they exit the stables and mount, Andie looks over at my house nervously.

"She's going to be fine," Katherine says.

"Did you ever find out about the girl in the picture?" I ask.

"A dead end. Either this guy is really good at covering his tracks, or he's not the one we're looking for."

"Of course he's the one. He's hiding his identity, moves from place to place, and has zero personal ties."

"He certainly fits the profile." They ride away. "Take me to the four-wheeler. I'll sit behind you so you can use one of my earbuds. If Victor sees us, it will look like we're on a date."

We follow Andie at a good distance. We're so far back, they can't see us, and Victor couldn't identify us even if he did spot us. They make a lot of small talk. I can tell she's trying to get him to open up, but he's not biting.

"Have you lined up any houses to look at?" he asks.

"Not yet."

"Why not? You like living here at the ranch?"

"It's not that. I've been waiting because I'm not sure what my future holds."

"What do you mean?"

"I might want a house big enough for more than just me, but you've said you won't be here forever."

I bring the ATV to a stop. "Turn it up," I tell Katherine.

"Are you saying you might want to live together?" Victor asks.

"This is good," Katherine says. "It might actually work."

"Buying a house is a big decision. I want to know where I stand is all."

"Andie, we haven't even slept together. This is coming out of left field."

"I know, but I have to know if you're going to stay."

"I want to. You know how I feel about you. But I'm not sure I can promise anything."

"Why can't you? It's easy."

"I can promise to try."

"What does that mean? You're so cryptic sometimes. I feel like I don't even know you."

"It means I want to stay, but there are reasons I might not be able to."

Katherine grabs my shoulder. "Nice. Keep him going."

"Like what?" Andie asks.

"I can't talk about it."

"Can't or won't?"

"I've done things I'm not proud of. I've hurt people. I don't want to hurt you."

"This is it," I say. "Let's go." I start the engine and take off.

"Slow down," Katherine says. "This is not a confession. Wait, Maddox."

I ease up on the throttle and listen intently.

"Can we get off the horses?" Victor asks. "This is not a conversation I want to have when we're six feet apart."

"Don't do it," I say.

"Michael, do you have eyes on them?" Katherine asks.

"Affirmative."

"But we're almost there," Andie says.

"Andie, you all but asked me to move in with you. I think this conversation is a tad more important than the sunset. Now will you please get off your horse?"

"Okay."

"Stupid, stupid, stupid," I say. "We have to get there."

"Michael's on top of it," Katherine says. "Let this play out."

"I'm off my horse. What do you want to say?"

"No matter what happens, I'm in love with you, Andie Shaw."

Bile rises when they go silent. He's kissing her. Possibly even hurting her. They're in the middle of nowhere. He could do anything.

"You're not going to say it back, are you?" he asks.

"I like you or we wouldn't be having this conversation. Maybe one day I could love you. When I feel more secure about who you are and what you want."

"I want *you*, Andie."

"For now. You want me for now. Until you have to move on. What are you running from, Victor?"

The silence coming through the phone is deafening.

"Answer the fucking question!" I yell, driving faster.

"Stop here," Katherine says. "We should be able to see them."

I get out my binoculars and look toward the base of the ridge. "There, over by the oak tree."

Victor is pacing. The horses are tied to a tree branch. Andie is looking around, trying to spot us.

"You have to tell me if there's any chance of this working. Are you hiding from someone? Who did you hurt? You have to let me in."

He shakes his head over and over. "I can't. I'd be putting you in danger."

"Why would I be in danger? Are you running from something? Is that why you have to move around? Someone is looking for you?" She pretends to be surprised. "Oh my god, are you married? Is your crazy ex stalking you?"

"I wish it was that simple."

"It *is* simple. Just tell me, Victor."

"Why are you giving me the third degree? You treat me like I don't exist. You make up excuses to get away, and now you want to know all my deep dark secrets so maybe one day we might move in together. Something's not adding up here."

"I'm trying to get to know you."

He traps her against the tree. "And I want to know you, babe. For months you've been stringing me along. Are you ever going to let me be with you? Do you know how much I want you?"

"Fuck, fuck, fuck," I say.

"Michael is close," Katherine says. "If Victor tries anything, he'll be there in ten seconds."

Andie puts her arms around him. "I'll give you what you want if you give me what I want."

"Are you bribing me with sex?"

She touches his face, and I cringe.

"You'll sleep with me if I tell you everything you want to know?"

"Yes."

He lets out a deep sigh, steps away, runs a hand through his hair, and paces. Then he stops. "I can't do this right now. Maybe not ever. I care about you too much to bring you into my problems."

"Or you don't care enough to let me in."

He unties his horse and gets on. "I don't feel much like seeing the sunset anymore. I'm going to ride back."

"Victor!"

He looks over his shoulder. "I'll call you tomorrow, Andie."

He rides away. I hop off the four-wheeler. "Motherfucker. Now what? She has to sleep with him to get him to confess?"

Katherine's phone rings. She steps away and gestures at Andie. "Go get her. I have to take this."

I wait until Victor is out of sight, then take off. She's sitting at the base of the tree, hands in her lap. "I was so close."

I sit next to her. "I can't believe you said those things."

"He's never going to tell me, is he? If you killed someone and then fell in love with someone else, would you tell her? It's ludicrous to think he would blurt it out. What was I thinking?" Michael and Katherine pull up on Michael's ATV. "What were *they?*"

She's right. I'd never confess if it were me. I stand and stomp toward them. "You were never expecting him to flat-out confess, were you? Why would he risk her leaving him? You wanted her to provoke him. You wanted him to attack her, didn't you? In a heated state, he'd say things about his other victim. That's what you wanted, isn't it?" I help Andie up. "They put you in danger. We're finished here."

"Yes, we are," Katherine says.

I spin. "What do you mean? You got something? You're going to arrest him?"

"We've got nothing. That's the problem. We're being pulled off the case." She holds up her phone. "The call I got was to let me know we're being reassigned."

"So that's it? You're leaving after everything you put her through?"

Katherine looks guilty as hell. "I really hoped he would give us something today, but we can't waste any more resources on this."

"But he said he hurt someone," Andie says. "He said he's running from his past."

"I know a thousand people who can say the same thing," Agent Watkins says. "Doesn't mean they're criminals."

I block them. "What if you leave, and he tries something? He's in love with her. If she blows him off, he might go after her."

"If that happens, you know how to reach us," Katherine says.

"Well, fuck you very much!" I yell. "You've gone and made things a hundred times worse. A month ago she was going to break up with the bastard. Now he's fallen in love. You think he's going to let it go? You have a duty to protect her."

She glances at the waistband where I keep my gun. "Looks like you have it under control."

"Unbelievable. Ladies and gentlemen, the FBI—fidelity, bravery, and integrity."

"I wish we could do more," Katherine says. "This happens more than you'd think."

I scoff. "You could have led with that a month ago. *You* talked her into this."

"If you feel threatened, Andie, call 911, then call me. We're based in the Dallas office, so we're not far away should you need us. We'll do whatever we can to help. But quite frankly, the man seems to have his wits about him. Other than him hitting the wall in frustration, I haven't seen anything remotely aggressive about him. And what guy hasn't put his fist through a wall over a woman? I'm confident you'll be fine. Break up with him. The sooner the better."

Andie takes off the ring and hands it to Katherine. She pushes it back. "Keep it. I'm sure Maddox will want to be close by when you give Victor the heave-ho." She taps on her phone. "I've sent you the info. Download the app and pair it with the device."

"You think she's going to see him again?" I say. "Fat chance."

Katherine shrugs. "Either way. I regret how this worked out. We'll leave the four-wheeler by the barn. Bye Maddox. Andie."

They drive off, and Andie and I stand here, stunned. She looks at me. "What now?"

I take the ring from her and follow the instructions Katherine sent.

"What are you doing?"

I put the ring back on her finger. "I want you wearing this at all times, just in case."

"What if I'm having a private conversation with friends?"

"Katherine said there was a way to turn it off."

"There is." She shows me how the stone in the ring turns counterclockwise.

"So keep it turned off unless there's a reason not to. I mean it, Andie. *At all times*. You never know when he might show up."

"I suppose it would make me feel better, knowing you'll be there if I'm in a bind."

"Me and the fucking cavalry," I say.

She looks in the direction the agents went. "The cavalry just left."

"That's not true. There are twenty ranch hands who would do anything for you."

"I appreciate that." She gets on Baby Blue. "But I only need one."

CHAPTER TWENTY-FOUR

Andie

I wake before dawn after a restless night and twist the ring around my finger. Knowing it's there gives me peace of mind.

I have to break up with Victor. Any normal person would do it face-to-face, but he's not normal. This relationship isn't real—not for me. I pick up my phone off the nightstand and draft a dozen texts. I send none of them.

As light starts to shine through the window, I put on my sleep mask, hoping for another hour of shuteye, but my mind has other ideas. I practically told him I wanted to live with him, and he said he loved me. Is he going to let me go? I have half a mind to ask Maddox to teach me how to shoot. Since I was a girl, Granddad has encouraged me to learn how to defend myself. He even bought me a gun when I turned eighteen, but I never unboxed it. I wonder if I should go back to my apartment and try to find it.

A loud noise outside has me jumping out of bed. My heart is racing when I peek out the window. Merle and the guys are working on a tractor over by the barn. Will I always be looking over my shoulder?

Maddox is drinking coffee on his porch. He sees me at the window and waves. He said he'd protect me, but for how long? After the ranch sells, he and most of the others will move on. What then?

I pick up my phone and text Maddox.

> **Me: Maybe if I told him the FBI was sniffing around, he'd take off.**

He reads it and looks up, then taps on his phone.

> **Maddox: Or maybe he'd do the opposite and hurt you.**

> **Me: I don't know how to do this. Do I send him a text?**

He gives me a scolding stare before he texts back.

> **Maddox: Yes, you send him a text. Are you crazy, Andie? You are not doing it in person.**

A truck pulling a trailer rumbles up the main driveway. I recognize it and feel like I might faint.

> **Me: Looks like I don't have a choice.**

Maddox sees what I see, jumps out of his chair, and goes inside.

Maddox: Unlock your back door. I'll be over in twenty seconds. Tell him you had a change of heart. If he presses you, I'll show myself.

Me: I'm scared.

Maddox: Do not let him in your house.

I throw on a T-shirt and yoga pants, and grab an iced coffee from the fridge, then head to the porch. Victor is almost to the stairs when I sit on a chair out front. He smiles sadly. "Hey."

"Hey."

He motions to the house. "Think we can talk inside?"

Behind him, Maddox runs to the stable. He's taking the long way to my back door so Victor won't see him. I shake my head. "No."

He sighs and takes the seat next to me. "You're ending this. I can see it on your face."

"This just isn't working for me."

"Yesterday we were talking about the future, and now you want to throw it all away?"

"We don't know each other. Not really. Maybe it's bad timing. I have a lot to deal with at work, and then there's my granddad and the inheritance."

"And Maddox. You forgot to mention him."

"What do you mean?"

"Come on, Andie. I'm not completely oblivious. I see the way you two look at each other. Melina or no Melina, he's got a thing for you, and you for him."

"It's not that."

"Whatever you say." He stands. "Listen, I came to apologize for taking off last night. I did a lot of thinking. What you said about timing? You're right. You have to figure out this thing with Maddox, and I obviously have my own stuff to work out."

I nod.

He holds out his hand. "So… friends?"

I'm shocked he's taking this so well. I figured he'd fight it. Beg me to stay with him. Maybe even share more information with me.

I shake. "Friends."

He holds onto my hand and leans down to kiss it. "If you ever change your mind, you know how to find me."

"Unless you move on."

He closes his eyes briefly. "Yeah, unless that."

He walks somberly down the steps and the walkway. He glances back only once before he gets in his truck. My heartbeat finally slows as he drives away.

Maddox comes out my front door. "You didn't turn the ring on, Andie."

I'd completely forgotten about it. "Didn't need to. Surprisingly, he was okay with it. I may have just had the most mature breakup of my life."

"That doesn't mean he won't come after you later."

I get up and go inside. "Thanks for reminding me."

"You can't let your guard down because he said he's okay with it. You should move to the main house."

"No. That's crazy."

"He could come back in the middle of the night."

"I keep the doors locked."

"He could break a window."

"And I could get hit by a bus on Main Street. Maddox, I'm not going to live my life in fear. I'm wearing the ring. I'm being careful. What more do you want?"

"I want you to be safe, Andie."

"Teach me to shoot then."

His eyes snap to mine. "Just say when."

"I have a gun. It's at the apartment somewhere. Granddad gave it to me a long time ago, but I never learned to use it."

He takes his gun from the rear waistband of his jeans, does something to unload the clip, then hands it to me. "Lesson one starts now."

It's heavy in my hands. "I didn't think it would weigh so much."

"Your granddad probably got you a lighter one."

I point it at the mirror across the room and squint.

He takes it from me. "Never put your finger on the trigger unless you're going to shoot."

"But you unloaded it."

"Doesn't matter. It's a good habit to get into, because you never know. Keep your trigger finger extended along the frame of the gun until you're ready to fire."

I hold out my hand. "Let me try again." I point and aim at the mirror.

He goes behind me and pushes my shoulders down. "Relax. Don't tense so much."

"Maddox, I have a deadly weapon in my hands. I hardly think I'm going to relax."

Our faces are inches apart. He gazes at my lips. I get tingly inside. Then I remember what I'm wearing, how I look, and that I haven't brushed my teeth. I hand him the gun. "I have to get ready for work."

"We'll go out on the hunting grounds. Today?"

I shake my head. "It's Monday. I have a full schedule."

"My cousin Aaron comes tomorrow, so I'll be pretty busy."

"Wednesday then. Late afternoon?"

He goes to the door. "It's a date."

"No it's not."

He leans against the doorway. "You're really hung up on semantics, aren't you? Now that you and Victor are history, there's no harm in me taking you on a real date."

"We're not dating, Maddox."

"Fine. A real *casual* date then."

I push him the rest of the way through the door. "No restaurants. No movie theaters. That's not what we do. We have supper. We hang out. Got it?"

He holds up his hands in surrender. "Got it, Doc. Shooting lesson, then supper on the ranch. Good?"

"Good."

"Then I've got work to do before Wednesday."

I eye him suspiciously. "What are you planning?"

He smiles and backs down the front steps. "Nothing much. Shooting then supper, like we said." He winks and runs off.

CHAPTER TWENTY-FIVE

Maddox

"I can't tell you how much I appreciate this," Uncle Griffin says from the passenger seat on the way back from the airport.

In the rearview mirror, I catch Aaron rolling his eyes. "Yes, thank you for agreeing to boot camp me for the summer. We're all so grateful."

"This attitude of yours better take a hike, son."

Aaron glumly looks out the window.

We drive most of the way in silence. Griffin probably wants to talk to me in private. I hope he knows how uncomfortable I am with this. Aaron may be almost ten years younger than me, but he's still my cousin. I don't want to boss him around.

I point right. "All this land is Devil's Horn Ranch."

Griffin whistles. "Incredible. Your dad's description didn't do it justice."

"This is nothing. The ridges the ranch was named after are fantastic, especially at sunset. I've never seen a more serene place in all my life, except in pictures."

"You really like it here, don't you?"

"It's a far cry from New York City."

"It sucks," Aaron says from the back. "It's hot and humid, and I bet you get crappy cellphone reception."

Griffin looks back. "You won't be needing it, so it doesn't matter if they get good reception or not."

"You're taking away my phone? What the hell am I supposed to do all day?"

"I imagine there will be plenty to do." Griffin pats me on the shoulder. "Isn't that right, Maddox?"

"There's always work to do on a ranch."

Aaron grumbles. "So now I'm a slave."

I have to bite my tongue. I don't want this to cause a rift between Aaron and me. We've never been close because of our age difference, but we always got along. I don't want him to see me as the bad guy.

"You reap what you sow, son."

"Whatever."

I pull into the driveway, and Griffin looks around in awe. "I'm sure glad I brought my camera. I'd love to take pictures of the ranch. Maybe get a nice one for your dad, so he can remember the place."

"That would be nice. Maybe I could get one, too."

I park and we get out. "Leave your stuff," Griffin says to Aaron. "I'd like a quick tour and then I'll wander around with my camera while you get situated."

Beau runs across the yard, coming to my side. "You like dogs?" I ask Aaron.

"Whatever."

"This one is Beau. He's a Border Collie. There's another one like him, Tron, that lives over by the bunkhouse, and an Australian Cattle Dog named Lassie you might see wandering the ranch."

We start at the stables. Griffin takes it all in. "There's some amazing scenery around here."

I take them into the tack room and motion to the boots. "Might want to pick yourselves a pair. It can get dirty around here." I hold a spare hat out to Aaron. "Try this one."

"Uh… no."

"My grandmother had a rule. Everyone on the ranch wears one."

Griffin tries one on. "When in Rome."

Aaron gives him a defiant shake of the head.

"Better get used to taking orders around here, Aaron. The boss says wear a hat; wear a damn hat."

I point to the others lining the wall. "If you don't like that one, you can choose another. Uncle Griffin, can I talk to you for a minute?"

We step outside the room. "What's up?" he asks.

"I'm not sure I'm comfortable bossing him around. I'm happy to have him here, but I don't want him to think I'm the boss of him. He'll hate me."

He chuckles. "My boy hates everyone these days. But I get it. I don't want to put you in that position. I'm sure you have someone around here who won't mind assuming the role. Now let's get on with the tour."

"You ever ride a horse?" I ask Aaron when he joins us.

He looks at me like I'm stupid. "I live in New York City."

"I'll take that as a no. I'd be happy to take you out later. There are guys around here who will help you out with anything. I'm sure you'll be a pro by the end of the summer."

"Oh, goody," he says sarcastically.

We hit the stables, barn, and larger riding arena. I show them the offices, the bunkhouse, and the pavilion. While Griffin is amazed, Aaron isn't the least bit impressed. I'm sure he sees this as his prison for the next few months. A shame, because for me it's been quite the opposite.

After we return to the truck, I help get Aaron's things out of the back. Owen goes by, and Griffin hails him. "You there, what's your job here?"

"Assistant ranch manager." He holds out his hand. "Name's Owen."

They shake. "I'm Griffin Pearce, Maddox's uncle, and this is my boy, Aaron."

"Oh, right. The cousin we heard was coming. Nice to meet you, Aaron."

Aaron huffs.

"It ain't that bad here. You might even like it."

"Fat chance."

"As you can see, my son is in need of some manners, among other things," Griffin says. "Think you're up to helping?"

"What'd you have in mind, sir?"

"Treat him like any other worker on the ranch."

I quickly intercede. "Let me amend that. He's underage, so no drinking or gambling."

"Or smoking," Griffin adds.

"Okay." He turns to me. "You don't want to be the heavy, do you?"

I shake my head.

Owen takes one of Aaron's bags from me. "Let's get you situated then."

He goes in the other direction when the rest of us walk toward the house. "Owen?"

"You want him treated like any other worker, then he's sure as hell not staying with you in the Taj Mahal." He moves off again. "The bunkhouse is this way."

Griffin hands Aaron his duffle bag. "Go."

"You can't be serious." Aaron looks longingly at the main house. "That place must have eight bedrooms, and you're going to make me sleep with the help?"

"For the next few months, you *are* the help."

"It only has five," I say.

"Oh, that makes this *sooooo* much better." Aaron storms off behind Owen.

"Don't worry," Owen tells Aaron. "The bunkhouse isn't that bad if you can get past Zac's snoring."

"You sleep there?" Aaron asks.

Owen laughs. "With that mangy bunch? Hell no."

Griffin hands me a phone. "You keep this. I'm not saying he can't ever have it, but I want him to earn it. Now if you'll excuse me, I want to get a few pictures before we lose the midday light. Maybe later you can take me out to those ridges you mentioned earlier."

"I'd love to."

He gets his camera equipment from the truck and sets up near the entrance to the north stable.

I put Griffin's overnight bag in the downstairs guest bedroom. When I get back outside, Andie is pulling up in her truck. She doesn't get out but gazes at the training pen, where Mickey is training one of the new boarded horses.

I cross the yard to her truck. "Hi."

She doesn't look at me. I look at the training pen again. Aaron is standing on the bottom rung of the fence, watching the horse.

"Andie?"

Whatever trance she's in is broken. "He could be your twin, back when you were fifteen."

"You think we look alike, huh? That's what our parents always say."

"It's uncanny."

I open her door, she gets out, and we go closer, standing on the other side of the pen from Aaron. "When I was a little younger than he is now, I fell in with the wrong crowd my freshman year in high school. Luckily for me, my best friend Sam wanted nothing to do with me when I was around the others. He gave me an ultimatum, him or them."

"What did you do?"

"I chose them. I partied for an entire month straight. Drank, fought, and did all the stuff delinquents do. My parents knew something was wrong, but I was good at hiding it. One night after sneaking out and getting wasted, I crawled back through my window to find Sam and my parents sitting in my bedroom. He'd ratted me out. I was grounded for two months."

She puts her hand on my arm. "Did you thank him later?"

"I don't think I did, but I should have."

"What happened to him? Are you still friends?"

"Aside from those two or three months, we were inseparable in high school. He was smart. Like genius smart. He went away to Tulane University. Last I saw on Facebook, he's doing his residency at the Mayo Clinic."

"He's a doctor?"

"I knew he would be. He never let anything get in his way."

"What did you want to be back then?"

"I'm twenty-five, and I still don't know what I want to do with my life. You're lucky you've known what you wanted since you were fifteen."

"I have, haven't I?" She straightens. "I'd better go. I only have a few minutes to eat before I'm due at the Double Duce."

"See you tomorrow then? Or tonight if you want to join us. I'm cooking for Griffin and Aaron." I chuckle. "Maybe not Aaron. Do you know my uncle has got him sleeping in the bunkhouse?"

"It'll be good for him."

"I hope Griffin knows what he's doing."

"Some kids need tough love, Maddox. It's nice when parents recognize that." She leaves.

Griffin comes over, his eyes following Andie to the guesthouse. "Got a renter?"

"She's a friend. I'm helping her out."

"A friend, huh? I'd say it's more than your grandmother's ranch holding your interest." He fiddles with his camera, then holds it out.

I shield the sun from the digital screen. It's a picture of Andie and me. Her hand is on my arm, and we're looking at each other. Our body language makes me a complete liar. She's more than a friend. Something inside me twists, no... hurts, when I think of leaving this place.

I hand him his camera. "I'd like a copy of that."

CHAPTER TWENTY-SIX

"It's getting dark," Maddox says. "We should go."

"Just a few more minutes." I line up the target and shoot. "This is fun."

"I think I've created a monster. But shooting in the dark, or even at dusk, isn't recommended."

I fire off one more round and hand him my gun. "Fine, but you have to agree to bring me out here again."

"With pleasure."

Maddox unloads the guns, packs them away, and straps the bag to Tadpole. I get on Baby Blue and turn toward the ranch.

"We're not going that way," Maddox says.

I draw down my eyebrows. "I thought we were going to have supper."

"We are. Follow me." He turns Tadpole in the other direction.

We're past the ridge, so I know we're not going on another sunset picnic. We keep saying we're casual. Friends even. But still, sometimes it feels like we're so much more. We see each other all the time. Have supper together almost every night. Tell each other about our days. We even fool around. But we've never crossed the line we both claimed we'd be okay crossing.

It's not like we haven't had opportunities. We've had plenty of them. I know why I haven't crawled into bed with him. Fear. Not the kind of fear I felt with Victor. I know Maddox would never hurt me—not in the same way Victor might have. My fear lies right in the smack center of my chest. Maddox is the whole package. Nice, handsome, generous. And I fear if we sleep together, my heart and my brain will travel so far past casual, it won't even be in my taillights.

A building comes into view, and I realize where we're going. "The hunting lodge? For supper? Maddox, it's probably filled with rodents and cobwebs, and there's no electricity."

"Oh ye of little faith," he says, smirking.

We tie up the horses out front. He holds out a hand, and I take it, carefully climbing the five steps to the porch while looking for the broken slat I once put my foot through when Viv and I were here a gazillion years ago. "Where's the broken step?"

"I fixed it."

"You *fixed* it?"

"I mend fences for a living now. One broken two-by-eight was a piece of cake."

The front porch has been swept, there are no cobwebs in sight, and two clean rocking chairs are facing west.

"In case we wanted to watch the sunset." We go inside. "Stay here." Excitedly, he runs through the grand front hall, lighting candle after candle. He disappears into another room and I see a glow there, too. A minute later, he's back. "What do you think?"

The place is empty, with the exception of an old piano covered with a sheet, a few paintings on the walls, and an ancient Victorian bookcase Vivian couldn't bear to part with. Light from the candles dances along the walls and ceiling. I step into the next room. A large blanket has been laid on the floor. There are champagne flutes, vases of orchids, a large picnic basket, and more candles.

What I don't see are rodent droppings, spider webs, and dust. "It must have taken an army to clean this place."

"Aaron helped. We started last night and finished earlier today."

"You did this in less than a day?"

"Only these two rooms and the porch. My uncle was with us. You should see some of the pictures he took of this old lodge. It makes me kind of sad that the new owner might tear it down."

I run a finger along an oil painting. I'm not sure why Vivian kept it. It's a portrait of the original owner and his family, which included Earl Thompson. She was never keen on the Thompsons, but she did respect history, and this old place has a lot of it.

"Why did you do all this?"

"You said no restaurants, and I was getting tired of eating in."

He opens the picnic basket and pulls out clear wrap-covered plates of cheese, berries, and bread. "Are you hungry?"

"I'm starving."

He smiles, reaches into a cooler, and pulls out a bottle of champagne. It's not the only bottle in there. My heartbeat speeds up. I tell myself this is all an illusion. It's temporary. This can't go anywhere. It's *casual*. But why, then, do I feel like Cinderella going to the ball?

"Let's go outside and watch the sunset," he says, handing me a glass. I follow him to the porch and we sit in the rocking chairs.

"It won't be as good as seeing it from the ridge," I say.

"I think you're wrong."

When I peek at him, he's not staring at the sky. He's looking at *me*.

Calm down, Cinderella, I tell myself.

He holds out his glass. "To sunsets and orchids and"—one of the horses neighs, and he raises his glass in their direction—"to horses." We laugh. He locks eyes with me. "To you, Andie."

I hold my drink up. "And to you for doing all this."

"To us then."

We drink in silence as the sun drops below the tree line.

He stands and offers me his hand. "We should probably go inside before the critters come out." He leads me back to the blanket and food. We sit on the floor and pick at the delicacies. I try to ignore how romantic this is. How perfect *he* is. How naïve I am if I think none of this is affecting me.

"Tell me about the guy who burned you," he says.

I pop a grape in my mouth.

"Oh, come on, Andie. I see you fighting it. You love it here, but you don't want to. You mentioned once you'd been burned. Tell me, who was he?"

I eat another grape.

"You don't want to talk about him, do you?"

I shake my head.

"Okay. Tell me what went through your head yesterday when you saw my cousin. It was like you were in a trance, the way you were watching him…"

"The resemblance between the two of you is uncanny, that's all. He looks exactly like you did at fifteen."

"I'm surprised you remember what I looked like. We only met the one time."

"I thought you'd come back," I confess.

He smiles. "So you thought about me?" I blush, and he laughs. "I thought about you, too. Hell, if I'm being honest, I did more than think about you. I was fifteen and you looked amazing in that pink cowboy hat. You were the inspiration for a large portion of my teenage fantasies."

Did he just confess to what I think he confessed to? "That might be TMI."

"Don't look so shocked. Are you telling me you've never, you know, fantasized about me?"

I glance away, embarrassed. "I was a young girl."

He moves closer. "Not back then, Andie. Now." I lean back, and he climbs over me. "After our night in the stable, I can't stop thinking about you." His gaze travels to my neck. His fingers linger on the top button of my shirt. "Truth be told, it's *all* I think about." He leans down, his lips barely touching mine. "I think about these lips." He kisses me, then he cups my breast over my shirt. "I think about touching you." His hand works down my abdomen, over my jeans, and settles between my legs. "I think how I might die if I don't make you come again."

I pull his shirt off over his head and touch his bare skin. He's right. I think about him. Dream about him. Fantasize about having him in every way. He removes my shirt, then my bra. He stares at my chest.

"You're beautiful."

I swallow. "So are you."

His hands cup me, kneading my breasts. I run my fingers along the ridges of his abs, then along the waistband of his pants. I skim a finger under his jeans, touching the tip of his erection. He draws in a sharp breath.

He abruptly stands, kicks off his shoes, and pulls down his jeans and boxers. I stare as if it's the first time I've ever seen such a thing. In some ways, it is. He's a man, a cowboy, a protector. He's everything I want and can never fully have. But he's here now, and I want him more than anything.

I get up and remove my jeans and panties. The way he looks at me makes my heart pound. I've never felt so beautiful. So wanted and utterly desired. If my skin looks as satiny beautiful as his does in the candlelight, it's no wonder he's eating me with his eyes. I'm not even embarrassed, just completely turned on.

"God, Andie." He steps toward me and we collide. His erection presses firmly against my stomach, creating tingles from head to toe. He pulls me so tightly against him, we practically become one.

We drop to our knees on the blanket. He traces my jaw, then weaves his hands into my hair. When we kiss, his penis jerks against me, and I'm reminded of my promise to reciprocate. I slip my hand around it. Moans escape his throat. I move my hand up and down, feeling a bead of wetness escape the tip.

We lay down, and he says, "I want that, but right now, I want this more."

His lips find mine again, then they travel to my breasts, where he toys with my nipples. I squirm and groan. He smiles deviously before going farther south. His tongue skims across my stomach. I shake in anticipation and then feel a finger inside me. I press down on it. His tongue is on my clit, and I shudder. "Yes," I breathe and arch into him.

His tongue does incredible things to me, running circles around the tiny bundle of nerves, then flicking it before lightly sucking as he works more fingers inside me. My thighs tighten and my insides burn, and I feel myself building. He lightens the pressure, giving me a reprieve, and I relax a moment before he starts again. I grab onto his hair and hold him right where he is. His tongue flits back and forth, and I explode, my walls pulsating against his fingers until he's drawn every last quiver from me.

My hands go limp and I drop my head to the floor. I'm languid, utterly spent. Deliciously satiated.

He gazes into my eyes. "I want to make love to you."

I bite my lip. "Yes."

The instant the word leaves my mouth, he's inside me, and the feeling is exquisite. He pumps slowly, then faster. He pulls out and starts again. He kisses my neck, my collarbone—every inch of skin his lips can reach. I can see he's close. He tenses. One last thrust, and he arches back and grunts loudly, then he collapses on me.

I groan under his weight. He laughs and moves to one side. "Why did we wait so long to do that?"

He awkwardly reaches behind him for our glasses and tops them off, then we lie on our sides facing each other, both perched on an elbow, and finish the bottle.

"His name was Bobby Monahan."

His eyebrows shoot up. "The one who burned you?"

"It was my own fault. I got too attached."

"Who was he?"

"We went to vet school together. He tried to hook up with me the very first day, but I shut him down. I shut everyone down. I was there to study. I didn't need distractions. So we became friends. By our third year, when he'd slept with every other woman in our class, he propositioned me. Said he wasn't looking for a girlfriend, and he knew I didn't want a relationship, making us the perfect non-couple."

"And you agreed."

I nod. "It had been a long time. I needed… stress relief."

"Did you get it?"

"For almost a year we had this incredible friends-with-benefits thing. It was nice not to worry about dating, but we still got to go on dates. He treated me nicely. We had fun together. It was perfect really."

"Until…"

I roll onto my back and close my eyes. "Until I went and fell in love with him. And stupid me, I told him."

"Ah, man. What did he do?"

"He freaked. He said I'd broken our promise not to let that happen. He was mad at me."

"Sounds like a douche."

"The thing is, he wasn't. He was right. He never led me to believe he wanted anything more. I knew I was going to end up in Texas, and he knew he was going to Wyoming. We swore we wouldn't develop feelings. It was all my fault, because even after I started having those feelings, I let things continue."

"What happened? Did he ghost you?"

"Quite the opposite. He remained my friend, but things were never the same. We couldn't talk to each other like we had in the past. He loved me, but not in the way I loved him."

"Are you still in love with him?"

"I haven't seen him since graduation."

He sits up and opens a new bottle. "You didn't answer the question."

"It's been well over a year, and we ended things six months before that."

"I take it your answer is yes then."

I sit up. I haven't thought about Bobby in months. "I'm not in love with him. In all honesty, I was more hurt over losing my best friend than losing a boyfriend."

"Was he the last guy you slept with?"

I shake my head. "Tony Ramsey, eight months ago. He was in town on a rodeo circuit."

"A one-nighter?"

"More like a four-nighter."

"Why, Dr. Shaw. Who knew you had it in you?"

I drink and spill a little. Wine tickles my belly as it rolls down my skin. I look down at myself and laugh. "Do you think it's weird that we're sitting here naked talking about my exes?"

He chuckles. "I'm enjoying it."

"What about you? You said you didn't leave anyone back in New York, but what about before? There must have been someone."

"A long string of nobodies is more like it. I don't date much. I can count on both hands how many times I've taken out a woman in the past year."

"So it's been a while for you."

"I said I don't date much, Andie. I didn't say I was celibate."

"What was the name of the last woman you were with?"

He looks off in the distance, like he has to think hard to remember. "Joanna Mills. No, Wells. Or maybe Willis."

"You don't remember her name?"

"We only went out once."

"When?"

"February, I think."

"Please don't say you took her out on Valentine's Day, slept with her, and never called her again."

"It wasn't Valentine's Day, and it was she who never called me."

My eyes wander down his body. "Foolish woman."

His penis twitches and gets hard. "Like what you see, do you?"

"I don't know. Do you like what *you* see?"

He brushes a hair off my forehead. "Hell yes, I do."

"Do you think you'll remember *my* name five months from now?"

He puts down his glass and mine and pins me to the floor. "Andie Shaw, I'll remember your name on my death bed."

My insides quiver, and I try to ignore the little voice in my head telling me that history is about to repeat itself.

I reach between us and grab his erection. "It's time I pay my debt."

CHAPTER TWENTY-SEVEN

Maddox

Sex with Andie has happened as often as supper with Andie. It's our thing. Supper and sex. Sometimes sex, then supper. Being with her is a whole new ballgame. She's unlike any woman I've ever been with. She isn't shy about her body. She doesn't try to impress me. She doesn't hide the fact that she likes burgers and tacos and extra gravy on her potatoes.

All of it may be a product of our casual relationship status. What does it matter if I'm impressed or not? But her not trying to impress me has made the exact opposite happen.

I'm totally screwed.

I sip my morning coffee, Beau at my feet. Andie dances down her front porch steps with a smile, and I wonder if she's always done that or if this is a new thing. She looks up. I tip my hat to her. She sticks her tongue out at me. Oh, how I love her tongue.

My phone rings. Dad's face appears on the screen.

"It's not too early for you, is it?" he asks.

"Up at dawn, Dad."

"That's a change. How are things going with Aaron?"

"He hates it here, but he's doing what he's told. Owen keeps him busy, and he's been helping me clean out the old hunting lodge."

"I didn't think your grandmother ever used it."

"She didn't, which is exactly why it needs to be cleaned."

"Sprucing the place up for the sale?"

I sigh. "Something like that."

"Speaking of the sale, I've been talking a lot with Hugh Jenkins. I know his offer isn't the best, but I like him. He knew your grandmother well and speaks of her fondly. I think he might be the one."

"I'm glad you're not considering the Thompsons."

"Not after what you, and frankly, everyone else, has told me. It'd be a cryin' shame to let all Nana's hard work be for nothing. What the hell would we do with an extra few million anyway?"

I choke on a sip of coffee. "Are you serious?"

"The ranch is worth a good twenty million, Maddox. Haven't you figured that out by now?"

"I… no, I had no idea."

"Don't get any ideas. You're still going to have to work for a living."

"Of course."

"Listen, I have a meeting to get to, but I wanted to let you know Hugh will be bringing his main guys over this week to check things out. Make sure he has access to everything: houses, land, stables, offices, even the books, if they want to see them. I trust him, and I want this to go smoothly and quickly. I know you must be eager to get back home."

"I don't mind being here, and Aaron is supposed to stay all summer, isn't he?"

"If probate keeps moving along at the current pace, it won't be long before the deal is done. I really have to run. You'll make sure Hugh has everything he needs? You'll tell Matteo and Owen?"

"Sure, Dad."

"I appreciate it. Enjoy the heat and humidity."

The line goes dead, and I stare at my phone. Twenty million? I'd considered asking him not to sell the ranch. To let me stay and run things—not that I really run things. It's the others who do it so well. But there's no way. Twenty fucking million. Maybe Hugh Jenkins will give me a job, but where would I stay? The bunkhouse? I'm not an experienced worker, and it's not like he'd give me a management job.

A truck pulls up, and my jaw tightens. I contemplate running for my gun. Victor exits and heads to Andie's door. Beau stands at attention. "Sit." I get up. "She's not home," I shout.

"Guess you would know."

I jump off the stoop and go over. "What is that supposed to mean?"

"Nothing. I have something for her."

"She's not interested in your attempts to win her back. She's moved on."

"With you?"

I don't answer, because I'm afraid the answer is no. He doesn't even seem mad. He seems… sad.

"Whatever you have for her you can leave with me."

He holds out a light-blue cardigan. "I found this in my truck. Thought she might want it back."

I take it. "I'll make sure she gets it."

He nods and turns away, but before he reaches the truck, he stops. "Treat her right, man. She deserves the best." He hops in and drives away, looking like he might cry.

None of this makes any sense. He sent flowers once, the day after she broke it off, but he hasn't called or tried to see her until today. I don't get it.

Andie comes out of the stable. "Did I just see Victor drive away?"

I hold up the cardigan. "He was returning this."

"I wondered where it was. What did he say?"

"Nothing."

"Nothing at all?"

"Pretty much."

"Huh. This is so not what I expected from him. Maybe he's moved on."

"He hasn't. He looked broken up about it." I glance at her hand. "I'm glad you still wear the ring. You never know."

"It's been over a week. You think he'll still try something?"

"If he's the lunatic they led us to believe, we have to assume he could."

Aaron stomps out of the stable and throws his gloves off. "I'm tired of shoveling horse shit."

"Nobody likes to shovel shit," I say. "But it has to be done."

"There are enough grunts around here to do it. I'd rather work on the lodge."

"How about you finish up the south stable and later this afternoon we can go over there?"

Andie's eyes light up. "You're doing more work on it?"

I shrug and tell a lie. "Thought we should fix it up for the new owners."

Her expression sours. "Of course."

"I know the way," Aaron says. "Been there a lot. I'll take a four-wheeler. You don't have to babysit me."

"I'm not babysitting you. I like to work on the lodge, too."

"I work better alone."

"You know what needs to be done?"

"Sand and paint, same as we've been doing all week."

"Okay. I guess there's enough for me to do right here then."

Aaron picks up his gloves and goes back to work.

"Typical teenager," Andie says. "Bitching about everything and not wanting supervision."

"He seems to be toeing the line for the most part. His attitude might suck, but he's doing the work."

She heads for her truck. "I'd better get going. Hugh Jenkins said he's got a colicky mare."

I follow and lean against the door when she rolls the window down. "About Jenkins. It seems he's the one who's buying this place. My dad has been talking with him for weeks."

She slumps. "That's good news."

"Hugh likes you, and you already work for him. You won't lose the ranch."

She looks at me. "No, I won't lose the ranch."

Our eyes don't stray from each other. Not even as she backs up. Not until she turns the truck and drives off. Even then, I swear I can feel her eyes on me in the rearview mirror.

Damn it, I'm just going to be another Bobby fucking Monahan.

CHAPTER TWENTY-EIGHT

"Why is Christina so late?" I ask Tara.

She picks up her phone and checks the time. "It's unlike her to miss one of our lunches."

I fidget. "I wanted to talk to both of you."

Tara studies me. "You look about ready to burst at the seams. What is it?"

"Okay, but when I tell Christina, you have to pretend you're hearing it for the first time."

"Got it."

"It's Victor."

Her eyes roll up. "Oh my god, you finally slept with him."

"No. Quite the opposite."

Her jaw drops. "You broke up with him. Because of McHottie?"

"You don't even know the half of it, girl."

The waiter tries to interrupt us but Tara shoos him away.

"How long do you plan on keeping me waiting? Spill."

"I'm not even sure where to start. More than a month ago, the FBI showed up at the ranch."

"What?"

I lean close and whisper. "Turns out Victor may have killed someone."

"Killed someone?" she repeats loudly.

"Shh." I glance around nervously. "He still doesn't know he was being watched."

"Was? I'm confused. What does this have to do with you?"

"They used me to try to get information from him."

"You're messing with me."

We order drinks, and I tell her the whole story. She listens in disbelief. I can't believe it myself sometimes.

"So he's just walking around free as a bird, and that poor woman is still missing?"

"They don't have enough evidence to arrest him."

"Are you freaking out? I mean what if he tries to hurt you?"

I open my purse and show her what's inside.

"You bought a gun?" she whispers.

"Maddox has been teaching me how to use it, but Victor—or whatever his name is—hasn't bothered me."

"But he said he loved you."

I check the time. "I'm worried. Christina hasn't answered any of my texts. Maybe we should run by her house."

"Can't. I have to be at work in an hour. She's probably shopping in Dallas and lost track of the time."

"But she hasn't texted me."

She picks up her phone. "I'll call her."

Maddox walks in and goes to the counter. He pays and then leans against a barstool, waiting for his food. I think of last night and the night before that. And the one before that. Each time we have sex, it's in a different place. His house, my house, his bed, my couch, his stairway, my bathroom vanity. I squirm.

Tara laughs. "You should wipe up the drool."

"I'm not drooling."

"Your eyes are bugging out like one of those cartoons when their eyes jump across the room at the sight of a steak dinner."

I glance at her phone. "She didn't answer?"

"Nope."

Maddox sees me and waves.

"Oh my god, Andie. You're totally into him. He's one hundred percent hot, but I've never seen you like this."

Maddox joins us. "Ladies."

Tara pats the chair between us. "Sit."

"Thanks, but I'm waiting on my order. I'm picking up lunch for the troops today."

"Feel free to wait with us," I say.

He sits. "Aren't you missing the third musketeer?"

"She's not answering our texts or calls."

Maddox studies my face. "And that worries you."

I nod.

"McBride!" someone shouts.

He holds up a finger to the guy behind the counter. "How about I run this to the ranch and then we go check on her?"

"You don't have to do that."

"You're sweet to offer," Tara says. "I've got to get to work, but the two of you should definitely go." The waiter puts our sandwiches down. "We'll take those to go, please."

Maddox stands. "I guess we're off then. I'll get my order."

Tara and I pay, get our to-go bags, and follow Maddox out. He puts a large box of food in the back of his truck. "Follow me home, and I'll drive us from there."

Home. I know it's a slip of the tongue, but deep down I wonder if that's how he's starting to think of it here.

"Nice to see you again, Tara."

"You, too." He drives away. She stares at me. "Oh, you've got it bad."

"I do not."

Tara's phone pings with a text. Thinking it could be Christina, I look over her shoulder. It's Owen. I suddenly feel guilty. "We didn't even get to talk about your date."

"Haven't had one yet."

"But he's texting you?"

"Bootie call."

"At one o'clock in the afternoon? And why is he texting you for a bootie call if you haven't gone on a date yet?"

"I said we haven't gone on a date. I didn't say we haven't had sex."

My chin almost hits the pavement. "Tara Wegley, you never cease to surprise me."

"He came by the diner the other day to ask me out. Said I smelled like bacon. Things escalated from there. We had a quickie in the men's room."

"Gross."

She laughs. "Who do you think cleans the men's room? Me. I knew it was spotless. Anyway, we both decided we didn't want to be tied down. I have Trey. He has a lot going on at the ranch."

"You're sex buddies?"

"Nothing wrong with that, and boy has he removed those cobwebs. You should try it." She glances in the direction Maddox's truck went. "Maybe with him."

I look at the ground and shuffle some dirt with my boot.

"You already have, haven't you? We are going to need another lunch and soon." When I don't say anything, she narrows her eyes. "Jesus, Andie, you're in love with him, aren't you?"

"It's casual."

"You are totally in love with him, otherwise you'd have said you were sleeping with him. Remember when you hooked up with Tony? You couldn't keep your mouth shut about it. You're tight-lipped about McHottie, though. I've got your number, sister."

"I am not in love with him, and I don't plan to be. He's leaving as soon as they sell the ranch. News flash. It looks like they're selling it to Mr. Jenkins. So there you have it."

She shakes her head back and forth, staring at me. "Good luck."

"With what?"

"The not falling in love part."

I stomp toward my truck. "I have to go. I'll let you know when I find Christina."

"I want details!" she shouts after me.

I wave and get in. While driving to the ranch, I wonder why I haven't told my friends about him. The week I was with Tony, I told them all about it. Every last detail. I rationalize I was waiting to give them the news about Victor. I didn't want them thinking I was sleeping with two men at once.

At the ranch, Maddox is leaving the offices when I pull up. He motions to his truck. I grab my lunch and join him. "That was fast," I say. "Did you even have time to get something to eat?"

He starts the engine. "I'll grab a bite later."

I unwrap my sandwich and give him half. "Take this."

He smiles. "Thanks. So you think something's up with Christina? As in her asshole husband won't let her out of the house?"

"Maybe. It's happened before."

"She's a grown woman."

"Who is controlled by the richest family around."

"Why does she stay?"

"Wait until you see her house."

He turns up his nose. "No house is worth putting up with people like that."

"I agree, but she doesn't. Christina didn't have much growing up. Her parents barely scrape by. I'm fairly sure she gives them part of her allowance."

"Allowance?" he says in disgust.

"You're starting to get the picture."

"How bad is it?"

"Bad, I think. She's good at hiding it. Turn here."

"I know where she lives."

"You've been there?"

He shakes his head. "Just need to know my enemies."

"And Joel?"

"I know his address, too."

"Do you think they'll ever get in trouble for the poison or the hay?"

"I doubt it."

"I wonder if they'll do anything else."

"You know them better than I do. Do you think they'll give up without a fight?"

"Sadly, no."

We pull up to Christina's palatial estate and stop. "How will we get past the gate?" he asks.

"Press the button."

A minute later, I hear Christina's voice. "Yes?"

I lean over Maddox. "Open the gate, Christina."

"Andie?"

"You missed lunch."

"That was today? I must have lost track of time."

"Open the gate."

"I'm kind of busy."

"Is Jon home?"

"No."

"If you don't open the gate, I'm going to scale the wall and probably break my leg. Is that what you want?"

The line goes dead, and the gate opens.

"You think she's lying?" Maddox asks.

I nod.

We park and go to the front door. We wait for minutes. I call her but don't get an answer. Finally, the door opens, and I understand the delay. My jaw clenches. A deep, dark bruise is evident on her jaw even under the heavy makeup she used to try and hide it. I walk in without an invitation. "That bastard."

She sees Maddox. "Uh, hello."

He focuses on the bruise. "Jon did this to you?"

She touches her chin. "It was an accident. We can get a little rough, if you know what I mean." She tries to make it sound like they have an adventurous sex life when I know it's anything but.

"Stop lying, Christina. Did he take your phone, too? Why didn't you answer my texts?"

"No, he didn't take my phone. Am I nine?"

I take out my phone and call hers. I don't even hear it ring.

"Where is it then? I've never seen it out of your hand or pocket."

"I must have left it in the bathroom."

"Mind getting it?"

She goes over to the bar and pours herself a drink. "Why are you doing this? Can't you leave well enough alone?"

Maddox grumbles. "From the looks of it, nothing is well enough around here."

"Maybe you should mind your own business, cowboy." Three short beeps sound through the alarm system and she's suddenly terrified. "You have to go right now."

"Why?"

"That's the gate opening. Jon is home."

"At two in the afternoon? He's checking on you?"

"Go. I mean it."

"My truck is out front," Maddox says. "He already knows someone is here."

"If you go out the side door, you can run around and get in and leave after he comes in the house."

"I'm not running away," Maddox says.

"Do you have a death wish?" she asks.

Tires screech to a stop outside. My pulse races. "Maddox, don't do anything."

The door flies open. "Who the fuck is in my house?" Jon sees me and Maddox and turns to Christina. "Mind telling me why this asshole is standing in my living room?"

I step forward. "I came over so we could plan Tara's birthday party."

He glances at Maddox. "And you needed an escort for that?"

"We were just leaving," I say. "Christina, how about you come back to the ranch, and we can plan it there?"

"She's not going anywhere," Jon says. "Are you, babe?"

Christina shakes her head.

"Did you invite them over?" he asks.

She shakes her head again.

"Then they're trespassing." He sneers at Maddox. "I could have you arrested."

"I'd like to see you try."

Jon laughs. "You forbid me from coming on your property but somehow you think it's okay to come onto mine? You think you're better than me?"

"Oh, wow. Where do I even start?"

Out of nowhere, Jon's fist connects with Maddox's jaw. Christina and I scream.

"I'm calling the police," I say.

Maddox stops me, rubbing his jaw. "The first one was free."

Jon laughs. "As if you could stop me."

"Christina might not fight back, but I will."

"Are you threatening me?" He puts an arm around Christina. "In front of my wife?"

"Maddox, let's just go."

"You want to come with us?" he asks Christina.

She shakes her head, but I can see she's frightened.

"She ain't going with you." Jon squeezes her shoulder hard enough to make deep finger indentations.

Maddox's jaw tightens. "She is if she says she wants to."

"Well she don't want to, so why don't you get the fuck out before I make y'all a matching trio." He looks pointedly at my jaw, as if it would give him pleasure to hurt me.

Maddox pushes me behind him. "You really are a sorry son of a bitch, aren't you?"

Jon pulls out a gun. "I may be a sorry son of a bitch, but you'll be a dead one if you don't get your ass off my property in the next thirty seconds."

Maddox reaches behind him, and I stop him from pulling his gun. "It's his house. We need to leave."

"Better listen to the dumb bitch," he says.

I drag Maddox to the door, looking back at Christina. "I'm all right," she says.

Jon kisses the side of her head, then pokes her bruised jaw. "Of course you are. Why wouldn't you be?"

Maddox backs out, never taking his eyes off Jon and never letting me out from behind him. He closes the front door, and we hurry to the truck. Once inside, he closes his eyes. "Holy shit."

"Drive, Maddox."

He hesitates.

"There's nothing more you can do here."

He moves slowly down the driveway, viewing the house in the rearview mirror. "She's in real trouble."

Tears escape my eyes. At the terror of having a gun pointed at us? At the thought of what he could be doing to her this very second? "I knew what was happening. I just didn't know it was that bad."

Maddox grabs my hand. "You can't make her leave him unless she wants to."

"I've been asking her to leave him since the day I came back from school. She likes the money and the status."

"But what if it gets worse? At least now she gets to do things like go to lunch and shop. You think she'll give a rat's ass how big her house is when she becomes a prisoner in it?"

"You almost pulled your gun. What were you thinking?"

"I was thinking he hits women."

I close my eyes. "I hate it too, but getting yourself killed isn't the answer."

"The next time you do lunch, I'm coming. Better yet, invite her to the ranch. We'll have one of those intervention things. You know her parents, don't you? Bring them. I'm sure they have no idea how bad things are for her."

"If he ever lets her out again."

He squeezes my hand. "You're shaking."

"And you're injured."

"It's nothing," he says, touching his jaw. "He hits like a girl."

"For Christina's sake, I hope you're right."

"Promise me you'll never go back to that house."

"What if she needs me?"

"If she's in trouble, tell me. I'll get the guys together, and we'll think of something." He briefly takes his eyes off the road. "Promise me."

I want to ask him what I should do if she needs me after he's gone, but I don't. It would sound desperate, and I've no intention of letting on how my heart stopped when Jon pulled a gun on him. How it made me feel when I thought Maddox might die. How my life without him flashed before my eyes, and I didn't like what I saw. Because then he'd know I *am* desperate. Desperately in love with him.

I let my head fall back against the headrest. "I promise."

CHAPTER TWENTY-NINE

I look at myself in the living room mirror, angling my face so I can see the bruise on my jaw. I lied to Andie. He did pack a pretty good punch, and it sickens me to think he probably doesn't hit Christina more lightly because she's a woman.

Aaron walks up behind me. "What does the other guy look like?"

I flinch. "Don't sneak up on someone like that."

"Did you think I was whoever hit you?"

"Forget about it. Listen, the reason I wanted to see you this morning is I need you on your best behavior today. The buyer is bringing his guys by this afternoon to check the place out."

"Owen already read me the riot act. Something about putting his boot up my ass if I act like a delinquent."

I try not to smile. Then I hear buzzing. It sounds like a phone, but it's not mine, and Aaron's is in a drawer in my bedroom. I look at his pocket. "Want to tell me why your pants are vibrating?"

He sidles toward the door. "I have to get to work."

"Aaron. Answer the question."

"It's a goddamn phone, okay? So sue me."

I hold out my hand. "Give it to me."

He crosses his arms defiantly. "No."

"Damn it, Aaron. I don't want to be the bad guy here, but it's only been two weeks. Your dad was very clear. If you don't cut ties with the people you were hanging out with, nothing will change."

"Good. I don't want anything to change."

"You enjoy getting suspended and having fights?"

His eyes go to my jaw. "Guess we have that in common."

"If you think working on the ranch sucks, wait until you experience military school, because that's where you're going if you don't shape up. Are you going to hand over the phone? If you don't, I'm calling your dad and that's on you, not me."

"You'd fucking rat me out? Your own cousin?"

I stare him down.

He pulls out the phone, throws it on the floor, then stomps out.

"Who gave it to you?"

He keeps walking.

"Which one was it?"

He yells over his shoulder, "Unlike you, I'm not a goddamn tattletale."

I pick up the phone and take it to the stables, where I find Owen with a clipboard. I put the phone on it. "One of your guys gave this to Aaron."

"No they didn't."

"How can you be sure?"

He puts down his pencil and gives the phone back to me. "Because they know their faces would be a lot more messed up than yours if they broke one of my rules."

"You run that tight of a ship?"

"Damn right I do."

"Then how'd he get it?"

"Beats me."

Aaron drives past the open door on an ATV. He's going to the hunting lodge again. He spends part of every day there, sanding and painting. It should be close to finished. "I'm going to get to the bottom of this."

"Get to the bottom of what?" he says. "Figuring out the mind of a teenage boy?" He strolls away, laughing.

I decide on an ATV instead of riding Tadpole. I have to be back well before noon to make sure everything is ready for Hugh Jenkins. On the way to the lodge, I pass the run-in shed Andie and I holed up in during the rainstorm. It makes me wonder how couples can go from doing romantic things like that, to hating—and hitting—each other. Maybe Christina and Jon never liked each other. Maybe it's a marriage of convenience. Andie thinks so. How anyone can love money more than their pride, more than their safety, is beyond my comprehension.

Did I just think of Andie and me as a couple? That's ludicrous. Or maybe it's just impossible. If she wanted to be a couple, she'd ask me to stay. I could do that. I could work for Jenkins, and if he wouldn't hire me, I could find work as a bartender. Unless she doesn't want to be a couple. She seems perfectly fine with the way things are. Could be the situation with Victor was so complicated, she doesn't want to do anything but easy.

When I get to the lodge, there's no sign of Aaron's four-wheeler. I go inside, and it's not much different than it was last week. Where the hell is he, and what's he been doing all this time?

I call Owen. "Have you seen Aaron?"

"Thought he was at the lodge."

"I'm at the lodge. He's not here."

"Anyone seen the kid?" he yells away from the phone. "He's not here. He go rogue on you?"

"I don't know. Call if you see him."

"Will do, boss."

"I'm not your boss, Owen."

"Maybe not, but sometimes I think you should be."

I get out Aaron's phone. It's a cheap one you can buy off the rack at any drugstore. I page through his contacts. There aren't many, and no names, only initials. Most of the area codes are from back home, except one, which is local. I contemplate calling it but decide to wait. I'm not that desperate. It's not like he's run away. He's probably off smoking weed.

I hop on my ride and take the long way back, planning to give him until noon before calling Griffin. Then I spot activity on the overgrown airstrip. Two trucks and... son-of-a-bitch, Aaron's ATV. I stay out of sight in the tree line as long as I can, then speed over. Aaron, three guys, and a girl are sitting around, smoking pot and drinking beer.

He's so drunk or high he doesn't seem to care when I approach. "Maddox," he slurs. "Hey, now I know I'ma supposed to be paintin' and all, but I jus' ran into some friends."

I pull out his phone. "Which one of you is Q.T?" All I get are defiant stares, so I press the call button. The blond kid's phone rings. "Why would you buy a phone for someone you just met?"

He shrugs. "Had some money to burn."

The whole bunch are as wasted as Aaron. "Who's driving?"

"Who cares?" one of them says.

I lean down in his face. "I care. You're all underage, and this is my property. That could get me into trouble. Unless you want me calling the cops, I suggest you hand over your keys."

"How in the hell are we supposed to get home?"

"Not my problem," I say. "Call Mommy or Daddy."

The kid stands up, swaying. "Yeah, right."

"Call an Uber then. From the looks of these trucks, you can afford it." I shove my chest against his and push him back until he touches the truck. "I mean it. Keys or cops. Your choice."

The girl hands me a set of keys attached to a pink lanyard.

"You think I was born yesterday?" I press the unlock button on the fob, which of course does nothing. I toss them back to her. "You have ten seconds."

Two sets of keys are thrown at my feet. I pick them up and make sure they unlock the two trucks, then I reach into the cooler and proceed to open and dump the rest of the beer. "Where's the weed?"

"Smoked it all," Q.T. says.

He's lying, but I figure I've made my point.

"You." I point to Aaron. "Get on the back of my four-wheeler."

"Jeez," the girl says. "You weren't kidding, Aaron."

"Told you he was a douche." His expression is belligerent. "I can drive."

"You're drunk."

"It's not like it's a car."

"Your dad would hang me by the balls if he knew I let you drive one of these things in your state." I grab the back of his neck.

Not hard but firmly enough to let him know I mean business. "Sit your ass down on the back of my goddamn ATV."

One of the guys whistles. "He's not as big a pussy as you made him out to be, Pearce."

I stuff the keys in my pocket. "You can pick them up at the house when you're sober." We drive off, and an empty beer can flies past my head.

Back at the stable, I find Zac. "I had to leave one of the four-wheelers out at the airstrip. Can you take someone out there and fetch it for me?"

He glances at Aaron and snickers. "Sure thing."

Aaron gets off. "Does everyone here fucking hate me?"

"I don't know. You live with them. Do they hate you?"

"They're all robots. Some of them even have stupid Devil's Horn Ranch tattoos."

"They aren't robots. They're good workers who have respect for the job and their superiors. You could learn a lot from them."

"Not likely."

"Take a shower," I say. "Drink some coffee. You have until noon to shape up. I want Jenkins thinking you're as happy as a pig in the fucking mud, or I'll report everything that just happened to your dad."

He looks surprised.

"I was your age not so long ago. I understand more than you know. I want this to work out, so I'm giving you a pass—but only if you turn things around. That means no more partying. I mean it."

"Fine."

"And no more going off on your own. Someone will accompany you whenever you leave the stables."

"So now I really do have to have a babysitter."

"You brought it on yourself."

He heads toward the bunkhouse. "I thought you said you understand."

"I do, and that's why I'm going to help you. Just not in the way you think."

"I hate this fucking place." He storms off.

"Trouble in paradise?" Andie says behind me.

I slump against the stable wall. "I'm never having kids."

"You don't mean that."

"No, I don't. Can I amend it to I'm never having teenagers?"

She laughs. "Kind of goes with the territory."

"What are you doing here? I thought you worked over at the Double Duce on Friday afternoons."

"Mr. Jenkins wanted to get my opinion on some of the horses you own. He's going to have to decide which ones he's keeping."

"Kind of a conflict of interest, considering you work here, too."

"That's what I said. I love all of them. Even Kingston, and you know he's a handful."

"I'm more worried about the staff."

"I'm sure he'll be more than fair. It's not like his guys can run both places. He'll need workers."

"But not Matteo and Owen, and probably not Miguel. He'll want his own managers."

She turns toward the guesthouse. "I'm going to eat. Make you a sandwich?"

"Sure. I have a minute."

I wash up as she makes lunch. After we sit at the table, she touches my jaw. "Does it hurt?"

I hold her hand to my face, and we gaze at each other. I push my sandwich away and pull her onto my lap. "It hurts less now."

She leans down and kisses me. I am instantly hard. I unbutton her shirt and play with her breasts. We make out like teenagers at a drive-in. It's the best five minutes I've had all day. A knock on the door ruins it.

"You get it while I deal with this." I point to the bulge in my jeans, and she giggles. I splash cold water on my face in the bathroom, then stare at myself in the mirror. "Just tell her, you pussy."

"Did you say something?" she yells from the other room.

Owen is in the living room wearing a shit-eating grin. "Didn't mean to interrupt anything. Jenkins and his guys are here."

I check the time. "They're early." I scarf the sandwich in three bites. "Thanks for lunch. See you later?" She nods, and I notice why Owen was looking at me the way he was. The buttons on her shirt are mismatched.

He and I leave, and Owen pats me on the back. "You're not fooling anyone. We all know what's going on with you and Doc."

"You don't know the half of it," I say. "Victor, the guy she dumped, was being investigated by the FBI."

"No shit?"

"This is more than a thirty-second conversation. I'll tell you everything later."

I walk slowly across the driveway.

"Looks like you're not thrilled about the Jenkins visit either," he says.

I've come to love the ranch more than any place I've ever lived. "Thrilled? No. I'd say I'm far from it."

I approach Hugh with my hand extended. "Mr. Jenkins. Welcome to Devil's Horn Ranch."

He shakes. "Thank you for taking the time to show us around."

Matteo and some of the others lounge along the arena fence. I motion to them. "Since there's so much to see, I thought we could match up our guys. You know, have my ranch manager show your ranch manager around, and so forth."

"Sounds good to me. That'll leave time for you and me to talk. How about we take a quick ride around the property? I'd like to check out the buildings before getting into the nitty gritty."

"Sure thing. You good on a four-wheeler?"

"Son, I've been good on ATVs since they had to be started with a hand crank."

For two hours we tour the ranch and end at the main house. "I think Thelma might like it here more than our place. I might just let Wyatt run things back home and take Devil's Horn for myself. I'm not so sure about the hunting lodge. The wife thinks hunting is sacrilegious. She won't hear of it. We may have to tear down the old lodge and expand the cattle business."

I know he means well, and he's most definitely the lesser of all evils when it comes to buyers, but hearing him say he wants to tear down the lodge makes me sad.

"You'd be okay with that, wouldn't you, sonny? It's been empty for years, as I hear it."

I swallow what I want to say and opt for, "That'll be your choice, Mr. Jenkins. None of us will have a say in the matter."

He opens the door under the stairs and notices hash marks and dates. It's where Nana measured my dad's height over the years. He runs a finger along one of them. "Must be hard for your family to think of givin' this up. Lots of memories here."

I don't want to go down that road. "Should we join the others?"

"Let's."

Two trucks pull up out front, kicking up dust when they stop abruptly. Joel Thompson gets out of one, along with his daughter, Karen. Two of his cronies exit the other.

"Looky what the cat dragged in," Hugh says under his breath.

Joel sees me and makes a beeline over. "Want to tell me what business you have taking the keys to my grandson's truck?" He sneers at Hugh. "What the hell are you doin' here, Jenkins?" He sees Jenkins' men exiting the stable. "Well, shit." He turns to me. "Your daddy done sold to this dimwit?"

"They're touring the ranch is all," I say.

"Bullshit."

I take two sets of keys from my pocket and hand them over. "I wasn't aware one of them was your grandson, but it wouldn't have changed anything. They were drunk and high and trespassing."

"They weren't trespassing if they were invited," Karen says. "Quinn says your cousin asked them to come more than once."

"Did you not hear the part about them being drunk and high?"

"They're teenagers," she says, like that excuses it. "Boys will be boys."

"Underage kids will not be doing that on my property. It wasn't only boys either. There was a girl there." I shudder to think what could potentially happen when you put four drunk boys and a girl together.

"Don't you mean *his* property?" Joel glares at Hugh. "What the hell is your daddy thinking? I know my offer beat Jenkins's by at least four million. You do something shady to come up with the difference, Hugh?"

Hugh laughs. "Not unless I learned from you."

"You better watch your tone around me."

I step between them. "You got what you came for. Take the keys and leave, and please tell your grandson and his friends they are no longer welcome anywhere on the property."

"Just who do you think you're talking to, boy?" Joel says.

"We both know what you and your men have done to this place. I suggest you leave before I have you arrested."

He chuckles. "If you could have had me arrested, you'd have done it long before now. Everyone in this town knows I'm above the law. Guess it's time you learned it too."

I pull out my phone. "Unless you're ready to test that theory, I recommend you get back in your trucks and drive away."

He spits on the ground. Some of it gets on my boot. "Heard you and that little chippy were nosing around my son's place, so you're hardly one to make threats. My boy give you that shiner?"

"He did. He's pretty good at giving shiners to a lot of people, including his wife."

"You best watch your place."

I hand my phone to Owen, who's joined me. "Owen, call the police. Tell them we have a trespasser who is threatening me."

Joel laughs. "You're new around here. I get that. But make no mistake, I get what I want. I always get what I want. Remember that."

"I'll be back in New York the day the deal closes, and you realize you're a loser. I really wish I could stay around to see it."

"Unless you find yourself six feet under before then."

Owen speaks into the phone, clearly having called the police. Joel motions for his men to get in their truck.

"We're not done here," Joel says. He glances at Hugh. "We're not nearly done."

He and Karen get in their vehicle and peel out, spraying pebbles and dirt.

I blow out a deep breath, relieved he's gone.

"Either of you need to change your drawers?" Owen says.

Andie appears, having wisely stayed in the stables while Joel was here.

"I don't know how you all put up with that family," I say.

"Y'all," Hugh says.

I narrow my eyes.

"Try it. *Y'all.* You live in Texas now."

"Okay. Y'all."

"Spoken like a true Texan."

Andie and I exchange looks. I get the feeling neither of us knows whether to laugh or cry.

CHAPTER THIRTY

I pick up the brochure and head out the door. As usual, Maddox is sipping coffee on his front porch, his loyal pooch at his side. I wave to him as I hop in the truck.

Maddox trots over and glances at the attached horse trailer. "Where are you off to?"

"Horse auction. Thought I might buy one to keep Baby Blue company when I get my own place."

His eyebrows arch. "Exactly when might that be?"

"I'm looking at a few properties next week."

"You mean *we* are. You said you'd take me with you. Can I come?"

I turn on the engine. "I thought we already established that."

"I mean to the auction. I've never been. Might be fun."

"Hop in."

He races around the truck and gets in the passenger seat, then picks up the brochure and pages through it. "You've circled five of them. I thought you said you wanted *one.*"

"I do, but I need backups. Buying at auction isn't a sure thing. You never know who will be in the market for what."

"What are these hip numbers?"

"Each horse has a sticker on their hip with a number. It's the order in which they will be sold."

"Why not just buy from a private owner? You looking for a bargain?"

I white-knuckle the steering wheel. "You know how some people get their dogs from the pound instead of a breeder? They are saving a dog from potential euthanasia. That's what I'm doing. A lot of horses bought at auction end up being slaughtered."

"Slaughtered? Why?"

"For meat."

He looks horrified. "People eat horse meat?"

"You'd be surprised what horse meat goes into."

His expression softens. "So you're going to save a horse today."

"That's the plan."

"If a lot of them get slaughtered, they must not be in very good condition."

"There are always a few diamonds in the rough."

"I suppose being a vet gives you a leg up at these sorts of things." He turns a page and laughs. "Princess Consuela. Jughead. Neidermeyer. Where do they get these names?"

"A lot of horses at auctions aren't papered."

"All you have circled are geldings."

"I thought Baby Blue might like to have a man around."

"Is she the only one?"

I can feel his eyes burning into the side of my head. I pull into the lot, which is pretty full. There will be competition for the best horses. Maddox and I visit the paddocks where the horses are being kept. I settle at the fence and start watching.

"What are you looking for?" he asks.

"I'm observing their behavior. They should be anxious about their unfamiliar surroundings." I point. "See the one over there by himself? The owners want you to think he's well-behaved, but in reality he's probably been drugged."

"Why would they do that?"

"When someone wants to get rid of an unruly horse, they drug them and take them to auction. Auction sales are final. By the time you realize you've bought an untrainable horse, it's too late."

"Unless you're using him for horse meat."

I sigh. "Yes, unless that."

"What happens next?"

"We examine the horses up close. Not every auction allows it, but it's why I picked this one. Then they'll be ridden one by one as they are auctioned."

"Andie?"

My heart skips a beat. I know that voice. I whirl around, speechless.

"It *is* you." I'm pulled in for a hug. "I was hoping I'd run into you while I was in town."

I take a step back to catch my breath. "Maddox McBride, this is Bobby Monahan."

Maddox looks slightly ill for a moment and then extends his hand. "I've heard a lot about you."

Bobby grimaces. "Shit, I hope you won't hold it against me." He appraises Maddox. "McBride, as in Vivian McBride?"

"He's Vivian's grandson. He's here to oversee the sale of her ranch. She died a few months ago."

His face falls. "Oh, Andie, I'm so sorry." He wraps me in familiar arms. "I know how close you were."

When he releases me, I rub the Texas necklace between my fingers. "Thanks."

"Sorry for your loss, man," he says to Maddox.

"What are you doing here?" I ask.

He points to a man standing against the fence. "I'm here with our head trainer. We're in town to look at some European imports but figured we'd check out the auction if there was time."

"When did you get in?"

"This morning. I was going to call. No way would I come all the way to Texas and not get with my best girl." He motions between Maddox and me. "Are you two…?"

"Yes," Maddox says at the same time I say, "No."

"I remember a time when you and I had one of those yes/no relationships," Bobby says, grinning. "Who are you here for? McBride won't be buying horses if he's selling the ranch."

"*Me.* I'm buying one."

He takes the brochure from me. "Which one?"

I snatch it back. "You better not have your man outbid me."

He clutches his chest. "Why, Andie, I'm hurt you think I'd do that. Tell me. I promise I'll steer him away from your favorite."

I glance at Maddox, who is impatiently waiting for this conversation to be over. "Hip twelve is my favorite. My next choice is four."

"Noted. They're letting people in now. We can look them over. I'll see you later."

As he walks away from me, all kinds of things are going through my head. Surprisingly, one of them is no longer infatuation.

"What are the odds of that?" Maddox asks.

"Of Bobby being here? Pretty good actually. He's a vet. Vets often go to horse shows to let owners know which ones to buy."

"But he lives in Wyoming."

"European horses are shipped to ports in Texas, not Wyoming. If they want their pick of the best, they have to be there when they arrive."

"What a lucky coincidence then that you were both here."

"I suppose. Come on, we only have a short time to view the horses before the auction."

I don't miss the way Maddox looks at Bobby. Is he jealous? And the way he said *yes* earlier, it was like he was claiming me. Then again, he's the one I'm sleeping with, and Bobby is my ex. I can't imagine what it would be like if the tables were turned.

We enter the paddock and come to my third choice first. I pat him down and examine his head. "Cross this one off the list."

"Why?"

"See here? He's got scars on his head and neck. Could be he was in a wreck. Might make him prone to panic."

My first choice, hip #12, is the next one I see. I'm happy to find out he's sound. "He's skinny, but I can fatten him up. He's still my number one."

We look at my other backups and cross another one off the list because of deformities and poor hooves.

"So you're down to three," Maddox says. "Numbers twelve, four, and fifteen. But since four isn't your first choice, how will you play it?"

"My budget is five thousand. I won't go over budget for hip four, but I will if I have to for hip twelve. I'd be happy with either, but I like twelve's coat better."

We are herded to the stands for the auction. Starting with hip #1, each horse gets trotted around the ring while being auctioned off.

My adrenaline spikes when the auctioneer starts talking. It takes a minute to keep up with him and hear what he's saying. People start bidding.

"Who just made that bid?" Maddox asks.

"Not everyone sits in the stands. Some stay behind the box. It can be intimidating for some to see who you're bidding against."

"Will it be for you?"

I nod. "Yes, especially because they don't use ring men here."

"Ring men?"

"In some auctions, you don't bid directly to the auctioneer, you use a ring man. Without them it's easy to let it become a battle of egos. That can lead to overbidding." I give him a look. "Don't let me overbid, okay? There will be other auctions."

"Five thousand," he says. "Not a penny more."

"Well, maybe a penny, but for sure not over six." Hip #2 comes out. "Let's watch these two. I need to figure out if the auctioneer gives a warning or just puts the hammer down."

Someone behind me shouts out a bid. It's Bobby's companion. Bobby smiles and winks. I smile back.

"Thought you needed to study the auctioneer," Maddox scoffs.

Bobby's man has the winning bid.

The next horse goes quickly. Then Maddox elbows me. "Show time."

Hip #4 comes out. The auctioneer gives the description of the gelding and opens the bidding at three thousand. It quickly escalates higher. I raise my hand. "Thirty-eight."

"Four thousand," a woman yells.

It's Karen Thompson. I pinch the bridge of my nose. "Oh, no."

"What it is?" Maddox asks.

"Forty-two," a man down front says.

"Karen doesn't want a horse. She's a killer-buyer."

"She's going to sell to a slaughterhouse?"

"Forty-four," Karen yells. She looks directly at me.

"Forty-six," the man says.

It goes quiet for a moment. "You don't want to go higher?" Maddox asks.

"I do, but I don't want to bid forty-eight."

"Why not?"

"Because then I can't bid five thousand, and that's a psychological cutoff for some. I want to be the one to bid it." I think I see the auctioneer raise the hammer, so I blurt, "Forty-eight."

Bobby taps me on the shoulder. "Mistake."

"Shut up."

"Five thousand," the man says.

Maddox grabs my right hand, the one I've been raising with each bid. "Don't do it. You said you won't go over five for this one."

"But if she wins, he's dead for sure."

"Fifty-two," Karen yells.

I try to lift my hand. "Andie, if she doesn't get this one, she'll get another. Hell, she might leave here with a dozen. You can't save them all."

"Fifty-five!" the man in front shouts and my heart calms. The hammer comes down, and I feel relief.

"That was intense," Maddox says.

"If you think that was, wait until number twelve. I might have a heart attack."

"Is this the first time you've ever been to one of these?"

"I've been to many, but as a vet consult. Never for myself. Huge difference."

Hip #5 comes out. The bidding starts at eight thousand. Bobby's man bids when it hits ten.

"What's so special about this one?" Maddox asks.

"Stallion," I say. "He's good, but too rich for my blood. Plus I want a gelding."

"I thought you said a lot of these horses are sold for slaughter."

"They are, but some people want a quick sale and don't want to mess with private showings. There are some good bargains to be found if you look closely."

Karen Thompson buys two horses. With each one I find myself saying a little prayer. I know their fate. At least with most of the others, I can hope or pretend they will take their new horses home to live a long happy life.

Hip #12 comes out. I watch him closely. I like him even more. His gait is ideal, and he seems to enjoy being ridden.

The auctioneer opens the bidding at three thousand. A man bids thirty-two, another thirty-four. I wait for the price to go up before raising my hand. I lean over to Maddox. "If I wait as long as I can, maybe they'll think that's my opening bid, and I'm willing to go much higher."

"Good strategy."

One of the men drops out of the bidding.

"Forty-four," Karen Thompson says.

My heart falls. "Not again. I'm not letting her get this one." I raise my hand. "Forty-six."

Nobody says anything for a few seconds.

"I have forty-six hundred," the auctioneer says. "Forty-six, forty-six, do I hear forty-eight?"

I start to get excited. I grab Maddox's hand.

"Forty-eight," Karen shouts.

I wait a few seconds and then say, "Five thousand." I lower my voice. "Is she looking at me?"

He peeks around me. "Yes."

"Crap."

"Five thousand," the auctioneer says. "I've got five, do I hear fifty-two?"

The guy down the way shakes his head. This is going to be a face-off between me and Karen.

"Fifty-two," she says.

I close my eyes tightly and listen to the auctioneer try to drive up the bid. I have to hesitate so I don't seem too eager, especially with her. She might outbid me just out of spite. Spite for what, I have no idea. Liking Vivian? Being friends with Christina? Working at DHR?

But I can't hesitate too long, or he'll drop the hammer. I raise my hand. "Fifty-four."

Karen immediately outbids me. "Fifty-six."

"I can't bid fifty-eight," I say. "If I do, she'll bid six, and that's my limit. What do I do?"

Maddox raises his hand. "Fifty-eight."

I gape in surprise.

"What are you waiting for? Do it," he says.

"Six thousand!" I swallow and say a little prayer. "Is she looking?"

"She's talking with the man next to her. He's shaking his head. Andie, I think you've got him."

The hammer drops, and my heart soars. I hug him. "Oh my god. I did it!"

Hands land on my shoulders from behind as Bobby squeezes me. "Congratulations."

Someone appears and hands me a buyer's contract. "Fill this out and give it to the cashier to finalize your purchase."

I gladly take it. "Thank you."

I get out my driver's license and fill out the contract while other horses are auctioned. I ignore what's going on until Maddox gets my attention. "This is the other one you would have wanted, right?"

I glance up and see they are showing hip #15. "Yes. I hope someone good gets him."

He motions to my left. "Someone good is definitely not getting him."

Karen is bidding again. I turn around. "Bobby, you should bid on this one."

"We don't need another Quarter Horse. If he were Arabian, we might be interested."

Another man and Karen drive the bid up to forty-four hundred. I put my head in my hands. "I can't watch. I spent a week studying the brochure. I can't help feeling connected to the horses I picked."

Maddox raises a hand. "Forty-six."

I pull down his hand. "I can't buy this one, too. I'm not prepared to care for three of them."

"I know that."

"Forty-eight," Karen says.

The auctioneer rattles off the numbers, baiting Maddox, and I feel sick to my stomach.

"Five thousand," Maddox shouts.

Karen opens her mouth to speak, but the man at her side stops her. She turns up her nose at Maddox as the auctioneer slams the hammer.

My jaw goes slack. "Maddox, what are you going to do with a horse?"

"Keep it at the ranch. We have the room."

"And you can pay for this?"

He pulls out his wallet. "As long as they take credit cards."

Someone hands Maddox a buyer's contract.

I'm aghast. "I can't believe you did that."

"You like him," he says. "I didn't want you to think of him being trailered to a slaughterhouse like the others."

I stand. "Let's go."

"Why? This is fun."

"Because I like a lot of the horses. You might end up buying a dozen more if we stay."

He laughs.

I say goodbye to Bobby, who follows us out of the stands. "Andie, wait. Can we meet for a drink? I heard about this place over in Ft. Worth that sounds fun."

I glance at Maddox, who is silently brooding.

"Bring Maddox. Bring anyone you want. The more the merrier. What do you say?"

"Okay."

"Great. I'll text you the place. Eight o'clock?"

"Sure."

"Great."

"You already said that."

"I must really mean it then. See you then."

Maddox doesn't look happy. "What?" I say innocently.

"You're going drinking with him?"

"We were both invited."

"But he only wants you. Obviously."

I stare him down. "You're not jealous, are you?"

"Don't be naïve, Andie. You and I are sleeping together. You *used* to sleep with him. You know there's going to be a pissing contest if we go drinking."

It's not lost on me that he failed to answer the question. "That's ridiculous."

"Wait and see."

"So don't go then."

"Oh, I'm going."

I roll my eyes. "Can we please collect our horses?"

He studies his buyer's contract. "Did I really just agree to buy a horse?"

"You really did. Maybe now you'll have a reason to come visit after your family sells the ranch."

He looks like he wants to say something but doesn't. Seems that's been happening a lot lately.

CHAPTER THIRTY-ONE

What does one wear when going drinking with the guy who was the love of Andie's life? I grab the white shirt, put it on, button it, and roll up the sleeves. The contrast between my tanned skin and the white shirt makes me look good. Not that it's a competition or anything.

Except it totally is.

I put on my dress boots, laughing at myself because I actually have dress boots. It's hard to believe three months ago, I didn't have *any* boots. Now I own them for every occasion. On my way out, I pick the black cowboy hat, but just because it's the only one without dirt on it.

Andie comes out of her house the same time I do. She's wearing a skirt. *A skirt.* I didn't even know she owned one. I suppose I saw her in a dress at Nana's funeral, but that's completely different. She's wearing this for *him*. Cowboy boots accentuate her shapely legs, and I follow a line from the top of her boots to mid-thigh.

"You look nice," she says.

"You look… different."

She scrunches her nose. "Way to give a girl a compliment."

"It's just interesting how I've never seen you in a skirt before, and the second Dr. Bobby shows up, you run to put one on."

"Maddox, you're being absurd. I've never worn a skirt because we don't go out."

"We go out."

"No we don't. We eat at our houses. We ride horses and have picnics. We occasionally go shopping. We've never gone out to a restaurant, club, or bar. If we had, I'd have worn something like this. You have nothing to worry about."

We get in my truck. "Why would I be worried?"

"Exactly." The whole way to Ft. Worth, she fidgets. First with her necklace, then her ring. Then she smooths her skirt obsessively.

"Why are you so nervous?"

"I'm not."

"You're trying to impress him."

"And you're reading way too much into this. Wait until you see what Tara and Christina are wearing. Girls like to dress up to go clubbing, Maddox."

It's more than that. She's usually more talkative on our drives.

"Have you named your new horse yet?" I ask.

"No, you?"

"Yes. Shawshank Redemption."

"After the movie?"

"It's a play on words. You wanted to save the horse, and your last name is Shaw. I thought it was kind of clever."

Her mouth opens and closes. "Actually, I think it's pretty darn appropriate. Also sweet. I still can't believe you bought him, but you can't call him that for his barn name. It's too big a mouthful."

"So I'll call him Shaw or maybe Shank."

"Shank sounds barbaric, and Shaw is too obvious."

"How about Doc then?"

She shrugs. "It's your horse."

I can tell she's secretly pleased and I feel a smile coming on. "Now let's name yours. I was thinking since I named mine after you, you should name yours after me."

"You want me to name him Maddox?"

"When I was little, people called me Mad Max."

She turns up her nose. "I don't think so. Makes him sound like a bronc."

"McBride?"

"Too stuffy." She bites her lip in thought. "I've got it. His name is Connecticut."

"I like it." I laugh. "But if I'm standing next to him, the two of us might get confused."

"That will hardly be a problem after you leave."

I sigh.

We pull up to our destination. It's huge. Hundreds of cars already fill the massive lot.

"This is a *bar*?" I ask, examining the massive building that seems to span a football field.

"It's more like a sports complex," she says. "Wait until you see inside. There are games, dance floors, even a bull-riding machine." She narrows her eyes at me. "I'm surprised you haven't been here yet."

"I'm a bartender in New York, Andie. The last thing I want to do in my spare time is go to a bar."

"Fair enough, but I promise this will be unlike anything up there."

After combing the lot for an open space, we go inside. No way will we be able to find her friends here. She pulls out her phone and texts one of them.

"Follow me," she says.

We pass two or three long bars, a few smaller dance floors, a Dave and Buster's-like game room, and finally see her friends. The three of them run to each other and squeal and hug. I am glad to see Christina is still able to do things like this.

"Girl, you look hot," Tara says to Andie.

"Speaking of hot." Christina walks around me in a circle. "You sure do clean up like a nice southern cowboy."

Owen appears and shakes my hand.

"I didn't know you were coming," I say.

He motions to a high-top. "Some of the guys are here. Thought we could blow off some steam. Maybe ride the bull."

"You go ahead. I'm not breaking an arm to ride some piece of junk tin can."

"That piece of junk tin can cost this place about two hundred grand. It's the best around."

I grin. "I'm still not riding it."

We put in a large order of drinks and pull a second high-top over to where the guys are. It's loud here. Part of me hopes Bobby What's-his-name won't be able to find us, and Andie forgets to check her phone. But ten minutes later, he walks right up to the table.

"Maddox," he says, offering me his hand.

"How'd you find us? This place is huge."

He holds up his phone. "A long time ago Andie and I set up our phones so we could track each other's locations."

"Isn't that convenient?"

He kisses Andie on the cheek. Christina and Tara immediately swoon over him. He's the very definition of cowboy: rugged, yet refined—a cowboy with an advanced degree, a chiseled jaw, and a five-hundred-dollar hat.

The band plays, and Owen takes Tara to the dance floor. A few dozen other people join them. They all do some couples' dance in a counterclockwise motion, perfectly in sync.

Andie leans toward me. "Want to try it?"

"Are you kidding? I'd step all over you and make an ass of myself."

"You can't come to Texas and not learn the Texas Two-Step."

Bobby butts in. "Someone better take her out there."

Andie gives me one more look. I must hesitate too long because Bobby drags her out on the floor. Feelings bombard me as I watch them dance together.

"Gotta be quicker than that," Merle says behind me.

"I guess so."

I can't stand watching, but I can't tear my eyes away. I finish my beer, call the waitress over, and order a shot.

The song ends, and I figure so has my misery, but another starts, and they stay out there. "Keep 'em coming," I say when my shot is placed in front of me.

"You really like her," Christina says across the table.

"Why aren't you dancing?"

"Are you kidding? I'm sure Jon knows a dozen people here who would report back to him if I so much as accept a drink from another man."

There are many things I want to say to her, but now is not the time.

Everyone finally comes back to the table. Andie eyes the empty glasses in front of me. I ignore her judgmental stare and turn to Bobby. "When are you heading back to Wyoming?"

"Day after tomorrow. This was a short trip."

"That's too bad."

He smirks. "As if you didn't want me out of here yesterday." He moves closer. "I saw you watching us out there."

"Yeah? So?"

"A man doesn't look like he wants to kill the guy dancing with a girl unless he's in love with that girl."

I glance at Andie. She's having a conversation with her friends. I shove a shot glass at Bobby. "You need a drink. You're seeing things."

He raises the glass to me and tosses it back. "I assume you haven't told her how you feel then."

"I'm leaving Texas soon."

"Oh, that's right. Well, shit. Things are starting to make sense. It's me and her all over again. She must really be a glutton for punishment."

"What are you boys talking about?" Andie says, joining us.

"Maddox was just saying how he wanted to learn how to line dance."

Andie looks surprised. I'm about to enlighten her when a song starts, and she and Tara and Christina pull me out on the dance floor.

I try resisting. "I don't think you want me to do this."

"It's the easiest line dance in the history of line dances," Andie says. "Cupid Shuffle. Just do what we do. Right four steps to the count of eight, then left. Then heel tap eight times, turn left a quarter turn for a count of eight, then start over."

I try to wrap my brain around what she told me, go the wrong direction, and run into her. "I told you I'm terrible at this."

She laces our elbows together. "Do it with me."

I follow her lead, watching my feet the entire time, counting to eight out loud and then repeating.

"Look at you," she says. "You're doing it."

She removes her arm from mine, and I try and keep up. I turn right a quarter turn instead of left and am facing the back when everyone is facing front. Owen and some of the guys are laughing at me. I bump into the guy next to me and he gives me a biting stare.

"First time. Cut me a break," I say.

The songs ends, and we return to our table.

"Thank God that's over," I say and slam down another shot.

Bobby says, "There are plenty of men willing to dance with her if you want to sit the next one out."

"Meaning you."

"Sure. Why not?"

There are a hundred reasons I can think of, but I keep my mouth shut. I check the time and wonder how long we have to stay. Andie and I came together, so I'm stuck here until she decides to leave.

She and her friends go out for another line dance while Bobby and I hang back and drink. I don't miss how he's watching her every move. I try to distract him, because I really don't like the way he's staring at her. "How're things in Wyoming?"

"Not as hot as they are here," he says, throwing back a shot.

Is he talking about the weather? "Do you work for a large ranch?"

"It's about a hundred thousand acres."

"Impressive. How many horses?"

"Five hundred. Do you really want to talk about my job?"

"Just making conversation."

"She told you about us, didn't she?"

"She did."

"Probably didn't paint me in a very good light."

"On the contrary. She said she was the one who broke the pact."

He laughs sadly. "It was better to let her think that."

He has my full and complete attention. "What do you mean?"

"We were getting too close. We both had plans that involved us being a thousand miles apart. It was easier to pretend she was another casual affair than to tell her the truth."

"The truth?"

"Maddox!" Andie yells from the dance floor. She's waving me over.

Several couples start doing the Texas Two-Step again. I shake my head.

Bobby stands. "I'll go."

I get up so fast, my barstool almost topples over. "I've got this." The other couples effortlessly dance together, and I wonder why in the hell I agreed to this. Maybe it would have been better to let Bobby dance with her than for me to look like a complete idiot.

Andie pulls me aside. "It's pretty easy. Quick, quick, slow, slow. Your body keeps moving at the same pace, but your feet follow the quick, quick, slow, slow pattern. Lead with your left foot. Try it here and then we'll join the others." She shows me where to put my hands. "When you move forward, I move back."

I study the couples dancing for a minute and then we try it.

"Good. Again."

"This isn't that hard," I say.

She pulls me out onto the dance floor. I keep the beat in my head. Quick, quick, slow, slow.

"Okay, now do a promenade," she says.

"There's more?"

"We open up our stance and move in the same direction, like them. Four steps and then back to the first part."

Although I feel like I have two left feet, I'm able to do it without tripping us both.

"Now spin me."

"Do you want to end up flat on the floor?"

"Do it, Maddox."

I fail miserably, run into her, and have to catch her before she topples the couple next to us. She laughs like she doesn't care that I just embarrassed us both.

The song changes to a slow one, and she puts her arms around my neck. I sigh with relief. "This I can handle."

"You weren't bad for a first timer."

"I wasn't good either."

"You have to start somewhere."

Bobby's watching us. If looks could kill, I'd be hanging on a meat hook. If I were a betting man, I'd say his feelings for her haven't changed.

"I'm glad to see you two getting along," Andie says.

I chuckle. "If that's what you call it."

"You're not?"

"He still has a thing for you."

"He never had a thing for me, Maddox. It was all about sex."

"Mind if we don't talk about Bobby right now?" I pull her closer and smell her hair. I feel her body against mine. This is the closest we've ever been to being on a date, with the huge exception of her ex also being here. "This is nice."

She gazes at me sweetly. "Yeah."

She settles her head against my shoulder. Her thumb tickles the nape of my neck when she moves it back and forth. I quid pro quo by circling my finger in the small strip of skin showing between her skirt and top. Her chest heaves, and I smile. Part of me wonders if Dr. Bobby is watching, and part of me doesn't care, because the way this feels right now is indescribable. She's in my arms. She fits against me like every curve of her body was made to match every curve of mine. I might be enjoying dancing with Andie as much as I enjoy sex with her. It's a feeling I've never had with any other woman.

The song ends, and I curse in my head as we go back to the table and *him*. I order more shots. I sit and listen to Andie and Bobby reminisce about vet school. I drink and order more.

I wait as long as I can before excusing myself to use the bathroom, because quite frankly, I question my ability to walk in a straight line. "I'll be right back."

Before I go down the hallway, I take a look at our table. Bobby scoots closer to her. I hope the line isn't long. I dart into the bathroom, do my thing, barely wash up, and hurry back. But they're not at the table anymore. Christina points to the dance floor, and there he is, his hands on her, dancing slow like she belongs to him. "Fuck that," I say, running into a chair on my way to them. I tap his shoulder. "I'll take it from here."

"Song's almost over," he says. "We're good."

I stand and stare, wanting to punch him in the nose, but as I'm seeing two of him, I wouldn't know which one to aim for. Couples whirl around me, and I almost lose my balance.

"Whoa, cowboy," Andie says, running over. "I think it's time we got you home."

"Now that's the best thing you've said all night." I pull out my wallet and throw money at the table as we go past, then get out my keys.

Andie takes them. "I'm driving."

We quickly say goodbye to everyone. Bobby follows us out. "You want help?"

"We don't need your help," I say.

"I was asking Andie."

"I'm fine," she says. "We'll be fine. We drove together anyway. It was nice seeing you again, Bobby."

"I can't see you tomorrow?"

"I have work and then Granddad is coming for supper."

"I'd like to meet Gerald."

"I'm not sure that's a good idea." We get to my truck, and she hugs him. "If you're ever back down here, look me up."

He kisses her cheek. "You know I will." He leans in and thinks I can't hear him when he whispers, "I missed you."

We get in the truck, and he moves back, looking defeated. I try not to gloat, but as we pull away, I lean over and wipe her cheek.

"Why did you do that?"

"Because I don't want anyone's lips on you but mine."

"You're drunk."

"Most definitely," I slur. "Doesn't mean it's not true."

The next thing I know, she's helping me out of the truck at the ranch. Once inside, I grab her. "Dance with me."

"I think we need to get you to bed, cowboy."

"I like that idea even better."

She swats my arm. "I mean so you don't fall down or puke all over."

She leads me to the bedroom, and I barely make it to the bed before I collapse. I pull her down. "Stay with me."

She doesn't answer, but the last thing I see before I pass out are her baby blue eyes, and I wonder if she ever looked at him the way she's looking at me.

CHAPTER THIRTY-TWO

Andie

Every time he moves, I look at him. I can see him clearly in the moonlight coming through the window. I didn't dare go back to my place. He got so drunk, I didn't want him to get up and chance falling down the stairs. I took off his clothes. Left him in nothing but boxer briefs. He's sleeping so soundly, I contemplate laying my head on his chest. This is the closest we've come to sleeping together, but I know it's not real. Even though he asked me to stay, he didn't mean it. Staying the night is definitely not casual. I inch closer so I can smell him, then drift to sleep.

Sunlight wakes me. Maddox is still dead to the world. Snoring even. I get out of bed and smell booze. It's all over my clothes. I should go home and shower. I glance in the bathroom and decide to use his instead. I go in his closet and pick out a T-shirt and sweatpants I know will be ginormously big on me, but I don't want to put on my clothes from last night.

I use his shampoo and realize I'm going to smell like him all day. I might like the thought of that a little too much. My hair is full of suds when the shower door opens, startling me. "Maddox!"

He slips in behind me. "If you're going to use my shower, you'd better be prepared for company."

He works his hands through my hair, massaging in the shampoo. My eyes close at how good it feels, and I tilt my head back, giving him better access. He takes his time rinsing my hair, making sure every strand is clean. I don't think I've ever had a more thorough hair washing. "Now you."

I squirt shampoo in my hand and stand on my tiptoes to reach the top of his head. He kind of half squats so I don't slip and fall. As I watch the suds run down his body, I can't help but see his erection standing at full attention. I look into his eyes and smile deviously as I drop to my knees. He knows exactly what I'm doing, and is ecstatic.

"Wait," he says.

"I thought you wanted—"

"I do." He reaches out of the shower for a towel. "But I'll enjoy it more knowing you won't hurt your knees." He folds the towel several times and puts it on the shower floor. I kneel on it.

I put my mouth on him. I've never been a huge fan of giving blow jobs, but right now there's nothing I want to do more. I run my tongue along each side. When I lick the sensitive skin under the glans, he draws in a breath. I rim the tip and then take him in fully. He grips my head just enough to let me know how much he likes what I'm doing.

I go fast, then slow. Then I stop and use my hand. With him in my mouth again, I play with his balls. He groans and moves his hips faster. When he lets go of my head and braces himself against the shower wall, I know he's close. His penis jerks, he grunts, and I pull away, finishing him off with my hand.

"Dang," he says, breathless and still recovering from his orgasm. "That was…" He helps me up and wipes a piece of wet hair off my face. "Thank you."

I blush, never before having been thanked for that act.

He squirts body wash in his palm and turns me around so I'm facing the wall. His soapy hands travel over my shoulders, down my arms, and across my back. He hasn't even touched me where it counts, yet this is already the most erotic shower I've ever taken. He reaches around and soaps my breasts, pinching my stiff nipples. I let my head fall back against his shoulder. Fingers blaze a trail down my stomach, and I arch into him, needing his touch. He leans over and lifts my right foot up on the shower seat, then runs a finger around my clit several times before inserting it inside me.

My moans echo off the tile walls. He kisses my neck and turns me around. He aims the shower in the other direction and sits me down on the seat in the corner. He moves the wet towel into position and drops to his knees in front of me, then opens my legs so I'm shamelessly on display in all my natural glory.

"Jesus," he says, appraising me like I'm a priceless piece of art.

I've never been so turned on and emotionally charged before. Does this man have any idea how much I want him? Not just for this. For everything. Does he understand how devastated I'll be when he leaves?

His mouth is all over me—my thighs, my stomach, my breasts. I'm about to detonate even before he puts it *there*. When I can't take it anymore, I guide his head between my legs. He chuckles and devours me in the most pleasurable way. Fondling my breast with one hand and working fingers inside me with the other, his tongue lashes my clit, bringing me to an explosive orgasm.

I sink against the wall and breathe through my recovery as he stands and aims the warm water towards us.

He takes a melodramatic bow and mimics Elvis. "Thank you. Thank you very much."

I swat his thigh. "Shut up." He pulls me up for a kiss. I can taste myself on his lips. The guys I've been with don't like to kiss after sex. When they're finished, that's it.

The water becomes tepid. He turns it off and reaches for a dry towel. He dries me off before drying himself.

The doorbell rings. "Who the hell around here rings a doorbell?" He grabs a dry towel and wraps it around his waist.

"You're going to the door like *that*?"

He winks and runs out of the room. I towel dry my hair and find a comb, then finger-brush my teeth and throw on the clothes I borrowed. Downstairs, Maddox is in the kitchen, staring at two large bunches of flowers on the table.

"They're for you," he says. "The delivery man tried your place, but there was no answer, so he brought them here."

"For me? Both of them?"

"That's what he said. Are you going to see who they're from?"

I pull the first card from a giant bunch of orchids, read it, and smile.

"Let me guess. They're from Dr. Wyoming."

"Yes." I hold out the card. "Want to read it?"

"No."

I read it to him. "It says: 'I may have forgotten what a good dancer you are, but I could never forget your favorite flower.'"

"If orchids are your favorite flower, why did he also send roses?"

"I have no idea." I pluck the card from the roses. "These aren't from Bobby. They're from Victor."

He snatches the card and reads it aloud. "'I miss you, Andie. I'm ready to tell you everything if you're ready to listen. I don't want to go another minute without you. Am I too late?'" He looks worried. "I thought we'd heard the last of him." The doorbell rings again. "I swear to God, if it's more flowers, I'm going to shove them down the throat of the delivery guy."

I walk over and peek through the curtains. "It's not. It's Wyatt Jenkins."

"Hugh's son?"

"Go get dressed. I'll see what he wants." I let Wyatt in. He looks like death warmed over. "Are you okay?"

"No, Andie, not really. My dad told me I needed to talk to Maddox. Is he here?"

"He'll be right down. Can I get you some coffee?"

He shakes his head. "I've had enough coffee in the last twenty-four hours to last me a lifetime, but thanks."

Maddox bounds down the stairs. "I don't think the two of you have officially met," I say. "Maddox McBride, this is Wyatt Jenkins."

"Good to finally meet you," Maddox says. "I hear you'll be taking over your dad's ranch when he and your mom move here."

Wyatt gestures to the couch. "Can we sit? I've been up all night, and I'm not sure I can get through this without collapsing."

"What's going on, Wyatt?" I ask.

We all sit. "My dad is in the hospital. He was in a bad accident yesterday."

"Oh no. Please tell me he's going to be okay."

His eyes glaze over. "Eventually he might, but he'll never be the same. He was trailering a new mare up from Austin and blew a tire." His voice cracks. "The trailer jackknifed and buckled on top of his truck in a ditch. Both Dad's legs are broken pretty badly, along with his back. He'll be in the hospital for weeks, need multiple surgeries, and then he'll be transferred to a rehab facility, where they hope he'll be able to learn to walk again. The mare was so badly injured, she had to be put down."

Tears fall, and I take Wyatt's hand. "I'm so sorry."

"He won't be buying Devil's Horn Ranch after all. He sent me over to give his apologies."

"He was in a terrible accident, and he's apologizing to me?" Maddox stands and paces. "I should be asking what we can do for you. Please let us know if we can help."

"I've got it handled, or I will after I get some sleep."

"Tell him I'm praying for him," I say. "And let me know when he's ready for visitors. He's always been one of my favorite clients."

Wyatt stands and shakes hands with Maddox. "I'm real sorry about this. I know you were hoping to sell quickly."

"Don't give it another thought," Maddox says. "Just make sure your dad is taken care of."

He leaves, and we stare after him.

"What now?" I ask.

"I don't know. I have to call my dad."

I go out on the porch, sit, and rock, trying to work off anxiety. "He'll sell to Joel Thompson now, won't he?"

"I promise I'll do everything I can to make sure that doesn't happen."

"But it's not your decision to make, Maddox. Joel is an interested buyer. Word is Dillon Patlinger, the only other half-decent potential buyer, has moved on to other opportunities. Not many people are in the market for a ten-thousand-acre ranch."

He sits in the chair next to me. "I'm sorry, Andie. I don't know what to say."

My phone rings. Bobby's face appears, and I hesitate.

"Are you going to answer it?"

I pick it up. "Hello?"

"Did you get the flowers?"

"They're beautiful. Thank you."

"I was up all night thinking about you. I didn't know how I'd feel seeing you after all this time, but the truth is I haven't stopped thinking about you since graduation."

I'm sure Maddox can hear Bobby talking. He gets up and goes in the house, slamming the screen door loudly behind him.

"What are you saying, Bobby?"

"Come back to Wyoming with me."

"Wh-what?" I shove my foot against the porch floor, stilling the rocker. Beau walks over and puts his head in my lap.

"You heard me. I want you, Andie. I've always wanted you. I was stupid to let you think you were the only one who had feelings back then. But I know what I want now, and I'm not afraid of it anymore."

"I, uh… my job is here, Bobby. My granddad."

"Bring him, and I'll get you a job. A good one. We could even go into practice together."

Maddox is staring at me from the other side of the screen door. I'm not sure whether to laugh or cry. Three months ago I was single with no prospects in sight, and I'd been perfectly fine with that. But now there are *three* men in my life. Two of them are all but declaring their love for me while the one I want is about to pack his bags and move two thousand miles away.

"Andie?"

"I don't know what to say, Bobby."

"Don't say anything. Just think about it. I couldn't leave town without telling you how I feel. You don't have to decide today or even this week. I'm not going anywhere. I want you. I... I love you." Someone says something to him in the background. "I have to go. Promise me you'll think about it."

"Okay."

The phone goes dead and I drop it in my lap.

"I knew it," Maddox says from inside. "He swooping in like a knight in shining armor?"

I'm still trying to wrap my brain around it. "Kind of. He wants me to go to Wyoming with him. Even offered to go into practice with me. He said I should bring Granddad too."

He shoves his hands in his pockets and sighs. "Sounds like a hard thing to pass up. With Jenkins pulling out of the sale, you don't know if your job is secure. Looks like he's offering you everything you ever wanted." He walks away.

"Maddox—"

I want to run after him, tell him maybe that *used* to be what I wanted, but now I'm not so sure.

"Andie!" Merle yells from the stable. "We need you. Old Man Kingsley fed his mare too many apples again."

Jerimiah Kingsley boards his horse here and this is the third time this month I've had to deal with this same issue. I think he's got dementia or something. "Be right there."

I peer through the screen into Maddox's house, but he's gone, so I head home to change before going to the stables.

I'm on my way to the guesthouse to get ready to pick up Granddad when he gets out of the back of a car in front of the barn. "I was coming to pick you up in thirty minutes."

"There's this thing called Uber," he says, showing me his phone. "They know right where you are, you input the address you're goin' to, and you don't even need any cash. It's genius."

"I know, but you shouldn't waste your money."

"You don't need to be drivin' me around everywhere. You have enough on your plate. Besides, I wanted to come early and see this new gelding of yours."

"He's in the south stable." We make our way back. "Granddad, meet Connecticut."

He looks at me with crazy eyes. "You named him Connecticut? That's a strange name for a horse, if you ask me."

Maddox exits the tack room. I haven't laid eyes on him since this morning. He obviously knows I'm here, but he ignores me and leaves the stable. "I think it suits him. Come on. I know you like to eat early, so I put a roast in the Crock-Pot. Should be about done."

We pass the arena on our way to the guesthouse. Maddox is watching Mickey train Shawshank or Doc or whatever he decided to call him. I'm glad he bought him; from the looks of it, he's going to make a fine horse. Mickey's lunging him, and he appears to be an old pro.

Granddad stops. "Maddox, join us for supper?"

Maddox avoids all eye contact with me. "Thanks, but I'm going to stay here with Doc. I'll grab something later."

"Suit yourself," Granddad says. "You're going to miss a fine pot roast."

"Nice to see you again, Gerald."

Granddad turns to me. "Something happen between you two? He doesn't seem like himself. Don't have that sparkle in his eye."

"He's preoccupied with his horse. It's the first one he's ever owned."

"*Hmmph.* If you say so."

Before we can go inside, a convoy of trucks pulls onto the property. Only one man in town travels with an entourage. "What do *they* want?" I glance at Maddox, knowing he won't be happy.

Maddox leaves the arena. Granddad and I stop and wait, out of curiosity if nothing else. Joel and Jon get out of the first pickup. Several broad-shouldered men exit the two others.

"He's not welcome here," Maddox says, gesturing to Jon. "And he damn well knows it."

"Hold on there," Joel says. "This is a friendly visit." He turns to Jon. "You gonna behave yourself, son?"

Jon leans against the car with a sneer on his face.

"He says yes," Joel says.

Maddox puts himself between them and Granddad and me. Owen and some of the others wander over. "Why are you here?" Maddox asks.

"Word is Jenkins had himself an accident." Joel shakes his head like he's sad about it, but we all know he's not. "A shame. Old guys like us don't heal as quickly as we used to. Heard he'll be out of commission for months, maybe longer. I'm guessing that means the ranch is up for sale again."

Owen says around a piece of straw in his mouth, "Rumor is that was no accident. His tire was shot out."

Maddox and I look at each other in surprise.

Joel laughs. "Now where'd you hear a crazy thing like that?"

"Two people ridin' horses nearby said they heard a few gunshots right before they came upon the accident."

"Oh, they heard gunshots, did they? They see a gunman?"

Owen shrugs.

"It was the tire blowin' out," Joel says. "You ever hear a tire blow out? Sounds damn similar to a shotgun. Happened to me once. Scariest thing I ever lived through. Shame about his mare."

"And you thought you'd swoop right in and buy this place?" Maddox says. "What makes you think we'd sell it to you?"

"Doesn't look like you have much choice. You talk to your daddy yet?"

"I don't think that's any of your business."

Joel chuckles. "I'll take that as a yes. You tell him I'm ready to negotiate when he is. The competition has dwindled, and I imagine I can get this place for a song now."

Granddad moves toward Joel, furious. "You backstabbing murderous bastard."

Jon pushes off the truck, scowling. Joel shakes his head, and Jon backs down like an obedient dog. "Maybe you better watch what you say, Gerald," Joel says. "I might have to sue you for slander."

"We both know that's a crock of manure after the things you've done. Blown tire, my ass. Which one of your men did the dirty work this time?"

Joel grabs Granddad's arm. "Watch yourself, old man." He glances at me. "If you know what's good for you and yours."

Maddox intervenes. "Take your hands off him, or you'll have me to deal with."

Joel backs away and laughs. "You and what army?"

Owen and half a dozen others move up behind Maddox and cross their arms. Joel's guys do the same behind him. My heart races, wondering who will be the first to do something stupid.

I pull Granddad toward the guesthouse, out of the line of fire, but he resists.

Maddox and Joel exchange a few more words and then Joel flicks his wrist. His men retreat to their trucks and leave.

We join the others. "You think Joel had something to do with Jenkins' accident?" Maddox asks Owen.

"He wants Devil's Horn Ranch. I wouldn't put it past him."

"Me neither." Granddad taps on his phone. "That family is toxic, and somebody best do something about it."

"What are you doing, Granddad?"

"Ordering me one of those Uber things." He kisses the side of my head. "Apologies, pumpkin. Can't stay for supper."

"Why not?"

"I ain't hungry. Remembered something I need to take care of."

"You're scaring me."

"Nothing for you to be worried about. Everything will be fine."

Maddox says, "Gerald, you can't go after him. You'll never win. Not even if everyone here joined you."

"I don't plan on going after Joel—not in the sense you're thinkin'. I just need to take care of something that's long overdue."

For the next fifteen minutes, I beg him not to go. I have no idea what he's planning, but if it has anything to do with the Thompsons, it's a mistake.

Granddad's ride pulls up. "You stay close to Maddox and the other folks here at the ranch. Promise me."

"Only if you promise you won't go after Joel."

"I promise."

"Or Jon."

"I promise that, too."

"And you'll call me tomorrow?"

"Sure thing. How about you put your pot roast on ice, and we'll get to it then?"

"I'll pick you up. No more wasting your money on rides, okay?"

"It's a date." He turns to Maddox. "You'll come to supper too, won't you?"

Maddox glances at me. "I suppose."

"Whatever bugs you two got up your butts, work 'em out by then."

He gets in the car, and it drives off.

"Where do you think he's going?" I ask.

"Beats me. Does he own a gun?"

"Not since he moved into the retirement home."

"Well at least there's that."

"There is no way I'll be able to sleep tonight."

"I could keep you company."

"You mean after giving me the cold shoulder all day, you want to entertain me tonight? No, thank you. There are things I need to do."

"Things like figuring out if you're moving to Wyoming?"

"It's not that easy, Maddox. In fact it's pretty complicated."

He kicks the dirt. "You'd really consider moving?"

"I don't know what I'm going to do. There's a lot to think about."

"We were supposed to look at houses tomorrow. Is that still happening?"

"I don't know. Actually, yes. I want to keep all my options open."

"Options." He laughs sadly. "So Bobby is still one of them."

"I don't see anyone else offering." *Oh, god. Did I just say that?* "I have to go."

"Andie," he calls after me.

I'm embarrassed. "Forget I said that. Today has been weird. Let's meet at noon tomorrow, like we planned. Don't read too much into anything."

"Don't worry about your granddad. He'll be okay."

There is a twist in my gut. I feel strongly *nothing* will be okay.

CHAPTER THIRTY-THREE

Sitting on the porch, drinking my morning coffee, I gaze at the guesthouse. Is she considering Bobby's offer? He had some nerve coming down here after this long, thinking he could swoop her up and live happily ever after.

I contemplate bringing her coffee. It would be an excuse to see where her head is. I'll be seeing her at noon to look at houses, but I'm not sure I can wait that long. I sit not-so-patiently and wait for her to emerge, checking the time every few minutes. She's usually up by now. That she isn't might mean she was up late thinking.

Beau looks at the guesthouse and moans unhappily. He, too, seems to know her schedule.

Glowering, Owen strides across the yard. "Aaron stay in the house with you last night?"

I stand abruptly. "No, why?"

"He didn't sleep in his bunk. Nobody has seen him since supper."

I rub my temples. "The last damn thing I need right now is another crisis."

"Want me to send a few guys out?"

"Not yet." I set down my cup, put on my hat, and head for the barn. "My guess is he's out at the airstrip again. I'll take a four-wheeler."

He accompanies me across the yard. "Not to make a bad day worse, but you talk to your dad about Jenkins yet?"

"Called him last night."

"And?"

"I'm not sure what to tell you. There aren't many options left."

His shoulders fall. "Thompson's making sure of that, isn't he?"

"I hate it as much as you do." I scan the equipment when we get to the barn. "One of the ATVs is missing."

"You let me know if you need help with Aaron. We've always got your back."

"Thanks, man."

I drive away, thinking about what he said. He and everyone else on this ranch might be about to lose their jobs, but they still have my back. What a difference from the world I came from, where it's every man for himself.

The entire way to the airstrip, I wonder what I'm going to tell Uncle Griffin and Aunt Skylar. They expected planting Aaron at the ranch would shape him up, teach him values, but it's not working. I don't want to be the bearer of bad news. I've done enough of that lately.

There's no one at the airstrip. I don't know whether to be relieved or worried. I can't call him; he doesn't have a phone. If the Thompson kid picked him up, I'll have to deal with Karen or even Joel. My stomach curdles at the thought.

Following a hunch, I drive to the hunting lodge and see the missing four-wheeler. I pull up next to it and run inside. Aaron is sitting on the grand staircase next to an almost-empty bottle of whiskey I recognize as one of mine.

"You swipe that from my cabinet?"

"What do you care?"

"Are you still hungover?"

He holds up the bottle and takes a swig. "Still drunk."

I march over and take it from him. "What the hell are you doing, Aaron? Do you want to screw this up and end up at military school? You don't realize how easy you have it here. This place is fucking amazing if you think about it for two seconds. The people here—they have your back, yet you're doing everything in your power to leave." I glance in the room where Andie and I first made love. "And all I want to do is stay."

"There's a big difference between you and me, cousin. You think my life has been easy? Gracie is the goddamn golden child. She can do no wrong. She gets bad grades in school, and my parents blame the teachers, but the first time I get in trouble, they ship me here."

"The way I hear it, it wasn't the first time."

"You don't know shit. How could you? Your parents actually wanted you."

"What in the hell are you talking about?"

"I was never supposed to be my mom's kid. Did you know that?"

"We all know."

"My dad didn't want me either. Did you know that too?" I stare blankly. "I didn't think so. Erin was the only one who wanted me. After she was gone, my parents had no choice. Gracie's always been the wanted one. I was the one they had to deal with."

"Bullshit, Aaron. You can't sit here and pretend your parents don't love you. I've seen it. Birthdays, holidays, Sunday brunches. Gracie is younger, so she gets more attention. It's the same for my sisters. And they're girls—things are different for them. But don't mistake that and think your parents love her more."

"You have no idea," he says. "I found letters about six months ago."

That was when Uncle Griffin said Aaron had started acting out. "Letters?"

"Erin wrote them to my parents. Your mom and Uncle Mason held onto them, with instructions to give the letters to my parents under certain circumstances. One of those circumstances was if my dad ran away. Before I was even born, he decided he didn't want me."

"He'd lost his wife. Maybe you could cut him some slack."

"And my mom? She was never supposed to be my mom. She wanted to give me away. She had to be convinced to keep me."

I sit next to him. "You're fifteen. Life seems all black and white to you, but it's not that way. Things happen. Life throws you curveballs. Sometimes you end up places you never thought you'd be. That doesn't mean you shouldn't be there."

"You can't possibly understand."

I laugh. "Oh, really? Maybe you've forgotten *my* story. I spent the first seven years of my life thinking I had a deadbeat father who wanted nothing to do with me. You think I never thought about how my mom got pregnant with me when she was eighteen? That's the last thing she wanted. Does that mean I shouldn't be here?

Does that mean I should be mad at her? No. She may not have wanted a baby at such a young age, but guess what? She was the best damn mom I could have hoped for. Just like your mom is the best. We both hit the jackpot where parents are concerned, and I'm in no way talking about money. Our family is amazing, Aaron. Our mothers and Aunt Piper are about as close as three sisters can be. Our dads are best friends. We grew up with cousins, aunts, uncles, and grandparents who love us fiercely. All of us. If you stand back and look at the big picture, you'll see you have two parents who love you so much, they'd fucking die for you."

"Yeah, they sent me here because they love me so much."

I slap the hardwood stair. "That's exactly why they sent you here. Tough love, Aaron. Sometimes it's a parent's last resort. If they didn't care about you, why not let you drop out of school? If they didn't love you, why would they be worried about you smoking weed or hanging with the wrong crowd? Parents who don't care are happy to have you out of the house."

"If they loved me, they would let me find my own way."

"I wish I could record this and play it back to you one day. At your age, everything seems like the end of the world. It's not. You don't have problems, Aaron. Look around you. This place we've worked so hard to restore, it's probably going to be mowed down. Those horses you're caring for will be gone—boarded at other stables that may not be as good for them. Or they'll be auctioned off for horse meat. All those guys you've been bunking with these past weeks? They're about to lose their jobs, and who knows where their next paychecks will come from. Where will they go? Will they even have roofs over their heads? *Those* are real problems."

He rubs a knot in a stair baluster. "What do I do now? I kind of fucked everything up."

I hand him my phone. "Call your parents. Tell them the truth. Things will get better if you do."

He takes the phone but doesn't make the call.

"It's time to man up, Aaron." I stand and go to the door. "I'll wait outside."

I pace the porch, gazing at the old rusted cars beside the lodge. I wanted to haul them off, but Aaron thought they gave the place character. He might be right. But at this point, I'm not about to lift a damn finger to improve this place if Thompson is going to replace it with condos.

Ten minutes later, the door opens, and Aaron hands me the phone.

"So?"

"Dad is booking a flight tomorrow. Says he's clearing his schedule to come spend time with me."

I smile. "That hardly sounds like a father who doesn't love his kid. He's a busy man."

"Mom wanted to come, too, but Dad said we needed some father-son time." He places a hand on the porch railing. "Do you think he'd want to help me finish restoring this place?"

I want to tell him not to bother, but I don't. "I think it's a fine idea."

"Are you going to tell him I got drunk?"

"I'm willing to keep it between us if you promise to give him and your mom a chance."

He nods.

"Let's go, then. I have something important to do at noon."

Twelve o'clock comes and goes without any word from Andie. Her truck never left the ranch, so I wander through the stables. When I can't find her, I call Matteo. "Is Andie out in one of the pastures?"

"She's not typically here on Monday mornings. She should be at Thousand Acre Ranch."

"I know that, but her truck is here."

"Maybe she's taking the day off. She didn't seem in good sorts last night after her granddad left. You check her house?"

"On my way there now."

I knock on her door and wait. I knock again. I get out my phone.

Me: Are you at home?

I sit on her porch and wait for a reply. A few minutes go by, so I text again.

Me: Where are you? It's almost one o'clock. We were supposed to meet at noon.

A minute later, I send another.

Me: Andie, what's going on?

I get a terrible feeling in my belly. Did she decide to leave with Bobby? I run back to my place and get the key to the guesthouse.

"Andie?" I yell as I enter and look around. Everything appears to be in order except for the half-full glass of wine on the table and the open bottle next to it. The master bedroom door is open, her bed perfectly made. I check the bathroom and see her things on the counter. I peek in the closet and her clothes are still there. Part of me is relieved. Then again, where is she?

I sit on the bed and text her again.

Me: Andie, just tell me if you're with Bobby. You're beginning to scare me.

On the way back to my house, the phone rings. I'm overjoyed when I see Andie's face. "Hey. Are you okay?"

"Uh… yeah."

She sounds muffled, and I can tell a man is with her, but I can't hear what he's saying.

"Andie?"

"I'm here."

"What's going on? You didn't go to work today, and your truck is here. Where are you? Did he pick you up?"

"I… I need time to think."

"With *him?* You need time to think with Bobby? Don't do it, Andie. He blew you off. He only wants you because he saw you with me. That's how our brains are wired. Come back, and we can talk."

"I need more time." Her words are short, clipped.

"How much time?" I almost blurt out something stupid, like, "Forget him", or "I love you and I'll do anything to have you, including shoveling shit on someone else's ranch." Because it's true. I knew it before Bobby Monahan came here and threatened everything. "Andie?"

"I don't know. Just more time. And beer. I really could use a beer."

The line goes dead, and I almost throw up. She said beer. She said it twice.

I immediately try to call back, but it goes to voicemail. I page through my contacts and find Katherine. I get her voicemail, too, but on the way to my truck, I leave her a message.

"Katherine, it's Maddox McBride. You need to get here now. Andie's missing, and I got a strange call from her. She said she needed beer. You know what that means. I'm going to Victor's right now. Please bring whoever you can and meet me there."

Owen sees me running to my truck. "Where's the fire?"

"Andie's missing. Victor has her. She's in trouble."

He yells to Zac to bring his gun. "I'm not letting you go alone."

"Hopefully I won't be. I called the FBI."

Zac, Merle, and Matteo run over and get in the truck with us. Owen says, "I told you we got your back, city boy." He calls the police, and I hear a lot of back and forth. He's getting mad. He throws his phone on the seat. "They say they'll send the first available officer."

"First available officer? How long will that take? I fucking know who has her."

"I told him. He said it's probably a false alarm and that things like this happen all the time, and the missing people almost always show up."

"That's bullshit. She gave me the code word."

"I'm sorry, man. Hopefully your friend from the FBI will show up."

"Fuck." I speed and get to Victor's house in record time. "Owen, come with me. The rest of you surround the house." I try the handle; it's locked. I bang on the door. "Open up!"

"Move aside," Owen says.

I do and he kicks in the door. I run inside. "Andie!" Owen and I go through every room of the house.

"She's not here," he says.

I sit down and put my head in my hands. "I can't sit here and do nothing." Suddenly, I remember the ring. "Oh, shit." I bring up the app on my phone, but there's nothing. Either she can't activate the microphone, or she's out of range.

"Get inside the house, motherfucker," I hear from outside.

Matteo comes in with Victor, pointing a gun to his head. I pull out my own gun and aim it at him. "Where is she?"

"Where's who?"

"Andie. I know you have her."

He turns green. "Andie is missing?"

"Don't pretend like you don't know, *Tim Dorsey*."

He turns ashen.

"Yeah," I say. "The jig is up. We know you have her, and we know you killed Jennifer Grossman."

"What are you talking about? I have no idea where Andie is, and I had nothing to do with Jennifer's disappearance."

I holster my gun, walk over, and punch him. "Where the fuck is she?"

He spits blood and looks at me with eyes full of fear. "Jesus, Maddox, I don't have her. If she's missing, you've got the wrong guy, and we need to find her."

I force him to sit on the couch. "You expect me to believe you? We gave her a code word to use if she ever felt threatened. She just used it."

"What do you mean, you gave her a code word. Who's *we?*"

"The FBI."

He swallows. "You're with the FBI?"

"No, but Katherine is… uh, Melina. We've been watching you for months. We know you killed that girl."

"I didn't kill anyone! *Months?* And Andie knew?"

"Andie was part of it, you scumbag. Of course she knew."

"It makes so much sense now. All her questions, the prying and bargaining for information." He runs a hand through his hair. "I'm not who you think I am."

"You're Tim Dorsey. Before you were Victor, you were Neil somebody. We know all about how you move around to avoid the police."

"I'm not Tim Dorsey, and I don't move around to avoid the police."

Owen puts his gun to Victor's temple. "We don't have time for this shit. Tell us where she is."

"I'm telling you, I don't know! And I'm not Tim Dorsey. You have to listen to me so we can find Andie."

"You have ten seconds before I shoot you in the foot," Owen says.

"My name is Matt Cryer," he says, sobbing. "I'm running from my father, Nolan Cryer, who killed my younger sister five years ago. Look it up. She died in a fire. He set it but got off on a technicality, and it was found to be accidental. Google it. Do it now."

"What's your sister's name?"

"Megan Cryer. She was fifteen. We lived in Missouri."

I google *Megan Cryer dead house fire Missouri.*

I read the article. "You're lying. If you're Matt Cryer, you're dead. He died in the fire, along with his sister."

"That's it," Owen says, cocking the gun. "I'm shooting his foot."

Victor cries out.

"Jesus, he pissed himself," Matteo says.

"Listen to me," Victor says. "I wasn't in the house. It was my best friend, Tim Dorsey. My dad is a psycho. He beat me and did horrific things to Megan. I was almost eighteen. I could have left a hundred times. I even tried once, took Megan with me, but he found us. He's ex-military and had ways of finding stuff out. I was home when the fire started, but Megan and Tim were in the basement. I couldn't get to them, so I ran, barely escaping. The closest neighbors were half a mile away. I hid in the trees and saw my dad come out of the shed. Instead of running toward the house and trying to save us, he stood there and watched it burn. I swear to God, he had a smile on his face. It was that moment when I knew I needed him to think I was dead. He told Megan and me over and over, after he tracked us down, that he'd kill us if we ever left. Tim was my best friend, a foster kid who'd recently aged out of the system. It was easy to become him. We were the same age and we both had brown hair and brown eyes. I broke into his apartment and took what I could—social security card, some utility bills. Anything I could use to get a new driver's license. But one day when I visited Megan's grave, my father found me there. I never thought he'd go to the cemetery. Why would he? He'd killed us. But it was too late. He saw me, chased me, and vowed to kill me. He said he'd make sure people knew *I* started the fire that killed Megan and Tim. So I ran, and I kept running. Every so often I'd assume a different identity to keep him off my trail."

"You expect us to believe all that bullshit?"

"It's true." Katherine is in the doorway with Michael. "We hadn't gotten around to telling you yet, Maddox. Someone from

Missouri, one of Tim's foster parents, recognized a picture an agent of ours posted in the newspaper. The woman said it wasn't Tim but his best friend, Matt Cryer."

I'm stunned. "What do you mean, you hadn't gotten around to telling me yet? Are you fucking kidding me? You're telling me this asshole isn't the guy who took Andie?"

"I didn't take her!" he yells. "And you're wasting time sitting here with me when we should be out finding her."

"There's no *we*," Katherine says. "Just because you didn't kidnap Andie doesn't mean you're not in trouble. Matt, I sympathize with you, and we'll do everything we can to help, but you have broken laws."

"I don't care about that right now. You need to find Andie."

"We will," she says. "Maddox, she called you?"

"Yes, but when I called her back, it went to voicemail. I think she's wearing the ring, but I'm getting nothing from the microphone. Oh man, Bobby can track her phone. He said he used a tracking app to find her at the bar the other night. Bobby Monahan from Wyoming. Can you get his cell number?" I stiffen as something occurs to me. "Jesus, what if *he's* the one who has her? They used to be a thing, and he's in town. He sent her flowers yesterday and asked her to go to Wyoming with him."

Katherine gives me a sympathetic look. "Are you sure she didn't? That would explain a lot."

"She used the code word, Katherine. I'm sure."

"You seem to know her better than anyone. I'll have to take your word for it. We'll call Bobby, and we should talk to her next of kin. She has a grandfather in town. Can you take me to him? Michael will stay here and deal with Matt."

I take one last look at Matt as we leave and almost feel sorry for him. If all this is true, he really does love her and is probably as freaked out as I am right now.

I throw my keys to Matteo. "Zac gave Gerald a ride home once. Have him text me the address."

Katherine and I get in her car. I glare at her. "You could have just called, you know."

"And you would have believed me?" She gives me the evil eye. "Based on all the firepower you and your friends were brandishing, looks like I made the right call."

"What will happen to Victor, uh, Matt?"

"Stolen identity of a dead person is a crime, but it's not federal. It will be up to the state's attorney."

"Can you drive faster please?"

"We won't be of any use to anyone if we wrap ourselves around a telephone pole."

Twenty minutes later, we pull up to the retirement home and go inside. Katherine flashes her badge, and we're escorted to Gerald's apartment. He answers the door.

"Gerald, this is Katherine York. She's with the FBI."

"The FBI?" He seems pleased. "Damn, now that's service. I was thinkin' the sheriff done gone and ignored me."

"The sheriff?" I ask.

Katherine's phone rings. "It's Michael." She has a short conversation and hangs up. "Bobby Monahan can't track her phone. It must be turned off. He was at the airport waiting to get on a flight, but said he was going to leave and drive out to Devil's Horn Ranch. Michael said he seemed quite concerned."

"Where the hell is she then?" I turn to Gerald. "And why did you talk to Sheriff Wheatly?"

Gerald waves us in. "I'm old but not that old. What am I missing? You're not here about Vivian?"

"My grandmother? What does she have to do with Andie going missing?"

The color drains from Gerald's face. "Andie's missing?"

Katherine and I help him to a chair. "Now I'm confused," she says.

Gerald covers his face and sobs. "It's all my fault."

"What's your fault?" I ask.

"I thought you were here because the sheriff called you. I should have known better. Thompson has everyone over a barrel, including Wheatly, apparently."

"Gerald, please tell me what's going on."

Tears come to his eyes. "I'm sorry I didn't say anything sooner. You deserved to know. But they threatened Andie. That girl is my whole world. Yesterday, after hearing what he did to Hugh Jenkins, I knew it had to stop. I thought she'd be safe at the ranch."

"Safe from what?" Katherine asks. "Please, Mr. Shaw, we need details."

"It's Joel Thompson. If Andie is missing, he or one of his posse took her."

"How can you be sure?"

Looking guilty, he grabs my hand. "Vivian didn't fall down the stairs. One of his men pushed her, and last night, I finally told the police."

CHAPTER THIRTY-FOUR

Andie

My hands are tied behind me, so I doubt anyone listening will hear my whispers. My mouth is too far away from the microphone on my finger, but I try anyway. I try for what seems the hundredth time since a guy wearing a blue track suit and hoodie grabbed me from my living room late last night.

At first I thought it was Victor, but I have come to know his height, smell, and voice. Unless he hired someone to take me, it's not him.

I am extremely groggy. They must have drugged me. My voice is raw from screaming. I've probably been taken to a location where nobody else is around. My wrists are bloody from trying to break out of the zip ties around them. My back hurts from sitting in this hard chair.

"Hello?" I yell. Other than when I was brought here—wherever here is—and the time I was forced to call Maddox at gunpoint, I've been alone. It's been hours, and I really have to pee.

"I need to use the bathroom! Is anyone there?" I see a shadow move past the crack under the door. "Hey!"

The guy in the blue track suit comes in. He doesn't even bother covering his face, and I start shaking. If he was planning on letting me go, he wouldn't want me to be able to identify him. "Would you stop screaming, you stupid bitch?"

"I have to pee."

"No, you don't."

"Listen, you. I have no idea what time it is now, but I assume it's past noon. That means it's been well over twelve hours since I peed. *You* try holding it that long."

He leaves, and I hear muffled words. He comes back in and picks up a red bucket.

"You can't be serious."

"It's this or you piss yourself."

"Is that what Victor told you to tell me?"

"Who the fuck is Victor?"

I can't tell if he's lying. He did just kidnap me. I'm sure he's a brilliant liar. "I'm not doing it in front of you."

"If you think I'm falling for your bullshit, you're crazy, lady." He pulls out a knife, cuts the zip ties, freeing my wrists and ankles, and then quickly points a gun at me. "You try anything, and I'll hurt you. Maybe not that pretty little face, but a bullet in the arm isn't out of the question."

I pick up the bucket and glance around. "Can I at least go behind the bookshelf?" He doesn't look like he's willing to concede. "Please?" I beg.

He waves his gun at the shelf. "Go."

I walk around the old wooden bookshelf that must be a hundred years old. There's an inch of dust on the shelves. Tracksuit Guy is watching me through the slats. I put the bucket down, lower my jeans, and squat over the bucket. It's hard to get the flow going under such circumstances.

I try to take in everything around me, searching for clues; something I can use to escape or remember as evidence.

"You go yet?" he asks impatiently.

"Give me a minute. It isn't exactly easy this way."

I scan the lower shelves, and my heart stops when I see a collection of Russian nesting dolls.

"Hurry it up, lady."

I close my eyes and try to relax. Finally I'm able to pee. Muffled splashes echo in the large empty bucket. I don't suppose I can ask for toilet paper. I wiggle my butt and try to drip dry, then pull up my pants. I pick up the bucket and come out from behind the bookshelves.

He turns up his nose. "No. Leave it there."

I put it back. He's expecting I'll be here long enough to use it again.

I wonder if there's anyone outside. Would he really shoot me if I ran?

"Lady, don't even think about it." He points his gun at the chair. "Sit."

I hold up my bruised and bloody wrists. "They hurt. Can you put some gauze on them or something?"

"Do I look like the Red fucking Cross? Sit your ass down."

"Can you at least tie them in front of me? It's uncomfortable sitting here for hours with them tied behind my back."

"You think this is the goddamn Ritz or something?"

"Please? I promise not to try anything."

He laughs as if I've said the funniest thing ever. "Tell you what, you quit your incessant screaming, and I'll tie them in front, but I'll still have to secure your legs to the chair."

I sit and ball my hands into fists, tensing them as much as I can, with the hope that when I relax, the ties won't be as tight. He leaves to resume his post on the other side of the door.

Before he closes the door, I say, "You can report back to Jon that I'm a model prisoner."

He stops. This has his attention.

"Jon Thompson," I say. "This is his shed."

"Don't know what you're talking about, lady."

"You can drop the charade. I know where I am and who has me. What I don't know is why. I don't suppose you're willing to tell me?"

He steps out. I hear more muffled words.

I don't bother screaming again. If this is Jon's shed, no one will hear me. It's about a quarter mile from the main house, and their property is surrounded by trees and a fence and is well away from any neighbors.

The ring!

I lift my hand close to my mouth. "I'm in Jon Thompson's shed. I hope you can hear me. Maddox? I have no idea why I'm here. There is a guy in a blue track suit keeping watch. He's about your height, dark hair, slight beard. It's too dark to see the color of his eyes. Can you hear me? I'm in Jon Thompson's shed."

After several minutes of trying to break free of the zip ties, I sit back and consider why I could be here. It can only come down to one thing. The Thompsons must think this is the only way Maddox's family will sell to them. It's crazy to think this would work. Do they really think I won't go to the police? Do they think Mr. McBride will just up and sell the ranch to them and this will all go away like nothing happened?

But it does give me hope they won't hurt me. If they did, the McBrides definitely wouldn't let them buy it. For the first time today, I feel I might have leverage.

"I want to talk to Jon!" I yell.

Tracksuit Guy pokes his head in the door. "You ain't keepin' your end of the bargain. Shut up, lady."

"I know you can't hurt me. If you do, there's no way they will make the deal. Tell Jon I want to see him."

"Don't know no Jon."

"You're lying."

"Lady, I've been lying most of my life. Some days I don't even know myself what's true or not."

"That sounds like a sad existence."

"But it sure do pay well." He shuts the door.

I spend the next hour whispering into the ring. Who knew whispering could cause as bad a sore throat as yelling?

When I'm sure my efforts are fruitless, I try to figure out how to escape. My legs are tied, but I can stand. I saw tools in the shed that might help if I can drag the heavy chair over there. I lean over and examine the legs of the chair. They are bolted to the cement floor. Who bolts a chair into the floor? Chills run down my spine as I ponder not being the first one to sit here.

I hear sirens and hope surges. Tears flood my eyes, knowing this could be over in a matter of minutes. They heard me after all.

But the sirens fade. I sit down, tears falling from sadness instead of elation.

The door opens. It's not Tracksuit Guy. It's Jon. He sneers. "Thought someone was coming for you, didn't you?"

I wipe my face on my sleeve. "If you think they're going to sell to your dad now, think again. Kidnapping is a federal crime. You're going to be in a lot of trouble."

"You think this is about the ranch?" He laughs and paces around my chair. "We didn't take you across state lines, so it's not a federal offense. Everyone in Texas knows my father. He contributes millions to political campaigns. Do you think they'll give a rat's ass about one pathetic horse vet who went missing for a few hours?"

"So you're planning to let me go? And what do you mean, this isn't about the ranch?"

"I have to hand it to the old man for not telling you, but that didn't keep him from going to the sheriff. Too bad Wheatly's first call was to my daddy."

"What old man? Hugh Jenkins? I thought he was in the hospital recovering from his injuries."

"You do lead a sheltered life, don't you?" He touches my cheek, and I cringe. "What's the matter? Never been touched by a real cowboy?"

My whole body shakes. I feel sick as he runs a finger down my neck and between my breasts. His eyebrows go up. "No bra. Damn. Now I'm hard. What are we gonna do about that? I could untie your hands. If I untie your hands, are you going to try anything?"

Bile rises in my throat, and I can't speak.

"You're feisty. You probably would. Maybe I'll just lower my pants. You can use your mouth. I won't even have to untie you."

He goes for his buckle. "Anything you put in my mouth will get bitten off."

My face sears with pain from the slap he delivers. "You'll do what I tell you to do."

"Like your wife?"

Another slap and my face feels like it's on fire. "I'm going to bend you over the table over there, and you're going to take what I give you unless you want to find that pathetic excuse for a cowboy boyfriend of yours at the bottom of Eagle Mountain Lake."

He starts to undo one of my legs from the chair. "Jon, don't!" I scream, hoping someone hears me through the microphone.

Sick laughter erupts from him. "Keep it up. I like it better when they squirm."

He's armed. He's always armed. Will he kill me if I fight? When my second leg is untied, I kick him in the shin. He buckles but doesn't fall down. This time his fist connects with my cheekbone, and agony rockets through me. Blood runs down my face, and he chuckles.

I stand and try to knee him in the balls, but the hit is off-center. It's enough to make him double over, though, offering me the opportunity to kick him in the ribs. He grabs my leg when I run, and I fall to the ground. I slip my tied hands over his head and try to strangle him, but he's twice my size. He pushes me off him and stands up, then yanks me to my feet.

He pulls out a gun and shoves it against my head. "I'll give you points for trying, not that it's going to do you any good. I'm really fuckin' turned on now. Here, feel. You and my wife can compare notes later."

With the gun still in his hand he forces my palm to his crotch and grips my hair with the other. When I realize what's about to happen I throw up all over him.

"What the fuck?" He jumps back in surprise. I hear commotion outside the door, followed by a loud pop, and feel a searing pain at the back of my head.

Everything goes black.

CHAPTER THIRTY-FIVE

Maddox

I pace the waiting room, staring at the clock on the wall. What is taking so long? Why hasn't anyone come to get me?

"You're going to wear a path in the carpet," Owen says. "Sit down."

"She could be really hurt. I should have been there sooner."

"You're the reason she's getting help right now. This could have turned out a lot differently."

Gerald comes through the double doors. He seems to have aged five years today. "He cocked her head pretty hard with the barrel of his gun. She's got a concussion, and they are monitoring her intracranial pressure. The CT scan didn't show a brain bleed—that's good news. But she's still not awake."

I sag against the wall. "I have to see her."

"They only let family back there," he says.

I slide down until my butt hits the floor, then lower my head into my hands.

He touches my shoulder. "You know what? In my book you *are* family. Get up off the floor, and I'll get you to her room."

He goes to the nurses' station, talks with someone, and then waves me over. He walks me down the hallway and points to a room. I stare at the door before going in, terrified of what I might see.

"They didn't touch her, if that's what you're thinkin'," he says. "I mean beyond the damage to her face and wrists and a few bruised ribs. They didn't… violate her in any way. I was assured of it."

I breathe out a deep sigh and nod. Gerald hangs back. "You're not coming?"

"Figured you might need a minute."

I stop in the doorway. My chest hurts when I see her face. I stride over, my vision clouded when I see a cut under one eye and a clear handprint on her left cheek. She has wires coming out from under her gown and one attached to her head. Monitors of various kinds are next to her bed.

"You can touch her," someone says, coming up behind me. "I'm Janice, Ms. Shaw's nurse." She puts a clear bag of fluid on a hanger. "This is saline to keep her hydrated."

"Is she going to wake up?"

"I hope so. I've seen people recover from a lot worse. Pull that chair over and sit with her. You're her brother, right?"

"Brother. Yeah, that's me."

She winks like she knows the truth. "Take her hand. Talk to her. It might be nice to hear a familiar voice."

"She can hear me?"

"Maybe. Nobody knows for sure." She leaves.

I pull over the chair and sit. Hate sears through me as I stare at her battered face. I can't imagine what she must have gone through. What she was feeling for hours on end. It kills me to think she was trying to talk to me all morning, but we were out of range. It wasn't until I talked to Christina that we figured out where she was being held. When I told her Andie was missing, and Gerald had gone to the police about Joel's involvement in Nana's death, she said there'd been a lot of activity out by the shed that morning.

Katherine and I sped over. It gutted me to hear what Jon was saying to her when we got in range. She fought him with everything she had. I take her hand. "I'd never been so scared in my life."

My throat becomes thick when I think of how close I came to losing her. How I could still lose her if she doesn't wake up.

Her hand twitches in mine, and I stiffen. "Andie?"

"Uuuuuuuuh."

"Oh my god, Andie." I press the call button.

"Yes?" someone says.

"She's awake!"

Her eyes flutter open. She tries to focus. "Maddox?"

Ten seconds later, Janice walks in and goes right to the machines. Then two other people, one in a white coat, enter. Andie moans again, her eyes close, and her hand falls away.

"You have to leave now," Janice says.

I don't budge. "Is she going to be okay? She said my name, but then her hand went limp."

She urges me toward the door, practically pushing me into the hall. "Waking up is a good sign," she says. "She'll be in and out for a while, but we have to run more tests. This could take a while. Maybe you should go get something to eat."

She closes the door in my face. I don't want to leave, but there's nothing I can do here.

But there *is* something I can do.

I return to the waiting room and tell Gerald what happened, then I notice Bobby sitting in the corner. But it's not seeing Bobby that has my blood pressure rising. It's seeing Victor's face that does it. "What's *he* doing here," I say, sprinting across the room.

Owen holds me back. "Maddox, easy."

"He should be in jail."

"For what?" Owen says. "Running from an abusive father? Will you just let him talk?"

I let go of his shirt. He sits, rests his forearms on his knees, and blows out a breath. "Agent Watkins summoned the local police. They questioned me but said they couldn't arrest me because Victor James isn't a real person—at least not the one I was pretending to be. Because I didn't steal anyone's identity or use my fake identity to defraud anyone, they couldn't hold me. That's not to say I won't face charges. I have been earning money without paying taxes, and I did falsify a driver's license, but it wasn't a Texas one. I could face charges in Missouri for using Tim Dorsey's identity, but again, since I didn't do it to make money, I may not get charged with a felony."

Part of me feels sorry for him. He lost his sister. His best friend. And he's been on the run for a long time. But it's hard for me to think of him as anyone other than the criminal we've been fearing all these months. "Why are you here?"

"Just because my name is Matt and not Victor doesn't mean my feelings for Andie aren't genuine. I need to know if she's going to be okay."

"You think if she finds out you're not who we thought you were, she might have a change of heart?"

"No. I don't know. But she deserves to know the truth, don't you think?"

"And she will. I'll tell her. You're free to go. If she wants to call you, she will. But I imagine you'll want to skip town now that your real name has come out. Aren't you afraid your father will find you?"

"Not anymore. Agent Watkins looked him up. He died three months ago, so I don't have to run anymore. I can be Matt Cryer again… as soon as I figure out how to bring myself back from the dead."

I turn to Bobby. "No need for all of us hanging around. The nurse said Andie needs a lot of tests. We won't know anything for several hours."

"I'll wait."

Matt leans back in his chair. "I'll wait, too."

"Great." I pull Gerald aside. "I need to duck out of here for a while. I have some errands to run."

"Now? Can't they wait?"

"I've already waited long enough." I glance at Bobby and Matt who have started a conversation. "Besides, it's getting a little crowded in here. I have to take care of a few things. You'll call me if there's any news?"

"Sure."

I crook my fingers at Owen. "Come with me."

"Where are we going?"

"I'll tell you on the way." I get out my phone. My father answers on the second ring. "Dad, we have to talk."

CHAPTER THIRTY-SIX

I'm still unable to believe what happened. Victor is innocent—and his real name is Matt, not Tim. Joel is responsible for Vivian's death. Tears pool when I think of Vivian and how needlessly she was taken from us, all because Joel Thompson wanted to own her land. I gingerly touch the back of my throbbing head. "I'm confused. Jon didn't shoot me? But I heard a gunshot."

"That was *my* gun," Katherine says.

"Did you shoot Jon?"

"Not Jon. Joel."

"I… but it was Jon in the shed with me."

Katherine explains how Gerald never got the anonymous note Joel's cronies left at the front desk of the retirement home. Granddad didn't even know I'd been taken and that they were demanding he retract the statement he'd given the sheriff. Then she tells me about the call between Maddox and Christina. My head hurts, and I'm on information overload. "When we showed up at

Jon's, Joel was there. Things escalated. All hell broke loose, and he threatened Maddox with a gun."

My heartbeat shoots up so quickly, a machine beeps. "He's okay, though, isn't he? He was here. Or did I imagine it? Please tell me he didn't get shot."

"He's fine," Granddad says. "Torn up about what happened to you, but fine. He sat with you yesterday when you were sleeping."

A nurse runs in to check on me. After I calm down, Katherine tells me the rest. "When I drew my gun on Joel, he turned his on me and cocked it. I shot him in the leg. Then he had a heart attack."

"He's here in this hospital?"

"He's at the morgue," Granddad says. "Serves him right after everything he's inflicted on others."

"And Jon? Will the police let him out? His family has lots of connections."

"Without Joel, the Thompson name isn't worth much more than the paper his death certificate is printed on. The sheriff assured me that despite their millions, with Joel out of the picture, he's more than happy to take down his son."

"So it's true. Joel really did have everyone over a barrel."

"He was threatening the sheriff's family, just like he threatened Gerald with hurting you."

I turn to Granddad. "I'm sorry you had to carry this around for so long."

He takes my hand. "I'd do anything for you, kiddo. I should be apologizing to you for not giving you fair warning. It's my fault you're here. I don't think I'll ever forgive myself for this."

"My injuries are temporary, Granddad. Joel being out of our lives is permanent. It might not have happened if you hadn't done what you did. I think it was very brave."

He lifts my hand to his mouth and kisses it. "You're everything to me."

Katherine says goodbye, and I wait for someone else to arrive.

Granddad smiles. "He knows you're awake and talking. I promised I'd keep him updated."

I pick at my blanket. "He's not here?"

"He left the hospital last night. I haven't seen him since. Said he had some important things to take care of."

More important than this? I want to say but don't.

"There are others who've been askin' to see you, but only if you're up to it."

"Who?"

"Seems my granddaughter is one popular lass," he says. "That Bobby fella is in the waiting room—has been all night. The other one—I don't reckon I know his real name—he left and came back this morning."

My jaw drops. "Victor is here? I mean, Matt?"

"They've both been here all day. You feel up to seeing them?"

I try not to show my disappointment that Bobby and Matt have been here but not Maddox. "Bobby can come in. Seeing Matt would be weird."

"Don't forget, he's innocent in all this."

"You're right. It can't hurt to talk to him. Send him in first, then Bobby after."

He gives me a look. "You like the Bobby fella?"

"I loved him once, Granddad, but he never felt the same way about me. Then he showed up here a few days ago and asked me to go to Wyoming."

"After everything that's happened, I wouldn't blame you if you considered it."

I put my hand on his. "You know I'd never go anywhere without you."

He chuckles sadly. "I'm not sure I'm the one who would feel left behind."

"Maddox is leaving soon. If anyone is getting left behind, it's me."

He kisses my cheek and crosses the room. "I'll send in the first lad."

I pick up the hand mirror on the tray table next to my bed and check my appearance. I look hideous. At least they took the wire out of my head yesterday after my scans. I've been told I will need to take it easy for a week or so. No riding; it could jar my brain and cause further damage. They said I can go home later today though.

There's a knock on the door and Victor, uh, Matt, is standing there with flowers. I smooth my blanket. "Come in."

He scans the room. "Where should I…?"

I point to the side table. "There is fine. Thank you."

"I take it you've been told everything?"

I nod.

He pulls a picture out of his wallet. It's the tattered picture Katherine found of the young girl. "This is my sister, Megan. She's the only other person I've loved."

Guilt consumes me. "I'm so sorry you lost her."

He reaches for me, and I flinch. "You don't have to be afraid of me, Andie."

"I know. It's just that so much has happened today, it's hard to take everything in. But I'm glad you aren't who we thought you were, and I feel terrible for having led you on."

"It's not your fault."

"But I knew you liked me."

"I loved you." He inches closer. "Still do."

I shake my head and then wince, because it hurts.

"Should I get the doctor?"

"I'm fine. Can you sit a minute?"

He pulls up a chair and sighs. "This is when you tell me it doesn't matter that I'm in love with you, because you could never see me as anything but the monster you thought I was."

"I can't be with you, Matt, but it's not because of who you are. Before the FBI showed up, I thought you were a nice man, but then—"

"It's Maddox, isn't it? It's always been him."

I don't bother saying anything. I'm sure he can see the answer in my eyes.

He stands. "I like it here. Once I get my life back, I might even go to college. What I'm saying is I'll be around, Andie."

"Good luck, Matt. I wish you all the best."

"You too."

I lean against my pillow thinking the next one might not be so easy. I stare out the window, thinking about what Granddad said. A lot has happened. Maybe it would be easier if I went to Wyoming with Bobby.

He's standing in the doorway, looking at me, and suddenly I know my answer.

"Hey," Bobby says.

"Hey yourself."

He takes the seat Matt vacated. "You've had an exciting few days."

"I thought you were flying home."

"I was, but when I heard what happened to you, I left the airport. I'm not leaving you again if there's any chance..." He studies my face. "Is there?"

"Maddox is leaving soon," I say. "He'll be returning to New York."

"I know. All the more reason for you to move to Wyoming, don't you think?"

My lower lip quivers. "I love him."

"So it's us all over again." He takes my hand. "Except it's not, because I love you. I love you now, and I loved you then. If I had it to do all over again, I'd beg you to come to Wyoming. Or maybe I would have followed you to Texas. I was stupid, and I don't want to make the same mistake twice. You loved me once. I know we could get back what we had. He's leaving, Andie, and I'm right in front of you. I haven't even seen Maddox since yesterday, and *he's* the one you want?"

Everything he's saying is true. Tears flood my eyes. "I can't help how I feel."

"You're going to let him trample your heart?"

"Says the guy who trampled my heart."

"I can give you a good life. You know I can. We were good together."

"You really want someone who chose you second?"

"Well, when you put it that way." He stands and paces. "Yes, actually, I do. Come with me anyway."

"It wouldn't be fair to you or me."

"You'd rather be alone, and possibly lose a huge part of your income when the ranch sells?"

"I have to be true to my heart."

The nurse walks in. "Ms. Shaw, I'll need to go over wound care with you before you're discharged. We should have you out of here by sundown."

"So that's it?" Bobby says.

I swallow the lump in my throat, knowing exactly how he feels at this moment. I know, because I lived through it eighteen months ago.

"If I leave, I'm not coming back," he says.

"I know."

He crosses to the door. "Goodbye, Andie."

I put on the clothes Granddad brought me, still watching the door as if Maddox will magically appear. He hasn't been to see me since yesterday. Maybe seeing me injured was too much for him. Could be that visiting me in the hospital was too far across the line of casual.

Granddad pulls my makeup bag out of a satchel. "I didn't know what you'd need, so I brought whatever was sitting on your vanity."

"Thanks, but I'm not sure I need makeup."

"Thought you'd want to look pretty when you get released. You know, show everyone you're a trooper."

I take the bag, not feeling up to putting on makeup but unwilling to disappoint him.

He holds out a hairbrush. "Might want to run this through your hair, too."

"Do I look that bad?"

He cups my chin. "You're always beautiful. I thought sprucing up a bit might make you feel better."

I carefully run the brush through my hair, making sure not to touch the huge goose egg on my head. My concealer covers up the bruise from the slap, but nothing will hide the gash under my eye. I put on a little eyeshadow to appease him.

"Don't you feel better now?" Granddad asks.

I nod, even though it's a lie.

"Hey, now. Chin up, pumpkin."

I give him a sad smile.

Nurse Janice comes in. "You're all set to go. The doctor has signed off. You just take it easy, young lady. Someone will be by in a few minutes to escort you out."

As I'm wheeled out of the hospital, I wonder if Maddox will surprise me by pulling up in his truck to drive us home. Granddad doesn't have a car. But when we reach the exit, Maddox is nowhere in sight.

Granddad looks at his phone and then at the approaching car. "Ah, here's our ride, right on time."

"You're taking me home in an Uber?"

He smirks. "You expected a limousine?"

"No, I just… forget it." I get in the back and he sits next to me.

He takes my hand. "I'm proud of you, Andie. Your mom would be proud, too. You've grown up to be everything a mother—or grandfather—could ever hope for."

"I wish everyone felt that way," I mumble at the window.

"What's that?"

"Nothing." I squeeze his hand. "Thank you. I love you, Granddad."

I must have dozed off, because when I look up, I see we've driven past the main entrance to Devil's Horn Ranch.

I tap the driver's shoulder. "Excuse me, you missed the turn."

"No he didn't," Granddad says.

"I'm not up to going out for supper. I'll make a sandwich at home."

"We're not going for supper." He smiles when the car turns onto a back road along the west edge of the ranch.

"What's going on?"

"You'll see."

We pass the hunting grounds and drive up to the lodge. When I see Maddox standing on the front porch with a bouquet of orchids, my heart soars. Has he been here the whole time, fixing it up? But what's the point? He said it would most likely be torn down.

Maddox leaps off the porch and opens my door.

"What's all this?" I ask.

He holds out a hand. "Come inside, and I'll show you."

I take his hand and step out of the car. It pulls away with Granddad and leaves us alone. "You didn't come back. I thought maybe—"

"Whatever you thought was wrong. I apologize for not making it back, but I had a few things to take care of. Things that couldn't wait. I figured you were in good hands." He walks me to the front steps and holds onto my elbow as we ascend. "Careful."

When we walk into the lodge, I'm stunned. Lights are on, though they are dimmed and candles burn throughout the grand hall. It's been furnished with couches, tables, and chairs. Pictures hanging on the walls have been dusted and polished. A large area rug is in the center of the room.

"This is what you've been doing?"

"Actually, no. Aaron and the guys did this. I had other projects to work on."

I eye him curiously. "Projects?"

"Come." He leads me to the adjacent room, the one where we made love the first time. It's been furnished and decorated as wonderfully as the grand hall. More orchids in vases are placed on every surface. Candles burn even though the electricity has been turned on.

A bottle of champagne waits in a bucket of ice. "What are we celebrating?"

"A lot of things." He walks me to the couch and has me sit down. "One—you're safe, and the Thompsons won't be able to hurt you or this ranch any longer."

"Unless Karen tries something."

He gives me a sour look. "You're ruining my mojo here."

I laugh lightly. "Can I say something? You saved me, Maddox. When you kept texting my phone, I was told to call you and make excuses. They were holding a gun on me."

His eyes become glassy. "I'm amazed at how brave you were and smart to use the code word."

"I was hoping you'd remember. I didn't know if the ring was working. I've never been so scared in my life."

"Of course I remembered. You don't have to be scared anymore. Now, where was I?" He pops the cork. It drops to the floor. He kneels down to get it, then pours us each a glass. Still on his knees, he says, "I have a very important question to ask you, Andie."

My eyes bug out. "I... uh..."

He sees my reaction and chokes. He quickly gets up off the floor and sits next to me. "Oh, no. No, no, no. I mean not that I won't ever, but we haven't even gone on a real date." He shoves a glass at me. "Looks like you need this."

I sip, my heart rate slowing back to normal. "What was it you wanted to ask then?"

He seems nervous. Why is he so nervous?

"I know Bobby and Matt were at the hospital, so you have options. I wouldn't blame you if you wanted to leave, considering everything that's gone on here. It would be easier for you to start over in a new place, where you feel safe and the memories aren't horrible. Gerald told me Bobby slept in the waiting room last night. That's hard core, so he must really love you. But here's the thing, I think I love you too, so while I'm not exactly proposing—" He gazes longingly into my eyes, and my heart thunders again. "Andie Shaw, will you be my girlfriend?"

I try not to giggle. I'm about ready to say yes when it occurs to me we still have an issue. "Maddox—"

"Before you say anything, I want to show you something. It's one of the things I had to do yesterday."

He takes off his shirt. There's plastic wrap covering what I assume is a tattoo. "Please tell me you didn't tattoo my name on your back."

He removes the wrap and leans close so I can examine it. My breath hitches. It's a tattoo of the Devil's Horn Ranch brand. "You once told me this tattoo was a way to pledge yourself to the ranch."

I trace the edges. "I'm confused. Are you going to work here? How do you even know it will still be called Devil's Horn Ranch?"

He puts our glasses on the table, then he takes my hands in his. "Because that's the other project I was working on. We're not selling, Andie. My dad agreed that as long as the ranch stays in the black, we'll keep it. I spent the better part of the last twenty-four hours on the phone. Some of the undeveloped land will be leased to the same company that already has wind turbines on the east acreage. That alone will cover the mortgage, property taxes, and insurance. I'm going to expand the cattle business and maybe even put in another stable when we've saved up enough capital. I have a lot of ideas I've been thinking about for a long time. Gerald can live in the guesthouse. He loves the horses, and I know he'd be happy there. You could live with me in the main house, if you wanted. It would be great, Andie. *We* could be great."

I finally wrap my mind around everything he's said. "You're... staying?"

He chuckles. "The tattoo is permanent, Andie, so yes, I'm staying. Now would you mind answering the question?"

"What question?"

He frowns.

I laugh and climb on his lap. "I'm only kidding. Yes, Connecticut, I'd love to be your girlfriend."

His lips crash onto mine. He holds my head gingerly as his tongue swipes across my lower lip and into my mouth. It's a sweet kiss. A sensuous one. One that tells me he'll always protect me and keep me safe.

I pull back and look into his eyes. Those gorgeous eyes had caught my attention when I was fifteen. I run my finger across the small scar on his temple. I hope one day he'll be down on one knee again, asking me a different question, because I know I'll say yes. I've known it since the day we met.

He cups my face. "I lied earlier. I don't think I love you. I *know* I do."

EPILOGUE

Six years later

Mom raises a glass. "To family and Sunday brunch. May they always go hand in hand."

"Hear, hear!" Dad says.

"It's been so nice having you visit," Andie says. She smiles at Jordan and Caitlyn. "You have no idea how much I'm enjoying having sisters around."

I catch Andie's eye and raise my brows. She gives me a subtle nod. "We're glad you're here," I say. "Because we have news."

Mom can hardly suppress her smile. Tears are flowing before Andie gets out the words. "We're pregnant!"

Andie gets pulled into a hug. "The perfect ending to a perfect story," Mom says.

I laugh. "Must you always be thinking in terms of books?"

"Just you wait. I'll write your story one day."

Dad holds out his hand, palm up. "Pay up, darlin'."

"You bet on this?"

"It's been five years since you married, son. We've been not-so-patiently waiting for this day for a long time. Your mom usually wins the bet, but not this time."

Mom gets out her wallet and melodramatically throws a twenty at him.

Caitlyn laughs. "Don't you share a bank account?"

"You're missing the point, sweetie," Dad says.

"Which is?"

"I won."

We all laugh.

"When are you due?" Mom asks.

"September."

"Will you find out if it's a boy or girl before then?"

Andie glances at me. "We haven't decided yet."

"Says you," I say. "We need to plan, babe. I don't want our newborn having a bunch of yellow clothes. Yellow looks bad on *everyone*. And then there's the baby's room. What color will we paint it? I'm not painting it green and then re-painting it blue or pink."

Andie rolls her eyes. "Oh please, like there's not a dozen guys around here who would paint it for you. Aaron would do it in a heartbeat. He loves that kind of stuff."

"Where is he staying these days?" Mom asks.

"When he's not at Texas A&M, he stays in the cabin he built near the ridge."

"Aaron built a cabin?" Dad says. "Aaron, the delinquent kid who came down here kicking and screaming?"

"He's a good worker. He'll make a great ranch manager someday. He's even written up a business plan to start renting out the hunting lodge for small weddings, company trips, and bachelor parties."

Dad nods. "We'll work something out, like I did with you. Give him some equity in the ranch for each year he works here."

"He'd love that."

"Consider it done. When does he graduate?"

"Next year."

"I still think he should have gone to Baylor University," Mom says. "Plus, it's not far from here."

Caitlyn giggles. "That's just because it's where you got your name."

"Maybe so, but *someone* in this family should go there." She pats Andie's stomach. "Perhaps this little one."

"Don't forget *I* went there." Andie rubs her barely-there belly. "I'm all for keeping this one close to home."

Mom gets up to clear the table. "Come on, you three, let's put ourselves to good use."

Andie stands to help. "Don't make a fuss. I can clear the table."

Mom makes her sit. "You'll do no such thing. Not while I'm visiting."

I pick up plates and lean over to kiss my wife. "You should learn to accept help, babe. In a few months, you're going to need it."

Andie stays put, but calls out, "Don't forget to throw Beau some scraps."

Mom leans against the counter. "I don't want to step on anyone's toes, but I can't tell you how nice it was to have family around when Maddox came into my life. I don't know what I would have done without my mother. If you need me, I'll come and stay on the ranch for as long as you like. I can write my books anywhere. And I promise not to butt in where I'm not needed or overstep my bounds with parenting advice. I have no doubt you two will be incredible parents. I'll stay in the guesthouse if you don't want me in your hair." She goes over and touches Andie's shoulder. "Speaking of the guesthouse, I was real sorry to hear about Gerald. You must miss him."

"It was time," Andie says. "Thanks to you all and this ranch, his last five years were very special. I can't speak for Maddox, but I would love to have another pair of hands when this little one makes an appearance."

"It's settled then," Mom says. "It will give us plenty of time for me to interview you for your book."

"You're not serious," I say.

Dad laughs. "Son, when have you ever known your mother not to be serious about her writin'?"

"I've read your books," I say to her. "You are *not* getting details about our sex life."

"That's why they call it fiction, dear." She taps her temple. "I have all kinds of ways to fill in the blanks."

"Gross," Caitlyn says. "You want to write sex scenes about your son?"

Mom waves off her comments. "We'll all be laughing about this one day." She gives Caitlyn the evil eye. "We'll laugh about yours, too."

"Mom, stop it."

Dad pulls me aside. "What about that other issue? The parole hearing you went to? Is everything okay?"

"For another year anyway. He was denied." I glance at my beautiful wife. "Don't worry. I will do whatever it takes to keep her safe. To keep them both safe."

"How's Jon's wife doing?"

"Ex-wife," I say. "After more than four years and three different lawyers, they finally found a loophole in the prenup he made her sign. If she plays it smart, she'll be set for life."

"And Karen, does she bother you?"

"Karen bothers everyone. Did you know Aaron is friends with her son? When Aaron got his act together, so did Quinn. Whenever Aaron's in town, they're inseparable. Quinn even helps around the ranch from time to time, much to Karen's dismay."

He puts a proud hand on my shoulder. "Well, then. Sounds like you have everything in order. I sure made the right choice trusting you with this place." He heads to the back door. "I'm ready for a ride. Anyone else?"

Caitlyn, Jordan, and Mom follow him. On his way out, he touches Nana's old hat, a constant reminder of how Devil's Horn Ranch started way back in 1972.

I hold Andie back, wanting a moment to ourselves before we join the others. They are the first people we've told about the baby. If this didn't seem real before, it sure does now. I pull her to me. "They seem pretty excited."

"It will be their first grandchild. Someday it will be us, finding out this one is having *our* grandbaby."

"I look forward to each and every day between now and then." I wrap her in my arms and kiss her. "You really don't want to know what we're having?"

She smiles. "I already know. I had a dream last night, and it was so real, it had to be telling me something."

"Tell me then, what are we having?"

Her eyes well. "I think it's a girl."

My heart soars. I'll be happy with any child this incredible woman gives me, but the thought of a small version of her is enough to bring me to my knees.

"We should start thinking about names." I lead her to the back door, where we stop and gaze at the hat on the peg, then at each other. We smile. "Well then, I guess that's settled, darlin'."

ACKNOWLEDGMENTS

You've been begging for the Mitchell Sisters' next generation, and I finally had the courage to start writing it! I always knew Maddox would end up in Texas. It was so much fun watching him make the transition from city boy to cowboy.

If Texas Orchids was the first book you've read of mine, you'll want to go back and read about Maddox's parents in Purple Orchids—where it all started.

Being a city girl myself, I required a lot of help getting insight into horses and ranch life. A huge thank you to Jen Meador and Paula Quinn for helping me learn all the ins and outs. I couldn't have written this book without their guidance.

Thank you to my incredible beta readers, Joelle Yates, Shauna Salley, Laura Conley, and Jen Meador. You all have special talents you bring to beta reading.

To my alpha reader and quasi-editor, Ann Peters, I appreciate your dedication and willingness to do multiple reads without a single complaint.

As always, my editing team at Murphy Rae Solutions deserves a shout out.

I would be remiss if I didn't also thank my super-awesome assistant, Julie Collier, who not only does beta reading, but helps me in all things.

Next, I'm on to Aaron's story, Texas Lilies. I can't wait to see where that takes me. It will be my 20th book which just blows my mind. Thank you to the loyal readers who've stuck with me on this amazing journey.

ABOUT THE AUTHOR

Samantha Christy's passion for writing started long before her first novel was published. Graduating from the University of Nebraska with a degree in Criminal Justice, she held the title of Computer Systems Analyst for The Supreme Court of Wisconsin and several major universities around the United States. Raised mainly in Indianapolis, she holds the Midwest and its homegrown values dear to her heart and upon the birth of her third child devoted herself to raising her family full time. While it took time to get from there to here, writing has remained her utmost passion and being a stay-at-home mom facilitated her ability to follow that dream. When she is not writing, she keeps busy cruising to every Caribbean island where ships sail. Samantha Christy currently resides in St. Augustine, Florida with her husband and four children.

You can reach Samantha Christy at any of these wonderful places:

Website: www.samanthachristy.com

Facebook: https://www.facebook.com/SamanthaChristyAuthor

Instagram: https://www.instagram.com/authorsamanthachristy

E-mail: samanthachristy@comcast.net

Made in the USA
Monee, IL
21 September 2021